D1373877

Dead Alive

DEAD ALIVE

Eva Demski

Translated from the German by
Jan van Heurck

A Cornelia & Michael Bessie Book 

HARPER & ROW, PUBLISHERS, New York
Cambridge, Philadelphia, San Francisco, Washington
London, Mexico City, São Paulo, Singapore, Sydney

 For information address Harper & Row, Publishers, Inc., 10 East 53rd Street, New York, N.Y. 10022. Published simultaneously in Canada by Fitzhenry & Whiteside Limited, Toronto.

FIRST EDITION

Copy editor: Marjorie Horvitz
Designer: Mary Cregan

This book was set in 11-point Bodoni by The Haddon Craftsmen, Inc., ComCom Division, Allentown, Pennsylvania, and printed and bound by The Haddon Craftsmen, Inc., in Scranton, Pennsylvania.

Library of Congress Cataloging-in-Publication Data

Demski, Eva, 1944-
Dead alive.

Translation of: Scheintod.
"A Cornelia & Michael Bessie book."
I. Title.
PT2664.E47S313 1986 833'.914 86-45362
ISBN 0-06-039062-X

---

86 87 88 89 90 HC 10 9 8 7 6 5 4 3 2 1

For you: who else?

Contents

Dead Alive

Day One

When the man died, no one seemed to think it necessary to put him under the ground with all due speed so as bit by bit to get him out of the minds of the people who knew him. The last his wife saw of him was a zinc coffin resembling a bathtub, which two men, gray-clad and softly swearing, were twisting round and round the narrow spindle of the stairwell. Four stories to the bottom. His wife went on standing at the top of the stairs, so she didn't know what the vehicle looked like that they shoved the coffin into. Gray? Black? Probably some inoffensive color so as not to startle the people who stopped on the street below.

At first it was unclear where the coffin had been taken. No one asked where, not his parents, not even his wife, and it wasn't his friends' place to do so. Only when the time between the man's death and his final disposition dragged out unduly came a question or two about floral decorations and whether the priest was liberal-minded.

Eleven days and nights the man's body had been kept aboveground—not in dignified darkness, on a last bedecked bed, but, at first, inside a tin drawer; then on a table equipped with drains; next back inside a tin drawer; and only at the end inside a coffin. At least that's what the wife's inquiries revealed. If she hadn't had her suspicions, she wouldn't have asked.

What you do is, you make a cross-shaped incision over the breastbone, take out a little of what's inside, and put it through the tests you deem essential. The left-over organs are thrown away; then you stuff the body with excelsior and stitch it up again. No doubt that isn't hard to do, because by this time the body is long since drained of blood. The ancient Egyptians would have preserved the extracted organs in an intricately molded jar: the heart perhaps in gold. His wife had eleven unquiet days and eleven still nights in which to imagine things like this.

When the man died, on a sunny, cool Saturday in April, he was thirty years old. He died naked, and fast, if you think how much time some people take to do it. It took him no more than a quarter of a day to die. At least that's how it seemed on the first day of his death. He hadn't managed to get dressed again; maybe he didn't even want to. People who have trouble breathing like being naked, as if their skin had millions of little lungs to help them out.

His apartment had been left in semidarkness; only slivers of sun forced their way through the blades of the venetian blinds. When his wife reached the place after getting word that he was dying, the first thing she did was to let in light and air. The man wasn't yet fully dead, but already she was beginning to brush him aside, to mock his wishes. He had hated sunlight and fresh air, detested vegetables and walks on unpaved ground. He took to his heels at the approach of vitamins in any form. But today he was no longer able to defend himself.

Several men in white coats were standing ill at ease in the hallway of the apartment. The wife had seen a large ambulance waiting downstairs. No one spoke to her. She wouldn't have minded being ignored if the reason for this lack of interest in her manifestly healthy self had been lively activity, a zealous and diligent pursuit of medical care; but the helpers were helping no one, except possibly each other, with their murmured advice and words of encouragement. When the wife tried to go into the bedroom they held her back, united in their belief that this was impossible. She went to peer into his law office, stepping from the blue of the hallway into the office green. Only the door to the red bedroom stayed shut. Then, on this the first day of his death, his wife sat down on the outer staircase, so as not to interfere with the medical treatment she thought, but it was really with death.

Admittedly, no one said anything about death; they were all far too busy for that. And because the wife had resolved not to cause a disturbance, she wondered at how many men were now zooming past her into the apartment, not seeming to care if they disturbed things or not. They were good-looking, casually dressed males of the same age as her dying husband. All the men in the apartment were approximately the same age, except for the boy who stood in one corner sobbing and hiding behind his long hair. The wife recognized at once that the men bypassing her on the stairway and climbing over her head into the apartment, just as if someone had called for or even welcomed them, were police. The moment she realized what she was seeing, she knew that her husband was dead. If he hadn't been dead, she would have heard him make some protest; but there was silence behind the closed bedroom door and that wasn't like him. He wasn't resisting the cops, so he was dead.

The wife stood up and walked back into the apartment. It wasn't her apartment. She moved cautiously, notwithstanding her earlier trespass on the venetian blinds, and walked much more falteringly than the plainclothes detectives, who were poking their noses into all the rooms and opening the bedroom door as if nothing had happened.

"I'd like to see him," the wife said.

"There was nothing more we could do," replied one of the doctors—or was he a conscientious objector doing alternative service, or a Red Cross volunteer? He looked embarrassed. "Absolutely nothing. Had he suffered from asthma for a long time?"

The wife said nothing, just: "I'd like to see him."

"You can't yet," said another doctor or conscientious objector or volunteer aide. "You can see for yourself, the police are with him." Only then did it occur to her that her husband was Catholic and that by rights people ought to be saying "The priest is with him," not "The police are with him"; but it suited him all the same.

The boy was still crying, a feeble, wailing whimper. The wife did not comfort him.

"I'm going in now," she said. There were so many people in the apartment; who was to stop her? Besides, it was her right to see her husband, a dead thirty-year-old lawyer with whom she hadn't lived for three years, and whose friend over in the corner was hiding his snuffling tears behind a curtain of hair.

The wife had seen dying people before, and dead ones too, when she did night duty in the hospital. As everyone knows, in hospitals people die in the wee hours after midnight. For the most part, these dead had been dried out, emaciated, dangling from tubes that fed them with liquid, disfigured by large surgical dressings. Often she had felt glad when finally they had their dying behind them. The last tough remnant of life had worn them down so, they had had to toil so hard, and at the end were completely at the mercy of strangers. The wife remembered times she had had to hold shut a hole in a patient's throat so that he could speak, so that his voice could get its sound back. On the threshold of her husband's bedroom, she was determined not to be afraid of a dead man.

The cops kept harassing her, asking her questions that she didn't understand in subdued voices, and blocking her view of the big bed. He had bought the bed after the two of them separated. The bedroom was a fine, unevenly shaped chamber painted a warm red, with books and candy scattered over the floor, and a chair where the man's clothes lay waiting, with big shoes standing underneath it. The wife looked at a wall poster on which her husband had written the slogan NO POWER TO ANYBODY. She didn't believe he meant that. He liked power—his own, of course, not other people's. A record player kept her gaze from straying to the bed; a bookshelf, a pile of newspapers. A small table where little white prescription blanks lay in clear view. The nightstand with its half-open door revealed boxes of cookies, chocolate bars, bags of candy, giant lollipops, licorice sticks, pills, and a couple of porno magazines.

They hadn't even laid him out properly on the bed, and it looked as if only his upper body was resting, a rest it endured with reluctance. He looked like someone caught between standing up or lying down, it wasn't clear which: his feet already (or still) on the floor, and his chest and shoulders with their outspread arms still (or already) on the bed. It troubled the wife to see her husband's handsome body in such a helpless posture—the last movement he ever made, if she was to believe the men who now were fussing around everywhere in sight. But believing them wasn't so easy. Her husband had spent too many years proving that you couldn't believe them: neither the men in the white coats nor those in the green uniforms; neither those in black robes nor those in studiedly casual wear—no, them you could believe least of all. He lay there looking at no one, though he could not help but see the flurried throng in his office and his apartment. He didn't protest, and this, at first, was the only thing that made her believe he was dead.

He had died naked and they hadn't covered him up. The wife took a close look at the man's body. No part of it had been worn out. So why die, then, when the outer cover is still beautiful and can be used? The winter-white skin was still smooth, the bones firm and strong, the hair dark and unruly, and even the teeth still able to chew despite a taste for sweets that knew no bounds. To tell the truth, only his hair looked dead. It used to look that way sometimes when he was still alive, whenever he was dissatisfied or life wasn't exciting enough. That's how his hair was now: it was dead.

The wife needed time alone in the red room with her husband. She would have used the time to lift his feet onto the bed, would have found a clean sheet and covered him with it. Then she would have folded his hands and placed his crucifix between them, along with his rosary and the photo of the anarchist Bakunin from his desk. She would have closed his eyes. She would have draped cloths over the mirrors, opened the rest of the windows, and sent someone from the building to buy candles. Six candles, or even better, twelve. When the candles arrived, she would have closed the windows again—having allowed the soul time enough to depart into the open—and placed the candles around the bed; or maybe only at its head. Then she would have washed her hands, fetched a chair from the study, and sat down. She could have begun to say goodbye properly. But she had approximately sixty seconds of time in which to consider all this while she looked at her dead husband. Much of it wasn't thought but only the germs of thought; some was memory; almost all was deep-felt wish. Then someone took hold of her upper arms and pushed her out of the room.

She didn't resist, because it was still the first day—that is, the last day of the past—and she hadn't learned how to handle it yet. It used to be, in cases like this, where the authorities seemed to step out of line, that her husband would get her to sign a writ of complaint, which then legally empowered him to rage through the corridors of the courthouse, fling his lawyer's robes around him like the French tragic actor Talma, yell at public prosecutors, and speak in a threatening whisper to policemen called up to testify. Somewhere among all his papers there must be dozens of these writs lying around. They used to write one every time there was a protest demonstration, and her husband would draw them up for other lawyers, if he thought they were his friends.

Meanwhile the plainclothes officers in their casual shirts were beginning to conduct a more purposeful search. The wife knew that her husband's political cases were filed in pink folders; otherwise she was largely ignorant of the goings-on in these varicolored rooms, and of the material stored there. But it wasn't hard for her to imagine, and she didn't want the officers prying.

No more than three hours had passed since her husband's death, but the officers' scrutiny, their subdued questions and conversation, were getting bolder. Nonetheless, they repeatedly went over to the door of the room where the dead man lay, to assure themselves that it was staying shut. They jumped when an inexplicable bang came from the other side. This was the wife's only moment of joy that first day, because she had no doubt that her husband was responsible for the warning knock, though it sounded careless, as if he had other things to do. Notions like this kept occurring to her more and more often. All normal communications between life and the body behind the door seemed to have been severed, so she was obliged to devise new ones. One by one, a trail of superstitions came flitting by on soundless wings.

After her expulsion from the death room, the wife stood uneasily in the hallway, trying not to look over at the boy, who was now squatting in a corner, theatrical and reproachful as an Oriental widow, and just as noisy. It was on account of him that she couldn't cry, the wife told herself; he made a perfect excuse. One of the cops was trying to raise the boy from the floor and get him to answer some questions.

"I can't—don't you see I can't stand any more? Shut up, you filthy assholes!" the boy sobbed, and the officer let him go, relieved because at last the boy had rediscovered speech. Unbecoming and strange as the situation might be, at least his antagonist's language sounded familiar.

"Can you supply me with some of his personal data?" the officer asked the wife. The man was holding up a questionnaire, as if it were an official permit. She felt proud because she remembered all the information required, fact by fact, without hesitation. She could have told the officer their wedding date too, and the date of her husband's first state exam. All the days lined up in a row, each wearing its proper number. Her only regret was that the question session was so brief. Afterward she felt useless again, in this group of people who each knew what to do and what to look for. She recalled how her husband had trained her never to give in to them. "They're enemies," he had told her over and over. "You have to fight them with cunning, dignified means. Just silence is a strong weapon." All the same, the wife caught herself thinking that she would have liked to tell the searching men something about the dead man, just to make them feel ashamed or curious. But the warning still echoed from behind the door.

"Actually, you could go home now," she said to the boy. No chin, she thought; and that trembling gaze. "Why don't you leave?

Really, there's nothing more you can do here. Besides, it'd be better for you to get some rest," she added hypocritically.

The boy looked out from under his bangs, and would have loved to hate her, no doubt. She was sending him home because she didn't want to share her husband. Just this once, not to share him. She was a motionless predator ready to pounce.

"Where am I supposed to go?" asked the boy.

Problems of who inherits what cropping up already, thought the wife. She had managed to forget that the boy had been living with her husband in this apartment, except for the brief times when the two had a falling-out.

But the idea of a quarrel seemed to have been switched off; and no one there—not the wife, not the boy, not the officers either—would have dreamed of turning on the lights and peering a little more closely into each other's faces.

The wife noticed an obtrusive odor. No, not *him;* it was far too soon for that. But in the bathroom she saw the last thing her husband had done, which he had left there just as he had left himself. He hadn't had time to dispose of it. His wife did it for him, just as she would dispose of the man himself when the time came.

A dozen people were still jostling through the apartment. Even the medicos hadn't gone yet but were officiously discussing their procedures with the detectives. Occasionally they turned to the boy as if looking to him for information. But he didn't play along: the man had made sure of that. The boy would never talk with a policeman, never so much as even refer to one by so polite a word. The wife felt left out, but no bright idea occurred to her of how she could make herself the center of attention, at long last. After all, she was a widow now, *his* widow: she and not the boy, let that be clear once and for all. After death, things like the boy didn't exist.

Just by looking at him, she could tell that the boy saw through her; but there was nothing he could do to fight her.

"Where are the cats?" she asked him.

The man had had two cats, a nice normal gray tom and a thin female who bore the name Icru: International Center Red University—the poor beast. Right now, the cats were nowhere in sight. They, too, had learned the lesson of how to treat the state authorities.

"You'll have to take them back to your pad," said the boy.

"I can take you along too," she answered, feeling all swollen up with tolerance and solidarity. The boy nodded. Apparently he had expected to pass from the man's hands into hers, and seemed to have no objections.

Later she couldn't get over how the men had managed to get the metal coffin into the apartment without making any sound. No clatter, no creak announced the arrival of the mortuary tub. Nor did the dozen searching men pause in their work or mark a reverential silence; because of course it wasn't a real coffin but a corpse receptacle, with the same clean silver surface as the sausage tubs that butchers use. Suddenly the men were there, and one of the detectives said, "Take him to the medical examiner's office." When the wife screamed something, he laid his hand on her lower arm and told her soothingly that this was just routine in cases of death from unexplained causes; after all, she must realize that thirty-year-old men don't simply drop dead for no reason. The officer drew her gaze away from the closed door, through which the coffin-bearers had evidently passed: For not a sound was audible, and by the time she took in what was happening, they and the zinc coffin had already practically vanished around the first bend of the staircase. The boy moved to follow them, and so did she. They crowded each other with idiot haste at the entrance door. But she had no rights, and neither did he. The same event had overcome them both.

The wife looked down the empty staircase and noticed that the lights were on there, despite the blazing sunshine. Then one of the cats appeared from somewhere and tried to escape onto the stairs by crawling flat on its belly. It was the one called Icru, of whom there isn't much more to tell in this story except that she survived the man by only one year, died of the same malady, and was buried in the same grave.

But now, on this first day, the cat tried to take off in the wake of the coffin. At least that's what the wife liked to imagine, because it seemed so appropriate. She noticed that the apartment smelled somewhat of cats. The boy said, "I'll catch them for you when we leave. They'll both fit in the carrier."

Now that the dead man was gone, the plainclothesmen seemed to have lost interest in his office. But maybe they were only pretending, because the presence of the wife and boy must surely have hampered serious investigations.

"We'll have to seal the apartment," said a detective. "No doubt you'll want it sealed up too," he went on, turning to the wife. "It's important that no unauthorized parties enter the premises."

She had the feeling that she could hear her husband laughing one last time. She didn't have to consider how his laughter used to sound: She could hear it distinctly.

A grotesque procession made its way down the stairs. The white-clad medicos had finally made up their minds to come to the rescue of their forlorn radio beepers and bestow their aid on someone else. By now their bodies resounded with pleas for help from breast and trouser pockets. The medical force headed the procession. They were followed by the plainclothesmen, stepping briskly. One of their number remained upstairs to keep count of the participants in the minor exodus, both man and beast, and ensure that no one was left behind in the dead apartment. After the detectives came the boy, no longer crying. A couple of neighbors, who had been lingering in the corridor, accompanied the train. One of them, a woman who at last saw her long wait being rewarded, decided to make her own contribution by repeating: "We heard him scream, we heard him scream for a long time. My name's Sattler," she added, as if to prove that she had heard real screams because she could produce a real name. Then at the tail end came the wife, who ought by rights to have been screaming herself; but all she did was to carry the basket with the screaming cats inside.

Turning to look back, she saw the door guard carefully inscribe a small slip of paper and stick it on the door. So that was the shield, so flimsy, so mighty. In the *Arabian Nights,* the genies guarded their treasure caves with a single word. The wife tried to picture the word being used to guard her husband's apartment. No doubt it wasn't a magic word but officialese, a cop's word. She felt sure that despite the attentiveness of the watchman, they had all walked off and forgotten something inside the bedroom or the law office, something that was very important and hard to find. She racked her brains trying to think what it could be. It wasn't her husband: He was already on his way to a place she had never seen, and she didn't know if he could be retrieved from there or what shape he would be in if he could. No, her husband was gone, for the time being. But something else had been left behind in the apartment. Maybe his stories, abiding still and spellbound inside the pink files until someone came along to release them with a word and make them speak. But who could do that except her husband, who now was keeping still himself? At least for the time being.

"Time for us to go home now," the wife said. She said it to no one in particular and wouldn't have felt the least bit surprised if the detectives had cheerfully agreed to come along. The medicos climbed into their big, handy mobile clinic and drove away. "What's your name?" the wife had asked each of them in turn. But she had got no reply.

The wife's apartment was in a better neighborhood than her husband's. It was a beautiful apartment with a small garden, and it was filled with congenial objects. Only now and then, at night, the military planes would roar in low over the houses, reminding you that it isn't easy to escape the city while remaining in its orbit. Her husband's apartment was braver; it hadn't tried to escape.

The wife still stood downstairs at the entrance to her husband's building, looking over at the Israeli Bar just opposite. Now, in the afternoon, the bar stood open; at brief intervals, buckets of filthy water were poured out the front door. She could hear the nearby railroad and smell the soup herbs and vegetables from the neighboring Turkish greengrocer's. A thin prostitute emerged from a dark entryway. She had yellow hair that had been done to death with curling and dyeing, and wore a very short black leather miniskirt. In the old days, the wife had often laughed with her husband because in this district where he lived and worked, every person he met on the street was a real or potential client. "My clients have got me surrounded," her husband had said.

"Is it true the lawyer's dead?" the hooker asked in a friendly tone. "I got the word already at noon. Awful thing, such a young guy. And a real looker, you gotta admit. Sure, he was always a bit pale, but everybody's pale around here. It's not something you die of, not right away anyhow. Lemme offer you my sympathy."

She gave the wife her hand, turned, and went back to her station. Unfortunately the man hadn't had a chance to get so famous that the whores of the railroad district would take a day off to mourn him, getting their black furs out of mothballs.

"It's not easy to cope right after something like this," the last detective said to the wife, who was staring after the blond hooker. "Sometimes the family stands around on the street for hours, not knowing what to do next. If you don't mind me giving you some advice, what you should do is make a list."

She couldn't help laughing, and thought again of her husband's laugh. He used to gobble away like a turkey, Ho-ho-ho, so that sometimes you found it hard to believe there was any real merriment in it.

"And what would you put on the list?"

"Well, the names of relatives, of course," the detective said sternly. "Parents. So far I haven't heard a word about any parents. And a minister. A funeral home is absolutely the first thing."

The wife listened and tried to memorize the items.

"I'll get you a taxi," said the plainclothesman.

But a horde of taxis was waiting at the end of the street. Nowhere in the city did so many lurk in ambush as here, because nowhere else were there so many helpless people. Loaded with suitcases, or drunk, or towing a new girlfriend, or holding a scrap of paper inscribed with unfamiliar street names: the helpless victims of the multitude of taxis. No doubt one of the drivers had seen the coffin being carried out of the house and thought: There's a live prospect to check out later; someone else is bound to follow it eventually. So now she found them waiting; but not to ferry her across the river. Her husband was dead and she was obliged to stay with him, on this side of the river. She shoved the basket of yowling cats into the car. The boy started to climb in with her.

"Sit in front," she said, and the boy obeyed. At least he wasn't crying now. She didn't take offense if the cats cried, but crying people got on her nerves.

It was dark by the time she reached her building. Now it was no longer the first day but the first evening, a Saturday evening, the time when people normally go out. She entered the dark apartment and got back on friendly terms with the pictures and the colorful rows of books. The boy didn't stay in the hallway but went into the kitchen to get himself a drink of water, and then sat down in the living room. The husband's cats, now that they were free, began territorial fights with the wife's cats.

Who knows, or ever will, how news spreads, how an event travels from mouth to mouth? Does it happen at a measurable speed? All that people know is bad news travels much faster than so-called good news. For instance, a child's birth becomes common knowledge a great deal more speedily if it's illegitimate—and more speedily still if it's born with a defect. Yet as far as we can tell, no one actively spreads the word. It's carried by invisible electricity. At least so it seemed to the wife, because the telephone in her apartment rang so often that evening that she felt it was a good pretext for postponing certain urgent phone calls that she herself had to make.

Everyone who phoned knew that her husband was dead. They expressed their regret at his fatal drug abuse. They asked the identity of his murderer. They lamented their inability to have prevented his suicide. The wife felt almost ashamed at having to bring up the asthma and the cardiac arrest. And in fact, this explanation struck her as false the moment she first said it—false, that is, to the extent that she was still capable of thinking clearly. For as the evening wore on, her thought processes were becoming a bit clouded. "People always feel like that," said a doctor friend who was among the callers, and he promised to visit her.

"What am I doing, telling them he died of an asthma attack?" the wife said to the boy. "The others are right: murder and suicide, both at the same time—that's a much more likely explanation."

In that year, 1974, dying was something that no one did—at least no one who was young, political, and officially regarded as dangerous. No, they didn't die; they went down fighting. Only a few had fallen so far, on the battlefield of their honor. You could tell quite clearly which kinds of death they would tolerate in their ranks, and death in bed wasn't one of them. That first evening she allowed herself to dream that her husband had died a hero.

She had to phone her husband's parents, who lived a couple of hundred miles south. No one was home when she called. She remembered an old school friend of her husband's, a good-natured, fat little man whom she had met once and who she believed didn't like her. She and her husband had gone to visit him just after they were married, at his home in a village on the Pegnitz River. It was a small house, which smelled of food preserves. Her husband's friend had impressed her. He seemed to her kindhearted, poverty-stricken, and incorruptible, almost proud in the shabbiness of his farm dwelling. She had been unable to sway him with her nervous fluttering, her sympathetic bustle. He had gazed at her calmly, a slightly contemptuous stranger.

How old had this friend, Joseph, been when she met him for the first and last time? Older than she, already past his mid-twenties? He seemed to her ageless. That was six years ago. She was sure he would still be sitting unwaveringly in the same house, looked after by his mother and sister, like a Catholic priest.

The wife telephoned Joseph and told him her husband was dead. She asked him to track down her missing parents-in-law, because his home was near theirs and therefore he could do it more easily than she could. He barely said a word during their conversation: this wasn't the proper way to report a death. But a little later he called back to tell her that he had managed to find where her husband's parents were staying. "We could send over the local priest; it's a long way from here," he said. He knew the appropriate way to handle tidings like these. She asked him to go ahead and activate the network of priests. The priest where Joseph lived could inform a brother priest, and he in turn could tell the priest of the family where her in-laws were guests. The wife felt reassured. The men in black had reclaimed one of their own, and she could rely on their professionalism.

The whole lot of them were Catholic: her husband, his parents, his best friend, the country where he had been born but which he could not remember. He was in love with the myth of that country: altars to Our Lady and heroic Polish freedom fighters. For one brief moment on that first evening, the wife feared that the men in black, the Catholics, might take her husband's death out of her hands, whereas she wanted to keep it for herself and fathom it to its depth. Of course she couldn't understand it all this first night; so far she understood nothing. But already she was assuming a defensive posture, ready to fight to hold his body and soul in one place, to keep him with her, where, despite everything, he belonged. For it said in the Bible that a man shall leave his father and his mother, and shall cleave unto his wife—not unto a chinless boy with stringy hair.

Her husband's friend, Joseph Deutner, had managed to set the Catholic machinery in motion very quickly, for quite late that evening the telephone rang once again.

"What's going on?" asked her father-in-law's voice. "What's the matter there?"

By this time a crowd of whispering guests had collected in her apartment. The wife felt for the old man. He seemed to be trying to wipe out what had happened by sheer firmness of mind. It was an error of history, subject to correction. The wife stammered. She would be accused of murder, she knew that. All mothers of dead sons think their daughters-in-law are murderesses—even though usually they have left only a morsel for their daughters-in-law to finish off. The wife felt afraid. Her mother-in-law was the type who wouldn't let anyone put anything over on her. Blond and sturdy, with a tight little mouth. Once, her husband had shown her a youthful photo of his mother, in which she looked like a lady's maid in a comic opera. "Actually she ought to have had six children and a great big house," he had said of his mother, whose bustling energy threatened to tear the house down. Her grief for the death of her only son would threaten to tear the house down too. On the phone, the father-in-law had said only: "What's going on? What's the matter there?" More than that he would never be able to say.

"We're coming tomorrow," her mother-in-law now announced, while in the background the father was breathing heavily, maybe crying. "We're coming as fast as we can."

The wife could hear in the voice what her mother-in-law really meant to say: "We're coming, so that I can straighten out this nonsense. No son of mine is going to die on me. It's all your fault, all the muddles, and now this latest one. But I'll see to it that everything gets back to how it used to be."

Her husband had told her a lot about his mother, and the mother had had her own stories to tell. The refugee march out of Silesia! I can't tell you what I went through with that boy!

His version: "She made me pull down my trousers when I was eleven or twelve years old, just so some silly women could see the scars on my rear end."

Her version: "When we were fleeing the Russians I took him to a Russian doctor, a woman, and she gave him an injection without sterilizing anything. I tell you, they used every weapon they could against us Germans!"

And she went on citing the inexhaustible proofs of mother love during their flight from Silesia.

I wonder how people go about proving mother love when there isn't a war on, the wife thought as she continued to listen to her mother-in-law on the telephone. You make one of your own, I suppose. Once, the wife had foolishly lost her head and retorted to her mother-in-law: "Well, what other choice did you have but to take care of him on the journey? Or do you wish you'd just stuck him into a garbage can along the way?" Like all very forceful people, her husband's mother was capable of feeling deeply insulted.

"You hurt Mama," his father had said. Probably tonight, after the death of his only son, he would have liked to tell his son the same thing—if he could have got him to listen one last time: "You hurt Mama."

"See you tomorrow, then," the wife said into the telephone. She felt scared. She had just remembered her husband's scars, deep, painful-looking imprints on his right buttock, like those left by a torturer—in reality, marks of the treatment that had saved his life. Thinking of the marks, the wife became conscious of her husband's body, the distant body that no doubt was still intact except for the Russian scars on his bottom, the beautiful life-giving scars. Soon other wounds would be inflicted on it, but these would never heal to scars. The wife found she was trembling slightly, and her guests saw that she was having trouble holding her head steady. Feeling her head wobble uncontrollably, she knew it for a sign that she would grow old.

"That's how you get when you live to a certain age," she said to a woman friend. "Your head starts to shake. He's been spared that."

Some dozen people were sitting around her apartment, trying to decide which of the two bereaved parties should be accorded the role of widow. But the wife wasn't worried; people would recognize her generosity to the boy, and then forget him as quickly as possible. All her guests had brought her something to take "instead of flowers," as a woman friend said ironically: Valium, Librium, Tranxene. "I won't take any," said the wife. "There's enough stuff there to wipe out half the city." The same pills were stockpiled inside her husband's nightstand, the uppers and the downers, as if that was the only way you could stand it all. She drank a large amount of cognac. Everyone was chatting quietly, and some cried as they talked about the dead man. The wife couldn't think of anything to say. The rival cats had fought each other into exhaustion and were sleeping on the cupboards and bookcases.

People who had never got along, or who felt indifferent to one another, enjoyed each other's company that evening. Her husband had had few political friends among the members of his own profession. He, the anarcho-jurist, the systematic devotee of chaos, the left-winger who threatened other left-wingers with legal reprisals: craziness upon craziness. And all this at a time when dialectical materialism had only recently been pigeonholed and set up as the infallible touchstone of right action. But her husband had never submitted to it—not because he wanted to show it up as false but because, once you were locked in such a system, there was a limit to the wild-eyed fantasy you could indulge in.

Truth to tell, the man had not been perfectly serious. He disliked all systems that made their advocates look gloomy, and was bored by any politics in which there was no place for circular capes, wide-brimmed floppy hats, and emotional eruptions.

Early in his career, he had breached all covenants about the color of flag he wanted to fly. So his wife sewed him his own flag, using over four yards of shiny black satin attached to a new white broomstick. The two of them used to take turns carrying it at demonstrations. In one of the '60s battles to take over an American department store, they succeeded in hoisting their black flag higher over the building than all the red ones, then lost it, with honor, when the police took the place by storm. She had always promised her husband she'd make a new one—it's women's work to sew flags. But the department store battle had been back in '69, and in the years since then, she had always found some excuse to get out of the chore, because as time wore on she had begun to feel it was slightly ridiculous.

She still had one photo left from 1969. It showed the husband and wife looking earnest and excited, but also self-confident—he at twenty-six, she at twenty-five—both dressed in black, with the black silk flag draped over their shoulders.

"Go home and fuck yourself, you anarchist sow!" one of the Marxist-Leninists had said to the wife. She tried to point out the man to her husband so that he could bash him over the head with the flagpole, but then she lost sight of him. That had been five years ago. Now, on the night of her husband's death, she suddenly stopped feeling the flag was ridiculous and instead regretted that she had never sewn a new one. You can use flags to cover coffins with; flags and flowers. She couldn't for the life of her think of anything else that would suit him—not even the spectacular family coat of arms that he had often shown her.

Of all the people now in her apartment, who were spending this first evening together with her, the boy, and the sleeping cats—that is, with the man's surviving goods and chattels—not one had ever carried a black flag. And yet tonight they were prepared to excuse him for having done so. Death had made the man serious once and for all, as life had never been able to do. The people who sat here on Holy Saturday night had all achieved seriousness within their lifetimes; they were people you could rely on. Two of his female friends, for instance, intelligent, progressive women with biographies that commanded respect—one a doctor, the other a lawyer, both mature beyond their years. To the wife they appeared far away, as if she had suddenly become myopic. Their words didn't get through to her; she understood only fragments of the conversation and wasn't sure but that it might consist only of fragments.

Her husband's former law partner was there too, a huge, calm man who was older than the others and gave the impression of being levelheaded. He and her husband had quarreled and disbanded their practice; but here he was, crying. Seeing him now, you forgot that he was a schemer, vain as a young girl. His anguish was genuine. He had lost his alter ego, with his dark quirkiness, his glittering courtroom pleas, his glib ingenuity. How well all those traits of her husband—a younger man—had set off his own seriousness, his reliability, his greater maturity! Never again, never again. Big, heavy Paul pressed the wife against him with a groan, and at that moment she resolved to forget a lot of what she knew about the past. Scarcely was a man dead than the sunshine of affection beamed from so many unexpected quarters! Hookers got chummy, so did the comrades, and his business colleagues too. How harmless they all seemed to think dead men were! But time would prove them wrong.

When somebody dies, there is always a kitchen, and there are always women who are able to make coffee without ever having set foot in this kitchen before. What's a death without coffee? Usually, it made the wife uneasy when someone fiddled with her things; but a widow is expected to need care and be willing to let others serve her. The dozen people at the gathering were up on every detail of the modern world; yet now they imitated the old conventions, those that had always been used to ward off death or to bid it welcome. One person brews coffee. Another opens the door. Someone else admonishes the rest not to make so much noise. That evening they all behaved exactly the same as bourgeois citizens, peasants, or native tribesmen, and the wife was pleased and didn't try to resist. It wasn't easy for her to get used to the notion that she was a genuine widow. She tried to picture the "W" that you have to circle when filling out forms. S/M/D/W—single, married, divorced, widowed. Now she had experienced three of these states. She was glad she and her husband hadn't divorced.

The evening of the first day was coming to an end. Suddenly she felt scared that everyone would go home now; scared to hear the sound of the hall door, of them putting on their coats one after another; scared they would turn away and leave her house. It wasn't the normal fear of being alone. She simply felt that people hadn't yet talked nearly enough about her husband, as if no one had commented yet on his death, on all the things that were bound to happen as a result, on the void he had left, whose vastness would become apparent only with time. For without him, what would happen to the conscientious objectors? To the defenseless drug addicts? What would happen to all the victims of political persecution? Where could the Italian anarchists turn now, or the

Spanish trade unionists? None of them knew yet that they were orphans, left alone in a hostile world made up of reds and right-wingers.

The wife felt that her husband's true friends were not present with her that evening. Sure, his old partner Paul was there, and Hilde the lawyer, Saskia the doctor. They and the others were kindly and shocked. They had all known him, they had known that he and they were fighting on the same side of the barricade; but knew it not with the burning love of anarchists, only with the reason of Marxists or however else they classified themselves. Their doctrines had not given birth to any customs to express loving grief; their political structures had no place for a dead man. Disorder would only have cluttered the roads they traveled. Yes, there were the old conventions. There were no new ones.

Good manners, that's what they had brought to the gathering; and anxiety because lightning had struck so close to home. They were veilless mourners. Yet the wife needed to have them present. Bakunin was dead, Valpreda far away, García in jail. Plenty of potential mourners were in jail, locked in the bastilles of the various democracies and dictatorships; so she had to look elsewhere for comfort.

"Shall I sleep over with you tonight?" Saskia asked.

"Where would you sleep?" the wife asked. "The boy is sleeping on my sofa."

"Oh, well then, you'll have someone with you," said Saskia, relieved.

"Him?" the wife said in a low voice, so he couldn't hear her. "He's the last person I want to be with tonight."

But even as she said it she knew she was lying. She said it only because it agreed with the conventions. No doubt about it, this twosome was impossible, so impossible that twist and turn it however you liked, you couldn't find a word for it, either a left-wing or a right-wing word. True, you could dress it up a little: the term "solidarity" wasn't bad, or "minority-group work," or "supporting anti-authoritarian love"; but it was still disgusting beyond words.

"No, I'm only keeping him here because he doesn't know where else to go." She thought the lie must be written on her face for all to read—but people don't expect to see lies on a widow's face.

"It's incredible how you handle it," said Hilde. "I don't know if I could do the same." She had the imperturbable face of a

Kirghiz woman, her hair hung down dark and straight to her mouth, and the wife felt good enfolded in her plump arms.

"Of course you could," the wife replied, giving in to a fit of malice. "You've done much weirder things than that."

"Maybe so," the Kirghiz said, unoffended.

What a stroke of luck for the group! A new problem had arisen for them to grapple with, one they were better equipped to handle: sorting out a tangled human relationship to make it appropriate and clear-cut, or at least politically useful. They all felt on home ground now. Their voices rose a little as they discussed the wife and the boy, discarding any effort to keep him from hearing. They had abandoned the topic of the man's death with relief.

The wife thought that she would have liked to have Joseph Deutner there with her. He would have known how to mourn better than she did—in the proper, Catholic way. He could have got her to cry. Whereas now she had only an unpleasant bleary-eyed sensation under her eyelids. Fundamentally, she was one of those plump, vivacious women, a bit maternal without ever wishing to be a mother, good-natured and rather arrogant—one of those women who tend to cry easily when they go to the movies or listen to late-night radio talk shows. But on this first evening, and as the night wore on, her eyes were a desert. A couple of trial sobs, a feeling as if a rough brush kept scraping back and forth inside her stomach; but not a single tear.

"It takes time for people to let go and cry," Saskia had said.

He can't just vanish into thin air, not yet, thought the wife.

Paul said, "She's still feeling numb," and Hilde said something about the tears one cries inside. That made the wife feel like bursting out laughing, not crying. "Exactly the same phrases are being spoken a thousand times tonight," she said, "in thousands of households, at thousands of different tables. It takes time to let go and cry, she's still feeling numb, she's crying inside—thousands and thousands of times!"

"You shouldn't run away with that theory," said Paul, his gray-brown horsehair mane hanging down into his moist eyes. "Each person is a special case. Each is important to the revolution, and he, of all people, was someone we couldn't afford to lose."

"Hot air," the wife said softly, so that only the boy heard. He nodded to her with a look of understanding. And yet she didn't want his understanding.

"They're bound to take you in for questioning tomorrow," she said.

"I know," he answered, showing no anxiety. "I'm under suspicion of murder."

"Intimidation tactics," said Paul. "They're trying to split us all up. They spread rumors they can't back up, just to get people to knuckle under. As for him," he said, pointing his chin at the boy, "they're trying to make him suffer a little so he'll tell them what went on in the law office, who visited there, what the defense strategy was in particular cases. No doubt they'll get around to interrogating you, too, eventually," he said to the wife.

"Let them try," she answered. "I'm not afraid. I'm not afraid of anything anymore. Please don't go yet, any of you," she added without preamble. "Stay a while longer; I can fix something to eat."

But they all said no. People don't eat when someone has died. You can eat only after you have him under the ground.

It was easier to talk about his law cases, to act as if the man had only stepped out of the courtroom for a few minutes, as if he were away on a trip. They spoke about the big trial now pending, saying no one else could handle the defense as he would. This comforted the wife, even though she had always hurried out of the courtroom as soon as her husband got ready to plead a case. She had been as keyed up as if he had been a vocal recitalist or a high-wire acrobat.

She wondered if the news of his death had already spread through the prisons in spite of its being the Easter holidays. It would have quite a number of different prisons to spread through, because the defendants in the big trial were being detained at separate facilities to keep them from planning another of their spectacular joint protest actions. Yet this hadn't stopped them from planning incessantly all the same. Her husband had been angered by many of the things they did; but there were times when he would have dearly loved to join in. Poor lawyers, always condemned to stand by and watch while others acted, like so many hungry ravens.

She remembered her husband's theatrical voice, his cries, his whispers. Now the voice was gone. What exactly is missing when a person dies? she thought. At first glance, not much; but he has no more voice. She couldn't stop thinking of plump Joseph, who could have got her to cry and then could have consoled her. Besides, maybe he was the only one who had really loved her husband for himself, without his colors and his robes, without his powers and his cravings—just a man like anybody else. Joseph, she thought, had been so fond of him that it wouldn't have mattered to him if her husband had been an ordinary, tiresome person. She was sorry that Joseph had never liked her.

Time was passing too fast for her now. Her panic fear of being alone was edging closer. She had made all the phone calls, said all the phrases; there was nothing left to say. Everyone had voiced his or her suspicions, all the cognac had been drunk, the quest for normal, everyday life had been pursued and proved vain. Little by little it was dawning on her that something in the sequence of events was not as it should be. She was remembering that on the day after someone dies, the bereaved have the chance to wear themselves out with what is known as "settling the deceased's affairs." But she had been deprived of this opportunity. Next day was a holiday, a Sunday, Easter Sunday; and the day after that was a holiday too. The courthouse was closed. The cemetery manager's office, the bar association, everything was shut down. There were no newspapers where she could publish her loss. No police officer would come to remove the seal from her husband's apartment. And no one at the medical examiner's would start to dissect him. The whole world was holding its breath. Instead of diving into work, it paused for solemn festivities, stopped moving, turned silent. This seemed to her appropriate, but hard to bear.

The whole process had started up only to stop again. And that wasn't all: The wife felt an urgent craving to spread the word. District attorneys and hookers, judges and drug addicts, priests and conscientious objectors, relatives and lovers—she wanted to tell them all personally, and to reap from each her tribute of grief. Not one of them should get off without paying his dues. Not for nothing had her husband inhabited so wide and various a world, colorful and brightly lit at some points, monochromatic or twilit at others. As his wife, it was her duty now to walk through and inspect this world, even his secret Bluebeard's chambers, and the amusement dens she knew of only by hearsay. Her dead husband's world was hers now, and she wouldn't part with an inch of it. Her every curiosity should be satisfied. That was her right.

The boy looked at her as if he knew what she was thinking; but he seemed unafraid, of her and equally of the police. No doubt he, too, was picturing the country he was now fated to live in, alone with the memory of his dead friend, embedded in the curiosity and envy of others.

He belongs to me, now he belongs to me alone, she thought.

"He'll always belong to me," said the boy. "There's nothing you can do about it. What do you know, anyway, about the kind of person he was?"

"What do *you* know about the two of us?" she retorted, while the other guests tried not to listen.

"He told me everything,"the boy said spitefully.

The wife got up and went into the kitchen because she couldn't stand the way the two of them were tugging the man back and forth between them; because respect was not shown for the fact that he now lay stretched across her knees, invisible yet impossible to miss: the dead husband, the dead son, ennobled and made innocent in the moment life had left him.

"We're all out of clean cups," she said apologetically in the kitchen, holding on to the kitchen counter and swaying a little. This hunger for sympathy! Did you have to behave in such an obvious way to get them to understand at last what you desperately needed?

She swayed a little more, and someone she hardly knew, who had hitched along with somebody else, said, "Come and sit down. You're completely done in."

Admittedly that wasn't much, but it was better than nothing.

Paul had followed her as she came in. "Müllner is on the run," he said. "Has he already gotten in touch with you? We have to turn over his papers to another attorney as fast as we can; you and I still have to talk about that."

Paul and her husband had fallen out completely, for reasons that even they may have been unaware of. But they had left the whole city free to watch and listen in on their prolonged nighttime wrangles at the bar of the Berlinstube pub, where they would shout at each other as they split hairs over theories of revolution and courtroom strategy. In fact it was impossible for anyone in the pub to ignore them: both men standing over six foot three, one bulking large in his gray attorney's suit, the other in black, and slender, wearing a big slouch hat. Their happiest day had come when one of their clients, listening in on the police radio, learned that both lawyers were under police surveillance and were officially known by the code names Berta and Greta. Then, in a back room of the pub, the two would tune in to the broadcasts and regale themselves with reports about their own movements. So they were known to the authorities! They were considered dangerous! Berta, alias Paul, resolved to start wearing the same kind of big slouch hat as his colleague. Sometimes the men shadowing them would stand along the bar at the Berlinstube, reading the tabloids—something no one else who came there ever did—looking like old-time film detectives. Days of bliss for Berta and Greta!

Yet it couldn't be denied that the two men had quarreled definitively and split up. And now here was Paul standing in her kitchen, trying to play the role of her husband's heir, the faithful aide who would carry on his work, helping addicts and revolutionaries.

"He ordered him months ago not to set foot in his office," the boy said, motioning at Paul.

"In my day, they used to call that squealing," the wife said to Paul, feeling obliged to take his side because she didn't want to take the boy's and hadn't yet found a side of her own. Although, of course, being a widow was in itself quite a respectable status. Then suddenly, as she stood there in her kitchen, it occurred to her that she would never see her husband again. She felt a pang at a place under the breastbone, in her back, in her temples; it bulged like tumors. Catching a piece of skin under her left breast between two of her fingers, she squeezed it with the fingernails, so as to give a fixed abode to the pain that was roaming free around her body. But even now no tears came, not yet; so she welcomed the pain with relief, because she had already begun to fear she wasn't reacting normally.

"I know you two split up," she told Paul. "You have no idea what's happening with his cases."

"Neither do you," said Paul, "but let me remind you, I at least am a lawyer."

"We really do have to go now, it's after two," Saskia said, and the wife made only feeble efforts to stop the exodus. Hilde folded her in her powerful arms and pounded her back, as if trying to burp a baby.

"It'll all come right in the end," said the Kirghiz in a Swabian singsong. "It'll all come right."

"It'll never come right again," said the wife. "It'll never come right."

"Don't you want to take a little something after all, something mild?" asked Saskia the doctor. "It wouldn't hurt. If you aren't used to taking anything, even the mild stuff has a powerful effect."

"I won't take anything," the wife said, after a brief consultation with herself in which she tried to decide which would be more suitable to her new role: to slumber exhausted under a veil of white pills, or to lie awake all night dead sober—that is, with half a bottle of cognac inside her.

"You have until Thursday to think about how to follow things up at the office," said Paul, who was no longer crying. "Until then, our hands are tied anyway."

"After that they'll be tied even more," said the wife.

"See you tomorrow!" Saskia said just as always, and Hilde closed the apartment door with a vigorous click that the wife found painful.

The night was already turning into morning, the first morning. Not one of her thoughts had been rehearsed, so they all ambushed the wife from behind, catching her undefended. What did her husband look like now? Where was he lying? What was he wearing, or had they left him naked? How had he died? After a certain age, there was a place inside people's heads for questions like these, and maybe even for the answers. But the wife was twenty-nine years old and these weren't questions she was used to. She closed the door to the room where the boy had fallen asleep on the sofa. Her cats were acting up because they weren't used to the doors being closed, and because her husband's cats were lying in the places usually reserved for hers.

Her husband had never lived in this apartment. Several months after their separation, she had moved out of the tiny attic the two of them had shared, and found this beautiful bigger apartment for herself. She guarded her three rooms jealously, along with all the objects that showed people who she was. Every bit of this place was all her own, down to the last book, the smallest picture. Not one knife, one chair, one candlestick had been placed by accident. What people thought was important to her, though she would never have admitted it. It disturbed her deeply that the boy was now lying asleep on her sofa, his face covered by a fringe of hair, with his shoes, his worn-out boots, touching the brown fabric. She regarded this as an act of revenge from her husband. She opened the door again, to shut her husband's two cats in with the boy, along with some water and other necessaries, then closed the door. "Now at least they're all confined to one place," she said. "But how to get rid of them again?"

She was still waiting for the tears to come. "You're supposed to cry; it's only proper to bawl." The wife discussed the matter softly with herself. She had got into the habit of talking to herself since she started living alone.

Now, though, it wasn't just that they had separate apartments; now she'd never have any contact with her husband again. She could no longer call him up or sit with him in bars. She could never again bask in his radiant good looks, never again hide behind his political fervor, never again sleep with him in his law office, relishing the taste of sin this had had since their separation. She felt tempted, now, to turn him into a hero, to cut him off from himself—egocentric bastard, wild rebel, vain fag that he was. She went on thinking, all through that first night and into the morning—because if she had no tears to give him, at least she could offer a wakeful vigil—about what would happen next. Would her husband, finally, become an inseparable part of herself, or be cut off from her for good? She felt frozen as she lay in her big bed, and rubbed her hands over her body, pressing down on her hips and cheeks. Underneath the flesh, only a tiny distance away, sat the skeleton.

The wife knew that sometime or other the same thing would happen to her that had happened to her husband. And so, out of fear, she betrayed him again. She betrayed him in her thoughts, which were not about him but about the dead man. And the dead man wasn't him.

Day Two

Where had he spent the first night?

It was Easter Sunday.

The wife had been awakened by the wailing of the church bells and was trying to order her thoughts. It was the second day, his first complete day of being dead, and so far she knew very little. The sun was invisible. A chilly Sunday was announcing its arrival. The sky wasn't an Easter sky, although in the garden you could see pale green starting in the bushes. The crocuses sprouted yellow and white in the meadow. Her husband would never enjoy another holiday and would never see any more flowers, but she didn't feel sorry on that account. Things like flowers had only got in his way. He had loved places of a different kind—the caves of the city, for instance, and the palaces of the law where he was free to speak as he pleased, where he could make it known, day in, day out, that he was dangerous.

In the living room, the boy was still asleep on the couch. He smelled of dirty feet, and a trickle of saliva was etching a path from the corner of his mouth into his hairline. The cats were sitting in the corners, and puddles of cat piss were trailing off the furniture legs. The wife no longer recognized her castle, her cave, her sanctuary. Not only her husband had left her, not only he would decay, but her home too, her very own home!

Only then did she realize how dependent she had been on him, on his willingness to tolerate her being alone, and to accompany it with warm good humor.

Her husband had never entered her apartment without telephoning first, the way people knock first on the door of a small child so that she will feel important and grown up. When he visited her, he would invariably walk through all the rooms and list with indulgent amusement any changes she had made—new objects, pictures that had been hung in different places, altered colors. "You have a nice place," he would say. "It's really getting cozier all the time."

Meanwhile his glances would be saying: I don't need this sort of thing myself. Poor little woman, look how desperately she tries to build her ego into a dwelling so that anyone who walks in can see at once whom he's dealing with. Ah, poor hermit crab (his glances said), you cram your defenseless soft parts into a snail's shell that isn't yours, that has nothing to do with what you really are.

How different he was from her in this. He had only a couple of nails to hang his lawyer's robes on and his slim black leather outfits. His walls were colored mauve, red, and black, the paint laid on in streaks; and by tomorrow he might change them to green or silver. Yes, he had a clothes closet, but it had no shelves and housed an undifferentiated heap of weird-scented fabrics—bed linen and underpants, silk shirts and leather belts, a cutaway coat and a dozen white piqué bow ties. All his multiple skins were piled into a shelfless wardrobe and soaked in patchouli.

As for his bed, for a long time he had only a mattress laid on the floor. This was replaced by a huge red leather sack stuffed with Styrofoam balls. Whereas her bed was always neatly made during the day and embellished with bedspreads and pillows.

No matter. Now he was dead. His faraway body had suffered no change yet, she was sure of that. But her apartment, which he had tolerated with a superior smile, was beginning to decay.

She combed her dyed hair and applied makeup to her red eyes, her plump cheeks. There was no shortage of black apparel in her wardrobe; black makes you look slim and sexy, black is mysterious, the color of witches and seductresses. What about mourning clothes? For proper mourning you needed thin legs inside black woolen stockings, or the melancholy head scarves of Italian widows; black calico handbags with little shovels inside, to turn the earth in the cemetery; black knitted jackets that were wearing through at the elbows; black shoes whose leather had turned dull where the bunions bulged out. *That* was real mourning. The wife picked out a black silk skirt and sheer black tights, a black cashmere sweater. On this the second day, she saw no resemblance between herself and the elderly women, the professional mourners, whose ranks she would join in time.

The cats were meowing with hunger. Parceling out food among the bowls, she thought what an impractical color black was, because of the cat hair. The cats hissed and wrangled in front of their food bowls. She filled a bucket with chlorine water and washed away the puddles of cat piss.

It was eleven in the morning: no ordinary morning, by any means. The church bells wailed and swung without a moment's pause, while the boy just went on sleeping. In the kitchen, the wife was furious, with the repressed murderous fury of mothers making morning coffee. The cups rang out like pistol shots, the pot lids like rifle fire. Ping! went the tray. Isn't he awake yet, that pig? Why don't they ever have a bad conscience? The milk jug smashed on the stone floor and the frightened cats streaked away from their food bowls into her bedroom.

She heard the boy walk past the kitchen door into the bathroom. Into *her* bathroom! To use *her* towels! The two of them stood silently on either side of the wall, and she could hear the boy peeing, long and loud.

"That's too much," she said to the coffee cups, "too much. I won't put up with that."

"What did you say?" she heard the boy ask through the wall. She could feel water rising in her gullet, her throat, her eyes. A strangled sob came out instead of an answer. The boy looked around the corner into the kitchen while he fastened his trouser fly.

"Of course," he said. "You're just gradually beginning to feel it. After all, you're the one who knew him best."

The wife felt ashamed because she didn't know whether this rising moisture was being pressed out of her by grief or by fury.

"I'm only starting to feel it," she said. All these idiotic phrases! You feel numb at first, you can't take it in. All the idiotic phrases.

The boy hugged her. He was taller than she but not as tall as the man had been, and also thinner. Very skinny, just the way her husband had liked them; a chinless boy with delicate bird's bones and long hair. Her husband had bought him a pair of leather trousers. He was wearing them now, as he embraced her, while she soaked his dirty T-shirt with her tears. Do they all smell that way, she thought, is that how he liked it?

"How are you going to handle things?" asked the boy.

"What is there to handle?" she retorted suspiciously. "Paul still knows what's going on, and I need a lawyer. He's bound to know where everything's at."

The boy held her out at arms' length; she felt like an unwieldy cushion. "That's what you think!" he said. "He'll rise up out of his coffin if you let Paul horn in. A lawyer wouldn't have a clue. You have to go to his safe-deposit box at the bank; I know the combination. And you have to do something about the pink files. Besides that, there are a few people you have to notify so they can look around for help somewhere else."

"Is all that so urgent?"

"Stop acting as if you've got amnesia," the boy replied. "It was always urgent, every bit of it, except for stuff where they made sure it would drag on for years. Is that what you want? To be responsible for somebody losing a few years?"

The wife recognized the hallmarks of a little actor who had learned his trade from a big one, and she stopped feeling worried. The bells were silencing at last. She, too, wanted to be silent and just sit there quietly for a while.

"Do you have anywhere you can go?" she asked the boy.

"I already figured I was getting on your nerves," he said. "I'll take the cats with me; they're used to me. Icru won't be able to live without him anyway."

"Sentimental shit," said the wife. "It's only a cat, don't you understand?"

"No," said the boy. "It's *his* cat. But I'll take them both with me."

"Where will you go?" she asked, weeping with remorse.

"I do have parents," said the boy. "I've even got a brother. They might get a charge out of seeing me turn up."

She had always pictured the boy as a brainchild who had sprung into the world full-grown, like Athena from the head of Zeus. When she saw her husband and the boy side by side on the street or at some bar, she used to think: Sometime or other he popped out ready-made, skinny and dressed in black leather, from a cellar or a gully—born out of dreams, a bony fulfillment of innermost desire. It surprised her to hear he had parents and a brother.

"Did they ever meet him?" she asked.

"*Him?* No," said the boy. "Not that it mattered. It's just that I didn't want to mess things up—for my own sake, I mean. In a year I finish high school and take my college entrance exams. I'm an honor student."

He took his leather jacket off the hook, cordially drank half a cup of coffee standing up, thrust the cats into the carrier with an effortless motion, and split. The wife was crying again, softly and despairingly, and couldn't stop for a long time because again she had failed, again she had betrayed her husband. Throwing out the cats too—that was the worst of all!

Until noon she had managed to avoid the thought that her husband's parents were coming today and that they would call her to account for what had happened. She vacuumed the floor and restored chairs and dishes to their wonted order. Then she distributed relics around the apartment: a pillow here, a vase there, gifts from her parents-in-law. It was a gesture of subservience. She hunted for pictures of her husband. The only one she found was a childhood photo. His picture gazed crookedly out of a half-empty photo album. He had been blond then. She could hear her mother-in-law's voice murmur from far away, like a ghost: "He was such a sweet child."

His mother had said the same thing when he was alive. She said it reproachfully, like all mothers of sons, who wish they could turn their young into changelings, who would like them to be wise old men yet stay sweet little children, and sometimes to be young men, filled with passion for their mothers. In just a few hours, she would say again what a sweet child he had been.

The wife bent her head over the picture she was holding, and saw that he had not been a sweet child. A small blond boy in an imitation Tyrolean costume, with a little cap on his head. His laughter came too readily, eager to please, and revealed two rows of sharp little teeth. "Do you see his dimples?" crooned the ghostly voice of her mother-in-law. Sometimes in life you met with what seemed an advance echo: First came the echo and then the cry. So it echoed now: "Do you see his dimples?" Yes, she saw the dimples, but she didn't like them. They looked like makeup.

Outside, the day was trying to get dark again. The sun was making no effort to play at Easter and only the bells went on with their work. The multistory building that obstructed the view from her garden seemed very close and leaden gray. It looked as if it were leaning forward, trying to topple over into the hedge bordering the garden. A yellow light, like that preceding a thunderstorm, shone at the top floors. There were lights on in a couple of windows even though it was noon.

The wife had tidied everything. Her three cats, still affronted, were sleeping in a corner where they weren't accustomed to sleep. The gas heater gave out a soft hiss. Dust, she saw, hung in the folds of the curtains. She wiped brown cognac rings off the tabletop. Cigarette stubs floated in the toilet, refusing to dissolve. Humbly the wife readied her home for her husband's parents, just as if she and her husband had been living here together like a proper couple. Only there were no traces of her husband in this colorful female pad. The boy and the cats had been the only ones, and they were gone. His parents would detect little sign of their son here. That's the way it is: Sons leave you, dead or not.

The wife sat again, poring over the childhood picture of her husband, trying to find his face under the black-and-white baby fat. She could see no resemblance, even around the eyes. The only thing he had kept to the end was the all-too-wide, all-too-willing laugh. District attorneys and his more orthodox colleagues had many a tale to tell about that laugh. But they wouldn't tell them, not now that he was dead.

By now, he already had been lying wherever it was for longer than twenty-four hours. The wife found a newspaper ad that said: FUNERAL SERVICES, DAY AND NIGHT. She called the number, and even Easter Sunday did not deter the cordial man on the other end of the telephone from offering his immediate assistance. He could come right away if she liked, he said; yes, he could come at once. But she didn't want to share his visit with her in-laws: Even the undertaker belonged to her. Could he come on Easter Monday, she asked, and would the death notice be in the paper on Tuesday?

The man replied yes to both questions and asked the present whereabouts of the deceased. The wife was amazed at the cheerful way he received the news that the deceased was at the medical examiner's, awaiting autopsy. "Ah, yes, absolutely!" he said several times, as if this were a particularly fine and appropriate place for his clients to be stored until they came into his own capable hands. "That presents no problems whatever," he said. "The holidays, dear lady. Tomorrow we can take our time and talk about the date of the interment and so forth."

She was barely twenty-nine. After her conversation with the funeral director, who bore the somewhat sinister name of Mr. Sable, she had the feeling that she had grown up just in time for her thirtieth birthday.

The telephone rang. It had been silent far too long and she was feeling neglected.

"Is it true?" said a voice that sounded so far away that at first she couldn't tell if she was speaking with a man or a woman, a boy or a girl.

"Are you there? Is it true?" said the faraway voice, pushing its way closer. "Come on, say something! Or aren't you alone? Have they already been there? Have you got the stuff?"

As she stood there, still silent, the words of the voice started to outline a human figure. Yes, she remembered him: a man—he had a cover name—a lean young man with shoulder-length pale-blond hair, a trimmed beard, and pale eyes under lids he never opened all the way. He had white hands, and hollows under his cheekbones.

"Don't say anything," the voice said, almost kindly now. "Just tell me if it's true."

"Yes, he's dead," said the wife.

"Look out for our things."

She realized that he hadn't intended to say that. Death had thrown its monkey wrench into everyone's plans so abruptly that the group was forgetting its network of caution.

"You'll be hearing from us," the voice said, and that was all.

"You'll be hearing from us," the detectives had said to her twenty-four hours earlier, in the same noncommittal, intimidating tone. She hung up. "I'll be hearing from the whole damned pack of them," she told the empty space. "From everyone except you. *You* won't be saying a word from now to eternity!" She started racing around the apartment, cried into the fur of an indignantly resisting cat, and thought up curses with which to curse the dead man. "What does he mean—our things?" she murmured into the cat fur. "Damn it all, what kind of things am I supposed to look out for?"

By the time her husband's parents rang the bell, it had all turned into an impenetrable jungle.

The mother's rage, the father's bewilderment. How could it have happened? Only the last time I saw him, I said to him, You should get more fresh air, don't you ever eat any vegetables? And that apartment, with the shutters always rolled down! Have you got a hankie?

How his father had aged since she'd seen him last!

"Do you want to take him back to your home?" asked the wife.

"Think what it would cost to transport a coffin!" said the father, in a tone of melancholy reproach.

The wife was glad his parents didn't intend to take him away from her. She was acquiring him piece by piece, and no one had noticed yet.

"Then we'll hold the funeral here," she said, in the same tone of amiable gravity the mortician had used earlier, as if death were a daily visitor to her home.

"There's nothing more we can do," said her husband's mother. She simply didn't believe her son's death was genuine. The man who died wasn't her son, he was a traitor, a deserter, a coward. Occasionally, a look of dismay ran over her smooth face: Or was it her son after all? Her true son, the one with the Russian scar on his backside? The sweet child? The dashing student? The lawyer who graduated with honors? The handsome boy? Was it really him? Something overshadowed and protected her, preventing her from reaching clear conclusions. Seated meekly beside her was a man no longer a father now but doubly a husband, whereas she, now more than ever, remained a mother.

"It's hard on you too," the mother said forbearingly to her daughter-in-law, who promptly dissolved into tears again—this time from gratitude—and once again made coffee, only to find she had no milk in the house.

"It always was a strangely run household," said the old man, with a feeble attempt to be gruff, as he used to be.

"Drop it, for heaven's sake," said the mother.

Death sails on rivers of black coffee, thought the wife. Normally I don't make as much coffee in a whole month as I do now every couple of hours. Is coffee supposed to make you immune to death? Do people think that otherwise it's contagious? "The Indians burn some kind of fragrant wood," she said softly in the kitchen. "I always thought it was to stop the corpse from stinking, because it's so hot there. But here people don't keep the dead in their houses, yet they never stop drinking something with a strong smell, as if they had to drive away the reek of death."

His parents didn't look startled when they heard the news of their son's present whereabouts. "Can we see him?" asked his mother. But she didn't persist, and accepted the father's pleas to spare herself that. "Let's remember him the way he was," said the father. At that moment the same phrase was being uttered in hundreds of languages.

"The way he was! The way he was! I think you two don't have any inkling what he was really like," said the wife, even though she didn't really want to hurt the old people, at least not much. "I think you have a few surprises in store." She had decided to fight the pain—this pain that was spreading steadily through her, growing stronger all the time, and that she couldn't call grief because it was too harsh and grating and not dignified enough—to fight this pain with malice, with threats that she had it in her power to reveal or conceal her husband's true identity.

"Don't talk nonsense," his mother said sternly. "After all, I know my own son. No one else knows him like I do."

"No one can possibly know him the way you do because there's no such person!" answered the wife. And both women sat and waited for him to come; to listen flattered, but only for a moment, and then to put a stop to their quarrels about him.

"What's the point of you two arguing?" the old man said wearily. "You can't argue him back to life."

One day, five or six years ago, the wife had put on a suit and high-heeled shoes and gone into the courtroom to watch her husband at work. Back then he was still an apprentice lawyer, but no one who saw him striding rapidly, black and tall through the corridors, took him for an intern. At ten o'clock that morning he was going to argue a case for the district attorney. Proud of himself, he wanted to show his wife how well he could play the role of prosecutor, how he would manage to blunt the cutting edge of the system by harnessing its power. "I admit it's a pretty minor case. They won't let me get at the big ones yet. But to the people concerned, little cases like this can mean a lot."

The wife's head came just up to her tall husband's shoulder, and as usual she tucked it down a little behind and underneath the shoulder, where she could shelter from the rain. Draped over his other arm was his fine expensive lawyer's gown: his raven's wings.

"It'd be a shame if we stopped wearing robes," he had said, waving its folds affectionately. What really mattered to him was the dashing figure he cut in it, not the hierarchical intimidation of delinquents; or at least so she thought. His wife liked to see him in his robe.

"What sort of case is it?" she asked.

"Soliciting outside the licensed district for prostitutes," said her husband. "I told you, it's really a small case. But it's important to the prostitute they're trying to pin it on. And prostitutes are just the kind of people we need to win the support of, because they know more about exploitation than all the sociologists in the world put together. After all, they get exploited by everybody! You'll see. And if the judge won't accept my motion, I'll summon the entire vice squad to testify. They make the hookers service them for free; everybody knows that. We'll make them show up in court and tell us the real facts about the red-light districts and how they're controlled and who's getting the payoffs."

The wife said nothing, but experienced a pleasurable shudder. She and her husband were still living together back then. She was working at a theater, and their apartment was truly impeccable from the proletarian standpoint, with only about eleven by twelve feet of floor space, on the sixth floor with no elevator: a hovel you could show to one and all without a quiver of shame.

The courthouse was all that a courthouse should be. Not one of those pseudodemocratic glass-box jobs but a real mountain, a castle, a dungeon of wrath-red sandstone trimmed in gray basalt. The bars on the lower windows bulged threateningly and the doors were high and hulking, so that you had to lean your whole weight against them to get them to open. You could have driven a train of haywagons through those massive portals; although of course no one would have dreamed of letting a lowly haywagon through, for they had been built in a more forthright age, when the proprietors of the law, the old Victorians, saw nothing wrong in showing how important they were. A more modern extension had been stuck on later, but only succeeded in looking ridiculous by comparison. A sheet-metal motto was affixed along the extension's front. It spoke about the inviolable dignity of man and was the laughingstock of every passerby, until one night one of them at last took pity on it and stole the dignity and threw it into the river, where it has been well cared for ever since.

But back on that day, when her husband, acting the role of public prosecutor, undertook to protect a hooker from the exploitation and derision of the court, the dignity had still been in place.

Thank God this important albeit minor hearing took place in the old court building, so a suitable stage stood ready for his use. The wife wobbled along the gray-tiled corridors, unaccustomed to wearing high heels, and tried to think what the place smelled of. She recognized the odor, but there was an ingredient she couldn't identify. If lies had a smell, she thought, then this is what they'd smell like. But in fact it merely stank like all houses nobody loves. Houses take revenge when their inhabitants hate them: They do it by stinking. Law courts always stink the most.

She was alone in the space reserved for public viewers, and gazed admiringly at her husband, black-gowned and handsome, who had taken the public prosecutor's seat. The judge was rosy-faced and yellow-haired and had a dueling scar on his cheek that showed he had been to the right university.

The defendant was very fat. The wife could see her only from the back: huge bulging buttocks, pillows of fat sticking out behind her upper arms; round fat calves. She wore a gray jersey suit that had become too tight for her, with a thin fur collar and a wine-red imitation-crocodile shoulder bag. The white flesh of her feet protruded unhappily along the edges of her red sandals. The prostitute stated that her name was Hedwig S. Evidently she was taking out her anger at the court on her handbag, which she pommeled and squeezed without mercy. She had thin, graying brown curls fastened on the nape of her neck with an imitation-jeweled barrette.

The wife saw her husband smile over at Hedwig S. to show her that he was *her* prosecutor. This seemed to induce even greater fury in the accused. She hasn't an inkling, thought the wife. How could Hedwig know that he was on her side?

"It's all a big lie," the prostitute Hedwig S. replied to some question from the presiding judge. The wife hadn't understood the question because she was busy trying to imagine the face of the accused, and figure out who could possibly want to sleep with this woman, and be willing to pay for it to boot.

"It's all a great big lie. As for *him,*" she cried, jerking her chin to indicate the husband, thinly disguised as a public prosecutor, "I don't know him yet, but I'm bound to meet up with him before long. All of youse come along as customers, and the ones from the court are the biggest swi—"

The judge had interrupted the indignant Hedwig S. several times, and the wife, sitting in her solitary pew in the audience, several times made out the words "penalty fine" and "contempt of court." The defendant's fat shoulders heaved, revealing that she was sobbing, even though no sound could be heard.

"Please don't cry," said the husband.

"Up yours!" answered the accused. This last moved the judge to impose a fine of three hundred marks, or an alternative sentence in jail.

How wonderfully gutsy this hooker was! She refused any kind of bargaining and said it was worth the money just to get a chance for once to tell this shitty pack of liars, cheats, bribe takers, and sex molesters where to get off.

The wife was hoping to hear a little more about what Hedwig S. repeatedly referred to: the indescribably perverse sexual habits of the courtroom personnel. But the judge, who by now had cast several suspicious glances at the public prosecutor, bellowed his demand for case data on the accused; and this was duly supplied.

She had been born in Dresden in 1930 but had moved to Upper Hesse with her mother while still a child. Her mother had been a servant in a farming family. Her father, a Polish miner, had died in an accident in the pit. Yes, she acquired brothers and sisters later on, from her various stepfathers. Her mother had never married, but she'd been a good mother, considering all she had to cope with. She ended up with four kids. People don't like to hire servants with children.

While Hedwig S. told the story of her childhood, speaking fluently now and in grammatical sentences interrupted only by the occasional sob, the wife looked at her husband. She loved him dearly, because it was he who had taught her that stories like Hedwig S.'s were true, that they genuinely happened and genuinely made cripples of their protagonists. You're not to blame if your mother's a Hessian farm maid with four children by four different fathers; but then you're not going to get ahead in this world either. Everything was exactly the way books described it.

"Keep to the point," said the judge to Hedwig S. "We have a witness; let's get down to business."

Her husband reluctantly read out an indictment that he had not drawn up himself. You could see just by looking at him that he was suffering. His wife felt proud of him, because he was determined to express his convictions even via this horrendous agency of justice, the public prosecutor's office; and to communicate these convictions to defendants by his understanding attitude and by getting them acquitted. But that day the wife could tell by her husband's face that things weren't turning out exactly as he had intended. Very likely he had got the impression by now that Hedwig S. was going to bite the hand that was trying to help her. Admittedly, all prosecutors were alike: mere lackeys of state repression, and it was good that the prostitute Hedwig S. seemed to grasp this. But, on the other hand, *he* was here now, perhaps only for this one day, and his intentions for her were altogether different. So why did the accused fail to appreciate the miracle? The judge's face made clear that he at least appreciated it quite well, although he wouldn't have used the word "miracle."

The public prosecutor moved for a dismissal of charges on the grounds that it was a trivial offense. The judge asked, raising his voice somewhat, whether he had discussed this matter with his mentor. The husband put on a very haughty air and replied evasively. "But we haven't even called the witness Ramona!" said the judge.

The defendant had failed to follow the turn of events. "It's a big lie," she said.

The wife understood: Hedwig S. simply never heard the words of the black-clad men at the high bench. To her, it was as if they were speaking under water. The men's words were more foreign to her than the most foreign language. The wife gazed at her husband and felt sorry for him.

"That Ramona lies like crazy," said Hedwig S., whose face the wife had yet to catch a glimpse of. Hedwig had just heard the court usher bellow "Witness Ramona!" into the corridor. Him she could understand.

"What's *she* got to do with it anyway?" asked Hedwig S.

The judge looked toward the door that no one was coming through. Then he had an inspiration. He wanted nothing further to do with this uppity apprentice prosecutor, so he drew a bead on the only other person in the courtroom—a woman in the audience section—looked her over carefully, and asked, "Are you the witness Ramona?"

Now the wife saw the face of Hedwig S. for the first time, as Hedwig turned to look behind her. She had wild dark eyes and a mouth puckered with so many wrinkles that they looked like cloth gathers pulled together along a drawstring. A prolonged pause fell over the courtroom. The prosecutor took his time replying, seeming almost to savor the judge's question, as if he would have liked to hear it repeated.

"What's the matter?" the judge asked impatiently, bracing himself as if he were about to stand up. But instead it was her husband who rose to his feet, ran his beautiful long thumbs tenderly along the satin lapel of his robe, and said, "No, Your Honor, that isn't the witness Ramona. That's my wife."

Was this the sort of story she ought to tell her husband's parents today, on the second day of his death? Evidently they had never known him; so she was willing to share a couple of stories to show them their son, or at least a slice of him. But her mother-in-law went on and on describing the conditions of his birth and their flight out of Silesia, and over and over she would call down imprecations on the Russian doctor. She wasn't far from turning this Russian woman into the mysterious cause of her son's death almost thirty years later. While she spoke, the wife reflected that the two old people would hardly enjoy hearing tales like the one about Hedwig. What an awful choice you face when someone dies: The nice stories make you sad because there won't be any more of them, and the bad ones make you equally sad because you feel ashamed for the dead man after the event. What would the mother say then about her little boy?

"What about his cats—where are they?" her mother-in-law asked at that moment.

"I've left them with one of his friends," said the wife. "All they did here was fight with my cats."

"Ah, the cats," said the old man sadly. "I always felt sorry for them. They never got any light or air, and the one with the funny name was always so thin."

The father perhaps was searching for reasons, however far-fetched, for the death of his son. It must, he felt, have meaning, even bring benefit, to some one of earth's creatures; so terrible an event must somewhere have a good to counterbalance it. The old man looked as if he were pondering whether the welfare of the cat Icru could possibly be sufficient cause for his son's death.

"In fact, just imagine that—someone with asthma keeping cats!" the mother exclaimed. Where the father looked for justification, she was on the trail of the guilty. His asthma! Those Communists! Those cats! Ever since he had eluded her hands and her watchful glances, everything around him had worked silently and relentlessly to bring about his downfall. Yes, his wife too.

"Then there was that pro-abortion piece in the newspaper," said the mother, avoiding looking at her daughter-in-law. "Why did you have to sign your name to that? Maybe that's what killed him! I mean, not directly, of course, but it must have been awful for him."

Her husband had paid not the slightest heed to this project of hers. She was finding it very hard just now to think about him, the man and the boy, about their mysteriously linked and separated lives. Sitting beside her were the people who had conceived and given birth to him; but they had been blinded along the way and the wife couldn't get them to see, because if they had been able to see—who would there have been left for them to mourn for?

"A lawyer," the mother said, "can make a good life for himself. He always did enjoy a good quarrel. He could have gone on like that, doing just what he liked, and made piles of money at the same time."

Everything her mother-in-law said echoed her own feelings. That strenuous era, the late sixties and early seventies, had put an especially heavy strain on lawyers. Where it would be useful to scratch the law, they weren't allowed near it; they had to be well behaved, otherwise they couldn't represent people who weren't well behaved. Being a lawyer was so awkward. When something happened, you had to figure it out and think up reasons to tell the court why such and such was legal and not a punishable offense—when in fact it ought to have been illegal, and it was a punishable offense, at least in a bourgeois society. What a mess it all was! And in the middle of it all the Marxist training keeping the theoretical side of it all bright and untarnished, so you wouldn't lose track of why you were doing all this and putting up with all you had to put up with.

Yes, the wife used to think exactly the same things as her mother-in-law, but hadn't dared say so. Comfort, convenience, was the worst of all, and comfort wasn't what her husband had been after. In the courtroom, when he saw the sheep dogs masquerading as wolves, he didn't mind wrapping a fleece of lawyer's talk around them to make them look like lambs. She couldn't understand why none of the would-be wolves had ever fought back. At least not during his early trial cases. Later on, of course, this all changed, when the true elect, the most solitary of the noble house of left-wingers, were brought before the court.

The wife would so have loved to tell her parents-in-law stories about how heroic her husband was; to conjure him up in his robe, with his fashionably long mane, his white piqué bow tie, and his slightly stooping, aristocratic posture—the posture of very tall and slender men who tackle their opponents with their heads bent down and forward so that they look like giant condors. His parents had a right, after all, to a son who was heroic. Everyone has the right to embellish death with a golden halo: How else can you stand it?

As for the hooker Hedwig S., the wife simply couldn't get the story out of her mind. And yet she hadn't thought of Hedwig even once in the past five or six years, and couldn't imagine what heroism might lie hidden in the story that now came filtering back piecemeal into her mind. Nothing at all heroic occurred to her, and the tragedy she needed to nourish her imaginings—and to paint for his parents a pleasing picture of their dead son—was turning into a low farce.

The case of the hooker Hedwig S. had been her husband's first genuine political victory. The charges against Hedwig were dropped when the prosecution witness Ramona failed to appear in court—or rather appeared in the wrong guise. The system had made a mistake. The aristocratic judge proved too lazy and too self-assured to shoot down the notions of a junior counselor. No doubt he thought there wasn't much at stake, so why not stretch a point this once?

"But that's exactly how you weaken the system," her husband had said triumphantly after the hearing. For days afterward he would address her only as Ramona. "You have to get them where they're sloppy. That's how to take the struggle out of the universities and bars and into real life."

Her husband still had a few legalities to clear up, but the wife had followed Hedwig S. as she stomped down the courthouse stairs. She was slightly afraid to talk to Hedwig S., but she was curious to know how and where a woman of her sort lived, whether she was married or had a pimp. Hedwig S. heard the footsteps of her putative colleague and turned.

"Whadder *you* after?" she asked malevolently. "Such a load a crap! Ya can see that asshole judge ain't got a clue. *You* Ramona? He's a real jerk. Izzat really your husband?"

"Yes, he is," the wife answered, feeling proud.

"What'd anybody wanna go an' marry a guy like that for?" the hooker said reproachfully. "Couldn't ya find nothin' beddern that? Y'll be old and gray before you got any of the good stuff comin' in. Your man don't look to me like he has much of a knack for finance."

"You don't look as if you have either," the wife had said bravely. After all, what was she thinking of, this fat whore, to talk that way about her savior? He had descended to her from on high—hadn't she seen that? Was she too stupid and callous to recognize an archangel when she saw one?

Her mother-in-law started asking about the law office, the apartment, their financial affairs. Meanwhile the wife's conversation with Hedwig S. was coming back to her, sentence by sentence, the way an old role played years before suddenly reenters the mind of an actor.

"You're right there," said Hedwig S., and the hoop of wrinkles around her mouth split open in a laugh. "I ain't even got enough on me to buy a cuppa coffee. My friend was gonna pick me up. He figured it'd take longer. Or maybe he got held up somewheres gettin' soused. He's good at that."

"Maybe I could buy you a coffee," suggested the wife. It seemed important to talk further with Hedwig S., to find out more about her. Here was an example of the kind of life that so urgently needed changing. She saw an unexpected opportunity to understand at last what it was all about: the hidden meaning of the rallies, the sit-ins, the boring books. Her own life suited her just fine, but she knew little of other lives. The exploited were too remote; she had never seen one of them close up. The rich and the poor didn't enter her life. But Hedwig S.! She was fat and ugly and no longer young; she had to earn money by letting strange men on top of her. Now she didn't even have enough money in her purse for a coffee; and her friend, who no doubt was her pimp, had stood her up and was out getting soused. The husband had tried to give Hedwig S. some help; but stubborn Hedwig hadn't noticed.

As she pondered the case of Hedwig S., so long ago and utterly immaterial, the wife could hear her mother-in-law's voice like a musical note that swelled and faded and could equally well betoken comfort or alarm. "I'm sorry, what did you say? I can't seem to concentrate." Nothing was certain except that the husband was dead, the son was dead. But secretly his wife doubted even that; and his mother probably hadn't believed it from the start, even if her reasons for disbelief were quite different.

"I keep thinking of a story," said the wife, "a case he had once, back when he was still with the public prosecutor's office."

"What kind of case?" asked her mother-in-law, a mother greedy for the life of her son.

"It had to do with a hooker," the wife answered clumsily. "It was very funny—the judge mistook me for a hooker." Her parents-in-law stared at her with round eyes. "It was really very funny," she insisted.

"Maybe it wasn't the right profession for him," said the father.

"It was the only one he wanted," said the wife.

The mother, crying: "Anyway, he kept the wrong company, he led the wrong sort of life."

There isn't any right life, proclaimed the dead man inaudibly.

It's not at all how I imagined it, Hedwig S. had said then, six years ago, at the entrance to the courthouse bar, where the wife, out of curiosity, had invited her for a coffee. "It's really turned out a whole lot different than I figured."

The wife could readily imagine it had. There are many important professions that people don't choose, that choose them instead. No one gets out of school and says he's going to become a gravedigger, for example. No girl passes her finals and enrolls in a course in prostitution. The same for garbagemen. Actually, to start with, no one even chooses to be a judge.

"I wanned to be a nurse," said Hedwig S., and curved her hands around the hot cup of coffee. "But I got married instead. And then there wasn't enough money. But whadd'm I telling you that for; y'hear them kinda stories all day long."

This view of her greatly surprised the wife, who had just turned twenty-five. She sat back and looked around the bar; no one noticed her, despite the pride she was feeling. Hedwig S. took it for granted that the wife of the good lawyer—had she finally caught on to who he was?—was familiar with his work, with the suffering and oppression he was trying to end.

"I s'pose in a shitty job like that you get nothin' else to read, in all them files. That's why lawyers're all so funny in bed. They give ya a hard time."

She had understood nothing.

"But it's possible to change things," said the wife. "It doesn't have to go on this way forever, women being exploited by pimps, opinions being suppressed, the rich getting richer and the poor getting poorer."

None of this interested Hedwig S. She yawned, then remembered that the wife planned to pay for the coffee, and said for politeness' sake: "Yeah, pimps give ya a hard time all right; they sure do."

"What will happen to the law office now?" asked her mother-in-law. "I suppose you'll be able to sell it, and his lawbooks and the other equipment." The wife, surrounded by Easter bells that were striking up again, with a treacherous softness to start with, thought of the small slip of paper that had been assigned to guard her husband's apartment. She dreaded having to go there, but go she must, sooner or later—probably sooner—because she still didn't understand what the mysterious phone caller had expected her to find. She was determined to do something about it, whatever it was, because her husband would have done something. She intended to take over some of his functions.

And yet: As she talked with her in-laws and they all raised their voices to keep up with the howling of the bells, the glass door leading into the garden seemed to open wide and then open again, and instead of trees and bushes it gave a view of the courthouse bar on the day of Hedwig's trial.

It was in the morning that she had had her encounter with Hedwig S. She couldn't remember what the weather had been like. The bar had a reputation in the city and after dark it was considered notorious. Now, in the morning, it had to forgo the glamour of ill repute. The copper counter was damp and dull, yellow liquid dripped out of the beer spigots. The tile floor was covered with dried stains, the spoor left by hordes of desolate feet. Behind a pane of gray glass sat an enamel tray lined with hard-looking meatballs. It was a small bar, some six or seven tables, with four chairs apiece. The tabletops were stamped with a beer label, Muerten Beer, while the glasses advertised a different brand. All the tables were occupied that morning, each by a solitary person; but by chance or design, everyone was seated so that neither Hedwig S.—who couldn't have cared less—nor the wife, who felt decidedly curious, could see any of their features, only their coats and hairlines.

Today, here in her living room on Easter Sunday, the wife saw the whole scene down to the last detail.

"I don't know yet what will happen to the law office," she said, speaking with difficulty.

"You haven't been listening; we dropped that subject some time ago," her father-in-law said, with a vestige of his old sternness.

"Maybe I could still study law and take over his practice," the wife said dreamily.

"You certainly cannot," said her father-in-law, grateful to meet with a sample of avoidable folly. "It would take five years at the very least. Who's going to pay for it?"

"I would so like to take over his whole place, just as it is," said the wife. By now it had completely slipped her mind that for the past three years she hadn't been living in her husband's immediate milieu. Even the boy had been shooed from her memory.

Will I have to bring in some other lawyer to handle his affairs from now on? she thought. Because she wasn't equipped to act as his trustee; any of his friends would be better suited.

But when she tried to remember his friends, their names and faces, she drew a blank.

"What's Joseph Deutner doing these days?" she asked her parents-in-law. The only one of her husband's friends who came to mind was his former schoolmate, the one who had notified his parents, and whom she had seen only once in her life.

"He's doing very well for himself," said the father. "He's got his health back. He still lives at home. Well, you know that."

"*He* ought to have stayed at home too," said the mother.

"Your son would never have stayed at home," the wife answered cruelly. "He didn't stay at home even when he was with me."

"He wasn't the kind of person you say he is," said the mother, defending her dead offspring.

"I haven't said anything. You'll see soon enough what he was like. You'll get to know him by and by."

"I've always known him," said the mother. "No one knows a person better than his mother."

Her parents-in-law left late that afternoon. All of them were talked out, though not very much had been said.

The wife hadn't had to fight for possession of her husband's corpse, for no one else had tried to claim it. She even had the impression that his parents were glad to leave it to her to perform the final duties. Perhaps they had seen too many dead men during the war and while they fled their homeland—too many who were given no grave and just lay around nowhere in particular, frozen stiff and unwanted. Dead men without flowers and adornments. Now that her husband's body was dead, they no longer seemed interested in fighting to own him. This attitude suddenly struck her as shrewd and down-to-earth. She decided to emulate it, in the event that someone asked her plans. But for now she let herself go, abandoned herself to fantasies of tombstones, flowers, and funeral orations.

The wife was alone with her cats, awake now and still in high dudgeon; their mood didn't improve when they discovered that she had forgotten to feed them. In fact there was no food in the house. The wife pondered. She knew people who owned cats. All she had to do was call them up and they would have brought her cans of cat food by the truckload. Instead she decided that she had only two choices: Either she could go out to buy a roasted chicken, pretending that this was necessary in order to console the cats, and take advantage of the opportunity to drop into a bar; or she could go to her husband's apartment and remove the seal, the scrap of paper with the magic spell on it, and check to see if it was really empty or whether someone was there, either someone else or he himself.

The wife had never been superstitious, but now notions like this kept lodging inside her and refusing to budge. She would have liked to hold a séance and conjure up her husband, because after all he couldn't be far, not yet. She remembered a friend of her parents, a writer who captured the voices of the dead on cassette tapes. The wife realized that she intended to phone this woman, Lisa Engström, whether she believed in her or not. She must leave no stone unturned. How long it takes some people to see the light!

That evening, the wife decided in favor of the bar. She had to buy something for the cats, so no one could hold it against her if they saw her drinking a beer while she waited for her order. Yes, she had to organize her time with care now, because for the present, time seemed to have stretched out to an endless expanse that couldn't be measured.

"If anything goes wrong, if anything happens to you, be sure and tell us right away," the father had ordered her as her in-laws departed. A sad and nonsensical commandment.

"I'm glad I didn't see him," his mother had said. "I still can't take it in. I can't believe it." All three of them cried as they said a relieved goodbye.

The wife set out for a café not far from her apartment. She hardly ever went there because it was a place where you tended to meet whiners who always stood at the same spot along the bar, telling the same sad tales of missed opportunities and futile love affairs. It had a few tables and a rotisserie, so that if she did happen to run into someone she knew, she could always use the excuse of needing a chicken for the cats. Besides, the bar resembled the one where she had sat long ago with Hedwig S., trying to coax her into telling her story. Hedwig hadn't been a good storyteller, she remembered. But for that very reason, she would have liked to be with Hedwig now, because she could have talked to her about her husband. For back then, at the end of the halting conversation that the wife's curiosity had started up again each time it bogged down, the prostitute had at last expressed surprise and surly pleasure in the "crazy prosecutor," as she called him.

"He's a nut case. They all are, but he's different." She had said it tenderly, almost maternally. What seemed not to sit well with her was the fact that the wife was married to this crazy man who, she thought, was penniless, desperately poor.

"No good'll come of it," she told the wife. "I got a feelin' in my bones."

"*You* say that?" the wife replied, insulted. "When you can't even pay for your coffee, and your boyfriend has stood you up?"

"Don't matter none," the fat hooker said serenely. "That one, he stinks of money. Something'll come along, something big."

The wife felt abashed then, because she thought that someone who looked like Hedwig S. had no legitimate expectation of coming into money. Why should any man give her money, much less a lot of it? The wife didn't dare ask the details of what Hedwig had to do for her money, although she would have loved to know.

That evening, she had proudly told her husband all about her meeting with Hedwig. He, too, was curious and asked at once what exactly she had found out. He had come home tired from court, from his miserable little office where so far no one had recognized that he was a champion of justice and everyone thought he was just an ambitious, arrogant young man of striking appearance who tended to reach the most startling conclusions and to arrive everywhere late.

"She must have told you something," her husband urged. "Some specific details?"

"Not one!" the wife replied.

"The johns aren't to blame, you know," he said reflectively. "After all, you don't condemn somebody because he uses an artificial leg to walk with, or dentures to chew. Hookers are crutches. Perversions are crutches too. They're substitutes for something in people that society has destroyed. You can't despise people for using surrogate limbs."

"Who's that, 'society'?" the wife repeated for the hundredth time. "Society *is* your cripples on crutches, limping around, stammering and needing artificial limbs, and making politics because they don't know it's only crutches!"

"That's half-baked garbage!"

The wife was sitting alone in the café on the second day of his death. She sat at a table with a glass of beer in front of her, staring at the rotisserie where the pale fowls rotated slowly behind glass. Thank God they were still pale: That gave her a perfect excuse to stay here in the light, waiting for the cats' food to cook and hearing the sound of people's voices. Today she even enjoyed listening to the shipwrecked waifs along the bar. The scraps of conversation were like a musical accompaniment to the pain of remembering. The real blended with the imagined. Her invisible sister Hedwig S. intertwined with the figure of a dead freedom fighter, while the visible forms of the drinkers at the bar took on a ghostly look.

"You're dressed all in black," said the barmaid, coming over to her table. "Have you had a death in the family?"

It was the first time a stranger had asked any questions about it. The wife put on a face, to test the effect. "My husband died," she said.

"Gee, I'm sorry," the woman said, a bit perplexed. "I didn't know you was married."

I suppose I'll have to go on explaining and explaining about that, thought the wife. "We hadn't been living together recently," she said, drinking her beer.

"Well, then, it won't hit you so hard," answered the barmaid. "Shall I wrap the chicken up for you?"

The wife stirred uneasily, because now she had no reason to remain in the bar and because she had so hoped to meet someone she could tell about what had happened to her husband. Of course there were any number of people she still had to notify; but she wanted to spread the word of his death throughout that other world, more remote to her, which her husband had always claimed was the real one, the one closest to his heart.

The barmaid brought the bag of hot chicken over to her table, as a special service to a new widow. She seemed slightly more interested now. Maybe on her way between the grill and the table she had decided that nothing more exciting was likely to turn up in her bar this Sunday than the death of a young husband.

"Did he suffer a lot?" She held the bag in her hand like an object she was about to pawn.

"It all happened very fast; it was asthma," the wife said deliberately. She was rehearsing questions and answers. She didn't believe her answers.

"It's awful when somebody goes so sudden!" said the bartender. She was a short, slightly bloated woman who had long ago given up any effort to be pretty. Stolidly she wore her old-fashioned permanent wave and drab sweater, beneath which you could see the grooves of her bra. She was fortyish and tended to let the corners of her mouth droop when she felt no one was looking. When she'd just come back from the hairdresser, the steady boozers who lived at the bar would call to her: "Hey, Rosie, you're looking good! I wouldn't mind a little . . . How's about it?" And she'd answer contentedly: "Lemme alone, you old boaster!"

Now the wife didn't want to talk to her anymore. She'd become restless, the bar seemed tedious and phony; she wanted to get deeper into her husband's world, into his cubbyholes, from which he had excluded her with good-natured silence.

This world of his had a doorkeeper: the boy. But the wife wanted to try to get inside on her own. She wouldn't go there tonight, the night of Easter Sunday, because for now it was probably deserted anyway; but she intended to try it later, without companions. "Go ahead," she said to herself on her way home. "Go ahead and prove to yourself that you can do it." And she felt proud that she had developed a widow's obsession so fast, without even trying.

"I'm already chattering away to myself like an old woman," she whispered with satisfaction.

The cats tore open the greasy bag to get at the chicken, and the wife barely managed to snag a thigh for herself. The animals hadn't yet forgotten the intruders. All three of them, normally placid and drowsy, snarled over the scraps of meat and skin, ground up the thin bones between their teeth, and behaved like wild things. The tiled kitchen floor glistened with grease, and the wife went into the adjacent bathroom and vomited noisily, gasping for air. When the phone rang she jumped, and swallowed a mouthful of bile.

It was the same voice. This time she recognized it at once, even though they had a very bad connection.

"Have you checked it out?" asked the man with the cover name that the wife hadn't yet remembered. It was something like Worcester, but not quite.

"I still don't know what it is I'm supposed to be checking," she said helplessly, "and besides, I can't get into his office."

"Pull yourself together," the voice said angrily from far, far away. "This business is more important right now."

"More important than what?" the wife asked, insulted.

"Most likely your phone is tapped," said the man.

Then it came to her: His cover name was Gloucester.

"We'll get word to you. Be available Tuesday afternoon."

She felt hatred for the compassionless voice that seemed uninterested in the dead man. Maybe Gloucester hadn't even known her husband. Maybe he was the type who knew only himself, and knew others only insofar as he could use them.

The wife remembered a nasty quarrel she'd had with her husband. At the time, they were still living together in their tiny garret apartment. He had explained to her how he planned to defend a case, and she hadn't seen the sense of it. It seemed to her that he treated his clients too meekly. "You don't have to let them pull your strings as if you were a servant; you don't *need* that."

Some time had passed since she had hung up the phone, and she found herself wondering where she had got that bitter taste in her mouth and how she could get rid of it. Back then, as now, she couldn't stomach being a flunky. Even the voice of this guy Gloucester had sounded as if he were used to handing out orders —even now, when he must be up to his neck in trouble. "Where do they get that from?" the wife said to herself.

She cleaned up the kitchen, avoiding looking too closely at the splinters of bone and left-over shreds of skin. She racked her brain, trying to think what it could be that Gloucester wanted her to check out. Her husband had told her a lot, but he used so many elaborate paraphrases that she didn't understand him and had stopped listening. For years, it seemed, the Group's web of information, place names, procurements, supplies, rendezvous points, and code names had been growing increasingly fine-spun, increasingly unintelligible: a fabric full of knots, each of which behaved with incredible airs of self-importance. Somewhere, sitting at the heart of the web, was someone who perhaps could boast of an overall view. But the wife sometimes had the feeling that the whole thing was less like a web and more like a giant complicated machine that could be switched on or off only by itself. The machine satisfied no one's hunger, made no one wise or beautiful or happy. It moved nothing but itself—and by moving, at the same time it moved another giant machine, which was likewise incapable of anything but moving itself.

And how this second machine used to shriek on its hinges! The machine of the state creaked like mad and shifted its gears with ever mounting frequency, with ever mounting din. The wife had told her husband so. And now she wanted to tell him again and to ask him what this man Gloucester wanted from her, whether she should give it to him, and above all what it would be used for. But there was no one for her to ask. She didn't even know if her husband's ex-partner, big Paul, had been clued in on all these ramifications. What about his other friends? No one but herself came to mind, and that made her feel proud.

"I won't talk it over with anyone," she told the sleeping cats. "I'll make a decision alone."

Suddenly her night-shrouded apartment felt threatening; yet at the same time she seemed to be sitting inside a stage set, and her husband's death was just part of a play, a plot conceived by others.

She hunted through a box for Hedwig S.'s phone number. She had run across the number repeatedly over the years and knew for sure that she had never thrown it away. She remembered how Hedwig had given it to her, on the day of their strange meeting after the trial. Despite her surly manner, Hedwig S. couldn't seem to tear herself away from the prosecutor's wife, and an obscure need to communicate, which had been bottled up in her for so long, flowed out at the touch of the younger woman's curiosity. After the wife had paid their check, Hedwig S. asked her where she was going.

"I want to buy a dress," the wife had answered.

"I'll come along," Hedwig S. said, and the wife walked side by side with the fat prostitute, feeling no embarrassment. Actually, she didn't know anyone who lived near the courthouse; that was Hedwig S.'s territory, and the wife had now been placed under her protection.

In the department store they looked at all the dresses, even though the wife had made up her mind right away which one she wanted. The saleswomen were nobody's fools. The looks they cast at Hedwig S. were rigid with contempt, and clearly they thought the wife was an apprentice in the same profession. The dress she chose was a black jersey wraparound, with an inset belt that shaped it at the waist. "Do you have that in an extra-large?" Hedwig S. had asked the sales clerk, in a genteel voice, and upon receiving a supercilious negative, replied without embarrassment: "Too bad! It would of been so practical! None of that fuss undoing all the buttons and hooks every time!" The wife couldn't help laughing, and resolved never to set foot in this store again.

"You feel embarrassed, huh?" Hedwig S. had asked sulkily. "You'll have to get used to our kind, with your man in the profession like he is. He don't have nothin' to do with nice people, with little lambs like you. He's gotta deal with the red-light district, and worse. And what's more, he's gotta talk about it all day long and can't never get any himself. He wants to be a lawyer? Then he'll get the same dirty money his clients have made, only less!"

The wife had never forgotten what Hedwig said about the dirty money. Because however you looked at it, dirty money was better than no money at all. And when the people known as the comrades came demanding his services, they called the work he did "solidarity" and didn't pay a cent. You didn't dare ask them for anything. Of course there was no way for Hedwig S. to guess that the remarkable prosecutor to whom she owed her acquittal would end up as even more of a babe in the financial woods than she had predicted.

When the two women emerged from the department store, Hedwig S. was doggedly punching and squeezing her handbag. She seemed to want to stay by the wife's side, as if she had been entrusted with her safekeeping. She paused at the entrance to a narrow lane at the upper end of the shopping boulevard. It seemed to be trying to slink away from the main avenue and was lined with crooked little houses whose doors stood half open, revealing nothing but darkness inside. One house was painted pink, and from the windows hung boxes filled with dried fir branches. This little street had the cheapest brothels in the city. "Five marks for a stand-up job!" they used to say as schoolkids, whenever one of the boys boasted of having been there. The wife had often walked through it curiously and been treated to the weary curses of the hookers. But she would never have dreamed that someone she knew would actually live there—someone she had been chatting with for over two hours. The sound of hollow blows rang out from a café—the noise of cards being slammed down on a table—but it sounded as if someone was getting beaten up.

The wife had stopped walking and gazed along the short, slanting street.

"You mustn't come with me here," said Hedwig S., and then pressed a piece of paper into her hand. It had Hedwig's phone number on it. "There," she said. "It's always possible you could need somebody like me someday. Don't laugh, now. Person like you marries a guy like you done, one day maybe she has a sad awakening. You think your man'll look out for what's right? What I say is, he only lives off what's wrong, what's bad, like we all do."

Then she vanished into one of the little houses. The wife never saw her again.

And now, five years later, she was holding Hedwig's number in her hand and wanted to tell her what had happened. To tell Hedwig and no one else.

It was a long time before someone answered the phone. The wife had assumed it would be all right to call there at night. In that profession, people must do all their living at night, she thought.

When she asked for Hedwig S., the man on the phone said

nothing for a while. Was he trying to remember, struggling to wake up? The wife couldn't tell.

"You mean Hedi?" he said then. "You mean Fat Hedi?"

"I think so," she said.

"You're a bit late. Hedi kicked the bucket a couple years ago. Her heart or something. Love and booze, ha-ha," he said. "You a relative?"

"No," said the wife, and hung up.

It was so quiet in her apartment that she could hear one of the cats dreaming in the next room.

Day Three

Easter Monday. The wife was still confined within the unrelenting calm of the holiday, which made it seem as if everything were standing still. And yet time was passing. Today she really ought to do a bit of work. Her work was translations, literary and film reviews, and now and then a radio program. Free-lance work was pleasurable and afforded you the luxury of getting up late; so she had imposed on herself a stringent corset of deadlines to keep her from frittering away her time and energy and loafing on the job. Her husband, rather grudgingly, had admired the fact that after their separation she had achieved another separation, quitting her salaried job as an editor, and yet she had never brought up the question of support.

"There's no doubt he would have liked me to ask him for money," she said as she sat down by the window with a big cup of coffee and stared out at the Monday that looked just the same as a Sunday. "No doubt at all." It had wounded him that they couldn't play the classic married roles: himself as the breadwinner who makes all the decisions, she as an attendant who looked after him and stood by his side during protest demonstrations. "That's the way we were," said the wife.

Later that day she looked over some French theater journals. She noticed that she understood nothing and couldn't decipher the words. Today the foreign language stayed foreign; she recognized that it didn't belong to her. Sometimes her husband used to do translations too, of short political pieces written in English. He would sit hunched over the typewriter, his thick dark hair hanging down into his eyes, and his big back hiding the text so that you couldn't see what he was doing. From time to time his nose would make pecking motions and dart straight at the text. He would type fitfully and irregularly, sometimes racing along at a furious speed. Occasionally he would read something aloud in his theatrical voice and his wife would listen with envy. For him the foreign tongue was like his own. When he couldn't think of a word he would make one up. And yet, all the while he was typing and wheezing and reciting, and rustling and searching through his other papers, she would see that under the table his big toes were pressed together and his heels spread apart. Under the table, he had been afraid.

Anyway, she'd managed to get the funeral director to say he'd visit her today, on the holiday; she could feel that she was achieving something, making a small show of progress. He would help her, explaining everything she didn't understand.

No doubt a man in his profession has to tidy up deaths far more ghastly and complicated than this one, she thought. When somebody drowns and they can't find the body, for example. Or people burn to death and you can't identify who's who. She wondered whether she would have felt better or worse if her husband's body had been destroyed, truly obliterated so that it could never be put back together. Somehow that would have made more sense. He had been so handsome. No doubt he still was, wherever he might be now. She pictured his body lying stretched out, half on, half off the bed. The image was clear one minute, blurred the next. They hadn't allowed her enough time with him for it to become unforgettable. "Now he'll never get any older," she said to one of her grumpy cats.

Her husband had brown eyes under straight black eyebrows with only the hint of an arch. His nose was large and narrow, his mouth wide. He had been the exact image of what everybody thinks a Pole should look like. His shoulders drooped forward when he talked with someone shorter than himself. This seemed a mark of politeness but it wasn't.

Once, when the two of them were in their local bar, somebody asked him for legal advice about a rental problem.

"What are you studying?" her husband had replied.

"Medicine," the other man said, looking perplexed.

"I wouldn't lie down here on the bar and ask you to look at my stomach to see what's wrong with me."

"Arrogant bastard!" commented one of the onlookers. "He just talks big. He doesn't know the meaning of solidarity," said another. And her husband had smiled, happy that people were quarreling about him.

He used to make a lot of people mad. He could send them into unexpected fits of foaming rage: prosecutors and Marxists, bank clerks and Trotskyites, salesmen, hairdressers, bar owners and legal clients. Other people's rage was as indispensable to him as their love. The seamier types found it easy to love him. Motorbike gang members and drug addicts, delinquent girl runaways and male hustlers, took to him because he wasn't like them and never acted as if he were. He didn't speak to them tenderly. He couldn't master that tone of all-comprehending indulgence toward every form of social deviation that came into vogue at the end of the sixties. He spoke the same way to them all: nervous, rapid, impatient. His voice had a wide range of pitches.

The way he talked gave no clue to where he came from. When he chose, he could speak in a Frankish dialect so thick that you'd have thought there was more than a hint of peasant garlic on his breath. In court he would sometimes drawl out a phrase until it got the attention he wanted, while he chewed up others—things he was forced to say but didn't approve of—so that nobody could understand him. His wife had often observed these tactics with pride, at the same time feeling a little ashamed.

You can't help but be dubious about the whole profession, she thought as she stood at her kitchen window. Should anybody be a lawyer, either good or bad? But her pride in her husband had always won out.

One time, her husband had taken her along to a consultation with some of his clients. A motorcycle gang from the neighborhood had been charged with robbery, grievous bodily injury, and hit-and-run assault. Her husband was supposed to represent three of the group. He and his clients had arranged to meet in a neutral bar, so that neither side would have the home advantage.

"It's a weird dive," her husband had said. "Wear something plain. The guys who go there all run around in leather anyway."

"Including you?" she asked.

"Of course," her husband replied. "How else do you think I'm going to get close to these types? They have to learn to trust me."

"You just think it's chic wearing that kind of outfit," his wife had grumbled. "What's so special about leather? I'll wear leather too."

Her husband laughed. "Do you want to look like a leather medicine ball?" he asked.

This scene happened about six months before they separated. His remark had made her cry with fury.

"Never mind." Her husband tried to comfort her. "Wear anything you want; they'll like you no matter what."

He had looked somber and savage in a sort of motorcycle suit of soft black leather, his favorite clothes apart from his lawyer's robes. This showy outfit looked good on him, with his long legs and wide-slung pelvis.

How did he see himself in that getup? As Easy Rider, or a black angel, or the masculine incarnation of the goddess Anarchy? Certainly he always took care to set the scene and come up with a suitable costume. But this time his wife was determined to give him a run for his money. If he wanted to look dark and dramatic, then she'd go for a different look, bright colors and sunshine.

"We'll see which of us wins the hearts of the bikers," she muttered, putting on gaudy makeup. "They already know guys who look like you; that's the look they go in for themselves. But they don't know me. Their girls look like boys. I don't."

"An elderly lady of twenty-six," her black-leather husband said over her shoulder to her image in the bathroom mirror. "What are you doing, trying to seduce the Bones?" And he had laughed.

"Isn't that what *you're* trying to do?" she asked the mirror, applying sparkling eyeshadow. Of course he wanted to seduce them. But she'd settle his hash. "What did you say their name is?"

"They call themselves the Bones. They have some kind of big bones hanging from their belts. But you needn't be scared; they're as meek as lambs when they're clients. It's really funny to watch them: they come on like musclebound heroes and then suddenly they get scared stiff because they remember they're still on probation, or they're applying for some apprenticeship."

"Are they victims?" the wife had asked. "Everybody's always supposed to be a victim, aren't they?"

"Of course," her husband had reproved her. "Don't ask such silly questions! If you'd just read a single case history to find out their background and what they've been through, you'd see what kind of victims they are, and whose too."

The beer joint was deserted. It was a little cellar pub with slogans pinned up on the wall: USA = US ASS-ASSINS; DEATH TO IMPERIALISM; DOWN WITH THE FRANCO REGIME. A wooden bar occupied one corner, with crates of bottles stacked on the wall behind it. A pillar of paper cups at one end of the bar, and at the other a contribution box labeled "For Victory in the People's War!" The ceiling was painted dark red, the floor made of fresh, untreated boards. Armchairs and sofas covered in greasy red-and-green-patterned upholstery were ranged around low tables. The pub resembled a lot of the other mod leftist hangouts of that decade, like the endless lounges, the Republican Clubs and Club Voltaires of Berlin, Hamburg, and Frankfurt, the rendezvous spots, the local dives.

Even now, as she sat waiting for Mr. Sable, who was coming to take charge of her husband's funeral arrangements, she still felt a nostalgia for those bars. Most of them had disappeared without a trace. The rest had been redecorated and looked like frozen food.

Four years ago, when she and her husband went down into the cellar joint to meet the bikers, they found the clients already seated, their hulking bodies unsuited to the cocktail lounge armchairs left over from the fifties. They sat with their legs spread wide apart as if they were still on their bikes, their heavy boots pressed firmly on the floor. The bellies of two of them were bare to the navel underneath their sleeveless leather vests. Their midriffs and arms didn't look naked because they were covered with bright tattoos. The third client wore a thick gray-green leather uniform blouse that looked like military issue. All three had on roomy jeans, and indeed a bone hung at each right hip amid a cluster of switchblades and fur tails. Chains swung from their thick necks. Two of them had big swastikas dangling from their chains. The wife could still remember how shocked she had been. Back in 1970 you didn't see anybody wearing swastikas, not even Hell's Angels.

"Gettin' an eyeful, are you?" one of them said to her placidly.

"Get your act together," her husband said without a flicker. "This is my wife, you asshole." He turned to her and introduced them. "This is Mike, and that's Bennie, and Blutwurst."

"What?" she asked.

"My name's Blutwurst," the thinnest one said, the one with the leather blouse. "Somethin' wrong with that?"

The three hadn't bothered to stand when the couple came over. Her husband just stood there waiting, black and tall, taller than the three hulks. The one he had called Bennie stuck out his foot and dragged two stools over to the low table. "Come on and siddown with your old lady."

Her husband remained standing. "You'd better take a different tone," he said sternly. "Or I'll drop the case, and you know what that means. You won't find any lawyer from around here who's willing to touch a chickenshit case like yours. I don't much want to handle it myself." After that the three looked slightly abashed, and their faces and gestures took on something resembling politeness.

How she had admired her husband that evening! Meanwhile she had gone on staring at the swastikas for so long that at last Blutwurst asked her what was wrong with them, so she gave him a long lecture about children killed in gas chambers. Back in those days, both she and her husband were still up to delivering a rousing lecture. They thought you could talk the world into being good, or at least a sizable chunk of it. As for the three gang members, with their dread of the trial they made perfect victims for lectures. Sitting there with their splayed bikers' legs and their loutish hands, these immobile mountains of flesh had no way of defending themselves.

"Knowledge is power," her husband whispered to her. "Are you still scared now?"

"I never was," she whispered back indignantly. Her husband had conferred some of his power on her, and that evening she had been given a chance to enjoy it. In the end, Blutwurst got worn down and decided to flush the swastikas down the toilet.

"What year were you guys born anyway?" the wife asked.

"Nineteen fifty," Mike, the fattest one, answered morosely. "Anything wrong wi' that?"

"Postwar. Born yesterday. They haven't got the foggiest notion, but they run around wearing that Nazi crap," said her husband.

"Yeah, so what about you?" Blutwurst retorted scornfully. "You and all the rest of them college liberals! You walk around wearing your fucking parkas instead of minks so you can prove how proletarian you are, and always making out how you're so poor. Why do any of you bother to go to college anyways? So you can make more dough later on, that's why, and don't you try an' tell me any different."

"So far I haven't see hide nor hair of all that dough," her husband answered coldly. But his wife saw how his fingers were tugging at the knuckles of his left hand until they cracked.

That evening in the deserted left-wing dive, the two of them had been very much a couple, a pair of scared college graduates who were invulnerable because they were together. The wife had felt her husband's hand on her thigh repeatedly throughout the evening. Finally the two of them had cut the other three down to size. Drinking beer and exchanging scraps of conversation about their childhoods, they all felt closer, and after a lot of beer they even believed for a little while that they spoke the same language.

Still two hours to go before the funeral director would arrive. The wife looked out at the white street and felt the warmth of a cat's body rubbing against her legs. If only she knew the right way to go about it, what things to watch out for. Or did you pay the funeral director just so you wouldn't have to watch out for anything? Mr. Sable had had a cordial voice on the telephone. Of course he more or less has to, she thought.

But this is a really important corpse. Different from the rest. People had to be made to understand this, again and again, and who but her could tell them? She would be her dead husband's herald, his epic poet, a female minstrel to sing of his intelligence and beauty. "Bullshit," she said softly to her cat. "What's the right way to grieve? I'm not feeling the things I think I ought to feel. There's no one to tell me. And he's past caring." And yet she felt, more clearly all the time, that this wasn't quite true. A nearby presence kept saying to her: There's nothing he doesn't care about —no matter where he is, no matter what.

She resolved, for the hundredth time, to do everything properly, to attend to the smallest detail: to give the same devotion to the political files as to the funeral director; to the autopsy as to the law office, the parents, and the debts. All were equally important, and in fact, by rights, she ought not to allow herself any time to sleep, not even for an hour, so as to neglect nothing. Unfortunately she was sleeping very well. She recognized that it wasn't proper to sleep peacefully, and then on top of that to feel ravenously hungry, as she did this noon. Widows weren't supposed to sleep, they weren't supposed to eat, either. She felt ashamed of herself because it had crossed her mind that this terrible event might make her thinner and perhaps more beautiful.

"Hey, kiddo," her husband had said after their rendezvous with the bike gang, "they thought you were a real doll. I suppose they need something sturdy like you to hold down their motorbikes."

"Well, anyway, *you* didn't stand a chance with them," she answered tartly, "not even after wrapping yourself up in twenty pounds of leather."

"Are you crazy?" he said, laughing his overloud ho-ho-ho. "Me interested in those fat butchers? What I'm after is slender young ephebes!"

Well, what could she possibly do about that? she had thought. Now she thought it again this Easter Monday. What would happen if *they* came and tried to claim him for themselves? She knew she hadn't yet got rid of the body; nor had she defeated this special world that her husband had never explained to her, although admittedly he had never kept her out, either. A world that was closed though it had no walls, and inaccessible though it could be heard, seen, and smelled. Would she be able to get in now, using his corpse for a shield, his dead body for a key?

Ephebes! Sometimes she used to look at her breasts, thinking they were like vegetable baskets—necessary but unappealing.

"You're a silly goose," her husband had said right after delivering his insulting crack about the ephebes—the thousandth remark of that kind he had hurt her with. "You're a terrific woman. You're just right for a woman. You're just the kind I want, and you can damned well eat a lot more for all I care! Don't try to be a man in disguise. The thing between me and boys, that's something different. It has nothing to do with you."

"Everything has to do with me," she always wanted to say, but never did. It would have been so bourgeois, so square, to get upset by his polymorphous peculiarities. Actually, he had never tried to hide anything from her; he just seemed to know that she'd never understand. Why did Bluebeard bother to lock room number seven? Had he left it standing wide open, all his wives would have passed by with their heads turned away and never betrayed his secret.

The wife started to eat a big sandwich. She was so hungry. But she left half of it on the plate, and a little later she vomited. Afterward she felt proud and weak. She was learning to be a widow. That she could manage, even if she hadn't been a proper wife. She had walked out on him three years ago, on account of some now forgotten ephebe. But why had she left him, really? "That was wrong of me," she said to herself on the third day of his death. "Why didn't I ask more questions? Now I have to figure it all out for myself."

One of her cats bounded inaudibly onto the kitchen table, where she was sitting, and began to walk back and forth, back and forth past her lowered face, as if it knew that a cat sometimes comes in handy as a handkerchief. Back and forth walked the cat, brushing against the wife's eyes, and didn't seem to mind its fur getting damp.

She'd failed him, failed! She'd abandoned her husband. She'd given away his cats. She'd driven away the boy. She'd been unable to make the dead son understood by his parents. And yet how easy it would have been to make them understand! She thought of her mother-in-law's eyes, those disbelieving blue eyes that knew it all yet kept it firmly locked out. She thought of the dead eyes of her father-in-law, who had lost a son for no reason—that is, without a war. It wasn't her husband who had been the betrayer, the failure, but she. She, sitting there at the kitchen table dressed up in black clothes that masqueraded as mourning, drying her crocodile tears on a cat; she, who was playing the role of the widow.

Things were a bit dead this Easter Monday. The telephone was silent, the doorbell stayed still. Bach's *St. Matthew Passion* was playing on the radio and it didn't agree with her.

Her husband had been a complete blank when it came to music. He had sung so badly that he had managed to throw an entire protest demonstration off key with his own version of the "Internationale." His wife's love for her records had been a total mystery to him. He didn't believe that anyone could really love something like that for its own sake, and not simply to create an attractive image of oneself as a music lover. But there had been three pieces of music that he would listen to, a hundred times over. One was Nana Mouskouri's nostalgic song "Adieu Mes Amis." This afternoon the wife realized that she'd never be able to listen to that record again, that it would have to be broken over his grave or played at his funeral—but nobody would be able to stand it. Another was Scott McKenzie singing "If you ever go to San Francisco." Her husband always used to sing along with that, unrecognizably but very loudly.

And then surprisingly, he liked a type of music that his wife detested, and that he felt quite capable of producing himself, indeed had a positive talent for: Stockhausen and other composers of avant-garde, atonal, and electronic music.

"Maybe I should be a composer," he once said. "You love those consecutive melodies, where each note comes out of the one before. Music isn't supposed to follow along in sequence. Bach and that sort of stuff—I always know after every note what will come next. Boring!"

But they had never argued about it. She had always been too

ready to credit him with genius, however wayward its forms, to argue the point. So why hadn't he become a composer? Then he might still be alive! Instead he had immersed himself in the life of the hard-boiled utopians who wanted to change the whole world yet were incapable of showing the least kindness and affection to the people they met every day.

Strange as it seemed, there was nothing her husband had feared so much as the contempt of these reformers. They were the true wolves, a shy and beautiful pack for whom all other animals existed only as prey. He had admired them. That had angered her. What reason had he to admire anyone else?

By some peculiar trick, they had managed to reduce intelligent adults to the status of children. Whatever the Group said or did was received with this strange admiration and a craving for more. Back when the Group started, the husband and wife had been among their first admirers. The Group sounded just like the manifestos they'd read. They had searched book after book for methods and battle cries like the Group's. The Group could light up the world and set it on fire.

But over the years, the wife had noticed with growing bafflement that she never knew what it was really all about. Everyone involved—the sacrosanct inner circle, those farther removed from the center, those on the outer fringe, and those who made the scene only now and then—they all had an endless series of missions to carry out that seemed unrelated to any tangible gain: Handle this. Take a look around there. Watch that house. Get hold of that paper. Come and fetch this box.

But the purpose of it all escaped them. At some point, the wolf pack of the elect seemed to have lost track of it themselves. And yet in the early years, when they burned down the big department store in Frankfurt, you could somehow derive warmth from the flames.

She wished the funeral director would come, to serve as a scarecrow and drive off her flock of memories. She didn't want to think of her husband as anyone's lackey. Maybe he hadn't been. A doer, a perpetrator: that was the role she would have preferred—but he hadn't been that either.

She went into the living room and looked out the window. It was five minutes to three. A plumpish man in dark clothing was walking slowly up and down in front of the building, now and then casting a quick side glance at her apartment. He couldn't see her, only the rectangular panes of glass and the white stripes of the curtains. The wife knew that she was safe from his gaze. And yet at the same time how exposed her life seemed, how vulnerable! The man walked up and down, up and down, passing the houses next door with each circuit and then turning to walk back. He carried a flat black portfolio under his arm.

That sort always arrive on the dot, she thought. They give themselves time to spare so that they can get a good look at your present abode before they go in to offer you a final abode. The two have to match. He wouldn't recommend a bronze-footed oak chest to a family living in a welfare institution. He's watching my house like a bailiff or a detective, she thought. Her next thought was that she might be developing a slight persecution mania. She was an important person now, the widow of a left-winger, of a man with secrets.

The moment she stood face to face with the funeral director, she had the impression that his piercing gaze, sharpened on so many deaths, could see at once that this one was special.

"Where would you like to sit?" she asked. He chose to spurn the rocking chair, and draped his soft, dark coat over the back of a reliable-looking armchair.

"First let me offer you my condolences," he said. "Please don't think I'm saying that just as a matter of routine. In my profession you can't allow anything to get routine. But a man as young as your husband! It's hard to see any meaning behind it."

He sat there the way a woman sits, his knees pressed together, his plump arms folded in front of his chest. Nothing in his face gave you a clue to remember it by: no beard, no scars, no glasses.

"Grief shouldn't be marred by disorganization. But grieving people are incapable of organizing things. That's where we come in."

With a sweeping arm gesture he indicated his invisible helpers, summoned entities whose nature the wife couldn't begin to imagine. He made as if he had angels at his command. She wondered if it would be improper for her to light a candle.

"Would you like something to drink?" she asked.

"A drink makes it easier to talk," he said.

"What's the appropriate thing to drink when someone has died? This is my first experience."

"You're far too young to have acquired that sort of experience," Mr. Sable said politely. "I'd suggest a little sherry if you happen to have some. It's invigorating too. It looks to me as if you haven't eaten since the sad event, if you don't mind my saying so."

The wife nodded, feeling thin. She was grateful to this man for enveloping her in a solicitude that she could pay for afterward, that didn't obligate her to be grateful. He was a professional, like a masseur or a telephone psychiatrist. She also felt quite sure that once the afternoon was over, he would forget everything she had said to him.

Mr. Sable opened his black portfolio and took out a stack of papers. She could detect nothing suspicious on the top sheet. She had been expecting big colored illustrations of coffins and flower arrangements.

"Today is still the holiday, of course," said Mr. Sable. "I'll have to wait until tomorrow morning to contact the medical examiner about the release."

Release? What release? So her husband's body was a prisoner now. In jail for the first time.

"We'll get him, dead or alive," she murmured. Aloud, she asked Mr. Sable, "What does that mean, that he has to be released?"

"I beg your pardon?" he said courteously. "What was it you said a moment ago?"

"Oh, nothing," she answered; but she could tell from the polite, still, sable's face that he had understood her exactly.

"Ah, well, this question of releasing the remains always arises if there's even the slightest doubt about the cause of death," said Mr. Sable. "And in the case of your worthy husband, they really had to get to the bottom of it. With a young man like him, one can't just accept everything without asking questions. There have to be some explanations!" He was getting quite worked up.

She felt abashed, as if she had been making a sloppy job of her husband's death.

"It's horrible for me, thinking they're free to do anything they like to him there," she said. "And after they're through, they simply release him!"

"I understand just what you mean," Mr. Sable replied, stacking his papers in a different order. "In cases like this, relatives have an easier time of it if they're a simpler sort of people. They don't try to imagine what's going on."

"What do you mean exactly?" she asked suspiciously, and thought: This guy's a right-winger.

"The simpler sort of relatives have an easier time all around," Mr. Sable said patiently, "because they don't think so much about the past. They only think about what's going to happen next, especially if there's a business involved, or children, and no will. You won't have to think about any of that," he said reproachfully. "But I understand exactly what you mean. You just let me worry about the medical examiner. One can remove every trace of what they've done. You can remove everything without a trace, believe me."

She could feel a thought rising in her mind and tried to suppress it. It scared her to think it. It was this thing about removing all traces. Maybe you could do that for a little while, for the few days the body stayed aboveground. But then it went underground, and under the ground everything changes swiftly and soundlessly, incomprehensibly.

The funeral expert spread out his papers with a determined gesture, as if he were unfolding a fan. So there were to be pictures after all; but discreet ones, black-and-white. At first glance, everything she saw seemed petty and philistine. The coffins looked pretty much alike except that some were lighter, some darker in color, with more or fewer bulges, more or fewer metal fittings. Nothing there for her husband. No suitable last abode.

"But my husband is very tall," she told Mr. Sable proudly and desperately, as if she thought he might be carrying a second, secret portfolio for kings.

"In that case, we still have something suitable. No doubt you had something unusual in mind. But my dear madam, life is the time for the unusual. It's not what you need from me."

She selected a light-colored coffin. The picture gave her no impression of its size.

"That's a suitable model," said Mr. Sable. "That's just the sort of thing I'd have recommended."

"How much is it?" she asked, not so much because she wanted to know as because she thought it was proper to ask.

"I'm sure it will fall within the range covered by your insurance. I'll need to ask you to give me your insurance papers. After that, there's nothing further you have to bother with. That's what people like me are for. I suppose the deceased had a large family, numerous friends?"

The answer stuck in her throat; the "yes" just wouldn't come out.

"I don't know exactly about his family," she answered, like a schoolgirl replying to her teacher. "He has parents, a few aunts —I don't know. Legal colleagues, of course. And friends too," she said eagerly, feeling ashamed at the way she went on staunchly betraying her husband.

"I'm only asking so as to know how many cards we'll have to have printed up," Mr. Sable said soothingly. "I'll deliver them to you tomorrow. We can compose the text in a few minutes, along with the obituary notice for the papers. You'll be able to read the notice tomorrow."

"Do you think it only becomes real to you when you see it in print?" she asked.

"A lot of people feel that way," replied Mr. Sable, "especially young ones. It hits them hard when they actually see a friend's name in the obituary columns. And no doubt the deceased has left many young friends behind who will mourn his passing."

Two things came into her mind: the boy, the youthful mourner; and the idea that Mr. Sable belonged to that same secret nocturnal society as her husband and many of his friends. She couldn't tell by looking at him; his appearance gave nothing away. But she could sense it, in his smooth, gravely amiable face, his solicitude, his still eyes, his pale, plump hands, which kept reshuffling the papers. He's part of it, she thought, and felt reassured, as if this guaranteed that her husband's uniqueness would be respected. She would have liked to tell Mr. Sable what she felt; but perhaps he already knew.

"Maybe a hundred?" she asked cautiously. "One hundred cards?" Just at the moment she couldn't think of as many as ten people she wanted to send a funeral notice to. But they'll come, she thought.

"Fine. One hundred," said Mr. Sable, making notes. "And perhaps we could just talk about the outfitting before we go on to the text?"

"What outfitting?"

Mr. Sable leaned back in his chair, causing a modest paunch to bulge under his dark vest. "I mean what the deceased will wear."

Suddenly, in her mind, her husband was transformed into a tall mannequin who kept changing clothes, a different color each time. It was like watching a slide lecture. Click—she could see the pictures quite distinctly.

His evening suit with the black cutaway coat and the wide trousers. The thing had been so expensive. Back then they didn't have any money, but he had set his heart on it and wore it to his second state exam. The other students were so impressed they forgot to laugh.

His jeans, which he wore with an embroidered lilac-colored silk shirt. He liked to leave the shirt open at the neck, and you could see a couple of chest hairs. His neck chains. The cheap rings that looked expensive on his bony hands with their eternally cracking joints.

His tuxedo, custom-tailored, so elegant, with a flawlessly knotted tie. This, too, they had bought when they were broke: post-tux, they were really out of money. He had still belonged to his student fraternity, and never missed one of their silly balls.

Click, click. More and more slides passed through her head, showing her husband in all his costumes. His lawyer's robe. There he stood in the gown, his left arm raised accusingly, pointing at her. She could see his white piqué bowtie quite clearly. Was this the right outfit for him to lie dead in?

The tight, narrow, black leather suit, the costume for his night side. Now she would know more about it. That was the side of him he shared with the boy. If he wore that suit, he wouldn't be lying there alone, she thought.

What about his turn-of-the-century, bohemian-style cape? The Aristide Bruant get up, with the big slouch hat he used to wear, mockingly, to make it easy for the police patrols to shadow him?

His silver-gray flannel suit with the exceptionally narrow trousers. His wife had given him that as a present once when she earned an unexpectedly high fee. More and more pictures; and Mr. Sable waited patiently, seeming to know what she was seeing and feeling.

"What do you usually dress them in?" she asked clumsily. All the black or colored clothes had seemed to suit him, but only if he was alive; in none could she picture him lying down and not moving. His clothes weren't made for lying down in.

"There are several possibilities," said Mr. Sable. "Actually, only older gentlemen are buried in their best suits, or in a uniform. The classic apparel is the shroud, which once again comes in various qualities."

This was dragging out interminably. "What are they made of?" she asked.

"We have them in anything from paper to silk," answered Mr. Sable.

"Silk!" she decided. She thought she could hear her husband's laugh again, but already it seemed farther away.

"That's what I expected you'd say," returned Mr. Sable. "And you'd also like the finer coffin accessories?"

"Yes," she replied.

They still had to compose the obituary. The wife insisted on a simple announcement of impressive size. No extra words, no added remarks, no pious maxims.

"Do you want it to include the date of the funeral?" said Mr. Sable.

"I don't know when that'll be yet," she said, suddenly sobbing. "I have to wait for them to finish cutting him up."

"Tomorrow you'll find the funeral date in the newspaper," Mr. Sable said consolingly. "Don't give it another thought! Sable will do it for you!"

The wife didn't dare ask if Mr. Sable himself would dress her husband in the shroud. She ought to have insisted on doing it. But by the time he was ready to be clothed, he would no longer be all in one piece, and she was afraid to see that. She was left with a flat sensation, as if she had gone to an important gathering and behaved indelicately, used bad grammar, eaten with her fingers. She felt like a foreign tribeswoman, clumsy, crude, crassly alive in this kingdom of death; a newcomer who had arrived too soon. The suave, dark-clad Mr. Sable could see her entangling herself in invisible nets. A sense of shame spread through her. She didn't know if it was normal in this situation.

"I ought to know better, so many friends of mine have died," she said out loud.

"That's sad at your age," said Mr. Sable. "But what do you mean exactly?"

"I don't know," she said. "It's so hard to do everything right."

It had been different when Meta died, and Jürgen, and Tony. Then she was free to feel sad, or shocked, or angry. She hadn't had anything to do with the body and with what happens afterward.

"Couldn't you embalm him?" she asked. She remembered Evelyn Waugh's story about the death industry in Hollywood, where they used makeup to banish death. Her husband would have fit into the Hollywood scene. He could have played the part of a lawyer, no one more beautifully than he. The notion of embalming him was growing on her; why hadn't she thought of it sooner? He'd be like Snow White in her glass coffin, like the hero in the Hoffmann tale where the corpse lies petrified in the mine at Falun: a visible relic that would bring comfort rather than distress.

"My dear madam," said the expert, "I think you're getting some strange notions. That's not the custom here, and besides, it would cost a fortune. You'd have to fly in specialists from the

U.S.A. And I don't think you really have an appropriate resting place to keep him in. It's a rite that's not part of our culture," he added sternly. "We're not Egyptians, or Hollywood actors."

"But people do have it done sometimes," she protested.

"There are always eccentrics," said Mr. Sable, "and anything is possible. But you're a levelheaded young woman."

She felt it fatherly of him to admonish her. But he hadn't really understood how dreadful it was for her to let her husband be destroyed without a fight. Eventually he'd realize that her notions weren't so foolish after all.

She decided to spend that last quiet holiday evening drawing sketches of tomb monuments. Maybe her husband would sense what she was doing, as he traveled the road that was leading him away from all he had known. For she firmly believed that a man doesn't die all at once but needs some time to complete the separation.

Mr. Sable rose, restacked his papers for the last time, in an entirely new order, then put them back in the black portfolio. She gave him the insurance documents he had asked for.

"You can rely on us fully and absolutely," Mr. Sable said at the door as he took his leave. "Everything will be done just as you wish. There's nothing more you need worry about. And tomorrow you'll learn the date of the funeral. I assume you'll buy your own newspaper. I'll have a sample copy dropped off for you, and ten of the death announcements, to start with. You'll be needing those. I'll contact your insurance company about the payment. I'm sure you'll have nothing more to pay."

He offered a soft handshake and left her alone, with nothing to occupy her time.

All the previous deaths in her life had been dramatic, almost unreal; but this was different. This time she had to arrange for a body to disappear in the prescribed manner so that it would never bother anyone again. The clergymen say the body isn't important, but it is. Her husband's thirty-year-old body had been the place where his voice lived; his thoughts had been housed in the nut-shaped brain that people were now planning to strip of its shell; his body had been the home of his desires; his affection had lodged in his hands, his swiftness in his feet. Everything had had its home inside him. And he hadn't wanted to leave this home—not like her friend who years ago had let a train run over her neck; not like her lover who had shot himself; not like that friend of theirs who had gone to the most expensive hotel in Florence and there shot and killed himself. Those three had all wanted to separate from their bodies, and it is a merciful thing, and a light burden, to bury a body that died of self-inflicted wounds. But her husband hadn't wanted this separation. Never had he expressed any such idea, not even when suffering the sharpest throes of love.

"He'd have been afraid to commit a sin like that," the wife said to herself, now that she'd been left alone. "After all, he was a Catholic."

She had neglected to mention this fact to Mr. Sable, and Sable evidently had thought it unnecessary to ask. She'd have to have a priest.

When she had first met her husband, he used to keep a little altar to the Virgin Mary in the window of his tiny room in the students' dorm, and under his bed lay clouds of damp, crumpled-up paper tissues that he'd used to dry his penitential tears. From the window of his multistory dorm you had a view of green cornfields, where, as everyone knows, nothing lives except the corn. Occasionally rooks would cautiously patrol its borders. The physics department's nuclear reactor glowed milky white in the distance.

Her husband had owned a ravaged desk, a prayer rug (not authentic), and a very few personal toilet articles. The first present she ever gave him was a pair of small, expensive, bright-colored underpants. He had been deliriously pleased. Almost too pleased—but she had known that in some circles he was known as the Contessa, and it hadn't bothered her. It's a reaction against the strict Catholic background, she had thought, and the small-town upbringing. Books were full of that sort of thing.

He had been a considerate friend and an egotistical lover, no different from other men. That's just how they are, she thought, and I love him. Besides, the entire law school (his) and liberal arts school (hers) had been following the progress of his domestication, and this had made her very proud. They were a very visible couple, especially when the political scene hotted up in 1968. They didn't want to move in together, so they went on walking the long distance between her room, in an unfurnished villa, and his high-rise cell at the edge of the city, not even noticing extremes of weather.

Mr. Sable the funeral designer had stayed in her apartment for over an hour and he left emptiness in his wake. Now there was no one to whom she could talk about her husband. Yesterday she had longed for Hedwig S. as listener, confidante, and professional mourner woman. Today she suddenly thought about the members of the biker club, the Bones. She would have liked to see their faces when they heard about the death of their black-leather lawyer.

Maybe they'll come to the funeral, she thought. She pictured their motorcycles, draped in black crepe, banked in rows to the right and left of the coffin. But most likely they did that only for one of their own. Death was a familiar visitor in their ranks and they had learned to greet him appropriately. They wouldn't understand a death like her husband's. For them there was only one kind of death: a motorcycle death.

But what was the right sort of death for a lawyer? Especially a lawyer like him, one who had a night side?

It was all difficult and it was all wrong, and the wife lurched back and forth between pain and the next best thing she could find.

Then a couple of telephone calls came. People seemed to get up the courage to phone as evening set in, as if it were easier to admit death once it was dark out.

The wife heard her soft, phony voice on the telephone as if it belonged to someone else. It wasn't really she who said: "Yes, it's true. No, they still don't know the exact cause. Yes, I think the emergency doctors slipped up. I haven't taken it all in, I simply haven't reached that point yet." She heard herself say it, and at that very moment she thought: This same sentence is being uttered by thousands of the bereaved. "I feel numb. It all happened so fast. We were together only the evening before. . . ."

Actually that wasn't true. The last time they had been together had been a whole week ago, when they had met at a club. He had been sitting in a corner playing chess with the boy, although he didn't play well. He had hugged her and she had smelled his patchouli scent, stronger than ever.

"Hey, kiddo!" he had cried. "Sweetheart! You're getting more beautiful all the time."

The two of them had left the boy sitting at the chessboard and they stood together at the bar. They had talked about one of his court cases, and her husband had glanced behind him more often than usual. "We have to meet again sometime in the next few days," he had whispered, "when the boy isn't along. It's impossible to talk here anyway. There are a couple of things I want you to know. It's about the Shakespeare guy." She had understood at once what he meant and asked, "The usual place?"

There was a café downtown where they would sometimes meet to give an atmosphere of secrecy and importance to their discussions. And they did on occasion talk about things that it was better no one else should hear. They would argue in soft hisses about the Armed Struggle—which the wife thought was nonsense—and about ways of uncovering the growing neofascism. Both of them had bright ideas about that. "So when do we meet there?" she had asked, that last evening in the club.

She had felt no presentiment, sensed nothing out of the ordinary, seen no fiery writing on the wall. A deathly silence should by rights have come over the hubbub; a raven's wing ought to have brushed her face. But there had been nothing.

"A week from today, usual place," her husband had said, and then turned to the boy, who had glided over slowly and pushed his way between the man and the woman.

"Are you getting bored?" the husband asked the boy fondly. "I'm sorry. I'll be back in a minute."

"I've had enough," the boy said, not specifying what he meant. "There are other places we can go."

To the wife this meant: He and I are going to our own world.

She had felt then as if she had actually heard the boy speak these words, and yet he had said nothing of the sort, but only laid his thin hand on the man's sleeve, seeming to guide him. In fact he had smiled at the wife and said, "Coming with us? This place is dead." She had refused disagreeably, and the two men left. No voice inside her shrieked: Stop and look, this is the last time you'll ever see him! The patchouli scent didn't suddenly turn sinister, the radio didn't start to play ominous music. There was no sign. Her husband simply walked out with the boy, forever.

At that moment she had been curious about their upcoming "Shakespeare" talk, which, she believed now, would have had something to do with Gloucester. Was the Gloucester thing a legacy from her husband, a legacy she had still to redeem?

She wandered through her twilit apartment, feeling more and more tied down by the holiday. There was so much she needed to do. She had a suspicion that while she felt confined in her apartment, the detectives had long since ripped the seal off her husband's law office and were taking advantage of the holiday quiet to give the place a thorough going-over. Her husband's files would be forced open to reveal their secrets. But that mustn't be. The office must sleep, paralyzed and mute, until she came to awaken it. She was now the only person entitled to do so.

She didn't want the police to find out about all his people: The bearded conscientious objectors with their pockets full of leaflets, living on fruit-nut loaves, who stuck to their cause so stubbornly and with such gentle eyes. The ratty little drug dealers who would cut an ounce to stretch it into five and then set aside half for their own lacerated veins, and who acted no differently inside the slammer than out, with their paraphernalia of shredded tinfoil, small bags, blotting paper, and tiny spoons and scales. The sour spinster caseworkers who would care for their political prisoners to the point of self-sacrifice, writing innumerable senseless petitions to the attorney general's office on their behalf, until they fell in love with their charges and set about trying to marry them. The aging actresses who fought to get long-forgotten husbands to pay up their back alimony. The schizophrenics who had learned that fighting the political system was a necessary step toward mental health. No, the police mustn't be allowed to know them. They made up a silent army, protected inside the pink, green, and gray folders of the file cabinets as orderly as soldiers in a row. And yet it still wasn't clear to her what she must do to shield them.

One thing she knew: Whatever happened, all these people needed to acquire a new protector. They had to be warned. And their secrets had to be stashed away safely.

She was standing in her bedroom, looking out at the street. The forsythia bushes were turning yellow.

I ought to have studied law, she thought. Then she could have served as a relay runner who would take the torch, the legacy from the hero's hand, before the hand grew cold. And what had she done instead? Her work as a publisher's reader, her appraisals, translations, and critical reviews, struck her as feeble and lifeless. You didn't accomplish anything with all that literary stuff. Only if you were involved with people, with real life, did it make sense.

For a while, in the years of wildest upheaval, from '67 to '69, she had had a job in the theater. She and her husband would come off the street and plunge in to watch the performances, scrutinizing each play impatiently to see if it measured up to the storms of the times, or might even explain them. They weren't alone. Everyone was cheering and booing then. The theater went out onto the streets—they'd got hold of some Americans who were old hands at arranging avant-garde happenings—and the streets moved into the theater. Of course, working people didn't come—no more than they had come to the street demonstrations—but everybody talked so much about the working class that the ears of every giant manufacturer in Frankfurt, from Hoechst to MAN, from VDO to Cassella, must have been burning. This whirlwind transformation had all been a bit too sudden for the director of the theater where she was working. But he had a couple of young playwrights in his stable who knew what was what with the proletariat and Stanislavsky and the Theater of Cruelty and the use of sensory stimuli to stir up politics; and they took up the challenge. The aging director sighed, thought back to his classical theater days at the Hamburg Playhouse under Gründgens, and became part of the audience.

Her job at the theater was to write the program notes, and that brought complimentary tickets. Nobody minded if she hung around all day watching the rehearsals; nor did they object to her dragging her tall, handsome husband along.

Back then he was still a law intern and used to pay careful attention to the actors and pick up their techniques. His favorites were the ones who overacted, and were laughed at by their colleagues. He didn't care for the practice of sharing control of productions, which was just then in fashion. He would have liked to be a director himself, to have his own canvas director's chair and an army of ballet dancers, guitarists, and overwrought girls waiting to do his bidding. Still, he sat in on all the discussions that took place in the canteen after performances. He would wear a mocking smile and cock his head in one direction and then another, which made him look a little deaf.

Once, her own theater held an avant-garde festival, and from afternoon until late into the night the place was filled with a steady stream of Swedish and American, French and Spanish theatrical groups, waiting their turn to perform. When a horde of runaways from a Frankfurt boys' home broke in on the middle of one performance, the actors were delighted. The theater had been rescued from extinction: the culture-vulture middle-class theatergoers had stopped attending. At least they weren't visible.

The young runaways, whom Frankfurt student liberals had recently encouraged to break out of their institutions, were turning up in noisy groups all over the city: in the bars and on the university campus, in the theater and the student dorms. You ran into them everywhere, and if you talked with them individually, they were gentle and shy and found no words to describe the horrors they had experienced. Gathered in groups of four or five, though, they could sense the bad conscience of their sympathizers and would generously allow them to pay for everything, without embarrassing anyone with gratitude. Now and then they would lift one of the comrades' cars, or trash somebody's apartment.

An American troupe at the festival had just finished a performance. The actors wore shapeless, garish costumes of papier-mâché. Suddenly her husband was involved in a noisy confrontation with a man who had set himself up as ringleader of the boys'-home runaways. His name was Andreas Baader.

"Your group is holding on to these kids as if they were dancing bears," her husband had shouted at Andreas. "Each of you has his socially deprived misfit on the end of a leash. Why the hell do you drag them here to the theater? Can't you see all they care about is the beer they get on opening night? You're just a slick left-wing Fascist!"

Baader, who already had a spectacular arson to his credit and therefore had him outclassed, yelled back that the boys should take a good look at this creep who was trying to deprive them of access to the normal sociocultural communications media: a rank elitist, and that's the kind of stuff lawyers are made of!

Andreas was a slender, swarthy man with close-set, beetling brows and a beautiful, always slightly aggrieved-looking mouth. He was nervous, vain, and his voice became high-pitched whenever he was angry. No one knew exactly where he had come from. Of the four defendants in the big Frankfurt store-arson trial of 1968, he was the one who had attracted the most curiosity. He had served his jail time, but his fame was still fresh and glowing.

Quite possibly her husband had always been envious of Andreas Baader, the wife thought as she sat in her dark apartment in front of the mute TV set. For some time now Andreas had been back behind bars, confined to a special prison for his numerous outlandish misdeeds. But back in those days he was roaming free, and was training the young runaways in survival tactics. Get hard, latch onto some paid employment and capital, and never forget that each and every one of you has been cheated out of every human right. So why should you respect the laws, when you learned long ago that they only work to the advantage of the other side.

In spite of the quarrel between Andreas and her husband, some of the boys had approached the couple, and they were all able to talk with gentleness and friendship. The boys liked the way the wife listened silently when they told her about the things that had gone on in the institution.

"It's no accident that they always build these homes out in the middle of nowhere," one of them said. "It's not just to make it harder for you to run away. It's so other people don't have to think about the fact that such things exist."

Such things: The initiation rites when they were little boys, when their backs were beaten with sticks and then the older boys would urinate into the wounds. The teachers whose imaginations extended to nothing beyond devising new humiliations. And the contempt shown them by the village schoolchildren:

"Look, it's a home kid," they used to say. "The homes turn kids into criminals."

Or: "What work do you want to train for? You've got three choices: welder, lathe operator, or butcher. Only you're too dumb to learn any of them!"

She and her husband listened to what the boys had to say, but they never could break through to a state of burning rage. It was simply too far away. They couldn't hear the sound of the beatings. They saw the boys standing there drinking their opening-night beers, with American actresses fluttering all around them. The boys were tattooed and looked embarrassed, but very healthy. They couldn't imagine them as children locked into those houses of misery.

Now her husband was dead, and there was still so much left for her to understand. "No, the cops mustn't know about them, they mustn't laugh." Her husband's files held many stories like these, and the childhoods his clients described had been terrible, each in its own way.

The last day of the holidays was nearing its end. Farewell to Easter, on this the third day of his death. Things are going to get very sticky if I sit around remembering them all, all those freaks.

"Why can't you ever play with nice, well-behaved children?" her mother used to say to her.

She had never liked playing with nice, well-behaved children. All the same, she had never ventured far into dangerous terrain but had only watched curiously from the sidelines. One had to fight the nice, respectable children. And now she'd have to do it alone, without her husband.

The light shone out into her garden and lit up a little patch of lawn, the laburnum branches, and a few blossoms on a bush. Even the garden looked sick and weary. But tomorrow was the real beginning. Death had taken its holiday and now the workaday routine would set in, with death as with everything else.

The first thing she had to do was go to the law court and retain a lawyer. So many errands and arrangements that not even Mr. Sable could help her with.

What gave her husband the right to place all these demands on her? After all, we were separated. But now he belongs to me completely, as all husbands belong to their quietly triumphant widows. I'm only twenty-nine, she thought, and at that age it's not so easy to make all the proper arrangements; although of course people *do* feel sorrier for you than for an old woman whose marriage had worn out long ago, and for whom burying her husband is the appropriate last act. Probably that's why the wives usually survive the husbands: because they're better at arranging funerals. She thought about all the other people she had known who were dead now. Or who had disappeared, into prisons or into life itself.

Maybe after death all the people she knew would get together somewhere. The wife recognized the childishness of this notion, but had no desire to part with it. So far no one had made her a better offer. There was no point in looking to Marx for an answer: Death didn't happen in Marx. All the philosophers had always seemed to be at a loss on this subject: they said neither no nor yes. But so long as the question was left open, then no notion was more absurd than any other.

So she sat there in the darkness, imagining that her husband was now rendezvousing with the others, even those who had been her friends and loved ones and not his: a mute, cordial reception committee made up of a nineteen-year-old girl without a head; two men in their mid-twenties, one looking like a Savoyard prince and the other like the leader of a burglary team, both of whom had died of gunshot wounds; an elderly Siamese tomcat; and a charming, rather melancholy middle-aged lady. The wife found the image consoling.

Goodbyes always happen all at the same time. Each time you say one goodbye, you have to repeat all the others too, even those that are long forgotten, because you didn't get them right the first time or because you passed over them hastily and glibly. She had a debt of tears owing for her dead girlfriend, Meta; for her friend Jürgen; for her lover Tony; for her tomcat Angkor; and for her grandmother, whose voice she could no longer even remember, and whose love she had simply taken for granted like a sweater or a comfortable armchair. Gone, all gone. She suddenly perceived that she had never loved anyone enough—not one of those dead shades, not even her husband. Even if she were to start now, none of them would derive any benefit: for she felt certain that the dead no longer needed her but cared only for each other. Perhaps they even slightly despised the living.

The wife considered her husband's Catholicism. Would it help, she wondered, if I went to a church now and confessed all to a priest in some dark corner? She was going to have to get hold of a priest anyway, one who wouldn't be shocked when he saw her husband's friends turn up at the funeral. It would be best if the priest was a Socialist too; but that might be asking too much. "After all, this isn't South America," she whispered.

She really needed someone to help and stand by her; she felt sorry for herself. There was no one to feel the bite of her pain, and allow that to make up for the deficiencies of her love. She felt guilty for her halfhearted and lazy feelings; yes, but not so very guilty. After all, that's why everybody had such a good time, a few years back, championing the Black Panthers and the persecuted Vietnamese, the boys' home inmates and the convicts, the blacks in South Africa and the American Indians: because none of those had actually demanded love. You can be tireless at solidarity, and at group work, info sessions, teach-ins, sit-ins, picket lines, and all the rest, so long as you're not threatened by love. What was the Red Army Faction, the Baader-Meinhof Gang, but a society for the destruction of its members' dread of the threat of love.

Up until the very end of his life, her husband had never known whether he loved the comrades; but certainly he had come very close to loving them. Never—or only briefly and reluctantly—had he allowed them to dispatch him here and there at their whim, or to send him from place to place without telling him what they were up to. He had wanted to love and to belong to them; but he had also wanted to have a solid objective that didn't simply slip through your fingers like water the moment you touched it. "They ought to learn a lesson from the practical anarchists like Emma Goldman and Prince Kropotkin," he used to say. "I'm afraid this bunch are nothing but gun-toting Leninists."

But then they ended up reading everything they could get their hands on, and joining the street demonstrations to protest the comrades' conditions of confinement, arguing about tactics and strategy, world revolution and armed struggle, urban guerrillas and whether any of this could really happen in the sleepy towns of their country. Throughout all this time of upheaval her husband was the only person she knew who had tried to love the Group, to love it the way one loves a child, with all his faults, wishing him to keep learning and one day grow up to be big and strong. Her husband was the only person around who had understood that they were no longer simply Gudrun and Jan, Ulrike and Holger, Andreas and X, but one body, capable of thinking up things its individual members would never have thought of.

"Together, they really add up to more than the sum of their parts," her husband said to her once. He and she were separated by then and had made a date to meet in the city, like a pair of lovers. "Together, they're something else!"

"No, together they're less," the wife had answered heatedly, "because each of them is less than himself. They're like segments of a tapeworm. They don't work anymore, and they don't imagine anymore, and the rear end is miles away from the head."

They argued that afternoon—in this, too, they were like a pair of lovers—rather loudly, taking no precautions against possible eavesdroppers.

"Maybe *he* wanted to be a segment of a tapeworm too," she said to herself as she made up her bed on the living room couch and tried to wrap herself completely in blankets. "Or maybe he wanted to be its head. But in any case he loved the whole worm, the whole dangerous dragon, with all those lovable types who made it up."

She turned on the TV. An announcer said that this year's Easter holidays had been largely uneventful.

Day Four

The moment she woke up, she knew that something had changed. Those first mornings, she'd had to struggle to remember what had happened. She'd thought that it might go on this way forever, that she'd never be able to absorb the awful facts and let them into her life. But on the morning of the fourth day, she realized that all of it was now truly hers, and that she was going to spend days and nights in its company without a fight. She lay in bed and pulled the covers up to her mouth.

The cats had been avoiding her ever since the strange cats had been there. She missed the familiar warm fur beside her. She didn't want to get up. It was an ordinary day; she had things to do that she couldn't postpone and she had no idea how to go about them. She should empty his court letterbox. Sift through his mail. Hire a lawyer. Notify the authorities and the court of her husband's death, and tell his friends who would now be returning from short Easter vacations. Today she had to go to his apartment and clean up things there. She would have to try to find out what the mysterious Gloucester wanted from her.

Her blanket wasn't warm enough; she was trembling under it as she saw the day growing lighter behind the curtains. Half of her felt unable to move, while the other half felt restless because she didn't know exactly what was expected of her. "This isn't an easy role they've given me!" she whispered.

She was talking to herself now without any feelings of shyness, in low-pitched sentences interspersed with little cries of encouragement, the kind you use to urge on an animal that you are fond of but know to be lazy. Get dressed and do your hair: Today that meant wearing her hair up because she was going to the public prosecutor's office. And she'd have to wear black. She would have to buy a black coat. She clung to the idea of the coat, to save her thoughts from accidentally taking a wrong turn. Because of course, she wasn't the only one who was now resuming her place in the ordinary world. Not only she had to go about her business: so did the medical examiners and pallbearers, the police detectives and morticians, the coffin and shroud makers, the pathologists and chemists and prosecutors, the morgue cleaning women and the gravediggers. All this was bringing an end to her husband's peace. There's nothing harder, she now discovered, than to avoid thinking of something that's sitting in the back of your head trying to come to the fore. No, no, you mustn't think about what they're doing to him now.

She found she couldn't swallow her coffee. It puffed out her cheeks and lay inside her mouth like a liquid stone. She remembered the morning when her husband, still an intern, had to attend his first autopsy, a requirement for all young lawyers. Back then they were living in Mainz, not Frankfurt. Her husband had got up at the crack of dawn looking very composed. He told her that the cadaver was a Turk; thank God, a young man who had been stabbed to death and not a drowned corpse or some ghastly thing like that.

She had been curious but disapproving. "It's crazy for them to force you to watch an autopsy," she had said. "If one of you can't hack it and faints, does that mean he doesn't get to be a lawyer? After all, lawyers don't have to know how to dissect people!" She was getting worked up. "I'd send all you would-be lawyers to spend some time in jail instead; that'd make some sense. Four or six weeks of lockup, so you'd know what you're doing." Her husband had admitted she was right. He couldn't explain the requirement either; but on no account would he try to get out of it. "It's some funny kind of male puberty rite!" his wife had said at the end, and tried to go back to sleep.

When her husband came back later that morning, he had been white as a sheet and had run the water in the bathroom for hours. Later he threw away the clothes he had worn that day. "If I don't, I'll never forget the smell," he'd said. And now *he* was the one lying there in the autopsy chamber, and maybe other law interns were saying, "Thank God it's a young guy, dead only three days, and not a drowned corpse or some ghastly thing like that."

She telephoned Mr. Sable. "Don't worry about it," he said.

"I'm taking everything off your shoulders, remember? No, your husband hasn't been released yet. But we do have the date. The funeral can take place on April twenty-fourth."

It took her a while, but eventually it sank in that she was going to have to live for more than a week yet with her husband's body, with his indistinct presence. That's it, she thought; you're scared the way you're scared of very sick people when you don't know how much they still understand. Back in the days when she had worked night duty, keeping watch on gravely ill patients, she'd never overcome this fear. She had been afraid of the incomprehensible mumbles, the urgent glances, the creeping movements of the hands on the bedclothes. She'd been afraid and felt guilty for it. Now she felt afraid of her dead husband, and again she had a guilty conscience, because she didn't know if he had really left her and how far away he might have gone by now.

Hilde the Kirghiz phoned. "The seal is being lifted," she said. "We can go to his apartment right away if you want to."

She wasn't pleased by the news. It would have suited her just fine if they'd left the seal on, if in fact they had walled up the door of his apartment. Look at every one of his things? Their looks could kill. Each cooking pot, each handkerchief, each sock demanded a decision. It was beyond her, she thought; but of course you can always pay somebody to take that kind of disagreeable chore off your hands. The thought made her feel guilty again. Moving men rummaging through his apartment! Just think of all the things they would get to see! His insides were visible in those objects, lying like a peeled orange exposed to the gaze of strangers. She wasn't even sure whether she herself might not be an intruder. Yes, in fact she was. Three years after you separate from someone, you'll find no spoor in his cave but his own. But I'm permitted to read the spoor, she thought. He wouldn't have tried to stop me.

"Do I have to go there now?" she said to the Kirghiz, her lawyer.

"You have to convince yourself you want to," said Hilde. "I don't know yet exactly what we'll have to do and how we'll do it all. But there'll be plenty to do, that's for sure."

"Are you coming with me?" asked the wife.

"Naturally," said Hilde. "I'll call the cops. We'll do it as soon as possible."

The wife walked anxiously through her apartment, looking around for places to store her husband's stuff. If the same thing were to happen to me tomorrow, would they ever have fun cleaning up after me! she thought. She remembered her undefrosted refrigerator with the tainted preserves inside; the drawer full of old electrical cords, spools of thread, leaflets, foreign coins. Nobody lives permanently ready for death. Everybody leaves rubbish behind that others have to clear away. Letters and papers, rings and necklaces. Poisons and sweets, war and peace. The wife got dressed. How simple it was, wearing black. She had lost a little weight over Easter. Between that and the black clothes, she thought she didn't look half bad.

On the street and in the subway, she saw nothing but young people rubbing bodies and grabbing each other in as many places as it was possible to grab at once. Black couples and white were trundling along cheerfully under the ground, away from their ugly neighborhoods toward some park. They were cheerful because they were in pairs and because even the most downtrodden park was more beautiful than the neighborhoods they came from.

The wife was riding through the Yank district, or rather under it, but no one paid any attention to her. The pavement overhead had been ablaze in '68, but it had long since cooled off. What battles they'd all fought there! Back then, the subway tunnels hadn't been built yet. What marvelous retreat zones they would have made: just like in the movies. The wife got out one stop too early. She always did that when she rode the subway. After a while underground, she would be irritated because the automobiles above her were riding in the sun, while she slid past empty stations like a tunnel lizard.

She walked for half an hour through her husband's neighborhood. Hardly anyone knew her there, and she felt sure that even her husband had rarely glimpsed the fast-walking Turkish women, the orange-uniformed municipal workmen, the Italian vegetable dealers, and the clothes menders who inhabited the district at this time of day—half past nine in the morning. The people hurrying past her looked very middle-class and industrious, and the closed striptease joints were virtually unnoticeable. The photos of well-endowed women with their behinds sticking out, cupping their breasts in both hands, looked like illustrations in a medical book. Children were playing right outside a dirty shopwindow where plastic vibrators lay next to underpants with a fur-lined hole in the middle. The children didn't even glance in their direction.

Nowhere else in the city did so many differing time spans coincide within such a narrow range of streets. The sun lit up a house whose windows were ringed by red neon tubes. Greek caryatids stood at the corners of buildings, carrying massive stone escutcheons from which the emblems had been knocked off. At the end of the street rose the central railroad station, a simple modern structure of stone and glass.

At noon the street would change its image. Fur dealers and bankers moved in, along with travelers, who would stand at the postcard racks and laugh when they saw the one of the woman in a swimsuit who suddenly went naked and winked at you if you shifted your angle of vision. She often used to eat out around here with her husband. The restaurant owners knew him and greeted him warmly in Chinese, Italian, Russian. In the afternoon the cluster of streets known as the railroad district would become almost elegant: a cheerfully mendacious elegance made up of sports cars and hurrying prostitutes, on their way to the area's many beauty parlors. Her husband hadn't really belonged to any of these worlds, although it wouldn't have taken much.

It occurred to her that she could live in his apartment now if she chose to; in this neighborhood she'd be much closer to the real world than she'd ever been before. She could install a young lawyer—it wouldn't require too much money—and study law herself. She hadn't yet managed to exorcise this idea.

The real pain came when she saw the gleaming nameplate beside the door of his building—the building where he died. There was his name and the inscription "Attorney at Law," just as if nothing had happened. Well, of course it was still there. She was not unprepared, and when she turned the corner and caught sight of the plate from the furniture shop at the end of the street, she felt the time had come when she ought to look a bit shocked. (The nameplate disappeared after that Tuesday, but the little holes in the wall where the screws went in are still there.)

Her lawyer stood waiting, her face turned to the sun. "Don't think I like having to go up there," Hilde the Kirghiz said. "But I couldn't let you go alone." She was used to helping people, she liked to help. She enjoyed having others need her. She was suspicious if someone could manage on his own.

The wife felt grateful. She wouldn't have known what to do if she'd come by herself.

When somebody deeply loves his home, or is too tired to move, people say, "The only way he'll leave there is feet first." But she didn't know if they had carried her husband down the stairs feet first or not. Hilde put an arm around her shoulders, even though the wife was much taller than she. "Have you lost weight?" she asked.

A plainclothes cop stood waiting outside the apartment door. This time she was truly shocked. She felt she couldn't hold her head steady on her neck. But it turned out that the cop was only there to remove the seal. Solemnly he tore off the scrap of paper. Now she would never find out what magic word had been written on it. A couple of documents had to be signed, and then he vanished without even trying to enter the apartment. Probably they'd had all the time they needed there during the holidays. Most likely the word on the scrap of paper had been powerless to protect the place.

"I don't think they've been inside yet," said Hilde, while both of them stared at the locked door. "They're more bound by red tape than you think. For them, a holiday is a holiday, the same as for a factory or a . . . law office." She tried to laugh. "Do you have the key?" she asked.

The two women entered the apartment side by side, the Kirghiz holding her friend the widow very tight. The wife stopped in the hall to look at the closed bedroom door. Then she went back out into the stairwell, sat down on the stairs, and cried. A rustling was heard behind the door of the neighboring apartment.

"There's no point in crying," said Hilde. "You have obligations now. You have to tell me what to do about all this stuff. For now, let's just go into the office, only into the office. The files are there. That won't hurt so much."

If you only knew, thought the wife. The files are his stories, and he'll die if he can't tell them anymore, and change them and mark them up with colored felt pens. He'll die if he can't play with his electric letter opener anymore and his mini tape recorder. He'll die, thought his wife, as she walked into the blue room. But he's dead.

"Amazing," the Kirghiz said, "how seriously he took it all. And he called himself an anarchist! Orderly as a druggist," she said, looking around the anteroom and into the office. Both rooms were large, separated by a folding door that now stood open. In this apartment, as in so many homes and buildings throughout Frankfurt, upper-middle-class architecture cordially rubbed shoulders with its enemies. The anteroom was filled with heavy furniture she didn't like at all. Ranged in a neat row in a bookcase stood some two hundred elegantly bound volumes of pornography, representing the entire output of a politically very progressive publisher.

Her husband had been the firm's lawyer for a while. She recalled once watching three or four dozen of the films they produced, to write up thoughtful reviews. At parties later, she was surprised to run into the same girls she had seen on film!

The Kirghiz laughed at the husband's unusual legal trophies. "How often did their films get impounded, anyway?"

"I don't remember," said the wife. "But they were always thrilled to bits when they were served with an impound order. Then we'd hold press showings of the confiscated films, and the newspapers published long articles on artistic freedom. The whole thing made the public prosecutor's office look pretty sick. And the actors in the films would bustle around in chic outfits, saying that they'd never have acted in them if they hadn't been experimental art productions."

Both women laughed, and the wife saw that her friend had been right. The office wasn't as bad as the apartment. Here his stories were only asleep, not dead.

"Maybe I could make tea," said Hilde. "We have the time. You don't have to come with me into the kitchen. I'll find everything; I always find everything wherever I go." She *is* a dear, thought the wife. She's like a pony trekking up a steep mountain. Or one of those women who lay out the dead. She's one of those people who would collapse if you removed their burdens.

The wife started thinking about a big party at the porn publisher's. That had been back in '69 or '70, the era of reality. The guests sat drinking at long tables. Their host's models lit up the almost unfurnished house with their colors and sheen. The wife was trying to match drinks with the others and found it amusing. She and her husband behaved like a couple again, and he had hissed at her because she flirted and danced with somebody else. She felt warmed by his jealousy. She was wearing lots of jewelry, a black dress, a red shawl around her shoulders. She had bent her head back so as to look into his face and show off her round white neck and ample cleavage. In a pinch, it could pass for happiness.

She saw their host using a nutmeg grater to shred a greasy-looking ball of hashish into giant bowls of fruit salad.

"That little item cost you as much as all the rest of the party," her husband said sternly to his client. No doubt there was something still owing on his bill. But all the guests had seen the gesture, it made a big splash, and everyone ate some of the fruit salad. The wife swallowed only a little, because she was scared and because she preferred to get high on wine; she knew what to expect.

A crowd of children had been playing down on the ground floor of the newly rented house. Later on they were supposed to go to sleep on some mattresses there. Back in those days, it was common to have large broods of children and lots of mattresses at every party. After all, why shouldn't people be allowed to go out at night and enjoy themselves? They'd just take their children along. Little girls and boys played noisily and self-confidently with youngsters who were total strangers to them, in houses they had never laid eyes on, and no one had a pang of guilt.

One of the models—they called her Fatima; the wife had recognized her at once from the books of nude photos she'd seen—came up the stairs into the big dining room, rehearsing an eerie little song. "Blood," she sang unselfconsciously, stoned out of her mind: "Blo-oo-od!" She sang rather blissfully. The wife had looked enviously at the model. You could see nothing of her perfect limbs under her bright silk suit. Her foolish little face was absolutely flawless; like that of a ferret or an ermine. Piles of her curly hair were casually looped together. It's not fair, the wife had thought, pulling in her stomach. "Bloo-oo-od!" Fatima said to her in a friendly voice.

Behind Fatima, a very small girl with braided hair and stained red trousers was pulling herself up the stairs by the handrail. She had to stretch her leg out far each time she climbed a step, and paused to rest when she'd get the second leg up to join it. Despite her arduous progress, the little girl overtook Fatima and announced breathlessly, as she reached the dining room, "Please can somebody come? Pia has hurt her head."

The wife was startled; but you can't really feel frightened in a warm room crowded with people, when you've just eaten a lot and are full of wine.

She hunted for her husband, who was sitting cross-legged in a corner, letting himself be admired by several younger guys who looked like assistant directors.

"Come on," she said to him, "there's been an accident." He just looked at her sluggishly.

"No reason for jealousy, my love," he said. "Of course, it's one thing for you to crawl all over some rotten he-man type, and quite another for me to have a quiet little conversation."

"It's one of the children, one of the children has been hurt," she answered, knowing that she was on the point of screaming or crying with rage. "I don't give a damn about your pals here, you asshole! But one of the children has had an accident. Now come on!"

"Why didn't you go see what was wrong?" he asked as they crossed the room, where by this time people were undulating slowly like figures under water, to the accompaniment of some wailing music.

"Because I'm scared," she answered calmly. "Why do you think I came for you?"

They had found the little girl, Pia, lying motionless. Her husband tracked down someone with a car, picked up the child in his arms, and ten minutes later she was getting emergency care in the nearest hospital. He had drawn his black silk shirt around him to look like a lawyer's robe and delivered a small courtroom speech to the hospital's dozing doorman, charging him with neglect of duty. The three of them had made a fine-looking group.

Eventually the child regained consciousness and said with unruffled calm, "My goodness! Were you two at the party too?" And when the X-ray technician addressed her in a version of baby talk, she told him he should please talk to her intelligently, that's what she was used to.

Pia didn't cry but chatted with the lawyer, to whom she had taken a great shine, while he pointed out the dark shadows of her nose and eyes on the X-ray chart that dangled from the stretcher. "See, my head is flapping on ahead of me," Pia said. Then she spelled out her last name for the record and asked the husband, "Was my mother stoned on hash?"

He laughed and said no; he'd just been in such a hurry to get her to the hospital that he hadn't had time to look for her mother.

She gazed sadly at the bright rows of porn albums on the orphaned bookshelf. Hilde the Kirghiz was opening cupboards in the kitchen and there was a sound of whistling steam. The apartment smelled as if no one had been here for a long time. Everything was stifling, the books and pictures, the bed, the record player. Only the files still breathed.

Hilde arrived with the tea, and while they drank it she noted on a large slip of paper everything that had to be done, in order of importance.

"He did have a lawyer who used to fill in for him when he was away," Hilde said. "That same guy would be able to wind up his cases."

The wife gazed at the pink files. "But please, you have to handle the political things yourself!" she said.

"I'd have to know more about them first." Hilde was unaffected by her pleading tone. "He didn't exactly run with our pack, you know."

The wife tried once again to review her husband's friends. Where could she find one who was an ardent but order-loving anarchist, who would work for an honorable termination of his lawsuits, collect all outstanding fees, and act selflessly to guard her husband's memory?

"There's no such person," she murmured into her teacup.

"Who?"

"Somebody who'd do it all the way he would!" she said.

"Naturally not," Hilde replied impatiently. "No one will do it like him. By the way, have you called up his intern?"

Her husband had recently taken on a young lawyer to work in his office, a man who had specifically asked to train with him. He was dark-haired and unostentatious, but when he spoke, you felt as if you were reading a nineteenth-century novel. The wife hardly knew him, but she decided to ask for his help.

She was beginning to feel muddled, as she made a concerted effort to discriminate between the death of the lawyer and the death of the anarchist, the death of her love and the death of her husband.

Back there in the hospital corridor with its black-and-white tiled floor, carrying the little girl Pia in his black-silk arms and full of reluctantly consumed hashish, he'd taken on yet another of his many identities. The hash made him sleepy even before the doctors finished stitching up the child's head. He had fallen sound asleep on one of the emergency cots out in the corridor; life-support tubes swung back and forth over his head.

"You can't sleep here!" his wife had hissed at him, while young Pia laughed a little tremulously because she was in pain now and felt alone.

"When I'm tired I can sleep anywhere," he answered. Pia's body went stiff in the wife's arms and she kept repeating, "I want to stay with you! I want to stay with you!" So she placed the child in the ghastly high bed with its overhead gallows, and her husband and the little girl giggled and both fell asleep at almost the same instant.

The wife had felt helpless and furious. He was forever making scenes, doing things that attracted public notice. Breaking rules had always made her very uncomfortable and she avoided it whenever possible. She stood in front of the bed, staring down at the two sleepers with deep envy because they had simply done what they felt like doing, and because it was so unnecessary to feel you had to justify an obvious need.

"But that's not allowed!" came the voice of a nurse behind her. The wife had been expecting some such remark, and expected, too, that she'd be unable to wake either man or child.

"They're tired, you see," she told the nurse in an exhausted voice, feeling ashamed of how she must look.

"See that they leave at once," the nurse had said, weary and disgruntled. The wife was tired too. Suddenly, in amazement, she saw the checkerboard hospital floor begin to plait itself into long braids.

It's that goddamn fruit salad! she thought. It certainly had a delayed effect.

The twining pattern under her feet made walking almost impossible. Somehow she had managed to wake the little girl, who started crying and now looked frightened underneath her head bandage.

"You're really stoned!" she pronounced, and the wife wanted to cry too, because she felt sick and didn't know how she was ever going to get back to the party to deliver the child to her family.

"We have to take the kid back now," her husband said suddenly. He stood up with dignity and escorted his little borrowed family across the heaving floor and out the door.

They found the child's mother back at the party, which was still going strong, louder than ever. The mother was lying on a wobbly water bed, high as a kite and having an uncontrollable crying jag. She was frightened by the sight of her little girl in her white bandage. "Take her away!" she cried. "She's not mine!"

The little girl had lost all her assurance and clung to the husband's legs. "Pull yourself together, you stupid cow," he said to the mother. Then he told the little girl, "If she goes on like this, we'll just go back and lie down in the hospital corridor again."

Today, as she sat drinking tea like a guest in the dead man's apartment, the wife could no longer remember exactly how that story turned out. By the next day the whole city knew what had happened. Pia's mother sent a bouquet of flowers by way of apology, and sobbing, blamed it all on the fruit salad. The husband slept for sixteen hours straight, and woke up completely free of aftereffects. Only for the wife did everything insist on going wrong. Next day she kept seeing braids on the floor, and would laugh uncontrollably at nothing. She felt truly pitiful.

"I don't know how to be a junkie," she announced to the Kirghiz, who was sitting on the edge of the armchair, scrutinizing her narrowly. "I'm incapable of celebrating orgies, I don't know how to be a revolutionary and probably not a widow either. I wish I could turn it all into a class act," she said, shedding tears that burned like acid. "I wish I could, but I don't know how: only he knew how. He could take any old nothing and turn it into something great."

For the first time since her arrival at the apartment, she remembered Gloucester and his mysterious phone call. Now that she was here, she ought to search for whatever it was, the very important object that was hidden in the office. Maybe it was the key to something great; maybe she could finish a project her husband had started; maybe she could become not merely his widow but his successor, his heir. The Group represented greatness, and she had been part of it. But now she was shut out, the king's highway was barred, for the king was dead. The legal or the illegal: a left-wing lawyer was exempt from the need to choose between them, because without the illegal he'd be out of business. But unlike the judges and the prosecutors, he was in a position to love the illegal if he chose; whereas they had no option but to hate it.

"The people who make it worth my while are the ones who show me life—even if what they show me is that life isn't worth it," he had said.

How could the Kirghiz possibly suspect the real contents of the bright-colored files: all her husband's possible lives, all the lives he'd never had to live himself because other people had lived them for him? His clients had supplied him with lives. Her husband had arranged them and seen to it that they didn't lead to abysmal results. And yet the results were always abysmal. One year in the joint? That sounded like a lollipop sentence. But three hundred and sixty-five days smelling the stench of the men and the buildings; the same fifty-two meal cycles repeated like clockwork; the three invariable articles of clothing; the never-changing face of one's cellmate; and the innumerable times the kapok mattress stuffing squeezed out of the upper bunk into the lower—the ultimate in punishment.

"He was crazy about his job," said Hilde. "The rest of us

couldn't understand it. After all, you can't change the system by getting all worked up about it, and fussing promiscuously."

"But he wasn't out to change it!" his wife answered furiously. "First he wanted to find out just how it works. All of you thought you could work within it, as though it were some kind of halfway house that you could eventually leave for somewhere else. But it was never that way for him, never. He knew there was nothing else waiting for him outside. And he's dead, and all of you are alive!"

"You keep saying 'all of you'!" said Hilde. "But he didn't give a damn about being part of some group. He didn't believe there was any such thing as We; no way. Now, in retrospect, you and I talk as if there were a We. Anyway, maybe he got things just how he wanted them. At least you seem to believe he was right."

"He was," said the wife. "Dying always proves you were right."

The wife saw that she was causing her friend discomfort. That made her defiant, and she started to shift into the role of enemy, or at least of enemy's deputy.

"If we don't get on with things now," Hilde said amicably as she cleared away the tea things, "we'll still be sitting here when night falls. And I wouldn't like that so much."

"Are you scared of him?" asked the wife.

"No," the Kirghiz answered reflectively, "not yet. But he could be scary. When I think about how he used to carry on, threatening other lawyers with disciplinary committee hearings . . ."

The wife didn't like to remember that. At times there had been a kind of rage in her husband that she didn't understand. Then he would threaten anyone who sided with him only in a general way, not absolutely and unconditionally. He would prescribe for them punishments that he would never have dreamed up for his out-and-out enemies. He liked treating his genuine foes with Christian charity, but he could be murderously vengeful toward anyone he cast in the role of friend who then (as he saw it) let him down. He would conceal his fury under a veneer of ironical coolness that deceived no one, least of all his wife.

Arm in arm, the two women walked through all the rooms and noted randomly on the big piece of paper all the chores they had to get done: Phone the landlord. Look for insurance papers. Take away the flowers. Place ad about apartment. Remove office furniture. Reroute mail. Apply for inheritance certificate. Go over accounts. . . .

Inside a drawer they found a flat box about the size of a briefcase. The wife opened it and was amazed to see dozens of bright gleaming rings, set with glass stones of every color, stuck into rows of narrow black-velvet slots. Her husband's wedding ring occupied a small edge pocket. The wife took it out, felt confused, then clapped the lid shut over this night-side pomp, this phony glitter.

"Why are you gawking like a stupid cow?" asked the Kirghiz. "You knew all about that. That's why you left him, for heaven's sake!"

"That's what you all think," said the wife, "because it's so simple that way. But I didn't care about all that—no, it's not that I didn't care at all, but it wasn't a big deal for me. After a while you get so that these boys don't matter," she said, arm in arm with her good friend Hilde, who stared straight ahead, hiding all traces of curiosity. "They really don't matter! Most of them are incredibly stupid, and besides, there's such a fast turnover. Sometimes you don't even see their faces. I think that often *he* didn't see their faces. You don't really fight it. Maybe it's hard for you to imagine what it's like," she said, full of emotion.

At last someone was asking her about it! At last a breach had opened in the implacable wall of tolerance that had surrounded her for years. She and her husband had been a known couple with known peculiarities; but no one had ever mentioned the peculiarities. And why should they, after all? The revolution would see to it that irregular behavior like his was resolved, either blessed or abolished. Until then, it was unnecessary to have any opinion about it. It was a purely secondary conflict. And besides, that sort of thing didn't go on among the proletariat; well, hardly ever.

Now, on the fourth day, as the wife began her life with her dead husband, she was longing for an end to this attitude of mute tolerance. Not that she wanted sympathy. But in middle-class society, there are various established ways to react when your husband is unfaithful to you, ways that will help you to survive. On the fringes of the underground, no problem is acknowledged to exist.

"I've never been able to figure out how you put up with it," Hilde said in a puzzled voice. "You must react to it somehow or other; a person can't simply accept it."

How could she answer that? Could she have said that it would simply have been absurd to make a fuss, when you watched your husband go out and you couldn't think of a single question to ask him? That jealousy and possessiveness carried their own intrinsic absurdity.

"If you want to do some ironing now, I'll go to the sauna for a while," her husband had said only a short time after their honeymoon.

"Suppose I go and you do the ironing?" his wife replied.

"I don't know how to iron," he retorted amiably, "and you don't have to iron either. Just leave everything the way it is. I don't give a shit. So where would you like to go?"

"To one of those saunas," said his wife, unable to picture the graphic details—or determined not to picture them.

"Oh, do you girls have them too?" He seemed interested. "I don't believe it." And off he went, free as a bird, without allusion to the secret that was plain to anyone.

"That boy will probably want his rings," said the wife.

"You can afford to let him have them," Hilde answered. "It's a nice gesture, and you won't be losing anything valuable."

The wife felt his wedding ring in her hand. She had always worn hers, even after their separation three years ago. It made things different for her at the publishing houses and the broadcasting station.

One time her husband had visited her at the station, storming cheerfully into her cubbyhole.

"Hey, kiddo," he said very uxoriously, and drew her into his cloud of patchouli. "It's terrific to see you; I don't see you nearly often enough!" And he looked over her shoulder at a male technician and a female cutter who were fiddling mutely with some tapes.

Husband: a nice role, just as long as it didn't appear on the program too often.

"That's the guy you walked out on?" the cutter asked later, looking stunned. "You've gotta be crazy. Nobody splits on a guy like that. If it were me, he could do whatever he liked and you couldn't drag me away."

The wife had felt flattered, and allowed her husband to be praised in the indulgent way of parents with their children.

It was already afternoon, and they had managed to settle only one thing: her husband really had left his apartment. You didn't feel his presence there—at least not as long as the bedroom door remained shut. The wife was amazed that she'd been able to stay so long.

Even now she couldn't say that she knew the meaning of the word "grief." Her tears; the occasional frozen feeling that came over her when she recalled the past; the images that flitted through her mind when she held half-remembered objects, twisting them in her hands—none of this came under the heading of what she understood by "grief." She felt sure that one component of true grief must be an endless sense of the dead person's absence; but she lacked that. Sometimes she felt that he was close by, at other times that he was farther away, just as when he was alive. He seemed to abscond or to reveal himself whenever he chose, just as when he was alive. At first she had suspected that he might be helpless now. She hadn't been able to get that thought out of her mind on the first day; but today it was dispelled.

She had a feeling, which was growing stronger all the time, that she had been the victim of a setup. Gloucester, too, had a role in this enigmatic game. She tried to figure out where in the apartment she could search, and what she could search for. To comply with Gloucester's demands, and because she didn't want to say anything about it to Hilde, she decided to postpone the search.

She was sure that Hilde, too, must have her secret hero. But one didn't talk about such things; only writers and editors did—the type of people who borrowed adventures the way they did library books and couldn't keep their mouths shut about them afterward.

It had started four or five years ago. The wife, alone with her husband, had often poked fun at those vicarious adventurers who would brag about being put through some trifling police search or a visit from an officer with a warrant. The way they would make public their agonies of conscience, sucking away self-importantly on big joints of marijuana and saying: "Of course I would never identify myself with some of their goals. But I wouldn't inform on any of them either; not me. On the other hand, I do have a family. Besides, right now you can accomplish more working from inside the institutions." They kept sucking at their grass lollipops, cupping their hands around their noses. They all used to read Red Army Faction terrorist manifestos, and they tore into the husband and wife for saying they thought they were awful.

"That's barbed-wire language," her husband said, shuddering. "They make a barbed-wire fence out of words; that's how it starts. We all have to make a concerted effort to look behind it."

Everyone believed him because he believed himself. No one could get the better of him. Like a Shakespearean actor, he would declaim the propositions of his underground comrades, the white crocodiles invisible to all inside the big-city sewers, no more than a rumor in the mouths of the powers that be. Even their writings had been stripped of the messiness of life:

"the anti-imperialist struggle cannot . . . the war of national liberation is not . . . the absence of historical perspective has not . . . one-nation socialism will not . . . counterpart to the transnational organization of capital . . . the U.S. imperialist-dominated military pacts encircling the globe . . . the cooperation between the police and the secret services . . . the international league of the ruling elite within the power sphere of U.S. imperialism . . . is, on our side, the side of the proletariat of revolutionary class struggle of the third world wars of independence of the urban guerrilla in the imperialist metropolis: *Proletarian Internationalism.*"

"Play it again, Sam," his wife said to him one evening. "I don't get it."

It was at some party downtown, in a hot room with a swarm of these texts spread out over the floor. The two of them were already separated and had only come to the party together for old times' sake. She had noticed that her husband didn't despise the latest manifesto, didn't find it hollow and meaningless cant. It appeared he would have liked to compose such texts himself, speaking out of an abyss, out of invisible trenches in a world where the lay of the land was all too clear. The man was regretting that he, who stood in the no-man's-land between the bourgeoisie and their enemies, was not regarded as dangerous. And yet—she saw that then and saw it now—he was the only really dangerous person there.

The wife and the Kirghiz left the husband's apartment with their work uncompleted, and parted at the subway station without saying much. The wife only pretended to go down into the subway. She waited until Hilde had disappeared off toward the railroad station, then came back into the daylight to buy a newspaper. She wanted to be alone with it, for she believed Mr. Sable's promise that today she would see death in black-and-white. She sat down in one of the railroad station bars. Now, in the afternoon, this took no courage. The bored barkeeps were glad for an occasional traveler to ignore the overnight dirt and the clotted smoke in their places and order a coffee or a schnapps. The women of the station quarter were taking a breather. The action wouldn't start until evening. Frankfurt's red-light district was like a hospital garden, enjoying a midday rest.

Obituary notices are easy to find. The black-bordered squares arrest your gaze like graves. The wife saw at once that Mr. Sable hadn't misled her. She was startled by the size of the notice. Her name came first among the mourners. She had concealed the boy under the phrase "and friends"; that was a snug place to tuck him. She had not let her husband "pass away" or "depart this life." He had not succumbed to a "brief severe illness" or a "sudden and unforeseen" one. She hadn't sent him away with her gratitude nor claimed any depth to her grief. Sitting there at the sticky little table, she would have liked to read that she had been shocked by his death; but that kind of thing doesn't appear in obituaries. One couldn't be angry either, or glad, within these little boxes.

"How come ya keep readin' the obits?" said the barkeeper. "Your boss cash in?"

"My husband."

"Couldn't of guessed that, at your age," said the barkeep, unperturbed. "Have a drink on me. Did he live round here? Round here ya don't live to get old."

He was short and rather plump; the cord of his apron held up a potbelly. His shirt had a patch that bore his name in silver: Ewald. On a barstool across from him sat a plump white smooth-haired dog.

"Name's Pluto," said the barkeep.

The wife couldn't help laughing. She folded her paper so that the death notices were no longer visible. "The hound of hell," she said. "He doesn't look it."

"Was your husband from the district?" asked Ewald. "If so, I know 'im."

"He was the lawyer from the Elbestrasse."

Ewald was genuinely amazed. "I'd never of guessed it. I dunno what all went on there. Nothin' to do with us, that's for sure. No reason for us to mix. He had, whaddya say, a different sorta clientele. Willy used 'im once, in a bodily injury case. Said he was good. It's no fun listenin' to a guy bellow round a courtroom for a livin'. Maybe we would still of got together though, him'n us. Too bad. My sympat'y."

He set down a glass of colorless schnapps on the bar for her. She drank it off in a single gulp and ordered another.

So this was the start of her journey into the unknown countries her husband had traveled. Not yet the right start; a blind alley, she knew that. But already it provided a clue to what his friends and colleagues found hard to understand: the meaning, for him, of a courtroom trial.

"It's like being a dancer," her husband had told her once. "You're strictly limited in the movements you can make. But there are thousands of variations. You have your fancy costume. I don't know why the others want to give it up; they just don't know how to dance. They say that in a trial, the state makes you dance to its tune, but that isn't true. Trial law and the state police were invented in a moment of hubris. They didn't stop to think that the balance of power could change. Now we're making them dance to their own music!

"The others take offense at all legal proceedings because they keep seeing the state behaving like the state—while what they should do is keep playing back its own tune: the dignity of man, reasonable doubt, illegal search and seizure, and the failure to read you your rights. Along with the ballet comes an orchestra. You just have to know how to play the instruments."

In his dark eyes, under his bony hands, you saw the stage light up for a drama of ever-recurring suspense: a trial! Every trial had that quality for him, of music, of surprise. Whether a guy had swiped coins from a washing machine or was a gold smuggler, the play could begin: The curtain rises, let's see the theater of the state.

Back then she had neither understood nor shared his enthusiasm. She had simply preferred him to all the others, who were so hard and clever and so radiantly certain of their opinions. There was no room in their lives for theater; and if they were obliged to play a role, they did it with an aggrieved air, joylessly, without passion. Many of her husband's colleagues resembled charitable spinsters who had spent years doing good deeds for mankind and felt insulted if, on top of that, mankind expected them to earn a living.

"I *always* wanted to be a lawyer," her husband said, "that and nothing else."

Not until shortly before his death had he shown signs of weariness after some difficult proceedings.

"It's no use," he had said to her just a couple of weeks earlier. "It's all so cold!" And he looked searchingly at the sky. "By the time my clients get to me they're past saving; it's like closing the barn door after the horse is gone. What I do doesn't make any real sense. I'm not making a revolution; I just try to convince the state not to be mean to the people who are. That's absurd. What is a lawyer in this country? The nation's storyteller. Somebody who makes the adversaries palatable to each other. The constitution! Government by constitutional law! God, it makes me sick. It's all lies. It's just a kind of incantation you hear rumbling through the law chambers, but only when people can't think of anything else to say. I'm not an armed fighter. But I don't negotiate surrenders either. My profit margin is pathetic. And I don't even know if I'm corrupt; the system hasn't tried to corrupt me. Apparently it doesn't fear me. Maybe it's not afraid of any of us, maybe not even of the underground; maybe them least of all. Well, kiddo," he'd said at last, "sometimes I think it really hasn't paid off for me; only for the others."

The wife signaled Ewald for another white schnapps and moved cautiously nearer to the barstool where the dog Pluto was sitting.

"Times he likes being petted, times not," said Ewald, and poured the schnapps till it formed a slight mound over the rim. "You got a steady hand? He won't let a hooker pet 'im. Too proud. Try it if you want; he's lost most've 'is teeth!"

The wife stroked the smooth, hard dog pelt. Pluto didn't move, he just growled a little, and she left her hand on his neck.

Many of the Group were already in the slammer; others were planning operations; some were silent; some were dead.

A point had come when the wife and perhaps even the husband no longer knew what it was all about. Okay, there was this web of supply and reconnaissance, of running and surfacing, recruitment and shielding: everything the Group—and their enemies—used to call "logistics." There was an invisible standing army, a war treasury, there were ration sergeants and signal troops, trenches and dugouts, there was a rear zone and a front line, there were generals and foot soldiers.

Again the wife considered whether her husband's death had any place at all in this. Because what was missing, had been there only in the beginning, was the *motive* for the whole war. They were urban guerrillas, right? The struggle against imperialism. Down with the pig republic. But how was it all supposed to work? The motives for the war swelled up in their heads and mouths until they burst and collapsed. And little by little, the only thing left was that you didn't fink on the Armed Fighters. That was something you just did not do. And you didn't nag them with questions about what they were fighting for, because you knew that the answer would turn out to be another phrase as gigantic as it was unfathomable.

"You could say it's the necessity for armed struggle—reaching the level appropriate to our situation here in the German Federal Republic as a U.S. colony, a strategic subcenter of U.S. colonialism. A situation set up by the Red Army Faction. A concrete message to the city military commanders: the kidnappings have the material purpose of liberating the imprisoned freedom fighters. . . ."

This was what her husband had left her alone with, now and forever. Once one of them said, "The reason our heads are round is so our thinking can change direction." She stroked the dog. Not only heads were round in this business, she suspected; the whole thing went around in circles.

Someone gets kidnapped. The person who did it gets caught and charged. They don't understand his motives and they lock him up. If they had understood his motives they wouldn't have locked him up. Of course, if they had been able to understand his motives he wouldn't have needed to kidnap anyone in the first place, and so he would never have been charged. But there are others who do understand him. They rob a bank to get hold of money to free him. Three of the raiders are caught, charged, and locked up. The rest pick out one of their countrymen who especially disgusts them, kidnap him, and use him to free a few of their jailed friends. Some others are not freed. They go on a hunger strike and die. Some are tortured and kept from dying. A bomb is planted in another town to draw attention to their fate. Then for a while no one gets caught, but many are investigated, especially those who look as if they, too, might one day decide that they've had it. And in this whole process there is no beginning and no end. A strike is held at the Rosenthal factory that achieves nothing; at the same time there is an increase in the number of people playing the lottery, and in the number of investors in building and loan associations. The people on the agenda to be rescued can't be found.

The wife petted the dog and hunted for her dark glasses. "I blubber a lot these days," she said apologetically to Ewald the bartender.

"No problem. What runs out don't turn sour. That ain't what they had in mind when they said that, but it fits." He wouldn't accept any money. "Another time," he said. "You can pay next time. But today ya helped me pass the time!"

She traveled home with a sense of discomfort. Soon after her husband's death she had begun to feel continually uneasy, as if she had forgotten to turn off the gas or not paid an important bill. She felt neglectful and guilty.

They had always felt a bit guilty: her husband and very likely all the other people she knew. They didn't talk about it. A lot of what they all did and thought and schemed ran contrary to the giant, mute images of their parents, most of whom lived hundreds of miles away and exerted no detectable influence on them, yet never believed that they were grown up. "Being grown up isn't enough," her husband had often said. "You have to become dangerous, different. There must be no going back, not even if you want to."

Now there really isn't any going back, not for him, thought his wife, down below in the subway. Probably I'm already headed in reverse. Maybe others are too. Some were already showing the first symptoms, doing political campaign work, moving into civil service jobs, founding a business. They made lots of excuses; but they left a way open to go back, back to their parents.

Her husband would never take that way now. He had proved he was right by dying and no one could prove him wrong. He would stay young and flawless forever. I'm twenty-nine now, she thought. In a month I'll be thirty. I always thought that was a big deal, but now they've done me one better: Being thirty is peanuts compared to being a widow! But he'll always be thirty. He'll always stay young, never get sick, never have a gray hair. We'll grow farther and farther apart as time goes on.

She had been suppressing a certain thought all day. Today was Tuesday, a workday. Everyone was at work. It was three-thirty in the afternoon. That meant that the medical examiner's office was still open. "If I can't forget about it, if I can't forget about it," she whispered to herself like a half-wit, "then I might just as well go ahead and think about it." But she shuddered, because she didn't know exactly what the awfulness was. After all, what did happen afterward? Ashes to ashes, dust to dust. But this? What they were doing to him now wasn't ashes, and it wasn't dust!

"Should I have insisted that they cremate him?" she murmured to herself. The people in the subway had given up staring at her by now and turned her into something that wasn't there as far as they were concerned, the way one does with drunks and cripples.

She knew that her husband's parents would never have agreed to cremation. And her husband? She was sure he wouldn't have accepted any form of bodily erasure. Maybe something like a cross between Lenin's mausoleum and the pyramids at Giza!

"Why can't people simply disappear when they die?" she said. The rest is bad enough, without this too. He's gone, and without him there are so many things I just don't get. But his body is still here. Maybe by now it's impossible for me to separate the part I loved and knew from the part I can discard.

Her husband's voice emerged clearly out of the subway blast: "Aw, come on, kiddo! Loved me, you say? What kind of a posthumous story are you trying to fabricate?"

"I haven't any choice," she murmured softly. "Why did you run out on us? Now we're going to carve you up. Each one of us will take his own cut: the prosecutor's office and your pretty boys and your mother and the Catholics and the comrades and I. To each his own. That's what you get for taking off the way you did."

In her mind was a table. She wasn't sure where it was, maybe close by, but she couldn't stop thinking about it. Was it a white table? Or maybe metallic silver? The table where they had laid him or were about to lay him might very well look like a butcher's chopping board. She knew it had a drain. "Take him to the medical examiner's office," the cops had said. No doubt they were saying that for the thousandth time. Did they watch it being done? What spectators were permitted? Would they have let her send in a family doctor, who would watch to see that they didn't damage him, and that none of his parts got misplaced? She pondered whether she didn't need to get in touch with Mr. Sable again. He was the only one she'd credit with the savvy to treat death properly.

It struck her for the first time how alone she was, among all the comrades. "That loony Marx," she said. "In his world nobody ever dies." A man sitting next to her caught what she said, got up, and changed his seat to one near the door. Gradually it was dawning on her that people who got shot or died in a hunger strike were not the true dead, as she had assumed until now. True death—the death no Marx or Lenin could make head or tail of—was dying in bed. It didn't figure in their ideology, so they left you on your own.

"We have other fish to fry," her husband had said. "It's life we're concerned with. A life of human dignity, without exploitation—and the fight against imperialism, and so on."

"But none of that's any use to me now," she said as she got out of the subway car. "It's no use. Sure, death happens to everybody, only with him it was so damned quick on the draw. Obviously the comrades have figured out that they can't make this into a hero's death; otherwise they wouldn't be keeping it under wraps this way."

Later she learned that this wasn't quite true. They hadn't been keeping it under wraps at all. All over the city—or everywhere that counted—the comrades had been discussing the death of this admittedly dubious and multifarious character, who nevertheless had been a loyal member of their fraternity. As a rule, lone-wolfing was strictly condemned and, politically speaking, regarded as if it were a mental illness; but in his case, death had mitigated the fault, which could now be registered under the heading of a premonition. Now, in view of his early demise, resentment waned at her husband's offbeat reactions, his ridicule of political slogans, the way he had publicly danced a waltz to the music of the Communist "Internationale."

Not only that, they said; but now it was bound to come out which of the couple, the husband or the wife, had really been pulling the strings, and which had been only their nominal supporter. With most left-wing couples you could tell that, but in their case there had been some doubts. Now—sad as the occasion might be, of course—these doubts could be cleared up. When they tried to assess the couple's political abilities and aims, to decide which was the more active or passive, they fell into two factions, of approximately equal size.

All this was unknown to the wife today, the fourth day. And she wouldn't have cared even if she'd been told, because their debate wouldn't clarify what to her was the only topic of interest: what it was like to be dead.

She'd been aware for some time that someone had been following her ever since she got out of the subway. You can always tell. Her husband had taught her the knack, as well as how to shake off pursuers. One time she complained to him that she didn't feel like running away from phantoms, and her husband had got angry. It didn't matter if the guy on your tail was real or imaginary, he said. All it took was one real one that you didn't shake off; so it was important to train yourself to get away even from ghost pursuers. Her training took place at a time when they were no longer living together but used to meet almost daily, and when they were being shadowed in actual fact. Her husband was representing a group of Heidelberg mental patients who had formed themselves into a politically active patients' collective, and the collective was arousing a great deal of interest from the feds and their ilk.

She tried to locate her subway pursuer so that she could decide whether or not to try to shake him off. Meanwhile she recalled several members of the patients' collective who could be of help to her now. Back then they were helping only themselves, and that had been no small assignment. Many of them had already been convicted of crimes. The authorities had handed down whopping sentences, as they always did when faced with something they couldn't understand. That was the era of incomprehensible crimes, which brought no profit to the perpetrators, earned them no money, no prestige, no power. Why did they commit them?

In the Frankfurt train stations there are glass display cases that show you pictures of the zoo. You can look at the photos and see the faces of animals that were born in jail. If you want to, you can look into the mirror-like panes and comb your hair, as you check to see if there's anybody behind you. Between the head plumage of a crested crane and the blurred image of her own face, she saw a young blond man with a beard. She had never seen him before, but she could tell he wasn't on the wrong side. That much is definite, she thought; there can be only one right side, even if it sometimes looks like the wrong one. This guy was on the right side. She could feel her head trembling slightly. She stopped and looked around her, along the rumbling track and into the dark maw of the staircase. The man behind her did the same. Then he appeared to stumble a little and bumped gently against her back.

"Tomorrow evening at your place," he said. "You'll get another phone call."

"Your name is . . . Gloucester," said the wife, with simulated cool.

"No. Gladys," the man whispered, furious.

The whole encounter lasted only seconds. Then she continued without further pause into the cool tunnel. She had to walk its entire length in order to come up near her apartment. She saw no one, and she was sure no one had seen her.

Had the group behaved in this same theatrical way with her husband? Apparently most of her countrymen felt proud if they suddenly discovered traces of Mata Hari and jungle romance here in this boring country. But surely her husband would have laughed at anyone who whispered pretentious code names to him on the street. Or would he?

"Gladys," she murmured. "I hope they don't think I'm going to sit there with a gun at my feet, waiting for them to phone me."

All the same, she knew she would wait for their call, and that her husband would have waited too. What for? Most likely it had nothing to do with the world revolution. She didn't have the faintest clue to their ends, only their means. Her husband's mental-patient clients, on the other hand, had had a clear if unadmitted goal. They were avenging themselves for being sick. They had experienced the power of the state firsthand. No, not in the form of prison or torture; and the state hadn't let them starve or freeze to death either. They couldn't even complain that they'd been neglected. On the contrary! Sealed in a soundproof room, the room prescribed by their illness, they were never unwatched, even for an instant. But no one ever touched them. No one credited them with any ability. No one trusted them. It's rude to be sick when you're being treated so well.

The wife had seen these clients, the members of the patients' collective, only once, in her husband's law office. They'd been terribly nervous, as if for a long time they had been forced to listen to a deafening noise. She had felt guilty in their presence, and they had made her uncomfortable with their suspicious glances. But no doubt they were right to want revenge.

She discovered a neatly sealed envelope waiting for her at her front door. Mr. Sable hadn't let her down. "You'll find the notices in your mailbox," he had written. "The funeral has been set for 11:00 A.M. on April 24."

She did some quick arithmetic. This meant that her husband's body would remain visible for twelve days after his death. "That's too long," she said as she unlocked her door. "Too much change happens in that amount of time."

Day Five

As each new day of his death wore on, his wife achieved more of a feeling that their three years of separation were meaningless, a brief spell of disharmony canceled out by the new life she was sharing with him since he died. Never before had she felt so much a wife as now, in her new station, caught in the undergrowth of myriad unfathomable duties.

Her days were organized now from morning till night, a strenuous sequence of errands and conversations, all with a single aim and a single object: him, nothing but him. Her duties extended to both his day and his night sides. She really couldn't put off going to the daytime law court, and meeting his intern. She intended to see the boy again too, that creature of twilight. And finally her persecutors, the Group, the creatures of night, had announced their intention to visit her, via a messenger with the absurd name of Gladys. Their visit might turn out to be the high point of today: the fifth day.

Her mother-in-law phoned, and said she felt miserable. Her normally feisty voice was almost unrecognizable. She and her husband were old, and had nothing to do but think about the awful thing that had happened, and wonder what had really gone on and who was to blame.

"What's the point of getting them safely through the war, and helping them complete their studies, just to have them go and die on you?" asked her mother-in-law. She didn't have the energy to lift a finger, she said; she was just sitting around bone weary.

"We have a definite date for the funeral now," the wife told her cautiously. "It'll be on the twenty-fourth." She could hear her mother-in-law counting the days.

"My God, that's a long time," the old woman said. "This waiting is the worst part."

The wife asked after her father-in-law.

"Papa is knocked for a loop," said her husband's mother.

The wife knew that this was an understatement. She had seen for herself how it was. A deep crack had run through the old man. His son had always been a stranger, but now he'd lost him completely.

Her mother-in-law, fleeing into the world of routine, asked her to send some of the death announcements. "There are people who have to be told, people you don't even know, but I have to write to them and give them a chance to extend their sympathy."

Warmest condolences, thought the wife. The cards had to be addressed, but to whom? Where was her husband's address book? "I'll send you some cards," the wife told her mother-in-law. "They turned out lovely."

"Lovely!" said her mother-in-law. "How can anything like that be lovely!"

"I'm sorry," said the wife, and noticed that the two of them had exchanged roles in this surreal conversation. She'd spoken exactly as her mother-in-law normally did, and her mother-in-law had spoken just like her. Her husband had finally brought the two women together.

I'll keep right on getting older, the wife thought. In ten or fifteen years he'll be like a son to me. The three years she'd spent away from him were dwindling to nothing: three years of work and small successes; three years of going out, having men friends and occasional affairs; three years of little trips and of testing her independence. Three short years.

Her husband had got into a white-hot lather when she had men friends. "The filly is still in my stable," he'd said to her once. "And the stable door stays shut, have you got that? Otherwise you can take back your own name!" He had said it leaning on the counter of their favorite bar, the one where they both hung out, while all the time he had a black-haired drama student lounging beside him—another of those starved-looking down-and-out mutts he went in for, no doubt fully equipped with a psychoanalyst and the clap.

She'd been speechless with rage. He had always arrogated the right to operate on a double standard: Sure, he was an honest-to-God left-winger and an anarchist, but after all, a man's a man. He would laugh till he was red in the face at all the gloomy comrades who kept making themselves do things they didn't really want to, just to show how with it they were: getting up at five in the morning to stand around at factory gates, or doing the vacuuming and attending classes on infant care, or driving their girlfriends to weekend seminars, or running off leaflets for good causes.

"Why do you do that, for heaven's sake?" her husband had asked the comrades time after time. "Why do you go around pretending to be something you're not? It can't be good for the revolution if it goes that much against the grain."

"He isn't even an anarchist," a redheaded comrade had said with contempt. "He's a hedonist."

She could still hear her mother-in-law's voice on the phone, invoking his childhood, as if that way she could at least get the little boy of long ago to come back to her. "You don't know what it feels like; you've never had any children."

She was making it easy for the wife to cut the conversation short. "I still have so incredibly much to do," she said. "Please don't be mad!" And she hung up.

Her mailbox was stuffed every day now, even though she hadn't sent out the announcements yet. Letters were arriving from people she'd never heard of. She dropped them all into a box and put it in the kitchen. Later, later. First she had to go to the law court.

As she dressed with elaborate care, she avoided the truth: She was starved for recognition. She wanted all the hostile ravens who fluttered through the courthouse corridors to gather around her, pity her, show respect and admiration for her husband. At last, she thought, wrapping herself in a black shawl with a silver sheen. Now, at last, he'll get what he deserves. She didn't doubt for a moment that he was the best of the lot. Of course he was also the craziest. But there were crazies on the bourgeois side as well, and there, too, they were the best of the lot. You could see that looking at several very successful older defense attorneys.

Her husband's bunch of keys weighed heavy in her handbag. She was exercising her right, the power of the keys. At the courthouse entrance she asked the way to the lawyers' chambers, even though she knew perfectly well where they were. The porter didn't bother to look at her. "Third floor," he said sullenly. The anteroom was full of unimpressive-looking men and women with robes draped over their arms. No one took any notice of her, and she saw no one she knew.

"Where are the lockers?" The woman lawyer she asked merely pointed to the next room.

The wife had to search for a long time before she found her husband's locker. She got the now familiar jolt when she saw his name on the front; this time it hit her especially hard. Why isn't anybody trying to stop me? she thought. After all, I'm doing something illegal. His papers are none of my business; I oughtn't to be allowed to walk off with them! People next to her were opening their lockers, picking out bulky files, chatting as they locked up again.

"Stinking holidays," said one man. "Would you look at the junk that piles up!" "File it," said another, pointing his chin at a wastebasket. None of them felt that the files were sacred, none saw the file folders as garments worn by sleeping stories. But they're all old and past it anyway, the wife thought maliciously, glancing at their bald pates and potbellies. "The poetry of a file!" her husband used to say. "The rest of them complain all the time about legal language. But it's concrete poetry!"

She decided to read part of the stack of documents that she'd taken from his locker. Once again she felt sorry that she couldn't hold on to his law office, the playroom where he'd spent his time dreaming and bringing papers to life. Or was it the other way around? He was a Nostradamus of lawyers, one of those weird types out of the tales of Hoffmann, black-clothed and bony-legged, tall and hunched over, who thrive in a setting of magic tobacco jars and mysterious leather parchments.

She hugged the bundle of legal paper to her breast and left the lawyers' chambers without having achieved the recognition she craved. Outside the door she ran into a public prosecutor whom she knew slightly. He was one of many against whom her husband had fought dramatic courtroom battles, and after their scraps, her husband refused to make up with him in the traditional way, by joining him in a drink in the courthouse canteen. The convivial beer would have stuck in her husband's craw, because when he hated someone, he did it twenty-four hours a day. This prosecutor, Dr. Taubenmeier, hadn't been able to understand that. When he saw the woman in black he paused, pondered, then recognized her. Does my hair look combed? she thought, and felt embarrassed.

"Ah," said Dr. Taubenmeier, a short, rather plump man who could as easily have been thirty as fifty. "Ah, dear madam. As you know, your husband and I weren't the best of friends. But the

Great Master reduces us all to silence. I'm sorry, very sorry. Such a young widow!" He'd put his hand on her arm and was propelling her on an intimate stroll through the tiled corridors.

"There's a lot of talk going around, eh?" he said cheerfully. The wife kept her eyes on her feet and her mouth shut, to see what developed. "It must be really tough for you. Have you hired a deputy yet to finish things for him?"

"Not yet," said the wife. "After all, it's only been five days."

The prosecutor twirled her around to face him, as if he planned to give her a talking-to. "Well," he said, "his colleagues won't exactly fall all over themselves trying to get the job. But the law's the law. Even if your client's a kook!"

"I don't feel it's up to you to judge," the wife said, finding it hard to form the words. "I have to go now."

"Dear madam," said Dr. Taubenmeier, completely unruffled. "Rumor has it that our revered colleague is undergoing an autopsy. Is that so?" The wife was at a loss what to say.

"I expect it's true, and quite right too, with him dying so suddenly, at his age, in unexplained circumstances. My, my," he said. "Wouldn't it be nice to be a fly on the wall, and watch when they cut out that devil he had inside him!"

And Dr. Taubenmeier took advantage of her stunned amazement to make his getaway, taking off with bouncing steps down the corridor.

"Hey, you," the wife said to her husband, to maintain her equilibrium. "You know, he hated your guts." She spoke softly into the empty hall of the law court, knowing that she was talking to herself. But her husband had occupied a chunk of her, so she was entitled; if she talked to herself, she was talking to him too.

They really hate him, she realized, and thought of the notorious Group: They'd been the first to learn to marshal counterhatred. "I don't envy them," she told her husband, whose shade must surely be lingering somewhere in the empty hall—where if not here? "But I can understand them sometimes. I mean, I can understand their hatred. But not their strategy."

As she left the courthouse, her thoughts reverted to the patients' collective. That had started a lot of balls rolling. Back then, in '69, things had come leaking out through the walls of the mental clinics and into everyone's mind. But thank God, the walls were still there, because none of the so-called normal could stand to see so much suffering. And then the people on the inside, locked behind the walls and into their illnesses, started to besiege those on the outside. And when they swarmed out for the first time, the ones on the outside were afraid. There was a certain doctor whom the mental patients trusted. The wife, who had seen him only once, didn't trust him. She was scared of people who were absolutely sure they were right. And also of people who made her feel guilty whenever she was with them. Her husband hadn't known the meaning of fear—maybe because physically he was big and tall, or perhaps because people treated him with more caution than they did her.

One time, some members of the patients' collective had gathered in her husband's office. Six or seven young men and women were seated on the floor in a semicircle. Their renegade doctor, their organizer, hadn't been present. Her husband discussed his defense strategy with his clients. Several released patients had been arrested for possession of firearms and criminal conspiracy, and the others were trying to free them, but at the same time they wanted to show the pig state what they thought of it. Her husband should be present as their counsel, but not actually plead their case: There was no need to defend yourself against a system run by pigs.

At first her husband hadn't commented on their proposal. "What's the point of him just standing around doing nothing?" his wife asked one of the patient group, a thin, irate-looking girl. "I mean, the trial isn't a puppet show, is it?" "I think your old lady needs a PPCR," the girl said to the mute husband. "What's a PPCR?" asked the wife. "A private political consciousness raising," her husband replied with a straight face.

While the wife searched for the courthouse exit, she tried to think what else they'd said at that little group session, but she couldn't remember. Now, four years later, the only thing she could picture clearly was the way her husband had got angry—that is, the way he had made up his mind to get angry. "Well, I'm not your performing clown, that's for sure. If I appear in court, I'll plead your defense. If not, I'll drop the case."

"Go ahead," said the irate girl. "You'll be sorry. We're not dependent on you."

"That's what you think!" her husband had said. "You guys always think the courtroom is the greatest place to issue revolutionary proclamations. Get that notion out of your heads right now. All they'll do is stop listening and do whatever they feel like with you. At least they would listen to me. I've stolen their language. When I speak in court, I pipe back their own language, only in a different key. You guys all have your special jargon, your psychology lingo, your mental-hospital jive. They'll just switch you off. I know how to talk their lingo and I can represent you with it. Why the devil should I just stand around like a dummy, decorating the landscape?"

The group hadn't listened to him. Their minds were made up and they weren't about to change them. They had undergone the tortures of illness, and what was worse, the tortures of bourgeois experiments at healing. In the end they realized that their illness was other people, and that true healing was to destroy the others —at least a little. This lawyer of theirs was part of the illness, and so was his wife. Both were outsiders. The outsiders had to be destroyed—at least a little.

Now he'd really been destroyed. Or had he? She'd have loved to know what the patients were saying about his death—the ones in the prisons, and the ones in the underground. For him, death had meant the end of captivity.

The wife walked along the Zeil, Frankfurt's main shopping boulevard, and passed the windows of the big department stores. She was looking for black clothes, but all the colors were saying spring. Entering one store's mourning-wear department, she found that the dresses and coats were bulky and heavy, made for old women who always felt cold. She bought a black raincape that looked like a stage costume, or a lawyer's robe. There wasn't much money left in her wallet. A colleague of her husband had told her that she was entitled to a funeral allowance from the bar association. She needed it desperately but felt ashamed to phone the association and ask.

If it hadn't been for the boys, she thought, as she crossed the Zeil wearing her new cape, if it hadn't been for the boys I'd have gone crazy with love. But he kept moving one step away from me, so I could get a clear view of him.

On her way through the city, she had eyes for only the adolescent boys leaning on the benches at bus stops. Sewed into tight jeans, they poked their thin backsides into the sunlight. She saw only the boys, with their long, rather greasy hair and self-assured gaze, gripping a bag of french fries or a cigarette. She'd never particularly noticed them before. In her husband's eyes, beauty had been solidly in their camp. When other men showed an interest in his wife, he felt it was not only rude but also strange.

"He did love me, he did," she told herself, pausing at the side portal of the cathedral. But as some kind of an added attraction: a mommy, a female friend. "You can't really talk with guys like them," he'd told her once. "They're birdbrains. You'd need to line up hundreds of them end to end to produce anything like a feeling."

"It sure is a rat race you guys are in," she'd said to him once, when she was already living on her own. "You all always seem to be in a hurry! And yet I can't ever figure out what you're looking for."

"None of us can figure it out," he'd replied. "We're searching for something that stays the same while it's always changing. Something the same as us. A twin brother who's somebody different. Equal parts trust and curiosity. And it all ends up with a hole in a toilet wall where you stick your prick through and you never know if the guy you can't see on the other side is going to kiss it or chop it off."

The wife had often been hurt by her husband's frankness, and at the same time felt somewhat honored. He didn't credit her with the ability to suffer because of the way he chose to live his life. She knew that if she wished, she could have been pals with all his ephemeral boyfriends. Her husband took her along to the gay bars, where she enjoyed an uncritical veneration resembling the love shown to aging female pop singers. Her husband had never lied to her. He'd never concealed the truth about himself. He had never spared her.

She went into the cathedral and sat down in one of the pews. It was dark and silent, and her black clothing was suited to the vast enclosure. She pondered: Was this cathedral Catholic or Protestant? Catching sight of the little tabernacle box on the altar, and all the statues, she realized she was in the right place for her husband.

She had to find a priest. "I can't take that chore off your hands no matter how much I want to," Mr. Sable had said. "Of course I'd be glad to do it, but no doubt you have something unusual in mind." As if one could choose a priest from a range of suitable models, she thought: one type for plain folk, another for the educated classes, or for intellectuals. Maybe it really was that way. The cathedral certainly wasn't making her feel any better. It's no use if you only go there once, she thought.

From a nearby phone booth she called a friend who had a doctorate in sacred music. "Do you happen to know any progressive Catholic priests, Dora?" she asked, and started crying for the first time today, the fifth day. Her friend named a name, a parish, an address. "That's where everybody goes who doesn't really want to go to church at all," she said. "You're sure to be less out of sync there than anywhere else. Do you really have to have a priest?"

"It's what his parents want," said the wife, sobbing in the phone booth. But as she said it, she knew she was lying. She wanted a Catholic service too, because she couldn't think of a better alternative. She had no other rituals at her command, and she couldn't tailor-make a funeral celebration especially for her husband, one capable of bringing him back to life.

"You really should do something offbeat for him, of all people," said Dora, through the wife's sobs.

The interval between his death and his funeral had seemed to stretch out interminably. Now, suddenly, it seemed to her hideously short, as if the remaining days had collapsed into seconds. It would take her weeks to prepare a funeral banquet worthy of him. And what was happening to the dead man in the meantime? Her thoughts strayed back to the wounds they were inflicting on his body—while she ran around buying coats and wondering about his hidden nature!

The pretty boys and the Group, the mental patients and the left-wing heroes—they'd all have to attend the kind of funeral celebration she had in mind. For one day, the prisons would have to fling open their doors, and the white crocodiles, the ones who'd gone underground, would rise to the surface. And at the very end, when it came time for the funeral oration, old graves would have to open, and the dead anarchist Bakunin would shake the earth out of his beard and bid his young comrade welcome into the next world.

I guess it has to be a Catholic priest all right, the wife thought sadly; there's no alternative. And to bend herself to necessity, she stayed in the phone booth and dialed the parish. She was given an appointment for that afternoon. Her surprise evidently annoyed the parish secretary.

"After all, it *is* about a funeral, isn't it?" the secretary snapped. "In that case, we obviously don't have all eternity!"

"I thought that was exactly what you were there for," the wife answered just as sharply, "for eternity. That's why I'm coming to see you."

"I'm sorry." The other woman's voice followed after a long moment. "I'm nervous today."

"I am too," said the wife.

"Well, then, so you'll come to see Father Lächler at his office at four P.M."

Still one hour before her appointment. She left the cathedral, not telling herself where she was going, and walked unthinkingly along the Main River, watching the ships pass under the bridges. If you held your head very still at a certain angle, the city looked beautiful, especially on a bright day like today. She came to a strip of lawn and shrubbery along the shore, known as the Nizza—Nice: just like the French Riviera.

She and her husband had loved the Nizza. She had fit perfectly under his right shoulder, in the crook of his arm, sheltered from the rain and wind, and warm in the winter. Now her right hip, where his hand used to rest, was orphaned and cold. At least twice a week her body had been able to take its customary place beside his. Walks had been a necessity of life for them: no one can listen in on you when you're out walking. Or did they have directional mikes good enough to pick you up now? Not here in the Nizza, where the bums slept wrapped in newspapers on the benches and the green necks of bottles jutted out from the trash baskets.

It dawned on her that she'd done more walking around today than on any of the four previous days—and still she hadn't finished all the errands on the day's agenda. Walking was a way to reassure herself: I can still walk, I'm not immobilized, I don't have to lie down. She just wanted to walk, nothing else. She'd thought of death as the end of captivity, but for her it had marked the start of a new spookier kind of captivity.

She saw that many of the streets were no longer made for people like her. Rejecting, choked with stifling air, mere rights-of-way, resembling canals. When you walked in them you felt deathly afraid. She hadn't noticed that for a long time. In the past few years she just hadn't taken in the change. Normally she traveled underneath these streets, or drove through them in a car, listening to music and smelling a man's shaving lotion. There were no shops left along these streets. Why should there be, when there was nobody left here to buy anything? The doors of the buildings were locked, the dirty windows covered with double panes of glass. No posters hung on the walls. The cars driving by seemed to be shaving away the narrow pedestrian path, making it narrower and narrower. After all, it wasn't being used.

Despite the cars, she didn't speed her pace. Clinging to the walls of the buildings, she let the draft from the vehicles blow over her, and drank in the hot smell of gasoline. Even the traffic noise didn't bother her. Her feet on the asphalt; the feeling of the cape blowing over her shoulders; the view of faraway trees promising an end to the highway—she enjoyed it all, now that her husband was dead. Every smell, every sound, was a proof of life. Every disturbance, every annoyance, every fear, showed that she was still alive.

The priest himself opened the door. She'd located the rectory at once behind the ugly yellow church. The priest's height left her speechless. He would have dwarfed even her husband.

"Lächler," he said, holding out his hand. "We haven't met."

It was a terse statement of fact. Naturally people like you and me have never met, he seemed to be saying. What business could we possibly have? You people come to me only when somebody dies. You've already decided baptisms are unnecessary, and half the time you don't bother to get married in church. You only come when there's a death; you always come then. As if it wasn't too late to do anything by then.

But of course Father Lächler voiced none of these thoughts. He asked the wife to come in, offered her a seat, and sat down at a desk that didn't accommodate his size.

"I'm not Catholic," the wife said awkwardly.

"That's not really important," he said good-naturedly. Then he glanced at some notes and reported that he hadn't been her husband's parish priest. Why had she come to see him in particular?

Frau Dr. Droste had recommended him, she said. Anxiety led her to stress her friend Dora's academic title, as if it gave her protection. She'd heard, she said, that Father Lächler was progressive. She couldn't bear the idea of empty claptrap being preached at her husband's graveside. She wasn't very much into Christianity, she said defiantly, but his parents were. And besides, her husband had considered himself a Pole.

The priest kept silent and stared into space with a deep melancholy that stemmed from causes unknown to her.

She began to talk about her husband, telling disconnected scraps of stories about his childhood, about the flight from Silesia. About the prayer rug he'd brought with him when they got married. About his work. Over and over she emphasized his left-wing loyalties, his love of anarchism. But she didn't say a word about the boys. She caught herself describing her husband as if she wanted the priest to mourn that he hadn't known him. To share her grief—no, not to share: to increase the sum of her grief with his own.

But the priest didn't ask any follow-up questions. Her stories flowed more hesitantly, then dried up completely.

"So what choice have I got?" she asked Lächler. "Believe me, I'd rather have organized a funeral for him myself. There'll never be anybody as crazy as he was—anybody who's everything all at once, the way he was. He was always Catholic. But left-wing too, and all the other stuff."

The priest didn't look at her, and she put on her sunglasses again to cover her eyes.

"By the way, can you refuse to do it if you want to?" she asked. She really didn't know. "Can a priest refuse to bury somebody?"

"If there are reasons against it, of course he can refuse," the priest said severely. "The Church isn't a public-service enterprise, even if it sometimes acts that way, out of opportunism. But in your husband's case, I don't know why you bother to ask. He was Catholic. You've dealt with the question of a church funeral. He's dead. Now, if you'll forgive me, we need to straighten out a few details, and if possible get a bit of information on his family."

Maybe the reason he's so tired is that he never gets to know people, the wife thought. He hears the stories of so many lives, and no doubt some of them are fascinating. He's curious about the people involved, but he never gets a chance to meet them. Besides, a priest is so dreadfully cut off from everyone else. And no doubt he's not always sure whether it's worth it in the end, to spend his whole life so alone.

Her next thought was that now, at this very moment, she knew more about death than the priest did. Her husband was around, whatever the clerics said. The priest was in the position of always having to tell people about death as if he really knew something about it, when actually the people concerned were the only ones who knew; and even they knew only for a short time, and only in one instance. Nobody can know every time and in every case, whether the dead are still alive.

"Was there any Bible text that meant something special to him?" the priest asked.

"Does it have to be from the Bible?" she asked uncertainly.

"It is customary," said the priest, smiling for the first time.

A series of passages whirred through her brain: texts that fit her husband and that she could pile around him one last time like protective ramparts. He hadn't read very much himself, but he knew a lot, and he always quoted accurately. She'd never been able to find out how he managed to soak up all those quotes.

"I love going to the movies," he'd said once. "But I only see films that I've seen before."

"The Bible," said the wife. "I can't think of a thing but that charity bit from Corinthians."

"That is an immensely powerful text," said the priest, once again stern and unsmiling. "It's unbelievably beautiful. And it's used at one funeral in every three."

"Do you have a Lutheran Bible?" the wife asked, thinking that at least she'd be able to find her way around in that.

"Did you think I wouldn't?" the priest replied. "Of course I do."

Lächler stood up and walked slowly along a bookshelf. All sorts of barbaric and pagan texts were running through her mind: Avanti popolo! or the Songs of Maldoror, or Come into the park that they call dead, or We are gods riddled with painful sores, or Fight and win the rights of man. Good grief, the Bible. But then the Bible, too, was barbaric in places. As the priest handed her his adversary's Bible, it occurred to her that she could ask him for some time to think about it.

"I'd really like to take it home with me and look it over," the wife said to the priest, whose face had regained its expression of austere, weary sadness. "I could phone you about it tomorrow morning."

"We have plenty of time before the twenty-fourth," said the priest. "By the way, why is it so long until the funeral?"

She realized then that she'd talked only of her husband's life, not his death.

"I don't know," she said as she went out the door. "They're doing a postmortem." The priest said nothing.

If you want to, you can use the Bible as an oracle. The wife did just that, when she finally got back to her quiet apartment late that afternoon. She got a cordial welcome from her cats, who had forgiven her for the disruption of their lives and were all three lying in their usual places. They stretched and purred softly when she touched them. She opened the Bible fairly close to the beginning, letting inspiration guide her to the right place, and without looking, placed the tip of her fingernail on a verse. Then she read:

"We will pass over armed before the Lord into the land of Canaan, that the possession of our inheritance on this side Jordan may be ours."

She sat down and pondered, because the meaning of the oracle wasn't immediately clear to her. But she could see it had something: something to do with her dead husband, with death in general, and also with fighting, or an uprising. There was that idiom "He's gone over Jordan," meaning he's died. And the verse said that we were to occupy our inheritance on *this side* Jordan. That meant in life, on the side of life.

"It's tricky stuff to figure out," she said to herself. Or maybe she was talking to her husband, whose shade, she felt, hadn't been so perceptible in the priest's office as in the law court earlier that day. "After all," she said, "I'm not a theologian."

But she liked the verse and she felt that a power went out from it.

Once, back when he'd helped prepare the case for the patients' collective and knew he was under police surveillance, her husband had told her that the two of them ought to go underground: Really, one had no choice. He talked about two of his legal colleagues who'd taken the plunge.

"That's bull!" his wife had said, dreading to think of the discomforts of life in the underground. "Going underground! That's not like walking down a flight of stairs, you know! What do you think you'd do in that scene? What work could you do? You're not wired in to the Armed Struggle. Just think how tall you are, for instance; you'd always stand out a mile. And your nose would be a dead giveaway! You don't want to have a nose job, do you?" And she'd gazed admiringly at his big nose.

It wasn't common sense that made her discourage him. Nor was it love for her husband that made her resist the thought of going underground. No, it was self-love, fear of a step that would turn what had been theater into real life. But she didn't admit that to herself, or to her husband either, though she sensed he felt the same.

It was one thing to observe the Group from the fringe, maybe even help them form their nets of self-concealment; or to watch them in the newspapers and on TV, to see their power in the anxious baying of the politicians. But it was quite another to live like them, in the same tangled undergrowth of never-ending tension and nonstop renunciation, false papers and true feelings; huddling in cold, empty apartments with closed shutters at the windows, in a decor made up of orange crates, fake auto licenses, and hair dyes, with no company but a dog who was going off his rocker. Yes, that was something else, that was a different matter altogether. That was no life for her husband: Nothing on earth could have made him cough up so much puritanism. Besides, he hated guns.

"You get such crazy pipe dreams sometimes," his wife had said to him, back then.

"You don't understand at all," he'd replied. "You just don't get it. It's a lot easier for you, with that artsy-craftsy stuff you do. You don't tell out-and-out lies; you just pussyfoot around somewhere in the vicinity of the truth. Sometimes you even manage to do something that looks like the truth at first glance, with your radio spots and your little films. And then you're proud and you feel good about yourself and naturally you think: What in the world would I do in the underground? But it's different for me. Much as I love what I do, I'm always bang in the middle of lies. I can't stop anything from happening. I've defended people who were written off from the word go. It wouldn't be farfetched to set up the files for their children the day they're born!" He'd looked really down that day.

"Besides that," he said, "there are some of them that I simply can't stand. It's no good telling myself a hundred times that they're victims of circumstance. That's exactly what they are—you know that yourself, kiddo—but even so, I just can't stand them. I have no idea how to go about liberating them. For myself, maybe I can destroy the thing that's destroying me. But I don't know what's destroyed *them.*"

It was extremely rare for him to have such moments of depression. Fate, or the arcane authority responsible for the assignment of public defenders, always stepped in to hand him a case that made him feel good and gave him another taste of the lifesaving illusion that he could change things for the better. At least that was still possible then, back in 1970.

Was it really 1970? she wondered, gazing out into her post-Easter garden. Surely it must have been later. But no; it was this same time of year too, between winter and spring. She remembered the azaleas, so it must have been between winter and spring. Her husband had just taken on a public defense case involving break-in and theft. He had brought the case documents to show her. He was already living most of the time in his office, but he took advantage of every opportunity to spend the night with her in their apartment. He had arrived that evening, and they stayed up very late talking over the new file. She remembered the case very well.

The accused was a man just turned thirty, a trained plumber-electrician who stayed afloat by doing odd jobs. He was charged with multiple burglaries, but all he'd ever taken was potted plants. The records of his interrogation said that he'd claimed he didn't steal the plants—he abducted them. He'd started his "abductions" when he was a boy. He removed half-dead plants from the windowsills of his school, from shelves in the dark staircases of public buildings, from tables in waiting rooms, from offices of every kind.

"They can't scream, you know," he'd said under questioning, and showed no signs of remorse. The police described his apartment as a virtual jungle, because he'd converted it, and an adjoining shed, into a plant hospital.

Among the documents her husband had brought home with him that evening was a rather long written statement by the young man, who begged to be released from pretrial custody on the grounds that he had to care for his sick plants and that he was the only one who was familiar with the individual cases. His signature at the end of the statement was written in a very legible script, neat as a row of beads: Christoph Koblenz.

The manifold suffering, the torture of the plants had always gone against his nature, he wrote. That leached soil of the pots with their dried-out edges, the yellow, drooping leaves, the pitiful blossoms! The ones that people thought were hardy, those suffered the most. If clivias or gum trees could produce sounds audible to human ears, no one would be able to hear himself talk: Those were his exact words. But the fate of individual plants wasn't the worst part. No, he'd often succeeded in restoring individuals, simply by carrying them off in their pots, nursing them back to health, and then giving them to trustworthy people. He had to give them away, for reasons of space if nothing else, he said. Naturally he'd never asked any money for the plants once they were well—not even for the giant camellia that he'd rescued from a hair salon just as it was on the brink of death. He'd got it out by telling the staff that he was a hired gardener. His only concern, he said, was the tender loving care of his plants. Occasionally he used to visit their new owners to see how his fosterlings were getting on.

Some years ago, he continued, he'd been satisfied with his achievements. But then the plants had started to move en masse into the supermarkets: arrays of half-dead African violets, plastic-wrapped poinsettias, wretched, half-smothered cacti. There was no point in even mentioning the Russian vines; they were very proud, sensitive plants that almost always died. It was very rare that you could save one. Ever since this new era, of the mass murder of plants, his own life had become more difficult. There was the space problem he'd mentioned before. He had carried away tortured plants from department and grocery stores by the cartonload, as many as he could accommodate on his bicycle. It wrung his heart to think of how many he'd had to leave where they were. It was clear to him, he said, that he'd never be able to save more than a tiny handful.

But one day, those who caused the pain would have to pay for it, he wrote. Eventually they would find out what it's like to have to sit with dead or rotting feet inside a prison, with no light, in air that wasn't fit to breathe.

"It looks as if what he has in mind is a kind of hell for plant-killers," the wife had said to her husband, while he leaned over her shoulder rereading Christoph Koblenz's letter. She'd been fascinated, just like her husband, and wanted to meet the accused.

His activist raids had climaxed with a break-in at a large discount market outside the city—the crime that had led to his arrest. It had been a challenging caper, and he'd prepared it like a general-staff commander. Everything had gone off like clockwork. By chance, Koblenz had seen warehouse workers unloading hundreds of palm trees from a truck. The fan leaves of the palms were hanging half torn off from the rough trunks, like the broken wings of giant birds, and the trunk tissue was riddled with large wounds. Some of the trees already were dead, due to improper watering or to frost during transport. The wounded roots had been cramped into gray plastic buckets. Koblenz hired an open pickup and alerted his friends. At night they broke into the discount store and kidnapped the ailing palms. There were no witnesses, but by this time the police had caught onto the plant savior's funny little habit. Now he was being detained pending trial. He hadn't betrayed his accomplices.

That evening, the wife had seen her husband start to glow over this case. Not that he actually understood Christoph Koblenz's obsession, much less shared it; he referred to all greenery by the blanket term "salad." He distrusted everything that smacked of good health, and for safety's sake he lumped potted plants into the same category. But he sensed that he and this gentle crank had something in common: a kind of cunning, a fight that always stuck close to the object being fought for. Koblenz's reasoning made sense, no one could deny that. The germs of his defense sprouted in her husband's head that very first evening. His plea would reveal the political aspects of this apparently off-the-wall case.

She tried to remember how the plant kidnapper's trial had come out. The state authorities hadn't given him a chance. That is, they hadn't taken Christoph seriously and had sentenced him to a term of probation for simple theft. They couldn't take his kind of fight seriously. They could afford to laugh off this goodhearted weirdo with his astonished eyes and his curly beard. They could afford not to understand him, they could even afford to act as if they really did understand him. They could afford it, because there were so few of his kind.

"I can't deny that his crime has a certain charm," the public prosecutor had said. "I grant that much to my learned opponent. But of course the fact remains that he walked off with someone else's property. You see what I mean. And heaven knows he's a repeat offender!"

The wife hadn't met Christoph until after the trial. Actually, she'd been a bit leery of the Plant Avenger. But that had changed, once she stepped into his green living room which smelled of the earth.

"I'll keep on doing the same thing, I don't have any choice," he'd told the husband and wife apologetically. They were perched rather precariously on an aged sofa, with the branches of some shrub hanging down into their eyes, and ivy snaking across the wall beside them.

"You don't see how much misery there is, until you've gotten into it," Koblenz said. "I expect you're wondering why I don't work to help children, or the third world. People always ask me that. But I'm doing what I know how to do. Somebody has to do it. Besides," he added with a touching flicker of defiance, "the ones who ask me that are always the ones who aren't doing anything, not for children or the third world or anything else! Sometimes it's all too much for me. But once I get the plants home and they gradually begin to breathe and stretch, and I can begin to hear them again, I get so much satisfaction."

"You can *hear* them?" her husband had asked.

Yes, he said, he could hear them. They sounded like a small, very soft string orchestra, or like lightly touched piano chords. He really couldn't explain. The husband had looked skeptically at his wife.

"Oh, cut it out!" Christoph went on. "You can hear them too, or you could if you wanted to. Only I hear them so loud that I can't just walk on by, especially when they're suffocating." He pointed to a pot that held a very yellow, discouraged plant with broad leaves. "I took that one from the courthouse, from the room where they had me for questioning. She's in critical condition. I was almost too late. But don't worry, nobody saw me take her!"

"I think you're going to become a long-term client," her husband had said to him fondly.

Christoph started to look embarrassed. "It's just on account of the money, you know—I don't have much. Maybe you can take this one with you." He reached out to a big clay pot that contained a plant nearly the size of a small tree, and stroked it affectionately. "He's in good shape. He looks a bit like you," he'd said shyly to her husband. She couldn't help laughing now, remembering the desperate look on her husband's face when he'd had to accept custody of a tree as a legal fee: a *tree,* when he'd never regarded any plant as more than "salad."

His wife had been amused. "I don't suppose you give one of your patients away to everyone?" she'd asked Christoph.

"No, only to the right people. And not every plant suits every person. This one suits your husband. He's sturdy too, and proud somehow. You'd have to chop him down to really hurt him."

"Why do you say 'he'?" she had asked. "Why do you call this particular plant 'he'?"

"I dunno," Christoph had replied after a long silence. "I've never thought about it. It's just that some are hes and some are shes. It's obvious!"

The fifth day was winding to a close. She sat there waiting for her mysterious guest, Gladys or Gloucester. Neither was a person; both were ghosts, mere names. Dangerous, that was for sure. But she couldn't seem to believe the danger was tangible.

She knew, of course, that it was now against the law to have anything to do with the Group. You weren't allowed to talk to them, much less help them. Even the wish to understand them was forbidden. Over the years, too, it had become increasingly unclear who "they" were. The lonely elect, the inner circle, had been in the slammer for quite a while, and recently the courts had opened a broadside of trials against the prisoners. Everybody was treating them like exotic, explosive bacteria cultures that had to be kept in isolation. You had to put on protective gloves before going near them, or their ideas. Special enclosures were built around them, they were encased in metal plates, concrete, tiles. Cubic yards of empty space separated them from other people, as if they had a contagious disease. Why had everyone invented the Group? The wife had known them only from a distance, curious and always a bit ashamed because she lacked the ruthlessness that was their hallmark. They knew it all. They dared it all. They'd taken on a deadly burden of loneliness.

She was eating an orange. She inhaled its fragrance before enjoying the moisture and acidity of the fruit. The veils had lifted from so many things since her husband's death. Since her husband's death, she saw less reason than ever why she should feel afraid to look over the fence, to make excursions into the night side. Their impending visit didn't frighten her; it only made her curious. Death demanded respect even from the Group—even if in their eyes his was an unworthy death, involving no visible battle, no visible enemy.

The women of the Group were even haughtier than the men. Whom did they love? Each other? The wife had often tried to picture that: Ulrike and Gudrun, Margit and Petra, Inge and Brigitte—such sweet names they all had. They must love each other, she thought, because it's hard to love men who have to spend all their time hiding.

Maybe I'm not seeing it like it is, she thought. But I expect the worst part of it would be having to be alert the whole time, having to give up laziness. "You can't think without laziness," she said out loud, "or without boredom either."

"You aren't really passionate, you know," her husband had said to her once in amazement. That was a long time ago, only shortly after they were married. "You only act like it. Actually, there's nothing that makes you lose control. There's nothing you'd be willing to die for, either." "No, there isn't," she'd admitted.

Was that still true? She'd said it five years ago. Was it true now? Not entirely. Now she was a widow. Now she had a torch to carry on, an idea to keep alive. She had a goal.

It was up to her to put a proper finish to the projects her husband had started. She could keep his name and make sure that the world didn't forget it. The world? In his case, that amounted to five or ten streets, and that ghastly courthouse with all its hidebound judges and prosecutors. The world: That meant the handful of boys with their bars and their daily fits of anxiety. The world: That didn't mean the Royal Danieli hotel in Venice, or the Amazon jungle; that didn't mean Angkor Wat or Denver, Colorado. Those worlds had never laid eyes on him. Her husband knew not the world and the world knew not him. And now it was all over, gone. The world and her husband would never meet.

I can go out any day I choose, she thought. I can do whatever I want. One day I may decide I have to fight. Or maybe I'll just stay an onlooker. I can choose either one. She was determined not to let her mystery visitor deprive her of her freedom of choice.

She didn't jump when the doorbell rang. The cats didn't even wake up. For hours now the whole apartment had been hiding behind opaque curtains. The light was dim, but there was enough so you could keep an eye on everything. The door leading out into the garden had had its hinges oiled, and anyone who chose could leave by that door and slip through to another street without being seen. Cowboys and Indians.

Outside the door stood an elegant young woman. She was tall, red-haired, and wore a black velvet suit with a casual spring coat. She held a small bouquet of roses. "Hello there," she said.

"Gladys?" the wife asked cautiously.

"Yes, of course!"

The wife invited Gladys to come in, in the deferential way people treat their bosses, and straightened a crooked chair.

"Would you like some tea?"

"Yes, please."

"A cognac?"

"No, thanks."

Gladys sat in a very alert posture, on the most uncomfortable chair in the room. She sat like a guest at a funeral—which in fact was just what she was.

"I expected to see Gloucester," the wife said boldly, and was amazed at the gracious way Gladys took it.

"We thought you might. He's not here, otherwise he would have come. So you've known him a while?"

"Yes," said the wife. They sat opposite each other like a pair of impoverished countesses, dignified and embarrassed. If she doesn't say anything, I won't either, the wife thought.

"I'll make some tea," she said. "Excuse me a minute."

"Oh, of course," Gladys replied politely.

By the time the wife came back from the kitchen carrying a

neatly set tea tray, Gladys had evidently decided to take another tone. She spoke very softly but distinctly, like someone who's learned to control her voice at all times to make sure she isn't overheard by the wrong people.

"Naturally we're sorry about him," she said. "But the same thing could happen to any of us, anytime, so we expect it. When we lose somebody, we just have to keep going. How much did he tell you?" she asked sternly. "Have you checked out any of our stuff?"

"He didn't tell me anything. I minded my own business," the wife replied tartly. "We had an understanding about that."

"There are two things you have to find for us," said Gladys. "I suppose the cops have already been in his pad?"

"Naturally," said the wife. "They got there almost before the doctors." She had a hunch that she was trying to snow this cool, elegant Armed Fighter. Fighter for what? She didn't dare ask. She was trying to manufacture a hero's death, or at least a demihero's. After all, it was only right for the Group to respect their lawyer —especially a lawyer who was dead.

"Did they take anything?" asked Gladys. "Did they seize any evidence?"

"Not while I was there," the wife answered, not daring to admit that on that first day she wouldn't even have noticed.

"Then it's still there," Gladys said, looking worried. "Then you have to check it out fast. When you find it, we'll tell you what to do with it. It's urgent, have you got that? Of course," she said in a more cordial tone, "I can't demand that you do it; you're under no compulsion. It's bullshit what the papers write about us. We don't pressure anybody. But this thing's important to us, you can see that."

"What is it exactly?" the wife asked, absolutely furious. "What am I supposed to be looking for?"

"It's only a bag," said Gladys. "Not a very big one. Black. Heavy. We can't get close to his office, but you can go there anytime you want; you have all his stuff to clear up."

"What's the second thing I have to find?"

"Gloucester'll tell you."

"What's in the bag?" The wife noticed that Gladys hadn't touched her tea cup.

"It's better for you not to know," said the Armed Fighter. "Your old man didn't know either."

"Didn't he ask?" the wife asked, still furious.

"No," replied Gladys. "He caught on quicker than you that there'd be no point."

"I haven't caught on at all," said the wife. At that moment, for the first time, she felt that her husband had deserted her. "And I don't in the least want to catch on."

"Cool off," Gladys answered good-naturedly. "I can see where you're coming from. But you've got to dig a little of what's going on—only not too much. It's for your sake too. With your old man kicking off the way he did, you've got the pigs swarming all over you. They think he's left a hole in our ranks where they can move in, where they can get a toehold and split us wide open. It's up to you. First you have to wait till the area around his office is clean of cops. It'll be a while yet before that happens."

As she listened to her distinguished-looking visitor's soft, distinct sentences, the wife considered all the places where the bag might be. Tomorrow evening she'd go back to his office again, pay it an official visit, wait there awhile and figure out the lay of the land. Maybe she'd start searching the place. She thought of Ewald the bartender. He might help her to throw off the police and whoever else was hanging around. People in the red-light district didn't ask many questions. She felt that the streets around the station could be relied on to keep a secret.

"I have to go," said Gladys. "I don't have much time." She pulled on a pair of elegant blue leather gloves. Her silk blouse was blue and so were her pumps. She looked every inch a lady. "I'm a real eyeful, huh?" she said. "We've gotten pretty good at playing dress-up by now. I can walk through a crowd of a hundred cops, within a foot of the Wanted posters they've got out on me, and all they do when they see me is whistle. I swear it's true."

The wife remembered the Wanted posters she'd seen, and scrutinized Gladys for any resemblance, the trace of something familiar. Nothing doing. This fashion plate had nothing in common with the somber black-and-white faces in the photos, one of which would be crossed out every now and then by an invisible hand.

It was evening, the evening of the fifth day. It had been a day of errands and journeys. And yet the wife didn't feel she'd made any progress. The more of her husband's unfinished business she had to deal with, the less certain she was about what role she should play. She considered the bag, and decided that if she found it, she was going to open it. These damned political nobles; they think they're so superior! They think they can see what's going on so much better than other people!

There was something like envy in what she said, in the senile little phrases that she murmured now almost nonstop. She rarely thought now how silly she must look to other people, chattering away to herself the way she did. "It doesn't matter when I'm home," she said. "But if I don't get over the habit of talking to myself at home, then I'll do it on the street too, and in the subway. And then they'll think I'm nuts. But maybe they'll forgive me if they see I'm dressed in black. The poor little widow woman!"

Now that Gladys's brief visit was over, her apartment was silent and dead again. She went on sitting in front of the cold tea tray, feeling like a guest in somebody else's house. "I want Gloucester to come," she whimpered like a child. "Gloucester will understand. A man, a man! Even one like him!" Today's journeys and errands weren't ended yet, she saw; not yet. Now it wasn't the others, it was she herself who couldn't stop inventing duties—so she wouldn't have to think.

She would go out to one of his favorite bars. People knew her there. He often used to take her along, and join in with her when she made fun of the customers. All the guys who swung his way tended to think they were unique. Each would run down all the others. She'd never seen a group where every person despised the others so, for traits identical to his own.

"Lay off the chichi accent," one guy said, speaking in an even more high-pitched, exaggerated lisp than the reprimandee.

"Will you just look at how she's rigged herself up!" a man wearing a lace shirt and gold belt said about one wearing a silk shirt and silver belt. They never stopped taunting each other—that is, taunting their own mirror images. Every haircut, every beard, every new pair of shoes, was the butt of hours of pitiless comment.

She took a taxi to the bar. As a rule, the gay bars were small and red, hosted by an exhausted and blasé proprietor who doled out endearments around the room with cold calculation. This one was no exception. The barkeeper here was called Geert. "Geert, with two *e*'s," he used to say whenever he introduced himself.

Her husband had represented Geert free of charge in a rental suit, and she and her husband had been valued, if rare, customers at Geert's bar ever since. Or at least she'd been a rare customer. She had no way of knowing how often her husband might have gone there in the past three years. The thing was, she now felt impelled to visit this world of his, and that meant she'd have to start with a relatively square hangout like Geert's, where the regulars addressed her as sweetie and dearie and wouldn't question her right to be there. And this was a place where her husband had been respected.

They had their reasons for respect. In the daytime all these gay birds lived in the straight world, working as clerks or hairdressers or messengers, or were unemployed. It was rare for a real live lawyer to stray through their ranks. Theirs was by no means a classless society, as her husband had often claimed. The only equality was in the identical costumes. The other barriers—who belonged to whom, who spoke whose language—were as evident here as everywhere else.

"I'm so horny again today!" one of them would declare. "My dear, haven't you got any manners?" they'd shriek at him. "Show-off, you haven't been able to get it off for three years!"

In the summertime they wore short pants and kept their stomachs pulled in.

They used to turn on the charm for the wife. They'd express their admiration nonstop, and keep exclaiming how thin she'd got —"However did you do it?"—and hold back obscene remarks. They used to tell her about their endless love affairs and their two-week vacations in Tunisia and Morocco.

That was the reason she'd wanted to go there this evening—to bask in their shallow, wide-open sympathy. The men down in the bar used to cry easily. No doubt they'd cry now, and make her own tears flow. The few songs her husband had loved were waiting there in the jukebox. She could listen to the songs along with the others, tell them about his death, talk about the hideous injustice. They didn't care about politics. If anything, they tended to be conservative. They hated rebels because rebels threatened the collateral worlds they had built for themselves over the years. She felt sure that none of them wanted to be liberated. They didn't care if they were the exploiters or the exploited, so long as the status quo was maintained: so long as there was still a day and a night world.

"Sweetie!" screamed Geert as she descended the stairs into the smoky atmosphere, treading warily because the staircase was steep. "Hey, I'm seeing a ghost! How can you still be alive? You're so skinny I wouldn't recognize you! How come you're alone today —have you finally told your old man to go to hell? I'll stand a round of champagne for everybody! Or is your hubby away, and you only came because you know nobody'll make a pass at you here?"

The wife had forgotten that the guys here never read newspapers, or at least not the newspaper that had published the news of her husband's death the day before.

"He's dead," she said, coming up to the head of the bar. Inside the jukebox, Marlene Dietrich was asking where all the flowers had gone. Oh, it was just what the doctor ordered: a dramatic silence, with an appropriate musical theme in the background. But then along came a slight hitch.

"Don't say another word; that's a no-no!" Geert replied in an irritated voice. "Oh, my God, I've got a migraine coming on! You don't need to tell us any of the details, dearie," he said to the wife, who by now was speechless. "For heaven's sake, a thing like that could spoil a person's whole evening!"

Day Six

On the sixth day—the midpoint of her twelve-day vigil—the wife had a feeling of hiatus, as if the events and encounters that had hurtled past since her husband's death were now massing somewhere into a threatening lump. There was no more orderly sequence in her plans, no more good or evil, day or night. Instead she felt afraid she'd have to do everything all at the same time, and bring together all the people involved with her husband, whom she'd seen in isolation until now. The priest and the boy, Gloucester and Koblenz, Ewald and her mother-in-law. Unless she got them all together, she thought, she couldn't go on, she couldn't come to a final understanding of who her husband had been. And until she understood him, she couldn't bury him.

Bit by bit, the long-drawn-out rituals of the ancients were starting to make sense to her. For it takes time to see a person whole and complete one last time, when his body is no longer in the way. It takes time to see him once more; how he was as a friend or a Christian, as a lover or an actor. There were witnesses to his every color and quality, and most of the witnesses had never met. The funeral, for instance, could be the ideal time to understand him entirely; but you'd need lots of time for that. Everybody would have to tell a story about him, including those who hadn't known him personally but had only heard about him. In fact maybe they would be the ones to think of just the right thing, the perfect thing to say about her husband.

Once she'd been in Singapore. She remembered the bright-colored tents lined with tables and benches. Wreaths of pale orchids hung from the tent supports, and a coffin stood slightly elevated, with a photo of the dead man leaning against it. An increasingly insistent odor came from inside. Because in Singapore it's the regulation thing that you hold a coffin aboveground for a week and keep the dead person company, eating and chatting, drinking and playing cards. Sensible, she thought; they're putting together his picture one last time. They really don't need his photo. And how fond they must be of him, to be willing to eat and drink so close to him in the damp heat, so close to his dead man's smell.

Her husband had been gone for six days now, or rather he'd become invisible. All she had to do was break into the medical examiner's office in the Forsthausstrasse, all she had to do was demand in a loud and determined voice to see him—no doubt they weren't equipped for visitors—and she could prove to herself that he still existed. In China, this would have been his last day aboveground. Here, he had been given yet another six days to wait.

Naturally, she would never have dared to enter the morgue. The people there might look at her and decide that she was a calm person with steady nerves, and might actually grant her permission to view her husband's remains. And that scared her stiff. It was all she could think about, but she didn't dare talk about it to anyone, not to any of the friends and colleagues who phoned to ask how she was and what had developed. She couldn't even have told the Kirghiz.

She felt sure that everyone who had experienced a death must have the same thoughts. But each was alone with his thoughts, and with the uneasiness they caused others. Even Mr. Sable had showed signs of not understanding, as if he'd caught her having lewd desires.

"Just think of the deceased's dignity," he'd said. "People simply don't put the dead out to lie in state anymore, not even in rural areas. Of course we can arrange for a coffin to be laid on a bier, if the case seems to warrant it."

Right now, early this morning, as she moved back and forth vacuuming and straightening her room and behaving perfectly normally, holding wakes seemed to her far less barbaric than the custom of people here—their way of clearing the dead out of sight so that no one could really contemplate them. Here, everything that might comfort you was dismissed as bad taste. She hadn't had much practice with words like taste and dignity.

Then she had an inspiration. The priest! He, of all people, was bound to answer her question, if anyone could. Not only that: He wasn't allowed to show it if he felt embarrassed or disgusted by her unwillingness to leave her husband's body, and its natural or inflicted changes, shrouded in mystery. And she had an excuse to contact him, after all—the Bible verse that she had chosen by oracle. The priest had actually asked her to phone him.

As she listened to the phone ring and then heard his voice—the slightly dragging voice so many priests and clergymen have—she pictured him to herself. To tell the truth, he was a damned good-looking man. Yesterday she'd only noticed his enormous height and the dismissive sadness in his face. Now she could still see that face clearly as she read him the Bible verse and asked if he could make anything of it. Two creases ran down from his nose to his chin. His hair was blond, and puffed up by a blow dryer. He had a beard darker than his hair, one of those short, rounded-off monk's beards.

"Curious verse, isn't it?" said the voice on the telephone. "But I expect it has more to do with you than with your husband. How are you feeling?"

"Actually, I'm not feeling so well," answered the wife. "I can't stop thinking about how he looks now, and what he's turning into. And there's no one I can talk to about it."

"I understand the thoughts you're having," said Father Lächler. "I had them too, when my mother died not very long ago. I suppose it wouldn't help if I say that the body is a garment, a piece of worn-out clothing that one simply leaves behind?"

"No," she said irately, "that doesn't help me at all. His body wasn't a used garment. It was very beautiful, even after he was dead, not one bit worn out. And what did I know about him anyway?" she asked the priest. "Or you about your mother? Their bodies, their eyes, the way they moved their hands! I don't really know what else there was, that could have survived. The only thing that was different after he died was that he couldn't talk anymore," she said, weeping into the telephone. "Otherwise he looked just the same. It's only now that he's changing. Or they're making him change, only I can't see it happening and can't help him now."

"We believe in the resurrection of the body," the priest said helplessly.

Surely that couldn't be true of everyone, she thought. In many cases the bodies really were pitiful, worn-out garments.

"I'm sure he believed that too," she said. "He'd have thought the next world too boring without his body. I imagine it must be awful for theologians, having to answer these same questions from lay people over and over," she said. She said it because she felt sorry for the priest, whom she pictured holding a pen and doodling tiny gravestones with crosses on them. "Several other people I was very close to have died too," she added hesitantly. "But I never had this feeling with them. Something of them survived, I'm sure it did, and it still does. But I didn't feel this concern about their bodies."

"After all, you two were married," the priest said in a dubious tone. "That makes for a special bond."

She had the same feeling she'd had at their first meeting, that Lächler wanted to say something quite different, something sterner, and held back only because that sort of thing no longer jibed with Church ideology. Maybe what he really wanted to say was: "Thou two wert married. Therefore, O woman, is thy gaze clouded by the inessential. Beautiful or ugly, young or old, what matters that? Thou didst not love him with true charity. Thou knewest not who he was. Nor didst thou help him to find his true self, and therefore hath the Lord God done it for thee. For a meaningless shell dost thou weep, instead of for thine own wretched soul. Thou seekest thy husband among strangers. Thou dost question, where thou shouldst be silent. Thou hastenest hither and thither, instead of submerging thyself."

That was how the wife had always imagined a priest would talk, and she felt sorry that this one, who looked just the type for it, was bowing out, and offering her words of lukewarm comfort instead.

"It's hard to talk about it over the telephone," the wife said, and Lächler seemed grateful for the bridge she'd built for him.

"You're free to drop by anytime you think I can be of help," he said. He spoke with the voice of a young student, sounding sweet and insecure, as if he didn't think himself capable of helping others: not when he was scared himself, with a fear probably not too different from hers. "Come anytime. And I'll give some thought to the Bible verse."

"Have you considered that it could turn out to be a pretty lively funeral?" she asked. "Polite types dressed in black won't be the only ones coming. His clients are bound to come too—and I told you he was a left-winger."

"I'm not worried about that," Lächler answered, still sounding tender and modest. "They all have to die. That's not something people can debate, or abolish or reform. And they all know that, even if they won't admit it. You see," he went on, with good-natured patience, "we have the arguments on our side. There is no argument against death! Only God. But I won't take that tack with you."

"No, go ahead and take that tack," she said. She could feel herself growing older, as if she had a clock inside her where time was whizzing past at a hugely accelerated speed—minutes, days, years. "Go right ahead. It makes everything simpler."

"Oh"—the priest sighed on the other end of the line—"that's the old mistake of all agnostics. God doesn't make anything simpler at all."

She said goodbye to the priest coolly, a little contemptuously. "They don't have an easy time of it either," she said aloud. "They can't prove anything." But Lächler, too, had skirted the issue that troubled her. She began to feel afraid that she wasn't quite normal, that her thoughts were a bit sick, because she couldn't stop picturing certain images.

"Today I'm having a day of standing still," she said as the phone rang. "Today I'm not budging from this spot. Today everything is coming to me."

"I'm calling about the flowers for the funeral," Gloucester's voice said from very far away. "Have you got them already?" The wife jumped with fright like a child, and couldn't answer at first. "I'm sorry for having to trouble you," the voice said gently.

"Please come over," the wife cried. "The flowers aren't here yet."

"Don't worry," Gloucester said, in the same gentle, faraway voice. "We'll find a way." And the line went dead.

"I'm going to his apartment," said the wife. "I'm going to his apartment right now. There's still so much stuff I have to haul away. If the place is under surveillance, they won't think there's anything strange in my being there. Probably they've already got everything they want. Or maybe they just don't know what to look for."

She had a job to do. Okay, maybe she didn't know yet what to make of the bag and the gentle, indifferent voice on the telephone; and maybe she couldn't help feeling that the Group thought everybody outside their ranks was a dope. All the same, her husband had started something, and she had to finish it. She had to find the bag and give it back to its owner.

She got dressed, wondering if she ought to buy a few things in the city first, or if it would show a lack of piety to walk into his dead apartment loaded down with shopping bags, as if somebody were still living and eating there. But the whole time that she dressed and wondered, she knew that she intended to open the bag once she found it, however much the idea scared her. This was just like her fears about the corpse—there was no one she could talk to about it.

Today, the sixth day, was rainy. Raindrops dangled from the trees. But she didn't take an umbrella. It's more suitable for widows to wear black kerchiefs. She felt dismay—a small, discomforting certainty that now, for the first time, she was going to find out what it meant to be alone. Being alone: That was to hoard thoughts and phrases without being able to give any of them away. That was the fear that others were bored by you or indifferent. How strange; she felt as if all her friends had edged away from her, now that her husband was dead.

The telephone summoned her back.

"Please don't think I was trying to ignore you," said Paul the Great. "It's just that the whole thing has bowled me over. I can't think of a thing to say to you. But life has to go on, and you need my help. You won't be able to manage on your own."

"The two of you hadn't been on speaking terms for so long," the wife said warily. "Do you think you could handle things in the office?" What she really felt like saying was: "You and he had such an awful blowup. He didn't want you in his office. Do you think he won't notice if we go against his wishes?"

But then she remembered the tears that Paul the Great had shed, how very fond he'd seemed of her husband, how maybe he even saw through him. Paul was ten years his senior, after all. She didn't say any of this out loud, but she didn't need to. The heavy, eloquent man at the other end knew the score.

"Listen," he said. "There are legacies at stake here, political legacies; let's get that clear. Of course I know what's going on at his office, and I also know more or less what's coming up for trial. Have you talked with Hardenberg yet?"

"He must be on vacation," she said apologetically. "I've tried to reach him I don't know how many times."

That was a lie, and she could tell that Paul saw through it at once. She'd thought of Hardenberg every day but postponed contacting him, as if she were saving him as a last resort. Last, but dead certain. She'd barely met Hardenberg, her husband's intern, and she knew nothing about him except that he talked like a nineteenth-century theology student and lived alone with a tame raven. And yet she felt that Hardenberg was someone who had really known her husband the lawyer—despite the fact that the two men, unlike virtually everyone in the left-wing scene, addressed each other formally even though they worked together every day. Yes, despite that, she'd been telling herself all along: If all else fails, I'll call on Max Hardenberg. He'll have the solution.

"We need to get him in on it too," said Paul the Great. "Maybe he's a little slow. But in many ways that's not such a bad thing."

The wife had been attentive to the undertones in Paul's voice, the pauses he made, the way he hesitated before certain words, certain names. How much did he know? Did he know anything, in fact? And what the devil *was* there to know? Was it better for the two of them just to continue on their separate but parallel courses, winding up her husband's business, straightening up after him, and avoiding discussion of what Paul had hesitantly referred to as his legacies?

This is my last chance, she thought. If I tell him now that I'm about to go to the office, and tell him why, then he'll come along, he'll want to help me. Then I won't be alone anymore with whatever it is. Then I won't need to make the decisions. I won't even be allowed to make the decisions.

She stood at the telephone, shifting from one foot to the other. She talked a little more, about money, about the funeral allowance, and asked if Paul could help her with that. It was painful for her to go and fetch the price they'd set on her husband's head; but she needed the money.

"Of course, I can help with that *too,*" Paul said meaningfully.

"Yes, well," she said. She'd reached a decision and there was no going back. "I'll just try again to reach Hardenberg. And then we can meet tomorrow or the day after to decide what has to be done."

You just stay out of it, she thought, listening to Paul's reluctant agreement. Just stay out of the little piece of life he and I have left. Maybe someday I'll be sorry, dear old Paul, for shutting you out of this story without even knowing a thing about it myself; but it's the last story he and I will have together. And nobody else is going to horn in on it: no one, not even Gloucester the Shade, or her husband's polite, taciturn assistant, Hardenberg.

Just before hanging up, Paul added, "If you change your mind and decide you do have something to take care of in his apartment or his office before we meet, don't forget that the place is probably being watched. Ciao."

When she finally left her apartment, she paused at the door to give the phone a chance to call her back one last time. But it kept its trap shut, and left her with no more excuses.

Outside, a storm was driving the rain ahead of it, and people were struggling with their umbrellas, which resisted and tried to escape. She saw no faces, only hurrying legs spattered with raindrops up to the calves, which looked as if they were dancing. She was going to her husband's apartment all alone for the first time, and she was afraid, with the kind of fear children feel, fear grounded in ancient superstition. If you cross a graveyard at night, a dead man will nest inside you. If you hit your mother, your hand will grow up out of your grave.

Had he ever hit his mother? She didn't know, but she wouldn't have put it past him. He had liked the barmaid at their neighborhood pub in Mainz; but when the woman got on his nerves, nagging and trying to reform him, he'd suddenly pulled her dyed head down into the sink where she washed the glasses, and held it under water until she almost stopped twitching. He'd laughed in a friendly, good-natured way while he did it, and Mrs. Wiese, the bartender, hadn't held it against him. So would his hand grow up out of his grave? We'll see, his wife thought; he's not even underground yet.

She'd never been afraid of her husband's anger, of his fits of sobbing rage and his lust for destruction, which he always turned against things he loved. Nor had she feared his white-faced silences when he felt he wasn't getting enough attention, or his pointed remarks when someone failed to notice at once how brilliant he was. No, his wife had been afraid only for *him* when he got into a rage, not for other people. Because it was himself whom he injured and tore at with his teeth.

One night, when the two of them were still living together, she'd come home late after a premiere that he'd refused to attend. She found him sitting silent in the living room, clutching a kitchen knife, and hacking up all the pictures he'd painted over the last several years. She'd been so shocked that she forgot caution and grabbed one of the watercolors away from him. Her hand got in the way of his blindly slashing knife. When he saw the blood, he started crying, and then he looked at the heap of bright-colored paper shreds lying beside him, and touched them over and over. He wasn't a man who cried easily.

That evening, she hadn't dared ask him why he'd destroyed

himself like this, through something that he loved: his paintings. She had hugged him and let him bandage her hand. She'd never admitted that she felt it was her fault, and he'd never said he knew any reason for her to feel guilty. But she knew a reason: Sometimes his austerity got to be too much for her, and then she would go and look for plainer companions, easy successes. No love affairs, not yet. Even though she knew that her husband allowed himself every freedom, she couldn't live a life like his. Besides, no one's life could be like his.

She'd never been able to talk to anyone about the double standard she had allowed, and couldn't do so now when he was dead. Other women would have stoned her if they'd known how guilty she felt, because back then women were just beginning the redistribution of guilt, and they would never have put up with a dissident like her. But she knew that there was no such thing as fairness or equality—she'd known it then, and she knew it now, when there was no longer any need for her to make decisions about what was fair: There was only being alone.

In the entrance of the Israeli Bar, just opposite the door of the building where her husband had died, stood the same pale-blond hooker who had watched his body being carted off five days before and had offered her condolences. She waved to the wife. "Don't it give you the creeps?" she called across the narrow street. She was pressed against the bar door, seeking shelter from the wind.

"No," the wife said, lying through her teeth. "It's all over now."

The prostitute crossed the street, clutching a strip of fur tightly around her neck.

"Hey, dumbbell!" she said, and none too quietly. "I don't mean are you scared of the lawyer! He won't do no more harm. But the traffic round here ain't let up for a minute since he died. I've been working somewheres else the past few days; it was getting on my nerves. Don't matter to me, but you look out, hear?" Then she turned and disappeared into the bar.

The wife glanced up and down the street, up and down, trying at the same time to get a look into the second-story windows. Nothing but thick curtains. Where could the watchers be? That guy leaning at an angle against the wind, hurrying into the furniture store on the corner, was too old for the job. But how young did a shadow have to be? Or could it be a woman? A boy? Look at that minibus driving slowly past: You could see peering heads behind the glass. In the past, the wife always used to make fun of people who told tales of being under surveillance. "It's revolutionary's paranoia," she'd said. "You guys think that the more cops you have tailing you, the more important you are. And there's nothing to stop any of you from saying they're listening in on your telephone. After all, nobody can prove you're wrong."

At first she hadn't even believed her husband and Paul the Great when they said they were being followed: not until she listened to the police radio and heard with her own ears the two men's cover names and the report of their position. But now all that had changed. When her husband died, she had inherited the beginnings of stories, and now she had to hunt for endings to them. She was sure that she wasn't the only one who'd find the endings: The state was a storyteller too.

Maybe the spy was the saleslady who was coming out of the furniture store carrying a steel-frame chair, which she placed at the edge of the street for no apparent reason, and then sat down on it, despite the blustery wind and rain. Or could it be the woman's boss who was chasing out after her, shaking the chair, making her get up again? The wife knew him, but maybe that didn't matter. No, they were both making themselves too conspicuous to be spies. Or were they being conspicuous to throw her off?

Spies or no spies, she knew she couldn't put off facing the music. She had to climb the stairs at last, open the door, and see what was what. She'd watched the street theater long enough. Today she had no escorts, at least none that she could see. Upstairs, her husband was waiting to invisibly receive her. He didn't seem thrilled with the idea. "That's just superstition," she said softly, and a little breathlessly, on the staircase. But belief of some kind did insist on creeping into this business time after time—not triumphantly, but with a gentle persistence.

Nothing dies as fast or as disturbingly as an apartment. If someone were to visit this apartment today for the first time, not knowing what had happened here a few days ago, he would have smelled death. Not the man's death; the death of inanimate objects.

It was uncharacteristically bright in his rooms. She and Hilde had raised all the blinds on their first visit, and left them up. The customary darkness had been replaced by a gray glimmer: gray not only because the day was cloudy but because the windows hadn't been cleaned for months. The light lay on the furniture and pictures like a layer of dust.

She went into a genuine panic. Listening to all the noises—there were a hell of a lot of them—she heard none she could recognize. She left all the doors standing open, including the one into the hall, so that she could escape if she wanted—even if she didn't know from what. When you're as frightened as this, you completely forget to be ashamed, she thought. She did a tour of the various rooms. I ought never to allow the place to grow empty and alien, she thought. She would have liked to go on paying the high rent until the end of her days, to hold on to this sepulcher, which would grow dustier and dustier as time went on. Not that she relished the notion of a mausoleum; on the contrary, it disgusted her. But the bookcases and strongboxes, the bed, the record player, the easy chairs and the desks had the weight of ages; you could see their heaviness. Even a week-old newspaper, lying on the floor, looked as it it were glued down.

So preoccupied was she, trying to overcome her fear and paralysis, that she almost lost sight of her real reason for coming to the apartment. She went into the study, riffled through the folders, searched for bar association papers. She found a narrow yellow file filled with poems. The poems were all dated, and had been typed in several colors like advertising mail. She started reading, and forgot that she had intended to look for the missing bag.

The poems were more than two years old. Her husband's literary taste had always been either very conservative or completely far out. She found a poem dated August 26, 1972. When she read the title she started to cry, as if she were hearing a favorite piece of music that he had left her to listen to alone:

Peace and Tranquillity Will Bless Our Old Age

But, comrades, if she whom we waited for won't come,
the maiden who overturns all the world's warped ways,
she whom we pledged our hearts to, the buxom
beauty Revolution, whose bloody, sudden rays
kill pain, like a fairy from an old tale:

So what! We've still got red wine imported from Spain,
cars, TV news, pastries and ale,
books by old liberals that time will not stain
yellow with age, and vacation trips,
old-age insurance, shopping, and songs that burn
with struggle and victory from brave workers' lips,

all those ballads of the old days that never return.
At night we'll get high, and we'll fuck at first light,
and the class struggle will be somebody else's fight.

Underneath the poem her husband had written in longhand: "Recipe for a concrete Utopia: 1. Found a city. 2. Prepare for your first world war."

The wife tried to think back to what had been happening in August two years before, when he had written that poem. What had he been like then, where had she seen him, talked with him? Had she listened to him or not, had she avoided him? She couldn't remember anymore. At this moment at least he was succeeding in making himself heard. She had no trouble hearing his voice: even though it's the voice that you always forget first.

Then the phone rang. She felt as if her husband's voice had suddenly escaped from her head and started coming out of a loudspeaker. It was preposterous for his phone to be ringing! But the phone bill was paid, today was a workday, so why wasn't it ringing a lot oftener? She was stiff with terror. Then gradually her muscles relaxed as the phone went on ringing and ringing. Actually, it's not so bad, she thought. It'll give me a chance to talk to somebody. She answered the phone and identified herself in a tearful voice, giving her full name, first and last. She was going to let everybody know that his name and her name were the same, even if it was a bit late for that now.

"The flowers," said Gloucester's voice on the other end of the line. "They're ready." The wife felt her muscles contract again. Play dead, simply hang up, she thought. There's not a thing they can do about it. After all, he doesn't know if I'm alone. And yet he knows where I am, so where is he? Maybe he could simply sense her location. Or was he standing in a phone booth just a stone's throw away, watching the house?

There's this group and then there's the other group, she thought. I don't know what either one looks like. Maybe they look alike. Both sides must be after the bag, and whatever's inside, they're both up to no good. They're all in such a damned hurry, she thought. I stand here like a female weather vane, pushed in different directions. No, that didn't suit her one little bit.

"Okay, when will you want to deliver them?" she asked Gloucester, thinking how cool and clever she was. This time there was nothing she hadn't "caught" and "checked."

But Gloucester had hung up, very gently, almost inaudibly, and left her high and dry again, with nothing to show for it but a small fit of rage, which felt damned good. But she could tell this rage wouldn't go far. "The class struggle will be somebody else's fight," the last words of the poem had said.

"What a shame," she said. "I haven't the slightest idea how the class struggle is going." She felt that she was useless, but didn't quite understand how and why.

She was hunting for keys. Every apartment holds dozens of keys that no longer lock anything; people never throw out keys. Here there were even more keys than in other places, because her husband had had a mania about security and couldn't resist any new concealment device. All his cabinets and boxes were locked; so were the suitcases under the couches, the pantry doors, the cassettes, and the leather-bound diaries.

The wife was kept busy for more than an hour, fitting keys to locks. After that, everything was wide open and terrifyingly visible. She felt ashamed of her intrusion, even though her search revealed nothing beyond the fact that the momentous bag wasn't there. It wasn't anywhere in the apartment, and in fact her husband would have been a fool if he'd tried to hide it there.

What about the attic? she wondered. Or the cellar? There were still plenty of leftover keys that she hadn't found locks for, and some of them looked like the cellar type.

"We saw each other here last Saturday," came a voice from the hall door, speaking in a broad Hessian accent. "My name's Sattler!"

She recognized the neighbor who had so closely followed her husband's final progress out of his apartment, and who had told everyone how she had heard him scream. It was obvious that she was irresistibly drawn to the mysterious apartment. She was fortyish, wore a kerchief and pale trousers, with a gray sweater stuffed into the waistband.

"I was just cleaning the stairs," she said, "when I seen the door standing open. I was a bit worried, know what I mean? And then I thought how maybe I could help out."

As she spoke, Mrs. Sattler peered past the wife into the corners of the hall, stopped short at the wildly colorful paintings, and then looked away again as if that was just the sort of thing she'd expected to find: that and worse. Her eyes searched for the something worse, but were disappointed.

The wife was glad that she was wearing black. "Pardon me," she said to Mrs. Sattler. "Do you have a cellar here?"

Mrs. Sattler looked pleased as punch; at long last there was something for her to do, something for her to explain. "Of course," she said. "It's a real pigsty. The landlord won't even have it whitewashed. I don't dare go down there myself; I send my husband. Your husband kept files down there. 'Mrs. Sattler,' he says to me many times, he says, 'the rats are getting at them. And that's a violation of the landlord's legal duty, the duty to care for property!' "

The wife couldn't imagine that her husband had talked with Mrs. Sattler many times, but she certainly could see him doing it now and then. Sometimes he simply got a kick out of auditioning his act, no matter who the audience was. A bum or a car mechanic, a tired housewife or a waiter—anyone would do. At other times, he'd suddenly get an urge to insult somebody, no matter who. It looked as if he'd really had a field day with Mrs. Sattler.

"It's tough on you, huh?" Mrs. Sattler said, sounding shy now. "Sometimes it's worse if one of you goes when you ain't been livin' together. Sure, I can see that. He was somethin' special, he was," she added, looking at the wife with pink-tinged eyes. "Don't get me wrong."

"Would you be kind enough to tell me where the cellar entrance is?" the wife asked, not wanting to be outdone by her husband when it came to politeness.

"I'll take you down," said Mrs. Sattler, leaving the stairs to fend for themselves. "I can always clean the stairs later. Your husband didn't pay no mind to them neither, till he got that there Yugoslavian cleaning woman."

The wife had never heard anything about her husband having a Yugoslavian cleaning woman. A cleaning woman, imagine! And we were supposed to be in the middle of the revolution!

"You don't have to come down there with me," the wife said, with growing alarm. "Maybe you could just tell me which of these keys I need." She mustn't let Mrs. Sattler come along on the search, no matter what.

"I have the time," Mrs. Sattler said, warmly and eagerly. "Right now what you're doing is more important. Are you looking for anything special?" And she started down the stairs, holding the dead man's keys. As she sorted through them, she murmured, "It could be this one. Or maybe this one."

My God, she's going to end up as my accomplice, the wife thought in gentle despair. Just a few steps more, and by tomorrow she could land in the papers, getting equal coverage with all the other national devils! Yes, that was another thing to keep in mind as she searched for the bag: the kind and degree of trouble its contents could cause other people.

"Tell me," the wife asked, trying to curb Mrs. Sattler's zeal for action and keep her talking on the landing, a safe distance from the cellar, at least a little while longer. "Did you know my husband's cleaning woman?"

"She's a neat one," Mrs. Sattler replied. "Always kept the stairs real clean. Even cleaned the windows on the staircase. It ain't easy to find anybody who notices dirt there. Only thing is, she ain't easy t'unnerstand! There was times she'd tell you somethin', she'd be real excited, and you couldn't understand a word she said."

So that's it, the wife thought. That's why he hired her, of course; probably he advertised for a woman who couldn't speak German.

"I don't even know her name," Mrs. Sattler complained.

"I suppose she must still have a key," the wife mused.

"Her?" said Mrs. Sattler, and her smooth, kindly face turned malicious under its kerchief. "I wouldn't worry about that if I was you. There's a whole lot of other people who have keys!" She had dropped her dialect now and was speaking proper German, raising a barrier of formality between herself and the wife. "I'm telling you, you'd be surprised."

You'd be surprised too, the wife thought, smiling apologetically at Mrs. Sattler. If only you knew how close you are this very minute to the sensational junk you read about in the tabloids every morning!

How can I get down into the cellar without her coming too? The wife thought as she went on descending the stairs. She stepped very slowly, as if she hoped that in the end, Mrs. Sattler would get bored with the wife's company and remember her housework. But no, Mrs. Sattler was clinging tenaciously to the bundle of keys, and didn't look as if she had a mind to part from these tangible symbols of authority.

The husband had always been an object of curiosity, even as a student—in fact, even before then. His looks weren't the only reason. His mystery mongering was to blame too, the inimitable way he would feed curious people tidbits of information to egg them on. That was how he'd snared everyone, including his wife: a weaver of tales at the disenchanted university—a man of passion who could kindle emotions here, there, and everywhere and fan them to a brief but blazing flame.

Mrs. Sattler refused to leave her side: At last she was going to enter Bluebeard's chamber. Perhaps Mrs. Sattler had often brought the husband pieces of fresh-baked cake, and he'd just barely let her into the entrance hall, polish off the cake in two bites, and hand her back the plate—her best plate—without bothering to wash it.

"It's a beautiful apartment," Mrs. Sattler said as they climbed down the stairs oh so slowly, as if they were carrying a coffin. "I only got to see the front hall. But I know the layout. The Rosenzweigs live right below him, and I been to their place for coffee sometimes, and I go there to water the flowers when they're away."

Again the wife stopped in her tracks, this time firmly. "Would you say this is the right key?" she asked, and took the key ring out of Mrs. Sattler's hands. "If you like, we could have some coffee after I'm through. But now I have to look at some records. Please excuse me, it's confidential. You know, the legal duty to care for property."

She looked into the watchful eyes of Mrs. Sattler and for a moment had the feeling that the woman saw right through her.

"Yes, you've gotta keep a sharp lookout," Mrs. Sattler said, unoffended, but still making no move to head back upstairs. "Hear nothing, see nothing. Say good day and on your way, that's *my* motto. So just you go ahead and ring my bell soon as you're through in the cellar."

She turned to leave, and the wife was just beginning to heave an overloud sigh of relief, when the front door of the building opened. The wife could see a man standing in the hazy light: a lean, elegant figure wearing a raglan-sleeved coat, with a flat case under his arm and holding a rolled-up umbrella. The daylight, pushing its way in from outside, lit up a pale beard and even paler blond hair.

The wife couldn't see his face, but she stiffened as she recognized Gloucester's quiet voice. She stood listening as if walled behind a thick pane of glass. Meanwhile, Mrs. Sattler wasn't budging.

Gloucester greeted the two women and asked if one of them was the widow, or if not, where he could find her. Then he offered the wife his condolences, and said that he'd come about the flower arrangements. "I'll just go on upstairs, then," Mrs. Sattler said, disappointed. "So I s'pose we won't be having coffee today?"

"I don't know yet," the wife croaked, then coughed and repeated it.

A tiny muscle at the left corner of her mouth went independent, started twitching and twitching, and wouldn't stop. People must see when I do that, she thought: as if part of me was trying to grin. She turned toward the cellar door and began to poke around with the keys.

"I hope I didn't come at a bad time? But it's important, because we don't have much time left for the arrangements," said the well-dressed gentleman. The wife still hadn't got a look at his face. He didn't alter his voice or behavior even when Mrs. Sattler had moved out of earshot. He stayed just as quiet and polite and firm. And though she suspected the revolutionary of being quite a bit younger than she was, he made her feel childish and inexperienced.

"I was just about to go down into the cellar," she said like a nitwit, while the little muscle at her mouth went on twitching.

"No good here," Gloucester said, making no effort to respond. "Zoo. Cafeteria at the main entrance. An hour and a half from now."

I wonder if they go somewhere special to learn how to talk like that, she thought. By that time he was long gone, and she was left standing indecisively at the cellar entrance. The little muscle had finally calmed down. Do they have to learn those tones of command? They're like Prussians! But she was determined to show up at the rendezvous anyway. First she intended to search the cellar, successfully, because otherwise she'd feel even more the fool. The bag!

Alone at last. Abandoned by both Mrs. Sattler and Gloucester, she went down for the first time into her husband's cellar. The same things that generate emotion or curiosity in an attic—boxes, picture frames, trunks—look eerie, even nasty, in a cellar. What child is ever afraid in an attic? And what adult is ever completely unafraid in a cellar?

It was hard finding her way around down there among the partitions. But she found the right one at once, because she glimpsed her husband's calling card—his name again!—hanging there white and elegant, completely out of place in the cellar.

"Hey, you," the wife murmured into the dark partition. "Hey, I'm scared."

Starving spiders were hanging in the corners. No doubt her husband had never been down here himself; he must have left that chore to the boy. Her husband had been scared of mice, and of spiders too. It made no sense for her to invoke him down here.

Again she was hunting for the right key. She heard the pealing of a faraway bell, and tried to count so that she wouldn't be too late starting out for the zoo. "Why don't you ever wear a watch?" her husband had said to her, irritated whenever she asked him what time it was. "Because I can get along without one," she'd answered. "But if things go on this way," she whispered to the stale cellar, now that she'd succeeded in opening the catch at last, "I'll have to buy one."

Files. Stacks of them, piled up along a wall. Meyer versus the Federal Republic of Germany. His suitcases. One of them still had the little airline tag on it from his trip to Milan for the trial of the anarchist Valpreda. He had regarded it as a good-luck token and had never removed it. In another corner lay snow tires, for the Mercedes, perhaps, which had been destroyed by an arsonist. The whole red-light district had spent that night staring out the window at the flames. Only he, her husband, had gone on sleeping his imperturbable slumber. He hadn't heard the fire sirens at two in the morning, or the police. Not even his ringing doorbell had managed to wake him. Her mother-in-law used to say tenderly about her son: "You could march a regiment of soldiers over his blankets and he wouldn't wake up."

"Now he wouldn't, for sure," the wife murmured to the cellar, meanwhile pondering whether she ought to clear out these filthy tires, and whether it was remotely possible that the momentous bag was hidden under them. She was positive that she'd find the thing, but when she looked at the few square yards of floor space in the enclosure, she hadn't a clue where to begin.

Everything lay in full view. No bag. But then the weight gave it away. As she started to shift files, she noticed some large, shapeless bundles that seemed to be clamped together. Four or five of them had been artfully distributed under and between smaller file packets. The dust was so thick it made her hands feel numb.

One of the bundles wouldn't budge from the floor. She simply couldn't lift it off the ground. It squatted there with the same weightiness as the objects in his apartment. She was convinced that the leaden core of all this paper must be the bag she was after.

Dead certain as she was that the bag was there, she was just as uncertain what to do with it. For the first time since this whole thing began, she was at a complete loss what direction to go, what role to play. She dawdled over the bale of documents, tugging at one end until she glimpsed something black and shiny hidden deep under the paper. There it was! Her husband had hidden the thing so elaborately that it was as if he'd wanted it to vanish from the world, not just for a short time but for good.

She had to leave for the zoo cafeteria now. The man waiting for her there must be the punctual type, and he'd expect the same from her. Then she realized with relief that she'd have plenty of time on the way to consider what she wanted to do with her find. She would think not about what her husband would have done in her place, but about what she herself felt was right. Carefully she readjusted the pile, blew into the thick dust so that it would settle back over the documents, and secured the lock.

On her way back upstairs, she rang Mrs. Sattler's bell and, apologizing, postponed their kaffeeklatsch. She had to notify the owner of the documents right away that she'd been unable to find them, she said. He would be at a disadvantage in court if she didn't tell him now. No doubt Mrs. Sattler would understand. "Believe me," she prayed inwardly, "please believe me."

"I 'xpect you'll have to come here again, pretty often," Mrs. Sattler said, peering at her with ever-increasing alertness. "I'll be glad to help you out. Though I guess I wouldn't be much help with the kind of stuff you gotta deal with."

Is she threatening me? wondered the wife. "I just have to wash up a little," she said helplessly. "It's so filthy down there."

"Didn't I tell you?" Mrs. Sattler cried triumphantly. Most likely she hadn't credited the wife with the good sense to recognize dirt when she saw it. It created a sisterly bond.

"Don't it bother you, having to use his bathroom?" asked Mrs. Sattler. "It's bound to make you feel bad. If you want, you can wash your hands in my place."

She seemed indeed to possess a kindly intuition; how else could Mrs. Sattler know that the wife positively dreaded her husband's bathroom—his towels, the traces of him on the soap, his hair in his brush, the tiny, tender remains of beard stubble in the washbasin? That was his last beard. Or rather almost the last. Dead men's beards keep on growing. Had they shaved him since he died? She felt like flinging her arms around Mrs. Sattler's neck.

Mrs. Sattler's bathroom, lined with little pink tiles, had just about banished masculinity behind ruffled tissue boxes, chintz bags full of hair curlers, and empty bottles of cologne. A single container of shaving lotion stood shyly in the crowd, and a second toothbrush peeped out of a mug. The wife stayed in the bathroom for a long time, inhaling the fragrance of warm hair and soap, and putting on lots of makeup. She even went so far as to use Mrs. Sattler's mascara.

"She doesn't know it, but that's a declaration of love," the wife informed the mirror, and tried an experimental smile. "And unfortunately I can't tell her." She was really quite finicky. Used handkerchiefs disgusted her, and she would stop eating if anyone took food off her plate. She couldn't drink out of other people's glasses either, and had never used her husband's toothbrush. But now she'd favored Mrs. Sattler's mascara.

She was familiar with this route through the city. But though she'd lived in Frankfurt for years, she hadn't suspected that there were human habitations between the railroad station and downtown, the Zeil and the zoo. People did their shopping there, of course, putting up with the roar of the construction machinery. But what her husband had told her was true: There was more there, much more.

She walked past Ewald's little bar. His dog, Pluto, was sitting imperturbably outside. He recognized and greeted her but kept his cool. Four blacks were sitting on the bench at the streetcar stop, with the rain dripping into their bags of french fries. The storm had let up. Outside the department store on the Zeil, the legless woman had stationed her familiar little cart under a canopy and was laying out an assortment of cigarette boxes and Kleenex packs. Her dog wasn't with her. Maybe he'd died. His muzzle had been gray for a long time. It would be especially hard on her, losing her dog.

"You're missing a lot," she murmured to the nothingness, as if her husband was to blame for not seeing what was happening on the streets anymore. He'd preferred the night scenes, but he would have liked the weather today—the sixth day. He didn't like sun unless he was in the south, where sunshine belonged. "Germany is a gray, rainy country," he said, and saw no point in changing it.

The wife was walking slowly. She had plenty of time before her meeting with Gloucester. She still hadn't decided what to do. "There are two possibilities," she said out loud. In fact, there are four possibilities, she continued silently.

One: I can forget the bag and say I know nothing. Nobody'll go down into the cellar. It will be a long time before I rent his apartment and have to clear all his stuff out. Let it cool off, she mused. Just don't lift a finger. But *they*'d be sure to lift plenty of fingers, and once started, they'd never stop. It was something they hadn't foreseen: that one of their surface contacts would simply die.

Two: I can open the bag and see what's inside. And if I think it would cause trouble, I could get rid of it.

Three: I could decide I don't want anything to do with it. When I get to this damn zoo cafeteria, I could tell him I've found the bag, and it's their worry, not mine. Then they'd take it off my hands and lay their egg someplace else.

Four: I could talk it over with somebody. "Never," she said, and stumbled. "Four is out, once and for all."

It was damned hard to get a good mad on against the system, even if you happened to need it. Or at least it was hard for her. Enjoying life came easy to her, and she resolved so-called conflicts with a mixture of laughter and laziness. She became truly angry only in emergencies, although once she got mad she tended to stay that way for a while. Nazi acquittals were one thing that really sent her up the wall. Or somebody kicking a cat. Or when she thought about what it meant for six people to have to live in two rooms, and what caused it. She got furious when one of her employers said, "Hey, honey, we're just a wee bit late today, aren't we?" Or when she saw pictures of what was happening on the other side of the world. Yes, she thought, that would do it. But it was hard to just turn on the will to fight, analyze, question, despise, simply because you needed it, without actually *feeling* it first.

People were stopping on the street to stare at a thin little man who was slowly stripping his clothes off, piece by piece—dirty jackets, knitted vest, sweater, T-shirt—folding them, and laying them on the damp ground in front of him. Crowds jostled at the entrances of the two department stores just opposite the little man, then everything went quiet. She heard a teenage boy behind her say to his girlfriend: "Wait a minute. I just want to see if he takes off his pants."

She felt ashamed of herself and tried to walk on, but found she was rooted to the spot. The little man, his chest now bare, seated himself on his discarded clothes like a fakir. He gripped the sagging skin of his upper arm between his thumb and index finger and tugged at it so that it stood out in a pale fold, then let go and watched it hold its shape for a moment before it began to subside. She was standing too far away to interpret his look. Was he staring angrily at them, or desperately? She couldn't tell. "Pleasepleaseplease!" he called insistently, his voice growing steadily louder, followed by other words that she couldn't make out, and then again, "Pleasepleaseplease!" He was no longer young and really pitiful, an emaciated little white-skinned body with the rain running off it. Pleasepleaseplease. No one went over to give him anything. His begging drove people away. Though she tried, she couldn't penetrate his wall of entreaty. She continued along her predetermined route.

Once she and her husband had seen a beggar, an angry, surly man, who swore at everyone who put money into his hat. Her husband had walked over and asked him, "How much money would it take for you to stop swearing?"

"You ain't got that much," the beggar had answered. "Even you ain't got that much, mister." Her husband had given him a large bill.

"Are you crazy?" she'd asked, because they were still young then and took their money out of the bank a few marks at a time.

"He's one of the damned of this world," her husband had said. "Did you hear that? We'll never have as much as they need!"

She didn't see Gloucester when she entered the zoo cafeteria, although afterward she noticed that he had been in a position to check her out through the window with its café curtain. There were only a few other customers, mostly elderly women, and a few lonely salesmen eating soft-boiled eggs out of a glass.

It would have been wrong to describe Gloucester as disguised. The Group were always walking around in the enemy's plumage, in gray flannels and pinstripes, all of it just right, from their haircuts down to their socks. If you wear your enemy's clothes maybe you end up becoming a little like him, she thought. She admired Gloucester's junior-executive look. His coat lay neatly folded over a chair beside him. He was struggling to look interested and polite. Poor thing, she thought, and began to feel self-assured.

"So there you are!" she called softly. She was acting a little. A pair of illicit lovers—what else would fit this gray-flanneled young man in the rather seedy zoo cafeteria? Besides, she wasn't afraid anymore.

She waited until Gloucester remembered that people were supposed to stand up when greeting a friend. No one was watching them; they could play out their little scene in peace. The wife embraced him. He wasn't much taller than she was, about five foot ten. She put her arms around him tightly and laid her head on his shoulder. He was so thin! Nothing but suit and bones. They never get around to eating, she thought: probably it isn't approved for an Armed Fighter.

Gloucester held her rigidly, resisting a little as if he were threatened by a needless waste of time. He was trembling very slightly, like a taut wire from which a perching bird has just flown away: a movement not of fear but of alertness.

The wife took his dark-blue coat off the chair to hang it up. She felt something weighing down one side of it. Now more than ever she had the sense of acting in a play. Gloucester took the coat from her and put it on another chair, even closer to him. He was annoyed. Or maybe just under strain.

She had great trouble remembering what was wanted of her and how she was supposed to react. I didn't find anything, she decided, without thinking about why she had made the decision so quickly —or why it had been so hard. Because that dust-covered bag was sitting there in her husband's cellar, and it wouldn't go away all by itself.

"We have to talk about the transfer," Gloucester said quietly. He had accepted the little scene she had set up and was playing along, so he bent toward her tenderly. He's very handsome, she thought suddenly. There was no trace of malice in his thin, downy-bearded face, no trace of lust for power, no hysteria. Only huge resolution, stripped of everything else. He moved his eyelids less often than other people and his eyes were blue like shadows. A pity, thought the wife, not knowing exactly whom she pitied. The embrace had warmed her, the touch of his thin arms. Probably he always had that effect on women. But there was no trace of that in his face either, no coquetry, only a severe persistent self-regulating calm. You couldn't picture him laughing.

"We can't talk about a transfer," said the wife serenely. "I haven't got anything to transfer."

"Are you trying to make trouble?" asked Gloucester, not modifying his voice in the slightest.

She saw that no one was paying any attention to them, as if he had drawn her into his acquired invisibility.

"I have no intention of doing that," she said. "It's absolutely silly for you to think so. But have you stopped to think what I've been going through for almost a week now?"

"The situation isn't exactly simple for us either," Gloucester replied without sympathy.

Her husband had left a gap, an unfulfilled function. For the Group he wasn't a person, not a living, breathing being: He was what they didn't allow themselves to be—a sloppy, pleasure-loving revolutionary, a well-fed freedom fighter who got drunk once in a while; an affectionate, love-addicted world-reformer. The man had removed all their suspicions by dying—but what about her, his wife?

The longer she looked at Gloucester, the messier and lazier she felt. She lacked consistency, discipline, the willingness to make sacrifices. This sense of inadequacy made her grouchy.

"Of course, I'll go on looking," she said. "After all, I have no reason to keep something in the house when I don't even know what it is. Won't you tell me?"

"Believe me," said Gloucester, "the decision isn't up to me. No decision is ever made by one person alone. Each of us knows only his own bit; nothing overlaps. It's for everyone's protection."

"I believe you people don't credit anyone with any political judgment. You think only you know what has to be done. But how can you expect anybody to believe that, when every operation you carry out is to shore up the last one or lay the groundwork for the next? I don't see anything real in that."

I have no right to say that, she thought in horror. It's probably nonsense anyway. If she had her way she would have liked to run an underground camp to reeducate arms runners and police chiefs. And one left-winger would be assigned to each top capitalist, so each would have a left-wing shadow. The shadow would have to know more about the capitalist's life than he did.

The wife would never tell Gloucester such notions, nor would she ever ask him to think along similar lines. The bank robberies? Terrific! But they never led on to the next part of the story, the vital part, where the money gets handed out to the poor. She had always found these fairy tales without an ending very unsatisfying. And yet, she thought, this guy looks capable of handing out the money, and maybe he thinks about it too.

"Gun-toting Leninists," she said softly, and thought about the weight in his coat.

"Beg your pardon?"

"Nothing," she said peevishly. She couldn't get rid of a sense of inferiority, the same she had felt with the people from the patients' collective. They had seen the face of the system unveiled, its twisted grimace; they could hate, could fight without cease, without distraction.

"What if you think something the comrades do is wrong?" she asked. She noticed that she didn't want to leave Gloucester yet, didn't want him to leave her, without her having discovered a tiny crack in his mask. "If some operation seemed wrong to you, what would you do?"

In the same never-altering voice, he said that really wasn't the question now. "Of course I can't say such things don't happen. In an armed struggle contradictions naturally arise. And there are people who decide at some point that they can't do the job anymore. Then they turn back—or they try some other route, even though everyone knows that's impossible. Once you're in it, getting out can only mean a step backward, into the shit."

That's where I am, in the shit, the wife thought, or in what he calls the shit. And he's right. But I enjoy living, shit or no shit.

"I'll contact you again in the next few days," said Gloucester, signaling the waitress with a wave of his chin. "I think it would be a good idea for you to search harder."

Paying the check, he revealed a wad of bills. The wife was startled. Fortunately the waitress was half asleep. Gloucester removed his coat cautiously from the chair. Outside the cafeteria, they separated without saying goodbye and took off in opposite directions.

Day Seven

In the morning, after a sweat-soaked night of confusing dreams, she was grateful for the problem of the bag. The dead always give you a guilty conscience, and not all the bereaved are lucky enough to have a means to make amends. She really had her work cut out for her, she knew: She was about to take an irrevocable step into adulthood. She had to hurry and make a decision.

Of course there was no need to be too hasty; the problem was still sleeping undisturbed in the cellar. Her adversaries didn't know the bag was there. If they had known, they'd have started searching the cellar the day he died, and back then they wouldn't have met with any resistance from her. Instead their curiosity had confined itself to his office files, where they'd sniffed and found nothing; or at least nothing important, because the really important stuff wasn't in the files. In fact, it wasn't in the cellar either. Her husband had left behind nothing but strings, whose other ends were still firmly attached to his own hands. But his hands were no longer moving, so the events he controlled had stopped too. Now she was removing the strings from his hands one by one, rolling them up, putting them away. She had stopped calling on her husband for advice and aid. She had stopped sending whispers in his direction—not because she was discouraged by the silence from the other side, but because she had the feeling that he was silent out of tact, so as not to stop her from testing her own strength.

She had a lot to do that day, so she hurried off on her errand to the bar association, then to mail the death announcements, at last. But the most important chore facing her was to open the bag.

What would she find inside: the props, the concrete paraphernalia of warfare? That idea scared her, because she thought the discovery might make her hate the Group, whereas until now she had respected them, even if confusedly and at a distance.

"That would be a loss," she said—but not to her husband, who was still silent when she was near. She said it to herself: "Somehow I feel that would be a loss."

Everything the Group did when they first began to take action—everything from setting fire to a Frankfurt department store to bank robbery—was ordinary crime. So why had none of the politicians laughed when they heard this guerrilla band, the fighting troop that was the Group, proclaim an armed proletarian struggle? Quite the reverse: It was as if everyone had been waiting for a bit of action at last. As if the emergency staffs and special committees on terrorism had rescued them all from a numbing boredom, the boredom of a country without a war. On TV, you could see the politicians begin to walk differently, with springier steps, with a greater air of importance, ringed about by their growing cordon of security men, who looked like a bunch of cowboys from a Wild West film. It would never have occurred to any of the politicos to state publicly that he wasn't a dangerous man, to point out the absurdity of a guerrilla war in a nice, boring, fully clarified country like this. The urban guerrillas revealed to them that they, the legitimate leaders, were dangerous. And they liked the idea.

The Group, that mysterious body each of whose parts was steadfastly alone, made a deadly serious opponent. Friend and foe alike would have felt it a terrible sacrilege to ask what the Group had ever actually accomplished. The wife knew that her husband had recognized this, some of the time, just as she had. But they had never talked about it, and he was enough of a Robin Hood to get a kick out of fighting invisible enemies in invisible woods. Even so, he took the Group more seriously than his wife did. She'd always felt guilty when she recoiled from the hardness of the Group, their disagreeable way of talking, their indifference to basic comforts. She resembled a cheerful but spineless jellyfish, who'd lack courage even if there were ever a task she needed it for. She was on the side of life, life!

"Not theory, practice!" the members of the patients' collective used to say. "There's too much chatter going on. The answer to the question Is it right to organize the Armed Struggle now?

depends on only one thing: Is it feasible? You can only find out by putting it into practice."

"They still see people they can fight, everywhere they look," her husband had told her. "That's where they and I part company. How can you shoot a corporation? How can you kidnap a cartel? Being an urban guerrilla is all fine and dandy. Of course there are capitalist figureheads! But they're not people, they're character masks. They're manufactured somewhere, in some factory."

"There ought to be a guerrilla band made up of revolutionary barmaids," his wife had said thoughtfully. "They're the only ones the figureheads ever tell anything to. The girls could show them at the bar how terrible they really are and what a mess they're in. That's what I'd call a really neat guerrilla war!"

"You and your freaky notions," her husband had said fondly. "Anarchism, housewife style."

"Barmaid style," his wife corrected him stubbornly. She stayed stuck on the idea for a long time. Whenever she read about faraway countries and outlandish oppressions, she would picture a manager from Klöckner Coal and Steel, or a high-ranking demon from Hoechst Chemicals, pouring out his woes to a gentle revolutionary barmaid, lamenting the emptiness of his life and letting her convince him that he would be happy only when he admitted that he was partly to blame for the defoliated jungle on the other side of the world. Then he would blow up his factory—after carefully evacuating all the humans and animals in the area. But she stopped telling her fantasies to her husband.

Once, he had had the privilege of defending a legal colleague before the federal high court, and she could hardly remember his looking forward to anything as much. Some of his colleagues told her later how he'd shaken up the red-robed judges by demanding to wear the same kind of cap they had on, to show they were all equal. The gentlemen entered into a characteristically earnest discussion of this unreasonable demand, although, regrettably, they turned it down. So he put on a judge's cap anyhow—he had brought one with him! But after this diversion he pleaded his case with gravity and passion, and deeply disquieted the judges by his remark: "because, you see, my client still believes in justice—hard as that is to understand."

His wife had been very proud of him, even though she hadn't understood what it was really all about. She'd been proud, too, of the lawyers' hunger strike outside the federal high court four years before, though she hadn't understood that either. A fine hunger strike it had been! Wearing their beloved robes and looking very pleased with themselves, they'd smiled into the flock of cameras. They had called the federal judges Nazi brownshirt gangsters.

"Isn't that a bit strong?" they were asked immediately after.

"Otherwise nobody would listen," her husband had said. He had hated Nazis, really hated them, quite as much as if he'd ever really got close to one.

Once, in a bar, he'd met Bernwart Vesper, the lover of the Group queen Gudrun Ensslin, and they'd spent a whole evening arguing. Vesper had described his poet father, a Nazi-sympathizer: no one had been bigger or badder than he was, no one more homicidal. There was something like pride in the grief of the poet's son.

Her husband had stayed grumpy and silent. He didn't mention his own father, or his membership in one of the old-style, reactionary student fraternities, or his Catholicism. He could have spared himself all his extravagant detours, if he had only had the good fortune to be born Bernwart's father's son. That was something big, a great affliction! Not silent uneasiness, like what had existed in his own home.

The wife had hardly listened to the two men that evening. She was distressed when she heard, later on, about the suicide of the poet's son. He might have supplied some key. She remembered his pale, thin-skinned face for a long time: a face without color.

Today, the seventh day, the wife caught herself thinking occasionally of something other than her husband. Normally you don't analyze how names and faces crop up in your head and then disappear again. At first she believed that the dead man had taken a fixed and immutable abode in her thoughts, but that wasn't so. He moved around in there, just like living people, now growing clearer and now vanishing.

She had made up her mind to drop in on Max Hardenberg on her way to her husband's office. It meant taking a small detour, but maybe the intern, secretly or openly, could give her some advice. She didn't intend to speak the word "bag." She was quite sure what to do about the bag now. She would decide on her own how to dispose of the contents: she, not Gloucester, whom she no longer feared despite his tense, casually threatening manner.

So why am I going to see the raven man? she thought, and considered phoning Hardenberg before visiting. She hardly knew him; she'd just always enjoyed his weird stories about experiences he'd had, or claimed to have had, with his pet bird. "After all, I want to make up my mind alone."

But she wasn't used to making independent decisions. She and her husband had always discussed and weighed everything together. Sometimes they'd weave whole fabrics of justification in the course of their arguments. "We have to thrash everything out," they'd said. But in reality they had built a mutual support organization, so that they would no longer need to be afraid of failure or messing up. They'd made everything watertight beforehand and carefully spread the risk among as many people as possible, so that they were largely proof against surprises.

Her husband had seemed not to play along with the game, but he had predigested all her decisions for her: "I don't want you working just for the money." Or: "That won't help you politically." Or: "She's a little too much on the Marxist-Leninist line; you shouldn't be seen with her too often."

Back then, everybody used to discuss everything, from abortion to what their landladies were up to. Everything was out in the open, evaluated, made safe. And now? Her husband had left her alone, and his death counted for nothing but a topic for discussion in the bars. And nobody wanted his wife around for that: She'd get in the way of the gossip.

Hardenberg was her last hope. She had also thought of Christoph Koblenz, but he couldn't even stand to see a plant die, so she couldn't expect much help from him.

Every city, even the biggest, has hidden streets that look like the lanes of a village, where everything is done the village way. Hardenberg lived on such a street in the middle of the inner city. His little lane wound crookedly along the rear facades of several department stores, where all day you could hear the shouts of the workmen loading and unloading goods. The tall buildings held off the noise of traffic. A fountain rippled outside a little coffee shop. The day her husband died had been a typical April day, chilly and damp; but it had become warmer each day in the first week of his death. The whistling of thrushes and the splash of leaping water had a gloating note; fragrance wafted from primroses in big pots, drowning out the fainter smell of coffee. As always, the workmen were loading bales and crates onto conveyors, exchanging brief shouts. Today they were bare-armed. She hadn't noticed until now: This year spring seemed like an ambush.

"You see," said the streets and the loaders, the branches and the birds, "it's all over for him. If only he'd paid more attention to us."

The window of Hardenberg's room, on the second floor of a gray building, was standing open, and the wife heard the voice of the raven, which seemed happy about the spring and was scolding the birds outside.

"I have been thinking that you were bound to come," Max Hardenberg said from the door of his small, almost empty apartment. He always spoke quite formally. He wore suits, three-piece suits. At his most daring, he might put on a sleeveless wine-red pullover instead of a vest. He was shorter than the wife, dark and pale. He squinted attentively when he looked at people, and spoke slowly, using lots of subordinate clauses, like a poet. He looked very hard up. The wife saw a couple of chairs, a desk full of newspapers, an open wardrobe.

In the center of the room, magnificent and luxurious, stood a bright-colored tub a little over a yard in diameter and about a foot high, filled with fine sand. Out of it jutted a tree stripped of bark, which took up more space than anything else in the tiny apartment.

"My bird needs space," Hardenberg said apologetically. "Naturally I want to offer it the best possible conditions. I believe that I provide everything conceivable, from a bird's point of view—except freedom. But I think it's a smart bird and doesn't especially miss that. It's more concerned with its well-being."

"Croak!" said the bird, fluttering onto its master's shoulder and rubbing its thick, sharp beak against his ear. It appeared not to like the look of the wife. It turned its black head slowly from side to side, fixing her with the gaze of only one round, shining eye at a time.

"It has certain problems with women," said Hardenberg. "You'll have to forgive it. Because it's really a she and has emotions. Strong emotions! She's disturbed by any kind of intrusion. By the way, she was very fond of your husband. Your husband was brave with her, and she likes that. She did bite him once, but only to test him. She wanted to know if he'd put up with that, whether he'd turn away from her in the end. She checked him out, you see, very carefully."

That word again: "Checked out." It obtruded like a typo in Hardenberg's speech, garish and unsuitable in his gentle stream of words. Apparently he hadn't noticed.

"May I sit down?" she asked. "Or wouldn't the bird like that? What's her name, anyway?"

"Isolde," said Hardenberg. "Actually, I prefer Verdi. But she'll only answer to Isolde. I've tried out a lot of names. Yes, we do need to sit down; it may take us a while."

"I'm sorry, but how old are you?"

"I'm older than your husband—was," Hardenberg said quietly. "I was delayed in my law studies. But I learned a lot from him. It's not so important how old you are. The important thing is not to act like a kid," he added.

She didn't understand, but didn't dare ask what exactly he meant by "acting like a kid." Was he referring to all of them, even the Group? No, on the contrary, the Group's actions were anything but kid stuff. The Group's members were hard and sure of themselves and alone, even if they did sometimes act like characters from the movies.

"I'm interested in only one thing," Max Hardenberg said amiably. "I don't want to be a member of a group, or to talk about or be talked about by others. At my age, one no longer cares about being something special, becoming famous. All I want is the revolution. If necessary I'm willing to spend my whole life in some dark corner. Because the thing is, the revolution is right, even if we don't really like it. It's the only thing that's bigger than life. When you work for the revolution, you never have the feeling that you're wasting your time. And you never ask what you're there for. Of course, I wouldn't mind eating something tasty now and then too, or refuse a bit of affection." He spoke softly and gravely. "That's what other people spend sixty or seventy years pursuing . . . or sometimes only thirty. But all that has something finite about it. The revolution is infinite. And it's a good invention for agnostics. It enables you to get around the longing for God. And then, of course, I do have my bird," he concluded. The bird hopped over and looked at him, twisting and cocking its head affectionately.

She didn't understand exactly what Hardenberg meant. She could only sense that he was far off from the game—and to her it still seemed a game, despite the reality of death and urgent problems. He didn't stand apart from himself looking on; and he wasn't a Robin Hood or a gun-toting Leninist either. Maybe *he* was the real revolutionary! She was proud that she had actually met one after all, outside the books she had read so reluctantly and carelessly. She knew that he wouldn't approve of the business with the bag. So, serious and sure of herself now, she looked for a way to say goodbye.

"You mustn't have any illusions," said the intern. "His work on the Elbestrasse is over. His office died the same moment he did. It died as soon as his blood supply was cut off. That's how things happen with a criminal-law office. There are no successors."

"But what about all his cases?" she asked helplessly. "He'd started so many things. Somebody has to finish them."

"Don't worry, you'll find out which cases you can finish," said the intern. "Of course you will; that's why you're here. But there won't be many, maybe not even the most important ones. All the rest will continue, simply continue. But differently from the way he would have done them. That's normal. Death is something you can't calculate for, in revolutionary work. And yet it's certain to occur. You have to accept it, even if it seems to change the direction of things. Your goal remains the same."

Hardenberg used two fingers to stroke the smooth black feathered armor of the raven, which held very still.

"The best thing would be for you to turn over the political cases to the Kirghiz, or Paul. Then they'd be in good hands. As for the rest, I'd try to get some money if I were you. Or don't you need money? Have you got social security?"

"Imagine," she said wickedly, "a revolutionary asking about social security!"

"But one has to provide security for a wife," Hardenberg said, amazed. "The way you people always confuse revolution with sloppiness! The revolution will take many more generations. But sometimes it takes a leap forward."

"Was he one?" she asked shyly, feeling the absence of her dead husband.

"Was he what?"

"A revolutionary!"

"Oh, no, I don't think so," Hardenberg said good-naturedly. "I don't mean to be presumptuous, but he didn't serve, he didn't serve anyone or anything. He could be dynamite in the right cause. But eternity wouldn't have been his thing, not politically. He didn't need it. He was already Catholic."

"Was he really so very Catholic?" his wife asked suspiciously. "Did he talk to you about it?"

"He talked to me about a lot of things," Hardenberg replied. "I think he talked more to me than to his boyfriends." The intern said the word completely without malice, without a trace of incomprehension or disgust. "He wasn't the least bit afraid of me; after all, I wasn't competing with him. He knew that I was his equal as a lawyer. He thought of me as a welcome addition, and I believe he trusted me too.

"You see," Hardenberg said after a pause, "I want the revolution. So that's why, first, I have to gain a thorough knowledge of everything that's preventing it—including, for example, his Catholicism. There's no point in condemning him, or religions in general. They seem to be essential and helpful to a certain type of person. They have something that the revolution has to have too, in order to succeed. So I have to find out what religion has got. Or what luxury has got, or power, or adultery, or astrology. They've all got something that we have to make part of the revolution. Your husband knew that perfectly well. He had it himself, that . . ."

"Glamour?" the wife asked hopefully. "He really did glow when he got to talking and convinced himself that he was onto something!"

"Yes, maybe," Hardenberg answered hesitantly. He'd stopped scratching the raven Isolde, and the bird was looking angrily at the wife as if it knew she was to blame. "No, actually it wasn't glamour. It was something else. He was—forgive me—so mortal. He was simply very aware of his mortality—and not only of his own, of course. But he knew that we should enjoy it all while we're here, because one day it will be over. He knew that, and so he had his sweets and his leather outfits and his nighttime revels. Actually, he was perfectly right in all that," Hardenberg said eagerly. "And yet it's wrong. I just can't understand it myself, and I don't understand the people who do as he did."

"You don't understand what?" she asked.

"Accepting death," said Hardenberg. "Obviously. I don't want to be pleasure-seeking or powerful—but I don't want to die either. Or rather I don't see why I have to. If you can conquer death and the fear of death, that's how you rid the world of violence, meanness, competitive struggle."

The wife wondered if the lawyer's apprentice might not be a bit cracked. But then she liked a lot of what he said.

"How do you propose to do away with death?" she asked.

"Through the collective," he answered. "Very likely that's what the early Christians had in mind. It's just that it's very hard to put into practice. If other people are as important to you as yourself, then you become less and less afraid of death. That's the point we have to get to. As long as a person feels unique, it's horrible to think of simply ceasing to exist. You must see that."

The wife looked at the bird, which was still gazing at her with a compassionless eye. "He couldn't stand the collective," she said obstinately. "He *was* unique! It *is* unbearable that he simply ceased to exist."

The intern looked troubled, but he was sure of his ground. "That's why I believe the revolution will take hundreds of years yet! Material prosperity for all is only an intermediate stage. The Marxist comrades give it a false importance. Of course everybody has to be able to enjoy everything, to start with. Just so they'll see how unimportant it is. So that they won't be forced into renunciation by poverty. People have to be able to live in the Frankfurter Hof Hotel, long enough so that they can say, of their own free will, 'It isn't important.' "

I think he is indeed a bit cracked, the wife thought.

"I sound a little crazy," the lawyer's apprentice said good-naturedly, "but it only seems that way. I live with the exact same problems as anyone else. I feel unique and can't understand the necessity of my death. But I don't have the normal potential for finding compensations. Literature means nothing to me. I don't eat much and I don't care what kind of a place I live in. My bird will live longer than I will. Ravens live to be very old. Do you understand, it's only bearable if you pass over into the collective!"

She could sense her dead husband nearby, an unruly and incomprehensible entity, like a child complaining in a foreign language. "I have to go," she said to Max Hardenberg, who was scratching his raven.

"I know I haven't been able to help you," said the intern, "but that's not a bad thing. You'll do it yourself."

"I'm sick and tired of that," she said angrily. "Everybody's always saying, 'Oh, she can take it, she'll handle it. A crazy, left-wing husband, with all those boys, and dead to boot—she'll handle it.' But I still don't know what it's really all about. All I know is, I have to straighten out a lot of things I never started."

"We always have to do that," Hardenberg replied without hostility. "We always have to. We never start anything ourselves. Not even our own lives."

A crank with an immortality fixation, the wife thought. A funny sort of Communist he is. So he reads some radical paper every day as a penance. But she didn't want to say goodbye to him and his black bird.

"Where will you work now?" she asked just before leaving.

"I don't know yet. Any change will be hard. But I'll wait and see who'll be his successor—legally, I mean. I could lend somebody a helping hand, winding up his cases."

"Or you could put some sticks in their wheels," she said.

"Yes," Max Hardenberg answered. "That too."

It was now noon of a cheerful spring day, and she knew that she was being watched. She hadn't picked out yet who her shadow was: she was a bit nearsighted. But she was sure that Gloucester and the Group didn't believe her claim that she didn't know where the bag was. During her last conversation with Gloucester, she'd seen how desperately they seemed to need the bag, even though he never showed the urgency but concealed it by a casual, mocking tone. Even now she was free to discover the thing officially. She didn't admit to herself that her resolve to decide about the bag all on her own stemmed from wounded vanity.

They had never considered it necessary to inform the husband and wife about the how and why of things. The fetching and carrying the couple had been asked to do had got on her nerves. All this bustle on the fringe, without ever knowing the results; this feeling of a paper chase that could switch to terror, nobody knew when. The group hadn't been interested in her husband's death either. Their only concern was that leaden bag that now rested, protected, in the cellar as in a pharaoh's tomb.

Before she set out to investigate the contents of the bag, and if necessary got rid of them, she intended to call on the clairvoyant Lisa Engström. She'd started thinking about Lisa Engström right after her husband's death, as if Lisa could hold open for her a door on which the lock was just clicking shut. It was during those first few days, the days of superstition. So far, the only thing that had allowed her to resist her longing for the night world had been the speed with which the day world kept demanding decisions of her.

Lisa Engström was a writer. How old was she, how young? Somewhere in the middle. The wife had visited her on occasion and talked with her about parapsychology and politics. Lisa Engström was a meticulous woman, a meticulous writer, meticulously dressed and made up. The wife didn't phone her. She felt certain Lisa would know she was coming.

It wasn't far from Max Hardenberg's place to Lisa Engström's.

You could walk a distance along a narrow park with sand under your shoes, while the cars zoomed past the avenues of trees. She didn't know exactly what she expected from Lisa. Maybe some orders, short and to the point: "Do this! Do that! Forget this! Remember that!" Lisa Engström hadn't known her husband. She'd have an easy time of it.

Traversing the little park that stretched like a thin green scar through the inner city, she thought: What a strange idea to visit Lisa Engström! Of course, Lisa had called after the news of her husband's death appeared in the paper, and had offered her help in a deep, kindly voice. But everyone does that when somebody dies, and not one wouldn't be dismayed if you acted upon it. Lisa hadn't said a syllable about her special powers when she offered to help. She'd never be guilty of such crudeness. She had the Sight: The wife knew that from their past conversations. Lisa could literally smell illness or indecision, and would relentlessly describe any sort of threat to your well-being. She had shaken her head dubiously at the lawyer's horoscope. But the wife had never told her husband anything about Lisa.

"I'll try one more person, and she's it," the wife said to herself, tearing sprouting beech leaves off the trees as she walked along. "Though heaven knows what I'm looking for. Anyway, what's the point of her having second sight, if she can't figure that out?" She knew—or at least imagined—that somewhere her husband was laughing: The more days she and he spent aboveground together, the more difficult it became to grasp their separation. "Now, now, no need to get yourself excited about my superstitions," she said to no one in particular. "Reason hasn't done me much good so far."

Lisa Engström was not surprised at all when she opened the door and saw who'd come to see her. There Lisa stood in the doorway—how old was she, how young?—impeccable, her delicate skin faintly tinted, her gray-blond hair soft above her long lashes. She's fearless, the wife thought. But the wife was twenty-nine and wasn't too comfortable with such fearlessness. The two women embraced warily.

"I knew you were coming," said Lisa Engström. "But then it wasn't hard to guess. I looked at your star chart once. Good heavens. And it's all strange to you!"

They sat in the dark living room, with a gold picture frame, a bowl, a sherry bottle: sources of light.

"That seems to be everybody's favorite funeral drink," said the wife, referring to the sherry. "It's been dogging my footsteps the last few days!"

"You idiot," said Lisa Engström. "I think you can't afford to be so finicky. You've got too much else to deal with now."

So far she hadn't said anything that anybody else couldn't have known.

"Get rid of it fast," said Lisa Engström, taking out a pocket mirror and drawing back her lips in the way she had, while she wiped off a superfluous smidgen of lipstick. "Get rid of it, I tell you!"

"Get rid of what?" the wife asked, taken aback.

"I don't know," Lisa Engström said matter-of-factly. "But it's something your husband was ignorant of too."

"That includes lots of stuff," the wife answered noncommittally. "You open Pandora's box, and out come all sorts of juicy surprises. . . . You know."

"No," Lisa said. "His love life has nothing to do with you. You're only horning in there because you want to swallow him and make him part of you. The female spider eats the dead male. No, this is something else."

Even now she's come up with nothing beyond what anybody else could have known, the wife thought—anybody who can reason and read a newspaper, that is. Still, she felt chilled in the warmly heated room. The books along the walls made the room even darker. Lisa Engström's own books stood open, with their first pages showing, like little lanterns.

"You're not really in such a bad way," Lisa said sternly. "It's only that everything's a big muddle. I'm afraid that's making you whiny. But you're seeing for yourself that he's still very much present."

"What's the point," said the wife, "when they're cutting him up now? They're cutting up his face!"

"The outer skin," Lisa Engström said impassively. "They're taking a look at the outer skin, as if it meant anything. But it doesn't do any harm. They're not touching anything, really. The outer skin wasn't any more use to him. In Ravensbrück concentration camp I saw people who had nothing left of them but their outer skin, while they were still alive."

The wife didn't feel like talking anymore. She drank sherry and let Lisa tell her about a new parapsychological technique involving cassette tapes. "It gives you genuine taped records!" Lisa said, and her face grew animated.

The darkness and heat of the room had made the wife sleepy, and suddenly she couldn't help thinking about her husband's feet. She could see his feet as clearly as if he were walking up and down in front of her, in this very room. She saw his long toes and his extremely white toenails. A network of pale blue veins ran along the insteps. Her husband had been able to crack his toe knuckles the way other people could crack the joints of their fingers, and he used to like to pick rolled-up socks off the floor with his feet and toss them into his hand before putting them on. His feet, of all things! Now was the perfect time to say to Lisa: "I especially loved his feet. Why are they appearing to me now?" But that wouldn't have been true. Before now, she'd never thought about the shape and colors of his feet, and she wasn't aware of having felt for them any of that special tenderness that lovers, truthfully or not, express for each other's attributes. "Your eyelids drive me wild!" they whisper, or "I'm mad about your hairline!" "Oh, that little spot on your neck!" None of that applied to her. Up to now, she'd been pretty indifferent to her husband's feet. They were an insignificant part of his beauty. But now, in the half-darkened room of the clairvoyant, she was seeing his feet.

"Lisa," she asked, "could it be that the doctors left only his feet intact? Because there's nothing much about them to investigate? I can see his feet so clearly, only his feet. Maybe they've stayed just the way they were, and that's why I'm seeing them."

"You don't understand a thing, poor baby," the beautiful painted lady said to her kindly. "Forget his feet; they don't matter anymore. Probably he's using them to tell you that he's had enough, he's walking away now. After all, he's not at home yet with the language of symbols. Dead people have to learn how things are done over there."

The wife was intimidated by the tone of assurance with which the older woman talked about matters that demanded so much caution. So they have to learn the way things are done. The wife heard the sternness of women doctors in Lisa Engström's voice, and felt the same discomfort she'd felt for all her husband's previous bouts of disorderly conduct.

He'd never behaved properly! He hadn't died a hero's death. His professional conduct had involved too much hoopla and playing around, too much lone-wolfing and vanity. By the early seventies, people were still vain, but they'd also become grumpy. The world had decided not to release its critics from the obligation to be earnest. One's private life wasn't allowed to steal too much of one's valuable time. If you loved somebody, you had to give it revolutionary chic, make it look politically useful. Or at least it had to serve the hygiene that benefited political activity.

But her husband had broken the rules: with his flashy outfits and his theatrical courtroom pleas, his gay bars and the pretty boys for whom he bought far-out clothes, and whom he even let have their say at political discussions.

"You just can't do things right," whispered the wife. "And now you can't even behave properly in the next world!"

Lisa Engström had got up and now returned with a glass of water. She was holding a small yellow-and-black pill. The sight of the pill turned the wife's stomach: It looked like the legless body of a dead bee.

"You're really coming unglued," Lisa said kindly. "Take this; it won't hurt you. These little things help a lot. I'd have been dead long ago without them."

The wife didn't dare refuse. She consumed the dead bee and could feel it crawling around inside her esophagus for a long time afterward. "But I have to keep on my toes," she said, interrupted by hiccups. "There's still so much I have to do."

"Don't drive yourself crazy," said Lisa. "At the moment there's no danger. You have time. But remember, get rid of it!" She said goodbye with a light embrace designed not to smudge her makeup.

"At least that loony told me something concrete. She's the only one who has, even though very likely she hasn't the faintest clue what it's all about."

The sun stood low over the city, and people were in a hurry. The wife tried to pinpoint possible tails, but she saw no one who looked to be from either one side or the other. Probably the two adversaries wouldn't look all that different; neither would be wearing slouch hats and trench coats. Her husband had always been able to recognize a plainclothes cop. After all, it was almost a basic survival skill. A bar where there weren't at least two or three police spies was considered a dead joint. But no one appeared to be taking an interest in her as she made her way toward her husband's office. She felt offended and deserted.

Her route took her past a number of her husband's favorite night spots. Now, in the daytime, the bars looked dismal, and only a few grouchy boys were slinking around. Without thinking about it, she'd traversed several times the square-mile world where her husband had hung out. All his haunts were close together. The courthouse, the bars, the stores, the law office, the cafés, and the streets the demonstrators shoved their way through on Saturdays. Her husband had needed so little room. He'd gone on occasional trips, a shade grudgingly and reluctantly. It's hard to find your place when you're traveling, hard to make it clear to the people you meet who it is that they're dealing with.

About two years before his death, he had traveled to Milan a number of times on business. He was defending a thin, aging male dancer charged with planting a bomb in a Milanese bank.

"They think anarchists can do nothing but blow things up," her husband had said bitterly, "and so they belong in prison whether they actually did the job or not." The trial attracted a lot of attention, and after a long period of detention the anarchist dancer was finally released. To fight for his comrade, the husband had walked onto the plane in a gray flannel suit, with a polished little suitcase in one hand, and his wife had been very proud of him.

She suddenly became aware that she had been slowing down. All the people around her had weird faces that looked as if they had been painted with bright colors. Their heads had gone soft and hazy. She felt alarmed.

"It's that goddamn pill," she said softly, without moving her tongue. "Lisa didn't understand: I've got to keep a clear head. I've got to get rid of that bag and the stuff in it." And yet it was a pleasant feeling, like a down quilt between her and the bullets the day was firing at her.

Where was she going to get hold of some money? She couldn't care less. It would be a snap to carry the bag straight to police headquarters. She was no longer scared of stool pigeons: You could tell them by the color of their heads. The Group? She wasn't even sure they still existed, or whether they ever had. "They're all in jail," she said sadly, as an experiment to see if she could still talk. "Practically all of them are in jail." But Gloucester will come tonight, she thought.

"You have a meeting tonight with the boss," a voice beside her said softly and distinctly. The wife found it hard to concentrate on the young man's identity.

"Eight o'clock in the zoo cafeteria. As usual, if it's no go, make it an hour later, at the second rendezvous. And so on."

"Hold it," said the wife. "I can't."

"It's important," said the young man amiably. She had never seen this one before.

"What's your name?" she asked.

"Carol," said the young man. "I'm Carol."

"Where's Gloucester?"

"He's on the move. The meeting with the top brass is very important. Have you got that?"

"I don't think you people have any notion of the stuff I've got on my hands."

"Not true," said the young man. "We keep up on whatever we need to know. If I were you I'd reexamine my priorities. You coming?"

"At nine," the wife said bravely. "Nine o'clock at the alternate meeting place. Not before. Otherwise, same rules as usual. But I can't stand being followed. Please go in a different direction when you leave. Now." She was amazed by the courage the bee pill had given her.

Carol looked at her dubiously. "You've been popping something," he said. "That won't do any good. It'll wear off. Okay, so nine o'clock."

"He would have liked your looks."

"We already checked that out," said the young man, turning around every few moments. His dark, sleek, slant-cut hair hung over one eye. He wore silver-rimmed glasses. Under his arm he carried a bundle of books held by a leather strap. The collar of his leather jacket was turned up halfway, his jeans were immaculate, his shoes expensive and quiet. She couldn't understand why it wasn't clear to everyone that he was in disguise. Nothing belonged to him, not even his hair. The bundle of books clearly got in his way; anyone could see it didn't come naturally.

"You're not really one of them, are you?" she said.

She felt suddenly miserable, as she thought of everything they had already "checked out"; what sticky threads were being spun out of dark corners, threads she could neither see nor break. Fear. I'm afraid of him, she thought. He wasn't involved because he wanted to accomplish something. He seemed to relish his own sleekness, the bite of fear he could instill. A good-looking gofer, a swank little hired agent.

"The boss lady's in the slammer," she said dully.

"Yeah," Carol said maliciously, "the old one. But not for long maybe. Until she gets out, we've got someone else."

Once the wife had seen the old leader, Ulrike. They already had a warrant out on her, but she didn't in the least resemble the Wanted photos posted at every street corner.

"Really," the wife had said to Ulrike, "now I look more like you than you do."

Ulrike, small and lean, with curly blond hair, glasses, and a gray sweater, had laughed. "Everybody looks more like us than we do. That's part of the whole story."

Years before that, they had seen each other occasionally when they both worked at the radio station. The wife had been very awed by Ulrike. She seemed so incorruptible, so earnest, so full of indignation. The wife's indignation had always been so short-lived. No energy could be derived from it, only a bit of hue and cry. But this woman Ulrike: in her, indignation had turned into something solid and grand, into justice and people fighting for their freedom; even the girls she went to visit in reform school were part of the freedom fight. Her columns of print had been like swords, and she never appeared to wonder if everything was what it seemed.

The man had arranged a rendezvous between the two women years later, without telling his wife whom she was going to meet. She hadn't recognized the inconspicuous, very matter-of-fact person she encountered. The meeting was about an apartment, a reserve headquarters, a place to lie low. The wife hadn't for a moment stopped to ask herself whether she really wanted to help her "big sister." She had felt ashamed because she had failed to come up with helpful suggestions.

That was back in '72. Revolution in the West/ the challenge/ to the bastions of capitalist power/ is the dictate of the hour/ it is critically important/ in the present world situation there is no place and no power/ that is in any position/ to guarantee peaceful development/ and democratic stabilization/ the crisis is coming to a head/ to shut oneself into a parochial shell at this time/ or to postpone the struggle until later/ means being swept away in the maelstrom/ of total destruction.

The wife recalled those manifesto phrases like the lines of a poem. Not long before her husband's death the boss lady had been arrested. Now they had a new one. She looked at the sleek little revolutionary aide and wanted no more to do with the whole thing. She was tired and no longer knew what was right. She thought of the bag that weighed so many tons. And she realized that—as Lisa Engström had already divined with her psychic intuition—she wasn't going to let anyone keep her from carrying out her decision to get rid of it. Not even a woman ringleader, and especially not one she didn't even know.

"I'm going now," Carol said, vanishing instantly into the street teeming with shoppers. The wife felt weak and clung to her handbag with its big bunch of keys. "All that's missing now is the cops; then we could have a real showdown," she whispered. But she didn't look around, she just walked as fast as she could, without any detours, to her husband's dead apartment. She rang Mrs. Sattler's doorbell, and in order to forestall questions, told her that she had to clear out the cellar before she did anything else, because she was obliged by law to send back all their papers to the litigants. "It's going to be murder, hauling all that away," she said.

When Mrs. Sattler offered to help, she turned her down: She was sorry, but it was her duty to maintain client confidentiality. Mrs. Sattler would remember, she'd already told her she could be liable for damages otherwise. Blooming nonsense, every bit of it. But like most people when you feed them pseudo-legal jargon, Mrs. Sattler didn't stop to think twice about it. She simply expressed her sympathy to the wife for having to carry out this mammoth chore all by herself, and wished her luck.

"Heavens, just think of all them complications, when folks go and die that way. A person just don't realize," she said, as dutifully as you could wish. "And so young, who'd ever have expected it? I s'pose his parents don't live here abouts?"

"They're coming to the funeral," said his wife. "They're getting on; it was a great blow."

"Their only kid?" asked Mrs. Sattler. "Oh, my. What's the good of raising 'em?"

The wife was in a pleasant sleepy state. She wouldn't have minded standing on the stairs for hours, trading trite phrases with Mrs. Sattler; the same phrases over and over, soothing as a litany, soothing as a children's song. "He was so young!" "So good-looking!" "No doctor's worth a plug nickel!" and last but by no means least: "Life goes on. You'll meet somebody else, I'm sure you will!"

But the bag was lurking in the cellar, and the wife had to break off this agreeable dialogue.

"Come on up, if you want some coffee or to wash your hands!" Mrs. Sattler called down the deep well after her.

The cellar light was dim. She regretted not being able to lock a door behind her. But she'd hear footsteps long before anyone could see her: Neither group would overcome her defenses. By the time someone could ferret her out in the cellar, the bag would have disappeared again under the bunker of files and documents.

Nothing stirred. There was an occasional rustle that sounded like a mouse. She wouldn't mind a mouse's company; even a rat wouldn't faze her.

She peeled a paper wrapping off the bag. The zipper had what looked like a powerful clasp, a thick flap ending in a pinlock. She'd brought a strong pair of scissors, a knife, even a pliers, but she didn't need any of her tools. The bag was already open; the flap had been smoothly cut, the lock with its tiny keyhole stuck uselessly in its slot.

The sight startled her so that for a minute she couldn't move. The surrounding emptiness was crammed with sound—a radiator, a breeze outside, a distant vacuum cleaner. The silence roared and nothing came to interrupt it.

"It's no use; you mustn't try to figure it out now," she said softly. Her voice sounded to her like a bellow. "Maybe he looked in the bag after all. Or maybe they did it themselves, because one of them mislaid the key." For a moment she thought about a metal box in her apartment where dozens of these tiny keys lay dormant. Everybody had homeless keys. "It's too late now. I'll never know," she said. "That much is clear."

She tried to lift the bag to a different spot but could hardly shift it. It seemed to have become even heavier, as if the contents were multiplying by the minute. She pulled the zipper, which made a violent noise in the stillness of the cellar.

The first thing she saw in the bag was a pile of rough, gray cardboard boxes, the kind you keep screws in. The boxes were very heavy. Underneath were layers of large shallow packets, and bundles of varicolored paper. The bright sheets of paper looked so harmless that she felt relieved. She opened one of the gray cardboard boxes. Bullets.

That much was clear. It could mean only one thing. But the meaning of the papers was harder to unravel. They were large sheets of rag paper, heavy and tear-resistant, in driver's-license gray, auto-license green, and an orange she couldn't decipher. The blank paper represented scores of potential people. It must have been tough to get hold of that paper, the kind they use for official forms, she thought, and slightly regretted that she would have to destroy it. She considered that the time might well come when she herself might make good use of such forms. She felt no regret about destroying the ammunition. She stuck the ammunition boxes into an empty sack to take away with her. Then she repacked the bag, pushed it back under the mountain of files, and left with the sack camouflaged by an armful of papers.

She left the house without reporting back to Mrs. Sattler. Out on the street, she didn't look for possible tails. Her decision was made, and neither group could change it now. At that moment, she wasn't afraid of discovery or punishment, and she'd stopped thinking about the meaning of what she was doing. She meant to destroy the heavy weight in the sack, to get rid of it, just as the fortuneteller had advised her.

"There's nothing else you can do," she said to herself. Painful thoughts of her husband had retreated to the background for the time being. She felt it wasn't dark enough yet for what she had in mind, and although normally she avoided turning up late for any appointment, she thought rather nonchalantly about her meeting with the new boss.

"There's nothing they can do about it if I don't go," she said to Ewald, as she drank a cognac and petted his dog.

"Have you gone off your rocker?" the barkeeper asked. "Or maybe you're busy thinking what to do with all them files?" And as he dried a squeaking glass, twirling a towel inside it, he looked suspiciously at the bundle of papers and the sack, which she'd set down casually on a barstool beside her.

"Come off it," said the wife. "I only mean that nobody can force me to do anything."

"You can't be serious," Ewald replied, while the white dog Pluto stretched his neck under her stroking fingers. "Of course they can force you; anybody can. You're lucky if you even know who it is that's putting the squeeze on you."

What does he know? she thought, and watched it getting darker —and therefore safer—outside. The white dog made her feel guilty. He reminded her of the cats, her husband's legacy.

She'd decided on these absurd heroics with the bag, when the cats were much more important. And yet she relished the fact that she'd now joined the ranks of the dangerous.

"We still haven't figured out what kind of guy your old man really was," said Ewald, continuing his stern scrutiny of the loot, as if he thought it might jump down from the barstool if he took his eyes off it.

"He wasn't one of you," said the wife, feeling dizzy from the cognac as it encountered the drug the fortuneteller had given her.

"That's not the point," said Ewald. "It's just that a lot of people are interested in you two."

"I have to go," she said evasively. She paid and went out into the lit-up street, above which arched a sky turned ruddy brown by the streetlamps. She still didn't bother to look around. Music filtered from the bars, a confused hubbub like the strains from a fairground. The hookers had taken up their posts and greeted her gravely and pleasantly as she passed. She felt the weight of the sack full of ammunition on her arm; but it wasn't far to the river. A child had laughed at her recently when she said that she'd gone swimming in the river not too many years ago. "Hey, you crazy?" the child had said.

Time and again she'd crossed the river with her husband, breathing in the stink it had in summer. "Bridges give you a chance to talk," he would say. "What seems farfetched on one side makes perfect sense by the time you get to the other."

Her husband must often have crossed the bridges at night with his boys in tow, various newly conquered princes, feeling breathless and excited, wondering if they were capable of appreciating him as he did them.

When they turned out to be stupid, he always used to whimper and feel hurt. "You hardly ever get everything at once," he'd tell his wife. If a boy was really good-looking—to him that meant extremely thin, chinless, and dewy-eyed—he would conceal his hurt for a while.

"There's more to him than you think. He just isn't good at expressing himself."

The wife had usually met the boys when the love affair was over, and they treated her with respect. Now not one of them was around, not even the last in the line, the one to whom she'd turned over the cats.

She walked to the middle of her favorite bridge, which was only dimly lit. Here and there a figure leaned on the iron struts, staring into the water. The river lay black and still. She took out the first of the cardboard boxes, opened it, and let its contents slide into the water. The shells fell like a tiny hail of bombs, like a small, gleaming air raid, onto the motionless surface of the water. Taking no notice whether anyone was watching, she removed one box after another from the sack, which got lighter and lighter. Then she threw the empty boxes into a trash basket hanging from the railing. She felt regretful when she'd shot off all her ammunition. After the final shower of silver bomblets, the water lay dark and still again under the bridge.

It was too late for her to meet the substitute boss lady at the first meeting place. Her conscience didn't bother her for having stood up one of *them.* She didn't even think about it as she made her way to the alternative rendezvous. Instead she tried to calculate how many days she'd need to annihilate the mountain of paper in the bag. She regretted having to destroy it, lured irresistibly by thoughts of paper you could make people out of, use to invent names and stories. You stick a picture on top, and there you are.

But she'd made the decision to get rid of the bag. It was her first taste of power, the first time she'd ever had control over a snippet of reality, of reality as *they* had made it. She calculated how long she'd be able to hold on to her husband's apartment and office, because obviously he'd left her no money, and her own income couldn't pay two rents.

"I can manage it for one more month," she said to herself. "Five loads of ID papers and it'll all be gone."

But where to dump the paper? It might not burn, and where can you burn stuff anyway? Throw it in the water—but it won't sink. She pictured treacherous bright-colored sheets of the paper floating slowly along the surface of the black river, like corpses. No way! Bury it? Where? Her garden was the size of a handkerchief, and twenty families could look down into it whenever they had nothing better to do. She might just as well inter it at police headquarters. As she walked through the streets, she realized that a city makes it hard for you to get rid of anything. The earth has sealed itself, the hiding places are exposed, the nooks and crannies leveled flat. Where to put the stuff? She thought of a safe-deposit box. But only recently the police had found real treasure troves, digging into safe-deposit boxes. Trash baskets? They'd find the stuff there: the one group or the other.

Now, there sits a real disposal expert, the wife thought as she entered the appointed pub and caught sight of the waiting boss: I'll bet this is the first time any of *them* has been kept waiting. But unfortunately she's the last person I can ask. The boss sat grave-faced in the only spot in the pub she could have chosen. That was one trick the wife had picked up by now: Stick to where you can keep everything in sight.

She was a bit older than the wife had thought she'd be. Reddish hair hung down smoothly to her shoulders; she wore a gray coat and a light-blue sweater. Like everyone in the Group, she was thin. Her eyes had circles of thin dark skin around them. She looked like a tired secretary. Sitting to her right was a big handbag of soft black leather. The wife knew what was inside.

"So you did come after all," said the boss. In front of her stood a plate with the remains of some fried chicken, and half a glass of beer with traces of grease along the rim.

"Want something to eat?" asked a weary waitress.

"Just a beer," said the wife, who never drank beer. "Apparently you people can't imagine how hard everything's been for me since his death," she said to the unmoved, uninterested face of the boss. "I feel I'm being pressured; I don't think it's fair."

"We have the impression," the boss said very softly, "that you could do more than you are doing. That you've changed toward us. We're also pretty sure you know where the thing we're looking for is stashed. When I say 'we,' that's not strictly accurate. It's *my* opinion, and we've all discussed it. We can't proceed in the usual way; too many of us are into other projects at the moment. So we're depending on you. You always seemed to us more level-headed than your old man, less hyped up, less unpredictable."

The wife looked into the pale face, hating it. This woman had said something against her husband, who was not yet under the ground and who had fought with skeptical good cheer for these people who now dismissed him with a phrase. She tried one last test to see whether they took her seriously, whether they took an interest in her.

"What's in the bag?" she asked.

That was the moment to bring her in on it, explain themselves; to put her in danger. To treat her as a grownup, capable of making decisions.

"Stuff," said the boss without emotion.

"Why do they call you the boss?" the wife asked, filled with hatred. Ulrike would have understood what was the matter. She wouldn't have made the mistake of treating people on the fringe like children. "What are you guys after, anyway? At least, with the ones in jail, I thought I still knew. But what's gone on since? You're going in circles. Nothing's happening."

"You're not informed," said the boss, allowing no trace of feeling to seep into her voice. "I'm not laying claim to any position. Boss is just a name I use, it's not a function. We protect the people on the fringe by not telling them things. If you're feeling mistreated, that's some psychological hang-up of yours. It has nothing to do with us, only with the system."

"What's in the bag?" asked the wife again, hearing the voice of her husband, who no doubt had asked the same.

"Stuff," repeated the pale boss.

"I won't find it," said the wife, furious, and stood up.

"You have a need for authority figures," said the boss softly, putting some money on the table. "Soon maybe you'll get another chance to focus it on someone you think is the real boss."

"Not as soon as all that!"

"Wait and see," said the other, "wait and see."

Day Eight

On the eighth day, the wife began really to think about the past for the first time: not to lament what had been but salvage it. The days right after her husband's death had been spent sorting out problems. She had tried to take her husband's place. Now his place seemed to her a frigid zone, a completely barren spot that she'd never laid eyes on before. Suddenly her bustle of activity dismayed her. Her thoughts of him were getting more and more disagreeable, and for the first time, she started to see the date of the funeral as her salvation. Eating breakfast, she said with her mouth full of porridge, "It's time to quit. The important thing isn't whether some people in jail get freed, or whether some people who are free now end up in jail. The bag isn't the main thing either. It's his World Plan. I mustn't forget. We have to keep that, even though now it'll never be finished."

The World Plan had started out as a game between the two of them, before they were married. Her husband had imagined a place for people to live, and then furnished it. So many people were needed to do the job! The stage was important, and the actors and costumes were important, no less than the intermissions. The World Plan had no prohibitions, nothing was forbidden to anyone. But lots of people didn't fit inside, so he invented a sort of antechamber to the world, a waiting room. The stage lighting used to change as they talked, turning the world now into a hustlers' bar, now into an imaginary courtroom full of wise, bearded judges.

"The judges belong in the waiting room," she'd said. "In our world there aren't any more judges." But he hadn't liked the notion of a world without courts, and wanted to retain them for their entertainment value. In his World Plan, a lot of the old things were retained for their entertainment value.

Most important of all, his world wasn't allowed to serve any purpose. Nothing was permitted that suggested a meaning not inherent in the actors themselves. And that was the crux of the problem, whenever they talked about the World Plan: Once you started "permitting," the prohibitions were never far behind. Then the prohibitions naturally had to be lifted—but not as in the day nurseries and communes, where nothing moved in to replace the compulsory regulations of the past: nothing but boredom, which in turn was dispelled by trivia dressed up to look like something important.

The World Plan provided a rigorous training of the imagination. The wife objected that not everyone wanted imagination. What would you do with happy tax officials, for example, or contented military officers?

"That's easy; all you need is a little Confucious. If every person made one other person happy, everybody in the world would be happy. So the plan can work only if everyone who isn't liberated yet gets an ally who'll work to bring it about."

"Aha!" she'd said. "There's the Catholic thing poking through again. It sounds to me as if you're talking about a guardian angel, someone who'll watch over you from morning till night. So my question is, how do you know if a person is an angel or the one he's guarding? What about you? Do you need a guardian angel, or are you one?"

"What makes you think *I* need one?" her husband had answered, genuinely astonished. "I'm the one who made them up!"

That's one question I don't need to ask him anymore, the wife thought on the morning of the eighth day, while she washed. But no doubt that isn't the answer he had in mind.

She used to be jealous if he played World Plan with anyone else.

They both had figured out quite soon—around 1971—that the Group didn't have any world plan. But they didn't want to admit it to each other. Laziness played a big role in their World Plan, and so did self-indulgence. Power, they presumed, would be ruled out automatically by the fact that it impeded enjoyment—for both its victims and its wielders.

One time, after they were separated, they'd met in a bar: the husband with one of his boys, the wife with another man. That was the accepted way to do things, after all. But she'd cried in the bar toilet, and her husband had started a loud, stupid argument, while his companion smiled proudly and egged him on.

It had happened in a cellar pub where the entire left-wing crowd of Frankfurt used to gather on Saturday evenings—a sad cellar pub with wicked slogans on the walls and rattling music in the background. Everybody went: One had to be seen there. And usually the somber and austere expression that people wore in those years didn't leave their faces even when they were dancing.

Once, that evening, they had danced together. The Stones tape was interrupted by the strains of the "Internationale," and all the dancers froze, their fists raised in the air, like people in a fairy tale. The two of them smiled—they were the only ones in the room who did—because they saw that they still loved each other, or were just beginning to love each other again.

"What's his name anyway?" her husband had asked, smiling sourly and tenderly. "I mean that hulk you turned up with."

"His name is Tony," the wife had replied. "And what's the name of that ugly, skinny street hustler you're dragging around with you? Or don't you even know his name?"

"Eli," said her husband. "No jealousy allowed. He's petite, not skinny. By the way, I didn't know you preferred the wrestler type, but judging by present company, I guess you do."

The four of them hadn't managed to connect. And yet there they all were, bang in the middle of the World Plan. They hadn't even noticed, but among them they had formed one of its cells: Eli, who was studying something or other at the university and was too lazy to pursue women but just lazy enough to admire her husband; Tony, who'd spent ten years in jail for sixty bank robberies and laughed because he'd actually committed two hundred; these two, and the husband and wife.

They'd had the perfect opportunity to make it all come true, she thought while she vacuumed. If only they'd realized it then. Instead they'd turned everything into a tragedy; and tragedies are a dime a dozen. "A pretty absurd tragedy at that," she whispered to the roaring vacuum cleaner, as the cats fled into the corners.

Despite everything, Tony, this same Tony, had probably welcomed her husband to his new abode eight days ago. He was in the right spot: Tony had killed himself that year, 1971, and they'd all been responsible because they'd understood nothing. When Tony died, no one had seen that she was to blame, simply because Tony made such a great victim of the system. But the fact that no one blamed her hadn't consoled her.

"Terrific," her husband had said when she first told him Tony's story, turning the pages of his life one by one. "I don't suppose he's handicapped on top of all the rest? Then he'd be perfect."

"No, he's not," the wife replied, furious. "Nowhere near as handicapped as you!"

At that time, people had an inexhaustible receptivity to suffering. They made no effort to reduce the world's horrors, but collected them as evidence of the rottenness of the system. They wouldn't accept any affliction, any illness, as fate. Everything was the product of a victimizer, a human victimizer. And the victimizers were going to be found out and punished.

That was what gave the Group their romantic aura: They were the first to mete out punishment. They didn't just analyze and assign blame; they struck real blows and—like all the Tamerlanes and Robin Hoods of this world—forced many who didn't deserve it to share in the punishment. A lot of people feared their ruthlessness, though they said nothing. True, they had a vague feeling that no one has a right to fall upon sinners like a thunderclap; but that didn't stop a lot of them from at least aiding and abetting from the sidelines. After all, the avengers might turn out to be right after all, and they might just be cowards—because the system had made them that way.

Often it wasn't easy to straighten out the tangles of guilt that their whole generation seemed to see so clearly. They would lay the blame for a comrade's cancer at a banker's door, link a crippled child with an energy conglomerate, a shattered love affair to a giant insurance company. Dire poverty was somehow tied to the American army, and instead of being distressed by the crimes of prisoners in jail, people grieved for their own lack of guts.

Tony was the perfect incarnation of all the injuries that could be done to a human being, and at the same time, he showed up the real criminals. Her husband had grudgingly admitted this, even though in those days he was the only one around who used to shudder at the way the comrades made suffering into a collector's item.

She had met Tony at a party in '71. She'd arrived late and hadn't noticed that he was the main attraction. The hosts were a married couple, both psychologists, and the guests were their clients. Young actresses wearing baggy trousers sat around on the floor munching cheese canapés, while male sociologists and painters harangued them. The wife, who had come alone, started chatting with her hostess.

"I can understand very well why you two separated," the woman psychologist said. "It's much too humiliating for you to take indefinitely."

The wife had chimed in her agreement. "Tina," she said, "it's so hard because there's no way to compete with them. With other women, maybe—but not with them! You always feel so clumsy. And besides, there are so many of them. They get bored fast, of course. But then ten more pop up before you can turn the next corner."

The wife munched cubes of cheese like the others, and sipped Spanish wine, while Tina replied that she'd had the same experience with very young girls: There'd been a steady stream of them; they seemed to grow like weeds over her husband Philip's path.

It was really a great party, until Tina said, "Have you met Tony yet?"

"Who's Tony?"

He was sitting in a chair in another, smaller room. He sat there very large and massive, like an idol, his big hands lying on his knees, his hair hidden under a Bogart-style hat and his eyes hidden behind round black glasses. His friends and comrades crowded around him, sitting on the floor. Many of them spoke to him without getting a reply. He drank beer out of a bottle, fast but quietly. Every time he ran out, someone fetched him a fresh bottle.

"He just got out of the slammer," Tina said. "He's been inside almost ten years altogether, just imagine."

From the doorway he looked to her like a golem, with his black glasses and his bare feet, his white, naked feet.

That evening he didn't talk to anyone. All around him, women and men talked reverentially of the time he'd done, as if only his image were sitting on the armchair and not the man himself. The wife had been very impressed by this silent man. She was especially taken with his size and weight. Days later, she ran into him again, and only then did she notice that his hair was red, and realize that very likely he stayed silent only because he had trouble talking. It was shortly before Lent, and still cold, but he wore no shoes, not even on the street.

"My shoes are like two little jails," he'd said. He spoke a dialect that the wife had never heard before. It wasn't that his speech was native to a particular geographic region. It was, she realized now, the dialect of an interior region, with which she was unfamiliar. Tony would speak either very loudly or very softly; around the wife, he always spoke very softly so as not to scare her.

Often she felt surprised and embarrassed by his remarks, which were like the things a child or an idiot might say.

"You're like an old, dead castle," Tony said to her once. And: "I always have to hold my hands still because they're much harder than I am."

He'd been one of the youngest of ten brothers and sisters: the biggest, the most conspicuous, the hungriest. His mother had never touched him, as far as he could remember. His father, he said, had been a highly placed member of the SS.

"When the war trials started, you know, my old man hanged himself, the swine. It's 'cause of him that I'm with the left."

The wife never dared to ask him anything. By then, he and she were together every day. They'd bumped into each other accidentally after the party, but neither of them believed it was an accident, and after that they were hardly ever apart. When she was working at the radio station, Tony stood quietly outside the main entrance for hours, until she came out again. She had to do a lot of waiting too, to hear his stories, which took ages to get ready inside him so that he could tell them.

Today, she was sitting in her apartment, seeing the person she'd been in the Tony period three years ago: a vain, anxious-to-be-admired woman with a tame beast on the end of a leash. Probably she was at her most obnoxious during that period. Tony's mute, gigantic love hadn't seemed very threatening at the time. She had visited him in his room in a commune. She'd loaned him a little money. She let the bank robber protect and love her for nights on end. Tony would have killed anyone who hurt her.

The wife was busy getting even with men. She was getting even with her husband, whom she often ran into in the bars with her dogged friend and protector in tow, defiant, embarrassed, and proud. Tony never said a word in her husband's presence. He admired her husband.

"After all, you two were already separated," he'd said once. "I wouldn't have been able to take you away from him."

"There's nothing to take away," she'd answered mechanically, because it was the right thing to say; but actually she still believed in that stuff about being able to take people away. "That doesn't concern anyone but me," she'd added. But it was only words.

Her husband, on the other hand, never missed a chance to make fun of her and her new boyfriend, her only boyfriend.

"I should have known," he'd said once. "That's what you women want. Thick, dumb adoration. Being put on a gooey pedestal. The doggy eyes. All of you want that nasty, petty kind of power!"

"You too!" she had screamed. "You too, for heaven's sake! Exactly the same! Why else do you need all your stray mutts? So they can surround you with wagging tails. The highbrow stuff you cram into them is just a cover-up!"

Her husband had replied calmly to her screaming. "That's something different. They're little pieces of me. They know me a little and I know them perfectly. I don't deceive them. But you, you're deceiving him, your noble savage. The poor swine would die for you. We're not living in the nineteenth century anymore, you silly goose. What you're doing is extremely counterrevolutionary."

"No," she'd answered, though she knew he wasn't off base. "It's revolutionary. What's counterrevolutionary is when you leave me starving at arm's length, when you expect me to be your buddy, your sidekick, useful and impersonal, without any identifying marks. You put all the glamour and the exotic stuff into your nights and your saunas, while you have me run off leaflets and cook soup!"

"Nonsense, it was all nonsense," she murmured three years later, on the eighth day after her husband's death. "Actually, all four of us had a good chance to experiment a bit—Eli, Tony, him, and me. Maybe then all four of us would still be alive, and not just two. Assuming," she said to her cats, "that Eli is still alive."

Back then, they'd been a notorious twosome; and eventually they'd made an even more notorious foursome. But she had felt crowded by the dense presence of the bank robber. He was always near her, barefoot, gigantic, without money, without work.

"There's no point me doin' anything," he said. "Now I'm out of jail, I have to pay reparations for what I stole. Seventy-five thousand bucks, give or take a little."

Tina and Philip were trying to get the damages suspended by the court. "How can you resocialize somebody who has to live with a mountain of debt hanging over him?"

They were told that nothing could be done; after all, he *had* swiped the dough. But they refused to admit that that mattered.

And so Tony was able to survive in their midst, inside the

left-wing network. A job here and a little loan there; he'd always managed to get along somehow. But the wife had found all this objectionable. He was too poor for her. She had always earned her own money; that gives you pride, but it also puts a chip on your shoulder.

He used to sit in the sunshine outside the radio station, and write in his diary while he waited for her. "Once," he told her, "I was told to slaughter a calf. That's the first time I ran away from the boys' home. But before then I tortured cats," he added, while he stroked the wife's gray cat in her little apartment. "You have to forgive me for that," he said to the cat. "I know I'll have to pay for it. But I couldn't do it to the calf. How come?"

She'd said nothing. She noticed—now that they'd been seeing each other more or less daily for about two months—that she was finding his stories harder to take now than in the beginning. Nothing but dread: butchers' tales, stories about the reform school, about prison. Thanks to Tony, she now knew that you can get high on ballpoint-pen refill cartridges dissolved in tea, and that in jail, more or less everybody ends up more or less homosexual.

"But not me!" he'd added. "They was scared of me. They didn't dare try that with me. But I'm tellin' you, it's tough."

"Haven't you ever really tried to hack it on the outside for more than a little while?" she'd asked Tony.

"How? When my mother seen me, even a long ways away, she'd call the cops straight off. I never got no training, no education. Besides, I really used to like doin' bank jobs! It's got pizzazz. You're sharp as a tack while it's goin' down. It just blows your mind. Me, I never could help laughin' while I was doin' it."

"You must be an idiot," she'd said. "They were bound to recognize you; you'd stand out from a hundred other guys. A bank robber is the last thing you should have become."

She'd never stolen anything in her whole life, not even books at the Frankfurt Book Fair—even the professors did that—not even bouillon cubes, or sewing thread: nothing at all. She completely lacked the faculty for rebellion that no doubt is a necessary part of being a successful thief. But she didn't mind when other people had it, like her friend Tony.

"Will you do it again?" she'd asked.

"Never again, not as long as I live!" He'd gone white-faced as he replied. "I'll never go back in stir. The next time, they won't take me alive."

Sometimes they would walk through the city: the giant, and

right beside him the wife, who felt petite next to the bank robber and noted with pride the anxious glances of people who passed them on the street. It was like owning a rare, dangerous animal who obeyed only her, and always looked on her with gentleness. During her first months with Tony, she ran into her husband quite often at first, then less and less, and finally not at all. She didn't phone him either. He's hardly in a position to play Othello if a guy falls in love with me for once, she thought. Him with his thousand boys. But deep down, she knew he was right. She was playing a rotten, shady game.

After two months had gone by, she started to cancel an occasional date with Tony. She'd get angry when he waited for her outside the radio station. She had a lot of work, and in the evenings she frequently had meetings with colleagues. The barefoot bank robber was hard to overlook. Often he embarrassed her, although she was ashamed of herself for feeling like that. On the other hand, they were almost always together at night. But she preferred to go home early in the morning and sleep a bit more alone, between her own smooth sheets. By this time, her husband had his office-apartment.

Once she'd talked to Tina about it. "I've always been afraid something like this would happen," Tina said. "You were bound to fall for somebody really macho. A bank robber. It's understandable, but it's dangerous. You're holding a bomb with a wobbly fuse. Look out for yourself! That guy hasn't the slightest tolerance for frustration. If you dump him, he'll kill somebody—you or himself or both of you."

The wife had felt flattered. "I almost think you're right," she'd replied.

"Stupid as a woman," her husband had said once, in the middle of her Tony period. "You're stupid as a woman. You don't know anything about love. You think it's supposed to excise your brain so you don't need to be afraid. I never thought you were capable of that. You're supposed to be different!"

But she'd been stubborn, and despite her shame, she couldn't part from the robber.

She could always have justified her relationship with Tony on political grounds. He belonged to the left, he'd ventured farther than any of them into the enemy zone, he'd had a proletarian childhood, a career in the boys' homes. She couldn't imagine anybody failing to understand why she was with him, why she looked after him. Because she did help him: got him welfare vouchers, loaned him money, read the job ads with him, even if there was no point.

Only her husband wasn't taken in by her social worker facade. "Nothing but primitive lust," he said. "It seems women want that after all. You call it being left-wing, but you're just looking for the same old primitive stuff. Anybody who's fooled by you is a dope."

"He's gentle," she'd answered her husband angrily. "He loves me. He wouldn't let anything harmful get near me. So what's so bad about that?" *You* never protected me, she thought, but she didn't say so, because she was afraid she'd see amazement in her husband's face.

"Did *you* protect *me?*" the dead man asked her on the eighth day of his death. "When I had asthma attacks, you couldn't stand it. And you didn't protect me from my fear when I couldn't breathe. All you ever thought about was that I was trying to blackmail you with it."

My love certainly didn't go very far, she thought. If there had been enough, it would have stretched to both men, and to Eli too.

The wife was cleaning her floors. People always clean house before a funeral. She was listening over the cleaning noises for the sound of the telephone. Things had reached such a pass that she was scared of the phone, no matter which group was at the other end. She was also scared of green or blue envelopes with windows in them, the kind that contained bills. But she was scared, too, that there wouldn't be any mail and that the telephone would stay mute. She knew that she'd feel better if she could get out and play the widow for a little while.

"There's nothing so awful about craving a little sympathy," she said to the cats. "I've got it coming." She could go to see the friendly, fat porno publisher who'd fed them the hashish, or Paul, or Hardenberg.

Today, for the first time, she thought only briefly, almost arrogantly, of the bag. When it got dark, she'd take another bundle of papers out of the cellar and get rid of it somewhere. She planned to do this every evening, or sometimes even during the day. Pretty soon she'd pack some boxes too, and send them off to phony addresses. Even if they were opened at the post office, the pieces of colored linen paper would look pretty harmless cut up. She marshaled consoling thoughts so that she wouldn't notice how shabby and inadequate she was.

She'd met the bank robber around Mardi Gras in '71. He died in June of that same year, with a bullet in his chest that smashed his spinal column. He lived for ten days, paralyzed from the neck down. He'd had a urine pouch hanging by his bed. Vital and motionless, he'd smiled at his Korean nurses. On June 12, her husband's birthday, Tony the bank robber died of a pulmonary embolism.

She'd withdrawn from him two months earlier. Carefully, because she didn't want to hurt him, she'd let him know that she felt crowded by his omnipresence, by his mute love. Tony hadn't understood. He didn't understand how people could want to be free when they were in love. He wanted to be bound from top to toe, to be hogtied by her; he couldn't imagine anything lovelier. Who could want to be alone? He didn't understand that. He'd been so horribly alone all his life. Now he'd just learned to talk and was writing a diary. He wanted to show her every line that revealed his life. Why else was he bothering with the damned thing? Tony didn't understand her, and she began to go out of her way to avoid him.

She started varying the times at which she left the radio station; she stayed away from the bars they both hung out in. She began calling up her husband more often, and asked hypocritically how Eli was.

"Have you had enough of your orangutan?" her husband had asked her angrily. She thought of the gentle, red-haired apes and decided it wasn't a bad analogy.

"Do you think that now you can go back to business as usual? Is he going to upset your calculations! You're underrating him. You people underrate all your social welfare cases. One of you has got an ex–boys' home inmate on a leash, another a drug addict; it's great for your image. The only thing is, it's so hard to get rid of them. They're always wanting something. I know what I'm talking about. I see them in court every day. You can't give them affection for a month and then decide you're bored."

That Good Friday three years ago, she'd gone dancing in a fringe night spot. She was with a group of several women, they'd been drinking wine, they felt like shaking their bones for a couple of hours. The bar was very crowded. Everybody else had respected the holiday, but not the people here. They were having a wild, loud Good Friday, drowned in smoke and noise. The dance floor smelled of heat. She danced up a storm, checking every now and then to see if anyone she knew had seen her. She shook to Miriam Makeba and the Stones—the same music over and over, its bass notes hitting her in the gut.

It was very late before she saw Tony. He'd been standing in the shadows, half hidden behind a wall, watching her. She'd danced over to him defiantly, provocatively; after all, the orangutan was on a leash.

"Don't look like that," she'd said. "You could scare a person. Is that what you want? Do you want me to be scared?" Each stupid word left a visible mark of pain in his face. He stirred helplessly, as if he were receiving little electric shocks, like an animal in an experiment.

"Come on and dance," she'd said. "Dance with me." He danced very well, lightly and without anxiety.

"All right, if they play something good."

His favorite song came on: "My Sweet Lord."

"You can't dance to that," she'd said.

"Can't you? Come on, let's try."

The night was one long begging session, nothing but begging. It made the wife angry. Actually, she'd have preferred it if her husband had turned up there at the bar. Now, on the eighth day of his death, she knew that he, too, had often begged her wordlessly, mute as the red-haired robber. She stood on the dance floor, with Tony's big hands on her shoulders.

"You mustn't cling to me so," she cried above the music. "I can't stand you acting as if I'm the only thing in the world that you've ever lost."

"But I've *found* you," Tony answered. "That's the thing—I've found you."

Back then, on Good Friday of '71, almost nobody was in jail, almost everybody was alive.

That night, a big crowd ended up going on to Tony's place, where beer and a record player awaited them. Monkeyhead was there too, the great revolutionary, and Eli, but without her husband.

"I won't go to that stinking hole," her husband had said.

Eli laughed. "He'll go to another hole. After all, it's Good Friday."

The wife had talked with Eli, and with the others too. She knew everybody, everybody knew her. The music took the effort out of it. She didn't want beer. Tony mutely brought her a cup of wine. She thanked him and paid him no more attention. He sat on the floor in the shadows, watching them all. She put her arm around Monkeyhead and laughed at him. Monkeyhead was the greatest revolutionary of them all. Always at the very crest of any building occupied by demonstrators, crowing like a rooster. Or taking some French philosopher out for a drive. No, that wasn't then, but it was soon after.

Monkeyhead had a boundless admiration for her husband, his lawyer.

"It's crazy," he told her reproachfully that Good Friday. "You can't compare the two of them, your old man and Tony. I don't understand you."

"Oh, what do you know about it?" she'd answered. "For you, every word he says is gospel. You look at him as if you were reading a prayerbook. You don't know how remote he can be. Tony loves me, you can see that. He's just crowding me now, that's all."

Monkeyhead was silent.

"You could do a lot with him politically," he said after a while. "He's gotten the message. He won't let the pigs take him in again. But you and your old man don't need to resort to jails and boys' homes and shantytowns all of a sudden. That's not how you two got into the movement. So what do you want with Tony? Do you really think he's more romantic? And for that you're giving your old man the brush-off?"

"After all, he gave me the brush-off," she replied, offended, "with his little sewer rats. There's one sitting right over there; do you see him? They're sitting around everywhere you go, and you can't get rid of them."

"Oh, so that's it?" Monkeyhead turned to look at her. "But that's not true; that never mattered to him. All he did with the boys was take some of the load off you, the chore of admiring him, fussing over him. He needs to be admired and fussed over, but he didn't want to stick you with that burden. You ought to have been grateful to him. With me, the women always had to do everything, and that's why they always ran out on me sooner or later. But your old man had things so well organized that you didn't have to have anything to do with the mucky part. You ought to be grateful."

Eli had been listening to them and laughed. Tony stared at the chatting group from his corner. He couldn't have seen anything but the moving mouths, heard anything but the Stones, and sometimes Ennio Morricone. He had jailed himself in his corner.

Eventually, the wife noticed that her hair was damp and messy. She felt queasy and got up. A mattress was lying unused in the next room. Its usual female occupant had gone on a trip. The wife found a comb and a mirror. Monkeyhead had got up and left the room with her, and they'd said goodbye in the corridor. "It's two A.M.," he remarked, "and I've got to go away tomorrow." There were still four or five guys sitting in the living room; the door stood half open. She closed the door of the unoccupied room so that she could comb her hair in peace.

When Tony opened the door she let out a scream. She'd seen in the mirror the way he closed the door behind him. She saw that he was crying. She screamed again. She kept screaming the name of a boy who, she knew, was still in the adjoining room. She could tell that she was really in for it. The noble savage had broken loose.

She didn't try to talk to him. Such creatures can't talk, she thought—insofar as she thought anything. You have to run away from such creatures.

She was still screaming the boy's name when Tony put his hands around her throat and threw her onto the mattress. Suddenly she heard a clapping noise behind the door, which was repeated several times at irregular intervals. Digging her thumbs under Tony's palms in an effort to let some air into her lungs, she couldn't figure out what the noise was. It sounded as if the wind were playing around with a loose shutter. Then she understood: It was the sound of the front door opening and shutting.

The others hadn't heard her screams. Or rather they'd chosen not to answer them. They were leaving one after another. Not all at once. Five times she heard the apartment door close behind a potential rescuer.

For the first time in her life, she felt what it means to give up hope. The clapping sound had made her go still for a few seconds, still and meek. Just let him do it, she thought as she struggled for air; I did enough to him. All she could hear was the sobbing of the bank robber, who'd begun to pound, slap, and shake her.

She'd stopped screaming now. There was nobody to hear her. She could feel that her face was covered with a thick coat of slime made up of mucus and tears, and maybe blood from her nose. Tony kept repeating little phrases that she didn't understand, in a voice as if he were talking to a child.

She came alive again; her arms shoved, her legs kicked, her knees sought and found a mark on the other body. But he felt nothing. She was developing powers she'd never used before, because before she could really give up, she needed to be able to draw another breath, to inhale. Until she could breathe, she wouldn't give up.

She didn't notice when the door opened, and it was a while before she heard someone say, "What's going on here? Isn't Lisa home?"

A moment before, she'd felt as if something inside her were breaking, splitting in two. Now she wanted to kill the bank robber. Eventually she would. She'd stopped thinking that she was going to die tonight, on this stranger's mattress, under the hands of this howling man. She didn't realize that someone had come into the room until she felt the strength ebbing from Tony's hands.

"Are you people crazy?" said the boy who had come in and was gazing calmly at the wife's unrecognizable face.

She couldn't get up. At first she didn't even try to talk. Her handbag was still dangling over her shoulder. She crept very rapidly past the strange boy to the living room door, clung to it while she pulled herself to her feet, and headed out of the apartment. She moved faster and faster. First the hall, then the door. She scrambled down the stairs, holding on to the railing with both hands. All she wanted was to get to the street, only the street. Outside, everyone would be her friend.

The air was cold. She had the feeling that the slime on her face was freezing into a mask that would stop her breathing again. All she could think about was water, as much water as possible, the Main, the Rhine, the sea. She saw a brightly lit phone booth on the corner but didn't dare go inside. In her bag she found tissues and a flask of eau de cologne. The marvelous all-purpose handbag of the middle-class woman! She washed the mask off her face. It was like washing with fire. She cried because it burned so.

The farther away she got from the murderer's apartment, the more frightened she became. She summoned up enough courage to enter the next phone booth she came to, because everything was quiet and she had a clear view of the whole street.

She phoned her husband, who had been living in his office for several weeks. Describing her location, she asked him to come and get her.

"But don't say anything when you see me," she begged him. "I don't know where to go. I need to talk to you."

She felt ashamed about that. After all, she had been free, and everybody says freedom hurts. But surely not as much as this!

He had come very quickly, wide awake and very alert in his old pale-blue car. Like a swan, it floated along the street all alone, right up to the phone booth where she was standing. He started crying when he saw her. There's another one, she thought. One of them does a job on me and bawls, and the other one sees the results and bawls too.

He'd taken her home. No, they'd gone home together, to *their* apartment, the way they'd done a thousand times before. They'd wheezed up the five flights of stairs together; she had to stop over and over to blow clots of blood out of her nose so she could breathe. Her neat little apartment welcomed her. The light was burning in the living room, a vase of narcissus stood on the table. The bed was smooth, the dishes were washed, the cats sleeping.

"Go ahead and wash up," her husband had said. "But take a deep breath before you look at yourself in the mirror. I'll make you some tea. I'll stay here, kiddo. This just won't work."

She detected a tiny trace of satisfaction in his words. He'd never made tea before. She went into the bathroom and looked at herself for a long time while she splashed handfuls of cold water over her face, one after another. Her hair, looking exactly as usual, shone above a blue face that couldn't smile, eyes that couldn't see straight. Her nose had stopped bleeding and swelled up.

Was it my fault? she thought. Nobody can be wrong enough that someone is allowed to do this to them. "I'll make sure he goes back to jail where he belongs," she said to her ghastly mirror image. "And the other five too." But her rage wasn't authentic.

Her husband really did bring her tea. It was three in the morning. They sat side by side on the bed where they had slept together for years. She told him what had happened with Tony and the other five guys. He listened in silence.

"Monkeyhead was there too?" he asked. "No," she answered. "He left earlier." Her husband looked into her face thoughtfully and politely, like a lawyer, then went to the telephone in the next room. She couldn't hear what he was saying. Her shoulder hurt, and her face was swelling up more and more, turning into a solid, unfamiliar mass.

"I called Monkeyhead," her husband said, returning to the bed. "He's already on his way."

"On his way?" she asked. "On his way where?"

"To the other five guys," he said. "He'll take care of them."

"So you're back to getting people taken care of," she said sadly, the corners of her mouth smarting.

"Haven't you gotten the point yet?" he asked angrily. "Even now? Have you still got bank-robber fever? Are you still pining for some avenger of the disinherited to come along? Well, that's not me!" he said. "That's not what I want to be. You ought to have had enough of your Stone Age slumming by now! Monkeyhead knows the right answer. I know it too, but I don't want to be the one to supply it. You think a guy is being untrue to his principles unless he's behind bars. Things are easy for Monkeyhead. A gun, a couple of catchy slogans, a couple of easily worked-up pals, and someone to give the orders now and then, and off he marches to war, a loyal vassal just like that whole lot thirty years ago. I don't trust virtues like his! I don't know what a different type of society would be like—anyway, it wouldn't look the way you do at the moment. Unbridled passions make me nervous. Antiauthoritarian children make me nervous. And yet I always wanted to be just like them."

"You *are* like them," the wife said wearily.

She was more tired that night than she'd ever been before or would be again. Even now, three years later, after everyone else involved was dead or had disappeared into jail, or to nowhere at all, she still thought that she'd let slip a great opportunity that night. She and her husband could have got back together again, maybe on a saner footing than ever before, with their World Plan intact despite all the Elis, despite her own Stone Age cravings. They hadn't sat side by side and talked like that for ages. He had stroked her disfigured face. But even that rubbed her the wrong way, and she had accused him of being indifferent to how she looked because he didn't find women attractive anyway. A woman could sit there beaten black-and-blue, and it wouldn't faze him.

"You've turned into a real dope, on top of everything else," he said worriedly. "What did I ever see in you?"

"A sort of instant woman," she said, crying. "A soluble powder made up of mothers and women psychologists and pillows and record players. And so smart," she yelled, "so intelligent, isn't she? Everybody admires the kid because she can give such witty answers—for a woman. And she belongs to you and you alone. And then she gets involved with a bank robber and gets beaten up. And so they lived happily ever after!"

"There, there, there," he said, comforting her. "Come on, it's late. We both have to get some sleep. Tomorrow I'll take you for some X-rays. Maybe we should go away together for a couple of days."

She opened up the bed and hid there behind her husband's back.

That night, the night of Good Friday before Holy Saturday, everything was just as it should have been again. Little images of

Italian piazzas and small, bright-colored boats ran through her head. Maybe we could go away for a couple of days, he'd said. That's what she was thinking as she fell asleep on the night before Holy Saturday 1971. Three years ago that was. The plan had run into a dead end.

Her husband was kind to her, even made her coffee and forbade her to get out of bed. The first call of the morning came from Monkeyhead, who was phoning his boss to report the results of his mission. He hadn't gotten his hands on one of the five yet, he said; the guy hadn't come home last night. And with her husband's permission, he hadn't touched one of the others, Balthasar. The guy was only half a man, with a whistling lung. His big trap deceived you. That guy wasn't long for this world. He wouldn't touch such a sad case.

"Fine," her husband repeated every so often. "Yes, fine. And that guy? And him?" Then he listened again, for a long time, like a police detective or a fed. "Yes," he said then. "Okay, call me again."

"You heard all that?" he said to her, as she lay in bed trying to get the hot coffee inside her through her swollen, burning mouth. "He got three of them. I expect they look just the way you do right now. He didn't touch Balthasar, and one guy's still missing."

The wife clung to her cup, saying nothing. That was the name that she'd screamed over and over the night before: Balthasar. She knew he was a boozer and maybe a drug addict, skinny and cough-racked, toothless and gloomy. But she'd called out to him because he was the only one there who could have talked to Tony. He was smart, and smart was more important than strong. But he'd chosen not to deploy his weapon. He was the one who should have been beaten, he was the one who deserved to be hurt—he, not the others. The others had simply been blind and stupid.

But she said nothing. She sucked at her coffee and let her husband go on playing general. Their crowd was already buzzing with the news, as she could tell from the countless phone calls.

"I know which guy he couldn't find," she said spitefully, a while later. "Your Eli. He was there too. But I suppose that's not one of the qualities you think he needs."

"I know he was there," her husband said quietly. "He was with me when you phoned. No, that's not one of the qualities he needs."

"I don't ever want to see you again!" she screamed. "Leave me alone from now on. I don't ever want to see you again."

After he left, she stayed in bed, didn't answer the phone, didn't respond to the ringing doorbell. That first day, she wanted to die, to get revenge on them all. On the second day, her face began to discolor. But the swelling was going down and little by little she started to look more like herself. She ate nothing but packaged soup; she had nothing else in the house. It was the Easter holidays and the bells never stopped ringing. On the third day, the telephone rang only at rare intervals. The cats' litter box was starting to stink and she was scared that people were forgetting her.

She put on some clothes and went down the five flights to the garbage can. In her mailbox she found five letters from Tony. She opened one, started to read, got the drift, and sealed it up again. She didn't even open the others, just readdressed them to Tony.

The Tuesday after Easter, she took her first shower and carefully made herself up. Her eyes stood out bright and large from her swollen face. She wore one of her favorite outfits. But the man she wanted to be beautiful for wasn't going to see her. He hadn't come back. Maybe he'd phoned, but that didn't satisfy her. He ought to have come back and taken her out of her prison of shame and rage. He ought to have nursed her back to health: his wounded wife.

She'd cleaned the apartment and given the cats fresh food. She put on dark glasses so that people wouldn't see the bruises, the yellow shadows underneath her makeup.

The phone rang just as she was about to leave. It was the boy from Tony's commune, the one who'd rescued her. His voice sounded sleepy and indifferent. "Tony's in the hospital. He took a pill overdose." He had Tony's address if she wanted to visit him.

"What are you people thinking of?" she shrieked. "What kind of crazy ideas have you got in your heads? Do you think I'm supposed to feel sorry for him? He's the poor criminal and I'm just the shitty victim?"

"Yeah," the boy said, "sure, sure. He's in critical condition. We just wanted you to know is all. It's your business if you go or not. He asks for you a lot."

She hung up on him, went into town, sat for a long time in a street café, eating ice cream—one dish, then two—and then bought an expensive dress. A man started to strike up a conversation, but after looking attentively and kindly at her face, he let it go.

She'd walked into another world, and that sunny afternoon she intended to stay there: among the cafés and boutiques and people wearing suits, riding in Mercedes cars, going to parties. No more courtroom trials. No more heroes and no more fighting. What was there to fight for? The sun was shining. The Armed Struggle, the Victory of the Proletariat, and the Urban Guerrilla Mandate looked pretty unappealing at that moment.

But she knew the feeling wouldn't last, it would dissolve like ice. Her husband wasn't there, her husband, the only one she could have talked to about it, the only one: the one she didn't want to see again, because his boyfriend hadn't helped her, and because he approved of his friend's not wanting to get involved.

In the days that followed, she kept sending back Tony's letters. She went to work. The marks on her face were fading. She sometimes ran into her husband in the bars. They greeted each other coolly.

"Oh, kiddo," he said once, "you just won't learn. This isn't a drama we're playing, it's reality."

Sometimes she would read with pride his articles in the *New Law Weekly.* Usually she spent the evenings sitting alone in her tidied apartment, listening to music until it made her cry. There was no more love—not Tony's confused, disorderly love, not her husband's intelligent love. Love was like a switched-off light back in the spring of 1971.

On the evening of June 2, Tony's friends called her up again. They screamed into the telephone that he'd shot himself. Come right away, he's shot himself.

She ran out of the house still wearing her pink caftan, into the darkness of a beautiful warm night. People out walking slowed their steps when they saw her. She found a taxi in a hurry, then lost one of her sandals as she got out of the cab opposite Tony's house. An ambulance stood waiting at the entrance, its blue light flashing. She stopped short in the middle of the road. A passerby followed her and brought her her sandal. The people from the house stood around the ambulance, looking cold.

The medics carried Tony down the stairs. He was buckled onto a stretcher. His hair and beard glowed redder than usual against his white face. His eyes were open but he didn't seem to recognize anyone. You could hear his moans a long way off. She wanted to go to him, to ride with him to the hospital. Instead she stood stock-still, a ridiculous figure in a pink nightgowny thing in the middle of a main street, still clutching one of her sandals. The medics pushed Tony into the ambulance the way you shove things into an oven. Then she let out a scream.

Now, three years later, she no longer remembered what she had screamed.

Back then, she thought, as she waited longingly for sunset of the eighth day so that she could return to the contents of the bag, back then I hadn't made much progress yet. She remembered that she called her husband. And he came, slightly scornful but genuinely shocked. The game had a flaw now: the gunshot was real.

They couldn't learn anything at the hospital.

"We're still operating," the doctors said at four o'clock the next morning.

This time her husband was very sober and quiet in the night-shrouded hospital—not at all the way he'd been after the little girl Pia had her accident.

"I bring people bad luck," the wife had said after a while.

"I bet you'd just love that! For heaven's sake, don't start going neomystical on me. A robber captain is bad enough."

"And then he goes and shoots himself to boot!"

"It *is* pretty bad taste," her husband had answered in a good-natured voice, as if he'd really changed from her husband into her attorney.

She'd have preferred him to bellow or to take a swipe at her, or heap her with reproaches for cruel behavior. Instead her husband was stifling her with reason, and stealing the last shreds of glamour she could glean from this ghastly business.

"You'd never put up with that from *me,*" she said to him, as if he read her mind. He understood what she meant, and asked no questions.

Eventually they drove home together—together again: Tony had brought them together—and this time they were more careful. "Come along to my place," her husband had said. "It may be better there. You won't have any memories."

"How funny that is," she'd complained. "*Your* office, *your* apartment—and you say I don't have any memories there."

"Not again!" he had said, leading her out of the white, still hospital. "Not again."

"Is Eli staying at your place today too?" she'd asked.

"Aw, kiddo," he replied after a long pause. "What Eli? You may still find a pair of his pants somewhere, or a hashish pipe, or a Frantz Fanon paperback on revolution. But of course you won't find him."

Just as on the night when Tony had tried to kill her—her, not himself, that time—she was so tired that she wanted nothing but to lie down behind her husband's back and sleep where nobody in the world could find her.

"Let's go to your place," she'd said gratefully.

That was the next-to-last night she and her husband had spent together. She didn't know what he was feeling. She didn't like how she looked, her breasts embarrassed her, got in the way. The next-to-last night, her husband had concentrated on himself, luxuriously and joyfully, as if his wife appealed to him, as if the dying man in the university hospital didn't exist. Until it got light, the wife tried to be very close to her husband, to give him pleasure so that she would feel less alone.

I love him, she thought. Everything's okay. Tony will get well and leave town, and I'll go back and live with my husband again. Everything's okay.

Her husband's bed was unfamiliar; she couldn't find the right spot in it. The sun was blazing. Her husband slept on, without moving, in his royal attitude, with his arms crossed over his chest and his feet curving down, like a dead man. The wife showered and went to the hospital.

"You can't see him," they told her. An exhausted doctor held her back. "Tell your friend that if he shoots himself again, he should use a steel bullet. That lead-cased bullet exploded inside his body."

"What does that mean?" she asked.

"He's paralyzed from the neck down. It doesn't look good. We operated on him all night. One lung is destroyed. As for the damage to the spinal cord—well, maybe miracles do happen, even for a guy like him."

She halted in the white corridor and thought nothing, felt nothing, understood nothing. "Now I'll have to marry him," she whispered to herself, "now I'll have to marry him."

She'd taken on a film-editing assignment for the week after Easter '71. It was a movie based on a best-seller: *Love Story.* Now, three years and a death later, she couldn't help weeping when she thought of the film's aching title music. Back in '71, she'd sat crying beside the film-editing table. Tony was lying paralyzed outside the city, and here she was turning love into celluloid.

She hadn't dared to visit Tony. Her husband had withdrawn from her after their night together, as if he expected her to make a decision; but she didn't know what. Love Story. For days she lived behind a big pair of dark glasses. In the end she went to the hospital after all, carrying strawberries.

The bank robber lay in bed, looking the same as always. His speech was labored because of his shot-up lung. He got embarrassed when she burst into tears.

"It's not your fault," he'd said, a priest munificently granting absolution from his bed. "When it's all over I can retrain. Become a telephone operator or something. Everything'll be all right."

It was the first time that he'd talked confidently and cheerfully about work. She popped a strawberry into his mouth every now and then. She hadn't dared ask if he couldn't move at all, and he didn't say anything about it either. He ignored her inadvertent glances at the urine pouch next to his bed. The little Korean nurses busied themselves in his room and gaped at him in wonder. The wife left after an hour. The guilt hadn't been taken from her; no one could take it from her, not even he.

She'd called up her husband and told him about it.

"There's no reason for you to be concerned with him now any more than before," he'd replied coolly. "You've got to get that through your head. Don't tell me you've found yet another role to play—especially one for which you're so unsuited."

The morning after her visit, she got a phone call from the head nurse. Tony had died quietly of a pulmonary embolism during the night. "We're taking care of everything," the nurse said.

Three years later, the wife walked through the twilit city to her husband's apartment. She was calm now, wrapped up in her stories as if they could shield her from the present. She'd been punished for the only time she'd cheated on her husband—cheated honestly, indeed.

Today, the eighth day after her husband's death, the city had turned warmer: a false springtime. Her black clothing attracted heat and glances. But no one saw her go into her husband's building, no one observed the skill with which she picked the cellar key out of the jumble of other keys. Once again she stowed a bundle of ID paper inside a plastic bag. She would look for a propitious trash container. She was looking forward to her evening stroll through the city after her day of paralysis at home.

The Israeli Bar was already open. The girls were standing alert and restless at their posts, and greeted her amiably. Two corners farther on, the transvestites had finished their painstaking makeup jobs and were slipping with a sigh into their big high-heeled shoes. The Lamborghinis and Lancias were lining up slowly along the edge of the street, uttering threatening howls in first gear. The first pimps, dressed in fresh linen suits, gazed up into the evening sky.

The corner brothel, with its red-neon-bordered windows, looked like a fairy-tale castle. The white dog Pluto, sitting outside Ewald's bar, sniffed cordially at her shoes, picking up news of the cats. Turkish sweets shining with color and grease gleamed in a shopwindow. Skewered meat emitted its fragrance.

"It's beautiful here," she said to herself. "Did he really know how beautiful it is?"

The bag with the paper was very heavy, but she didn't notice. She couldn't help giggling when it occurred to her that if she chose, she could find enthusiastic and well-paying customers for her goods on these very streets.

In the yard of an audio-video shop stood a trash bin overflowing with packing materials and old electrical equipment. She stuck the bag in; no one saw.

On the corner, behind the glass panes of the shop, TV sets were twinkling mutely into the evening. The wife glanced at them, and suddenly saw the image of Gloucester, his sad, austere, beautiful face multiplied tenfold. The street was absolutely still. She knew that now he was dead too.

Day Nine

"Dear old Paul," the wife said on Sunday to Paul the Great, who was filling her in on the details about Gloucester. "Whenever we think it's taking shape and starting to make sense, they go and shoot somebody again, without thinking twice about it. And then the other side shoots back, or they blow something up, and it goes on and on."

"I told you on Easter Sunday that Müllner was on the run, and that he'd be in touch. Did he contact you?"

"No," said the wife. "But it got to me when I saw his picture on TV yesterday. He was so good-looking, he looked so serious."

"He *was* serious," Paul answered, "he really was. But as time goes on, I find it increasingly hard to see any use in that kind of seriousness. I'm almost forty. When you reach my age, you have to watch out that you don't start to look comic as a revolutionary. I want the same thing they do," he said, while he slowly ate grapes off a plate. "All people with sense want the same thing, but their type are a rarity. It's all a question of taking the overall view. You can't sort out Southeast Asia and the Guxhagen girls' reformatory, the Argentinian Fascists and the black schoolkids in Little Rock, all at the same time. For the Group, revolution is like pulling teeth. They think that all you have to do is find a point of infection and rip it out. It'll go on hurting awhile, but then it'll be all right because of course there's no more infection coming into the world."

The wife didn't want to hear all this, but she didn't dare ask for the details of Gloucester's death. The grape skeleton was lying in a little puddle of water on Paul's plate.

"Have you heard that they've decided on a lawyer to wind up his caseload?"

"How come they told *you* about it first?" she asked, offended. You could never be sure they were showing you enough respect.

"Because I know what's what and you don't," Paul answered cuttingly.

"That's not the point!" she said. "What will this guy do with the political cases? Do you know him?"

"I never even heard the name," said Paul. "But he must have known your husband. You can still deal with the political cases. If you want, just tell the clients to go see Hilde."

Why doesn't he say *he'll* carry on my husband's work? she thought. The two men had often fought, no holds barred, but that didn't matter now. Paul was the only one who could really carry on. Why isn't he saying anything?

Paul gazed at her with his little bear's eyes. "What you ought to do is turn it into a memorial foundation, or something like that."

"The Taj Mahal," she said. "Where's the money supposed to come from? Who's supposed to benefit? Do we want a museum for the generations after us? 'Look, kiddies, that's what life was like back in the seventies, when we made our last fight for liberty.' " She was furious because her husband's accomplice and partner had guessed her secret wishes.

"Hardenberg said something," she went on. "When a lawyer dies, his office dies at the same moment. You can't bring it back to life."

"We don't have to talk about that now," said Paul, acting as if he hadn't heard the last bit. "About Müllner: Probably they shot him from behind as he was trying to get into a cellar. It was only a couple of yards from our office, from the old office we used to share."

"But that was a couple of years ago. What did he want there? Was he alone?"

"I expect he was looking for something," Paul answered indifferently. "They don't need to justify liquidating people, you know. Right now he's probably lying in the same joint as your old man."

"It's been nine days now, nine days," she said. "It's such a terrible thing."

She wasn't embarrassed to say that in the presence of her husband's friend. He started to cry into his big hands. It made her happy to see someone else cry, as if she were collecting tribute, tokens of love that could be combined to form one great love. The tears and words, be they friends' or foes', kept adding ever more color and detail to her husband's image.

"What about the kid?" Paul asked.

"He hasn't gotten in touch yet."

"Surely it's obvious to you that he can't get in touch when he's at police headquarters being questioned nonstop, under suspicion of murder," Paul said sarcastically.

She'd completely forgotten about that. Of course the police had taken the boy into custody, as a pledge, a scapegoat. She'd been feeling her husband's silence for the past few days, feared that the special bond between herself and him had been severed. Maybe it was because she hadn't protected the boy. Nor the cats. Instead she'd thrown herself into the political stuff, because she saw a role to play there, thought she could still inherit some of the glamour he'd collected. She'd left his real legacy in the lurch. That she would never admit to Paul.

"What else am I supposed to have done that I didn't do?" she asked angrily. "It's not as if anybody's been helping me. There I am, stuck with his office, with all his things, with the funeral, and everybody just gives me silly advice or lambastes me with some theory. He was a hero, they say, so I should go and establish a memorial foundation. Or I should make sure he gets a funeral like nobody else's. I should let the comrades know once and for all just who he was. And I should rescue his boyfriend from the clutches of the cops. Okay," she screamed. "Why don't you all just do it all for me! Just let me grieve in peace at last, and all of you go worry about the trimmings!" Exhausted, she looked at the lawyer's broad face, tearless now, and saw that he didn't understand a word she'd said.

The truth was, Paul was sometimes overcome by a kind of deafness that literally kept him from hearing disturbing things. He was famous for the way he could plow ahead like a tank, impervious to attack.

Of course she'd have to see to getting the boy exonerated, Paul said. No one else's testimony would count as much as hers. All the signs made it clear that a lot of people were very interested in seeing this death disposed of quietly, and a guilty party found to cover the tracks.

It was Sunday noon, and she felt sad when Paul left. She'd felt close to her husband while she was talking to Paul: even when they hadn't told each other the truth.

"You have to be able to lie better than the system," her husband had said once. "Only you mustn't forget for a minute that you're lying. The dangerous thing about the system is that at a certain point it starts believing its own stories. That's why all the politicians gush so, and why the Group are so terse: They know every minute that they're lying."

"If they're lying," she'd answered, "if that's what you really think, then what do you want from them? Why do you bend over backward to help them, in your own weird way?"

"That's just it," he'd replied. "In my own weird way. The thing is, I do think they're right about one thing, and that's their abiding distrust of social reforms. If you can make something legal, if they let you make it legal, you might as well forget it, you're barking up the wrong tree."

"It sounds to me as if what you're after is suspiciously like the all-purifying flame," the wife said. "In the end everything is cleansed, but unfortunately it's been destroyed in the process."

"That's where my weird way comes in, kiddo. I know that opposites don't meet, even in infinity. On one side, you've got the pure ideals, the liberation of the individual from every form of imposed power, from exploitation and fear—and on the other side, there's eating black-currant tart in the Laumer Café, and a great fuck on a summer evening when you don't give a damn about exploitation. There are the slaughterhouses and the jasmines. I'll have to live to be at least ninety to find out how to piece them together."

Instinctively, she had kept the boy away from her while she was mourning. She was afraid to see a different image of her husband, a selfish, superficial one. The boy had known him well.

He phoned that afternoon.

"I just wanted to tell you I'm no longer under suspicion of murder. Absurd as it was for them to accuse me of hurting him," his voice said, "I was really down in the dumps. When people only have an outsider's view of things between him and me, it really does look as if I might have killed him. After all, even the comrades heard us fighting. But now it looks as if the cops have the autopsy results, so they've let me go."

"What?" she cried into the telephone. "What did they say the autopsy results were?"

"They didn't tell me," the boy replied, sounding surprised. "Why should they say anything to me? All they said was that I'm no longer a suspect. You'll have to ask them yourself. After all, you're his wife."

He said the word "wife" as if it were a totally alien concept, as if it were inconceivable for this word to designate any actual relationship.

She was angry again, this time without guilt. That rat, she thought; that little rat. That word people aren't supposed to use about each other, not even in thought, gave her a good feeling. She hated the boy's untouchable quality, the precision with which he observed feelings, seemingly without sharing them.

"How are the cats?" she asked. "I'd like to give you some money for their food."

"Do you think that'll make you feel better?" asked the boy. "It's not necessary. The tomcat is fine. Icru will die soon."

"Nonsense," she said. "She'll get used to you." But she knew as she spoke that once again she was lacking in love. She knew perfectly well that only exceptional energy would enable her husband's cat to survive. The cat was his true legacy, the four-footed International Center Red University.

That day, the ninth day, she realized that she'd be a lot better off if she could act without inhibition, without the megalomaniacal loneliness of the widow. (Of an inauthentic widow, that is.) Because even her attempt to clear up the business of the bag had turned out differently than she planned. Maybe she should have tried talking to Gloucester, showing him love and trust instead of subservient defiance. Once again she could feel his bird's bones the way she'd felt them when she hugged him in the cafeteria—not to disguise their meeting, she now realized, but simply because she had wanted to hug him. Only she hadn't been able to tell him so.

She was positive that he'd gone looking for the bag, that he'd tried to get from another building into the cellar of her husband's old office. Someone must have set him on that trail. Before long, there would be nothing left of the pharaoh's tomb in the other cellar but an ordinary bag, an uninteresting fake-leather bag with a severed flap. She'd have to cart away two or three more loads of paper at most. She felt that no one suspected what she was doing, that neither group had found her out. But she wasn't doing it for her husband, as she pretended; she was doing it for herself.

The bells were ringing the way they had on Easter Sunday. She felt unremitting guilt for everything that had happened, from the muddle surrounding her husband's death to Gloucester's murder, which was bound to trigger other events in turn.

The notorious dead man was the first item mentioned on the Sunday news. Few details were being released, the news announcer said, so as not to imperil further investigation.

She wasn't the least afraid. For a long time now there had been no connection between herself and her husband's old law office. Naturally, the police would manufacture a connection. The setting was irresistible. She remembered how some years back they used to joke about the subterranean passages connecting the buildings of the inner city.

"He's back on his Early Christian Catacombs kick," Paul the Great had said when her husband got enthusiastic about the idea of an underground community of anarchists.

"It'd be easy for you, you white crocodile!" his wife had said. "You'd just as soon spend all your time under the ground. Do you know how you picture the underground? A place where there are no vitamins!"

"That's how everybody must picture it," her husband had mused. "Only unhealthy things have sensual appeal."

But his white skin had looked healthy, she remembered, not sickly. He'd only been attracted to white-skinned boys. None of these suntanned types in the cigarette ads!

She looked out the window, thinking about Lisa Engström. She couldn't altogether give up hope that there was some truth to Lisa's cool certainty, after all. At any moment, her husband might appear to her outside the window, show himself from a distance, whisper a few words of encouragement. She certainly could use them. When the doorbell rang, she raised her eyes reluctantly from the empty street, as if she feared she was going to miss something. She hadn't seen anyone come up to her door.

Five or six people stood at the door, ranged one behind the other and standing still, as if they were just about to start singing or deliver a speech.

"Are you Mrs. D——?" the lead figure asked politely.

The wife knew at once who they were. The men, and the one woman hovering in the background—I expect she's supposed to come with me when I go to the toilet, she thought—wore exactly the same curiously conspicuous casual clothing as the plainclothes cops who had sealed her husband's apartment the day he died.

She held the door open silently, while behind her the cats slunk into another room.

"You know I am," she said.

"May we come in?" asked a second cop, as polite as the first.

What would they do if I said no? she thought, and remembered what her husband had told her: They'd claim there was an obstruction of justice, and come in anyway.

"The federal prosecutor's office is summoning you for questioning," said the first cop, while one by one they all pushed their way gently into the narrow hall. "Don't be alarmed; it's just a matter of a few items that have to be cleared up."

"We know you've had a bereavement," the second cop said, taking his turn again, while the others peered into all the corners, just as they'd done in her husband's apartment nine days ago. "And today's Sunday. But it's urgent. No doubt you'll realize that, and make our work easier."

She'd told them nothing so far. All the guidelines her husband had given her to follow on occasions like this started running through her mind. Don't say anything. Especially not if they're friendly. Give them your name and personal data, that's all. If they try to get chummy, don't fall for it. If they pretend to be understanding, don't believe a word they say. Remember, if they were really capable of understanding you, they would have chosen a different profession, and then people like us wouldn't exist, because there'd be no need for us.

"No doubt you can imagine what it's about," the first cop chimed in again. Evidently only two of them had permission to talk, and the rest were there to look.

"No, I can't imagine anything," she said.

"Couldn't we sit down?" asked the first cop. "We haven't introduced ourselves. I'm Müller of the Criminal Investigation Department. My colleagues, Detective Helms, Detective Gutbrod . . ."

The wife didn't hear all the names. She'd have to pull herself together. This was her first acid test.

"Do you plan on staying long?" she asked sharply, and was amazed to notice that her knees were knocking together very softly and her right foot was trembling. She had folded her hands so that each could steady the other, and she felt moisture under her arms. I'm scared, she thought, and was astonished.

The two spokesmen had sat down, while the other two men and the woman stood at the door, staring into the next room.

"Yes," said Detective Müller. "Believe me, I'm sorry. The holiday. Your terrible loss. Those are not just empty phrases." He gave her a direct and serious look. "We thought a lot of your husband. Of course he represented the opposition, but then one wants to have brilliant adversaries. And he was a brilliant adversary, I say that in all honesty."

The wife's trembling was subsiding; soothed by these earnest words, she was relaxing. Suddenly she realized with horror that she was betraying her husband's unwritten commandments, the only important commandments there were. She pulled herself together and straightened her back, placed her hands palm down on her knees.

"You didn't come here to tell me *that.*" It sounded like a line from a movie, and she felt pleased with herself.

"No, we didn't," said the second cop, whose name she hadn't caught. He was a gentle-looking, blond thirty-year-old who could easily have belonged to the Group. No doubt that was a clever ploy on their part. "It has to do with Müllner's death. It seems there are links between him and your husband. Your husband was his defense lawyer, of course. But there are other connections, including some between Müllner and you."

"I never saw him," she said, and coughed. "It's the cigarettes; I've been smoking too much the past few days."

"I can understand that," the blond said softly. "It's really an awful business. We certainly wouldn't bother you if it weren't important."

"You said the prosecutor's office wants me brought in?" she asked, and suddenly she couldn't manage to spread her breath evenly among the words.

"Yes, it's an investigative hearing," Müller said soothingly. "No doubt your husband would have been questioned too, sometime soon. It has to do with 129A."

"With what?"

"Suspicion of aiding and abetting a criminal conspiracy," the blond cop said cordially. "Sorry about those numbers. Nobody could fool your husband with that kind of thing. It has to do with Müllner's death."

"He was shot," she said. "I saw it on TV. Why did you shoot him?"

"First off, we didn't have anything to do with the way things turned out. The police were searching for him. I assume that one of our colleagues had him under observation and acted in self-defense. I don't have any information about it. The facts will be cleared up, you can be sure of that."

"Yes," she said, "I can be sure of that. And what's the purpose of your investigative hearing?"

She could feel her husband close beside her, could hear the way he'd laughed during the federal high court sessions in Karlsruhe; saw his tall figure wearing the robe, with the forbidden judge's hat on his head. Now he was here, helping her; he wasn't deserting her. The carved-up body inside the metal drawer, the body that was destined to go under the ground soon, seemed very far away now. His body might have changed, but *he* was the same.

"It's not *our* investigative hearing," the blond said, very sternly now. "There are several deaths involved, bank robberies, inciting to crime, the organizing of gangs, an underground movement. People have died!"

"Yes, people have died," she answered.

"We respect your feelings," the first officer said in a mocking tone. "But we expect you to cooperate. We're meeting you more than halfway. When was the last time you saw Müllner?"

"I've never laid eyes on him, as far as I know," she said, sticking to her story.

"It's been reported that Müllner visited you in your apartment," said the first officer, the one whose name was almost identical to Müllner's.

"Who says so?" she asked.

She kept feeling that she'd made a big mistake, but she couldn't figure out what it was. She felt numb.

"Is it okay if we look around a little in the meantime?" the blond asked, gently once again.

"Do you have a search warrant?" she asked.

"I thought your husband would have taught you better." The first cop took his turn. "We don't need one. Not when there's a possible obstruction of justice."

Yes, she thought. Everything's going just as we always imagined it would.

"I want a lawyer," she said. "I won't say anything more."

That was the important point she'd been forgetting!

"No reason you shouldn't have a lawyer," Müller said regretfully. "But I won't conceal that I think it's an unwise decision. After all, we're only interested in finding out the truth. So our interests must be identical to yours. Your husband was such a truth fanatic! Why do you want a lawyer now, instead of finishing our little chat here in peace? But of course, it's your right."

And he was silent, while the nontalkers in the group sped eagerly through her rooms, opened drawers, and tidily examined, then tidily replaced, their contents. They handled the wife's clothing and rummaged among her books, leafed through the papers on her desk, and peered into the dark interior of the cats' basket. She felt tears coming to her eyes.

"Oh, no, not that," she said to her husband. "Please keep me from bawling." And the lump in her throat dissolved.

"I'd like to call my lawyer now," she said in a determined voice. "You can't stop me."

"Who wants to stop you?" asked the blond. "By the way, who is the person in this photograph?"

"That's my father," she said, sick with rage. "My father twenty-five years ago."

Had she really thought that things would go on in the same comfortable way they had for the past few days, with her hours divided neatly and quietly between work and mourning, sleeping and waking? It had started out so deceptively, everything had seemed just as it should be: the parents and friends, the tears and memories, his body and his legacy.

But all that wasn't enough to win her immortality. The real combat zone still waited for her. The bag had been only a small decision, a feeble attempt at autonomy, a childish insistence on freedom. As if there were any such thing! As if the Group hadn't known all along that it didn't exist!

For years she'd struggled to figure out what kind of battle she wanted to fight, what weapons to use, against what enemy, and for what cause. She'd always just groped her way along with the others, sometimes genuinely furious but most often only mildly discontented, and always very scared. She'd felt more fright than enthusiasm for the struggle against imperialism, and its methods intimidated her. Nor would she have liked it if everyone had become like the Armed Fighters. But now the other side had finally fixed things so that she couldn't go on being lazy, couldn't just rest on her laurels after her husband's death, as if by losing him she had paid all her dues.

When the blond cop announced that she'd be taken to police headquarters after she'd tried to reach a lawyer—and she might have some trouble; after all, today was Sunday—she calmed down. Now she took care before every word she said, and took no trouble to hide it. They considered her guilty anyhow, guilty of something or other. The very fact that she knew so many of the wrong type of people counted as guilt. There was no reason for her to go on playing innocent. So while the mute searchers inspected cupboard after cupboard, bookshelf after bookshelf, without curiosity, picking up objects indifferently before returning them to their original spot, she undertook phoning a lawyer.

"Who do you want to contact?" asked the blond.

She had an inspiration. It might easily have been one of her husband's bright ideas, and she felt sure that he'd given it to her in the moment she went to the telephone.

"I want Schaaf." She saw the undisguised amazement in the officers' faces.

"Do you mean that?" one of them said. "He doesn't defend lefties!"

She couldn't resist the pun: "No, he's a defender of the right."

Schaaf had had a lot in common with her husband, yet he belonged to a completely different camp. He was a star, an actor, tall and stooping, with a fleet of expensive cars and a lot of tax dodgers for clients. Her husband had liked him. Both men played the same instrument, only in different orchestras. Schaaf was maybe ten years her husband's senior. She had seen him now and then in bars, where he used to tell stories in a loud voice, almost a shout, and pressed champagne and expensive food on his entourage. His eyes often looked tired. Sometimes she thought that he used to chase around the bars making a racket in order to keep himself awake. "He's a crackerjack lawyer," her husband had said, "a screwball. If only he were political. Our guys are mostly so dull."

The faces of the police officers told her that she'd scored a point. But she couldn't reach Schaaf.

"You can try again from headquarters," said Müller.

"I'll keep trying until I get him," she answered.

She didn't see any of her neighbors that quiet Sunday noon as the police drove her away.

Nobody takes any notice of what happens to people, she thought. I could disappear now and never be seen again, just like in South America. But this wasn't South America; they were only pretending. Weren't they?

On the way to the station, she realized that she would have to show some willingness to talk if she was to find out what they wanted to know. She didn't believe them when they said that it all had to do with Gloucester's murder. For them, Gloucester was only a way in, a break in the wall separating them from the Group. She mourned for Gloucester as she sat among his enemies, riding through the deserted city. She wished she could see her husband standing side by side with all the dead freedom fighters; and yet she was glad she didn't. The giant apparatus for warding off change pounced on every sign of life from that alien land.

At police headquarters, they stuck her alone in a very small room, with a little table that had a typewriter on it, and a telephone.

"I'll go on trying to reach my lawyer," she said.

The silent men had vanished, and so had the female officer. The blond cop and his colleague lingered.

"We'll tell you when you can phone," the blond said. "It'll be another minute." They left her alone.

The bare branches of a tree swayed outside the window. She looked down into the yard, where the police cars were lined up. A uniformed officer was walking across the asphalt-lined plaza, around which the station buildings formed a square. Almost all the windows were barred, including the one she was looking through. She lifted the phone receiver, but the line was dead.

She whispered her husband's name, and knew that he'd taught her enough so that she could pass this long-deferred test on her own. The only thing was, she still wasn't clear whose interests she was representing. Not the working people, of whom the Group said that they were just waiting for class warfare to break out, that they had only to see the light switched on in order at last to recognize clearly the face of their enemy. No, she didn't feel she was cut out for that job.

"The working people think we're too lazy and that's why they don't join us. But they need us as bridges," the Group said. For them, their rage is enough, she thought, but mine is enough only when somebody does something to me directly. I have to make the most of it while I've got it. The presence of the dead was less real to her now than the little room with its window and its mute telephone.

"They *are* doing something to me," she said aloud, to see if her voice still worked. She wished she wore a watch. Silly, when time did not exist. There wasn't a church tower to be seen, no matter how much she craned her neck peering out the window. Then they came back.

"Sorry," said the blond cop. "We had a few things to clear up. Have you talked to your lawyer?"

"The phone doesn't work," she said furiously.

"All you have to do is press this button." The other cop pressed it and held out the receiver.

Once again Schaaf did not answer.

"Don't you want to chat with us a bit in the meantime?" asked the blond. "We know you're not a terrorist. We just want to clear the matter up, for your sake as well as ours."

She felt like laughing. So that's how they do it. It was just as her husband had said: You can't trust them.

"I don't understand what you want from me," she said. "I'm employed, you know that. My husband died nine days ago and he still isn't buried. You shot one of his clients. So why have I been saddled with an investigative hearing? It's your colleagues who should be under investigation, all those who've shot somebody dead."

The two men smiled at her as if she'd just sung a song for them or told a joke. "Yes, of course," said the blond. "But we've no choice, we have to question you. You know, I want to be completely open with you."

"Look out," she heard her husband's voice say. "Here it comes. That's what they always say just before they start lying like crazy."

"We're at a dead end," the blond cop continued. "We have to follow up every lead, even if we pester people like you to do it. Of course it's even worse for you because of your personal distress. Anyway, we've gotten wind of certain plans that Müllner was supposedly involved in, and we're assuming that your husband might have found out about them."

"What kind of plans?"

"Plans involving the terrorists imprisoned at Stammheim. Do you have any idea what they could be?" The blond looked slyly at the wife as if she were his accomplice.

"No," she said. "I hear they're not in very good shape."

"Exactly, exactly. That's why there may conceivably be plans to change the situation. No doubt you'd approve of that, wouldn't you?"

She didn't reply, but thought about the possible relevance of the bag. Anyway, it had nothing to do with her. None of this did.

"I'd like to try again," she said.

"What?"

"To get hold of my lawyer."

The officers were getting impatient. "If you don't cooperate," said the blond, "if you refuse to give us information, naturally we'll be forced to investigate you. That would be embarrassing for you, at work and with your relatives and friends."

"That doesn't matter to me," she answered. "Very likely you'll go ahead regardless."

This time she reached Schaaf.

"What are you up to?" he yelled into the telephone. "It's awful what happened to your husband. Where are you? Where? Why's that? Oh, yes, aha, yes," he shouted so loudly that the officers could hear every word. "Then you just go along home now, right away. Naturally," he said, in answer to a question from her. "Naturally you mustn't say anything. What would become of us if we all talked with just anybody? No, go home! Maybe we can have supper together this evening and discuss the details! Good-bye, dear lady, see you soon!"

"Hmmm." The blond sounded disgruntled. "In that case, the only thing we can do now is get you officially booked."

She was startled. "Can I refuse to be booked?"

"No," he said, luxuriating in the moment. "Even your big-shot lawyer can't help you there. Go ahead and ask him."

She phoned Schaaf. Quieter now, he confirmed what she'd been told.

She was taken to a room resembling a laboratory, where a cheerful police clerk asked her questions. She hesitated before each reply. She knew she'd look awful on the photos they took of her.

"They're never especially flattering," said the clerk. "But we don't plan to use them for wedding announcements."

The two officers had disappeared.

Eventually she walked out of the police quadrangle, feeling numb, and stepped back into this Sunday where everything had changed all over again. For a long time, she didn't know in which direction she really intended to go.

Her husband's apartment was very near police headquarters. She listened to the rumbling of the trains and tried to figure out her next move. Then she noticed that she was so hungry it hurt. There was only a little money in her wallet. She peered attentively at the windows of the bars, where the food prices were inscribed with thick paint. Choosing a café, she ordered a cheap meal, so completely self-absorbed that she barely noticed the flip advances of the men in the bar. Her black clothing protected her—at least for today.

She took a scrap of paper out of her bag and jotted down her most urgent chores. She knew she might be under surveillance. If the cops hadn't been very curious, they would have waited until Monday.

"Bag," she wrote on the scrap of paper. "Christoph? Mrs. Sattler. Night. Medical examiner's." Isolated words: nothing connoting effort, only thoughts. She intended to get some rest. She chewed away at the thin, stringy meat. Someone else would have to carry on for a while. Her enemies had neutralized her, and she was almost grateful to them.

She walked out of the bar, oblivious of the men's invitations, and called up the plant kidnapper Koblenz, whom she hadn't seen for ages.

"I've wanted to call you for a long time," came the sweet voice of Christoph Koblenz. She started to cry with relief.

"You've got to help me," she said. "Please come. Please come."

"To your place?" he asked calmly. "Just quiet down now, it'll be all right, I'll help you, I'll do whatever has to be done. Shall I come to your place?"

"No," she said. "I'm at the train station. Let's meet outside the florist's shop."

"Oh, dear," said Koblenz. "All right. Seeing that it's you. I'll be there in half an hour."

As she circled slowly round and round the train station, dived into subway passages and then climbed back up again, locked herself in the rest room and then left by the back entrance and disappeared in a different direction, she was thinking that now she'd finally landed in the coils of that tricky game of cops and robbers that she'd always wanted to avoid. Suddenly the only thing that still counted was the game itself. The enemy's identity was clear. The enemy had the power and she had the brains. The enemy wanted evil: things remaining the same. The other group wanted change—later on, when there was time for it.

She kept looking behind her. No longer was she protected by her black clothing but endangered. She couldn't have been more conspicuous. But she didn't see any cops looking her way.

Only when she slowly approached the florist's shop did she understand Koblenz's hesitancy about meeting her there. In the shop, trapped under cold blue light and behind bars, suffered the victims he could not liberate—not in the middle of the train station on a Sunday! Unintentionally she was forcing him to look at them. She felt like a monster, and looking at the potted plants inside, she saw them as he must see them. Soon after, she saw Koblenz coming, walking with short, rapid steps and carrying an empty burlap sack over his shoulder. He'd got slightly heavier since the trial. She thought it suited him. When you looked at him now, you no longer felt you had to apologize.

"You look well," she said gratefully.

"I'm feeling well too," Koblenz said amiably, trying not to look into the florist's window. She suspected that he'd brought the burlap sack along just in case it proved easier than he anticipated to bring off a kidnapping.

She explained what had happened since her husband's death, and especially what had gone on that ninth day. Meanwhile they strolled slowly around the station like a couple.

Koblenz didn't say much and didn't interrupt her once. All he did was ask her a question now and then, to help her move on in the story. He had never had anything to do with the Group, whose actions were foreign to his nature. He seemed to have made up his mind very young to be a loner, and had laid out the exact precincts of his work. Now he carried on that work unwaveringly, and wouldn't allow it to be dismissed as silly or meaningless. Nor did he ask her what she or her husband had to do with the Group.

"A person has to do something, somewhere," was all he said. "Your husband had lots of opportunities. But it's tough when they're prefabricated. People always brought him a finished product. He had to justify what they'd done, whether he liked it or not. That wears you out, in the long run."

"You'll help me?"

"Of course," said the plant kidnapper. "It shouldn't be hard for me. Nothing but a half-empty bag to get rid of!" He laughed.

"But we have to get it done today," she said. "They won't let me out of their clutches again. When they'd finished booking me, a guy who escorted me out said something about my being examined by the district attorney. No, they definitely won't let up on me now. But they're out of luck. I don't know anything about this guy Müllner."

And that wasn't a lie, because as far as she was concerned, the dead man was and always would be Gloucester, Gloucester with his thin bird's bones, who had trembled a little, with solitude and discipline, the one time they embraced. She didn't know anybody named Müllner. Let them look him up in her husband's files, if they hadn't already done so.

"Don't invent excuses," said Christoph Koblenz. He had heard the inaudible, just as he did with his plants. "Inventing excuses will give you yellow leaves. The two of you wanted to do something for those people, and now you want to carry on somehow but you don't know yet where to start. You did the right thing with the bag. It has to disappear, and we're taking care of that now. I can't tell you what will happen later, but the bag will vanish along with everything that's still inside. You can count on that. Go to his apartment openly, don't try to hide. But don't go to the cellar. Wait upstairs until I get there. I'll bring my truck. Look as if you were expecting me. I don't think the cops will come in the next two hours. Probably they'll get a judge to approve a search warrant. After all, today's Sunday, so it'll take them a while. And by the time they come, there'll be nothing left for them to see. I've already figured out how to do it."

Koblenz didn't say goodbye to her, he simply vanished into the crowd. She'd have loved to have that knack. She thought of the funeral. Three days to go, still three more days. "You sure do know how to keep a person on her toes," she said to her husband, pretending he was present simply because she didn't feel that he was.

If only I knew what I'm going to live on for the next few months. Could her husband have hidden a little money somewhere? But where? The cellar was out of the question.

She climbed the stairs to her husband's apartment, hesitated briefly, unlocked the door, sniffed at the entrance before she walked into the hall. Some houses rot while others dry out. This one was drying out. It was turning into an office. Its other qualities were no longer perceptible.

She sat down in the waiting room and picked up some files, but didn't read them. She felt very far from her husband here. The only thing left of him were the endless repetitions of his fancy signature. In the student fraternity he still belonged to when they met, everybody sported signatures like that, full of curlicues with little dots inside them.

She began to be afraid that Koblenz wouldn't find the way. Her husband had still been in his old office when he handled Koblenz's case. Panic grabbed her. She heard a car drive slowly by on the street below, but she didn't dare go to the window and look out.

The sense of elation that had got her through the police interrogation was evaporating. She didn't know how much time had elapsed since her meeting with Christoph. The same wan light as ever filled her husband's office, even though the blinds were raised now.

When the doorbell rang, she was so startled that her heart missed a few beats. She heard a loud rumbling in the hall downstairs. "He's had a brainstorm," she said to herself. "He warned me."

Koblenz had arrived with an old flatbed truck that looked like a postwar model. The gentlemen in expensive cars, who were just then stopping off at nearby bars, stared at the vehicle in amazement. Koblenz was unloading a bunch of tall proud trees, potted plants, and setting them down on the street as if for a solemn occasion. When he finished, he grabbed a black carrier bag that evidently contained something heavy. Mrs. Sattler had come downstairs some time ago and was inspecting the stately-looking plants.

"Why didn't you take them straight to the cemetery?" she asked, making it clear that she had a complete grasp of the situation.

"But that's obvious," he answered Mrs. Sattler in a warm voice. "They'd be stolen there. He was a friend of mine," he said, with a sad glance. "They're my very best plants! They have to stand in the dark for two more days, so they'll be just right for the funeral. Maybe one of them will even bloom. I'll bring them to the cemetery early in the morning on the day of the funeral."

"Do you want to take them to the cellar?" Mrs. Sattler asked, thinking hard. "If the trees need to be in the dark? My, I guess nobody visited that filthy hole for years, and now since her husband died, folk can't seem to keep away!"

The wife had been standing there in silence.

"Why don't you just go back upstairs," Koblenz said kindly. "I can manage. I have the basins right here," he said, pointing to the bag. "Is there a water faucet downstairs?"

"Oh, yes," said Mrs. Sattler. "There's plenty of water. Shall I help you?"

"You can give it a try," said Koblenz. But when she tried to lift one of the tubs, it wouldn't budge an inch. "You see? Why don't you go back upstairs with her?" He looked over at the wife. "It looks to me as if she's not feeling too well."

By now Mrs. Sattler had found out everything she wanted to

know, so she tucked an arm sympathetically under the wife's elbow. "Would you like something to drink?" she asked.

"No, thank you," said the wife. "I'll be all right. I still have to talk over some details with the gardener."

"Oh, he's a gardener," said Mrs. Sattler. "I wouldn't have thought so."

"He was a client," the wife said cautiously. "He's grateful to my husband."

"Oh yes, a client," said Mrs. Sattler. "Your husband got to know all kinds of people, didn't he? An interesting profession."

"Yes," the wife answered, starting upstairs as she listened to the noises beginning to come from the cellar. "Lots of variety."

"Only I guess that one way or another, there's none of them are quite respectable people," Mrs. Sattler remarked, trying to dispel the Sunday boredom. "They all got some black mark against them, otherwise they wouldn't need a lawyer, would they? Don't get me wrong."

"Oh, Mrs. Sattler," the wife said wearily, "you'd be amazed how fast it could happen to you. You just don't know. Things happen by accident." She'd been climbing the stairs as she spoke.

"Where there's smoke, there's fire," said Mrs. Sattler. "People are always to blame for what happens to them."

"Maybe you're right," said the wife, already at the next landing. "But I don't think so."

Once again she was seated in the waiting room, and she still hadn't opened the door to the room where her husband died. This time she didn't jump when Koblenz rang the bell. He stood at the door empty-handed.

"Where's the stuff?" she asked.

"Switched," said Koblenz. "Don't worry. You know that tract of land by the marsh, where I grow aquatic plants? I'll stick it there later; it'll be well hidden. There's nothing poisonous in it, and there's no better place than a marsh to store the two pieces."

"Pieces?" she repeated, stiff-lipped.

"Down at the bottom of the bag!" Christoph said impatiently. "Inside the false bottom, under what's left of the papers. Two guns. Without ammunition."

"I didn't see them," she murmured after a pause. "And I'm sure he didn't see them either."

"Then neither of you really looked," Koblenz said relentlessly.

She was glad that the bag no longer existed for her. Someone else had taken over the responsibility. She'd done her bit.

"Do you suppose he needed those pistols really badly?" she asked Christoph, who by now was privy to more or less all her secrets. "Do you suppose that's why he ran straight into them that way?"

"Why would anyone have such an urgent need for a couple of guns?" Koblenz had no need to ask whom she was talking about. "I've never understood that. You can't do a single useful thing with them."

"But you can't change the world with cow dung and a few restored cactuses." For a moment she was forgetting to be grateful.

"Who says?" he answered amiably. "That's bull. *They* don't change the world either. And your husband didn't change it; he just went and died."

"Look," Koblenz said after a pause. "Sometimes you're as dumb as they are. So much is happening, while you're watching out for your old man and trying to carry on his business. Some Latin American tycoon is giving a party six thousand miles away, and an Indian woman bends down in the dirt to pick up the coins he throws her. I've seen that happen. You two once decided you'd learn to be hardhearted so you could hit the hardhearted where they live. But that never works. Because they're happy and know they're on the right side, and that's something you guys will never know. You can't even fight them. You only fight with their deputies, the cops, and you think you're really something; and the cops think the same, so they play along. Meanwhile the fat cats are sitting up in the box seats watching you all and laughing their heads off. Your old man was so smart; he really ought to have seen how it goes."

She hadn't realized that the plant kidnapper was capable of such a speech. It sounded as if he had been preparing for months.

"If you don't mind, I'd like to see where he died," Koblenz said. "I come from a village," he added, as if apologizing. "And in a village, places are very important. An uncle of mine drowned in a cesspool, and everyone felt ashamed. That's not a fitting place to die."

She felt like laughing, but she wouldn't have minded crying.

"He died in bed," she said. "I think that for him that wasn't a fitting place."

"There you go again," said Koblenz. "If only I knew what you people think you're going to achieve with your revolution! Don't you see it would be terrific if everybody could die in bed?"

She opened the door to the red bedroom like a museum guard. She was trembling a little; but nothing had changed. The wide bed stood, smooth and silent, next to the poster bearing the words NO POWER TO ANYBODY. Koblenz paused in the doorway and looked around the room. He seemed satisfied with what he saw.

"I've brought something with me," he said. "If you don't mind."

He went outside and fetched a small package that she hadn't seen before. Inside was a large white flower. He put it down on the pillow where her husband's head had lain.

"It bloomed only this evening," said the plant kidnapper.

"And you cut it off its stalk?" she asked, noticing that she felt a bit jealous.

"Yes," said Koblenz. "Just this once. It's fitting that a couple of plants should die with every human being. But they have to be special ones." He bent his head down to the empty bed again. "It's nice and cool in here," he said contentedly. "It won't wilt for a couple of days."

Embarrassed, the wife closed the door of her husband's bedroom, feeling that now it was more alien than ever.

"It's better if we go now," she said. "I keep thinking they'll come back."

"What do you mean, come back?" asked Koblenz. "How do you know they've been here more than once, on the day he died? No, surely they won't come today. And tomorrow let them come if they want to. You'll have to get used to them."

Down on the street, she watched him drive away in his rattletrap truck. "I have to go to the marsh now," he'd said. "Now is just the right time to do it."

Darkness had fallen some time ago. She walked anxiously past the bars. The noises and colors were rubbing her the wrong way. She took a taxi home, even though she had serious money worries.

When she got there, she thought her apartment looked grubby. There was a book that the cops hadn't put back in place; and a sheaf of papers was spread out. Her castle had been invaded by invisible assailants.

She started cleaning her dim rooms, she frightened the cats, and annoyed her neighbors by running the vacuum cleaner so late. She was exhausted by the time the boy phoned.

"Is something wrong?" he asked. "Were you out?"

"I had company," the wife said after a pause.

"I figured you would," the boy said, unimpressed. "They're pretty stirred up after knocking off Müllner. That was a blunder on their part; they'll have hell to pay for it. Now they won't get anything more out of that quarter. Serves them right."

Everybody seemed to understand more than she did. It was as if everything that happened were written in an unknown code.

"What are you talking about?" she asked awkwardly. "Is there something I ought to know?"

The boy spoke evasively. "I don't know any more than what the files say, but I can put two and two together."

"How are the cats?" she asked.

"Okay," he said. "Icru even ate a little."

"What do you mean?" she asked excitedly, glad that at last they were on a topic that she understood something about. "You mean she wasn't eating before?"

"I told you she won't survive. She eats just enough to keep from dying right away. She coughs quite a bit too."

"We'll take her to the vet," she said, crying. "Tomorrow we'll go to the vet."

"I already took her." The boy sounded unmoved as ever. "There are things that aren't curable."

Then he hung up. She didn't put away the vacuum cleaner but sat down in the dark and tried to think of nothing at all.

Day Ten

"The medical examiner isn't back yet," a woman's voice said. "May I have your name, please?"

The wife repeated her name.

"And what did you want to talk to him about?" asked the voice.

She didn't know what to reply. She couldn't very well say, "The medical examiner dissected my husband." "It's about a cause of death," she began.

But the voice interrupted her. "We don't give out information over the telephone."

"I'd like to speak to the medical examiner personally," the wife said.

So now I'm reduced to handling this sort of thing by myself, she thought. And I'm not allowed to be scared. But she *was* scared, and she knew that her voice gave her away.

"It's about my husband," she said. Maybe the other woman would feel sorry for her.

"I'll see what can be done. Phone back at noon."

In the last few days she hadn't been thinking so much about her husband. She'd sensed his presence, or at least she'd managed to imagine that she had. His body seemed to her just to get in the way, and she was glad that she didn't know where it was. Safely stored in some box, maybe already in a coffin, covered by the silk shroud so that you couldn't see what they'd done to him. The time left until the funeral seemed very short. She had to order flowers, and hotel rooms for relatives and for his parents.

In truth, she no longer had any desire to know the cause of her husband's death. This medical examiner could go right ahead and investigate blood and skin, and maybe bones and organs. But he mustn't be allowed to unravel her husband's death.

Asthma! There's no disgrace in having something take your breath away. But that hadn't been the cause. She would have liked her husband to have had a number of different deaths—dramatic or wise, as the occasion demanded. Had he departed as a victim, or of his own free will? The world would miss him, like a spice.

She sat down at her kitchen table with a piece of paper and stared at the trees outside the window. She was trying to draw up a love catalogue for her husband: a scale showing the degrees of love and hate that the various people she'd met had felt for him. Of course, it's easier to love a man when he's dead; but in his case, one of the main feelings was bound to be disappointed curiosity.

"They were scared of you," she said, looking at her piece of paper, which was proving difficult to fill. "Because you were so malicious." But the boys had paid him back for that, time and again. They had plagued him with their unreliability and their impudent little faces. "Maybe that's what they were good for," she said. She didn't write any of the boys on her list, except for one, the last one; she couldn't leave him out. "Other men have friends, but not you," she said. "You had to have lovers, no one else would do: only people who loved you, only slaves."

She thought of Joseph Deutner, her husband's childhood friend. "He'll go on the list," she said. "He'll go at the top. He didn't want to see through you, even though he may have been quite capable of it. He just liked you, simply liked you, without any theatrical fanfares and spotlights."

As she sat in her neat apartment, chatting away with her husband, the image of his dead body crept in again and refused to leave. "It's all very well for Lisa Engström to talk about castaway garments," she said. "The reason we bury the dead is that we're ashamed at how the body gets—so repulsive. Why do you suppose it gets that way? Why can't it just dry up neatly and cleanly, like a beetle?" She thought of those Italian catacombs where the dried-out monks stood around in niches. That didn't appeal to her either.

On the tenth day, her husband was very different from the dead hero of nine days earlier. For the first time, she thought of him with a kind of impatience. Now and forever she'd go on avowing he was right, as you do with a spoiled child. He was bound to stay young for eternity. His faults and errors were free to crystalize.

"That's how he was," she would say of him in a year or two. "That's how he was."

She thought again how she'd be thirty in less than a month, and then sometime she'd be forty, and then more, and her husband would progressively turn into a lover, then a friend, and finally a son, even a grandson. She had no doubt that she was going to live to be old. She wanted to live to be old. But today the distance separating her from her husband and his intelligence, his beautiful face, hurt her like a foreshadowing of things to come.

She was supposed to have telephoned the medical examiner long ago, but she wasn't sure she could keep control of herself on the telephone. "There's no way to avoid it," she said. "Of course I could have one of the lawyer clique phone for me. But that would be cowardly."

"Yes, you can speak to him now," said the secretary. Then she heard the voice of the butcher. It sounded impatient.

"Mrs. . . ." he said hesitantly. "Mrs. . . . ah, yes, here it is. Actually, we never give out information over the telephone. Well, it all dragged out a bit, didn't it? Because of the holidays. There's nothing one can do about that. Well. There's not a lot I can tell you. The autopsy findings showed insufficient cause for a fatal outcome. Well. Death due to person or persons unknown is so improbable as to be virtually ruled out. Well. Rather unsatisfactory. But that's how it is."

For that you cut him up like a chicken, she thought. For that you opened up his chest and peered inside his head. For that you removed his last meal from his stomach and opened up his heart.

"Why is he dead then?" she asked.

"Well," the medical examiner said again. "That's how it is sometimes. Even science doesn't know everything with finality."

"Could I see him now?" She felt angry.

There was a long silence on the other end of the line. "That's not customary," the medical examiner said reluctantly. "But it has nothing to do with me. That's the business of the undertaker."

"What do you mean?"

"Well," the said. "The funeral director is in charge once the autopsy is completed."

But Mr. Sable had all but forbidden her to see her husband. That was several days ago, and no doubt time hadn't made him readier to understand her wish, much less grant it.

After her conversation with the medical examiner, she didn't phone her parents-in-law as she had planned. The fuzziness about his death made her feel sorrier for them than for anyone else. It might have helped them if some illness had been found, some airtight explanation that they could have reported to their friends and relations. "At least he didn't suffer," they could have said, if the butcher had found a cancer, an insidious clot. But this way it looked as if her husband had died of nothing. In fact he hadn't died at all. The autopsy findings showed insufficient cause for a fatal outcome.

To the wife, it seemed that the baffled report reflected a flame of resistance from her husband. They hadn't been able to wrest his secret from him: not with scalpels and chemicals, not with patience and painstaking exactness. This dead man was truly keeping mum. It wouldn't have reassured her if the medical examiner had wised her up. But this way, she could allow herself to go on daydreaming about his multifarious deaths, without any scientific explanations to get in the way.

All the same, she did have to concoct an explanation for other people, to stop the proliferation of tales about murder and suicide. So far they were allowing her to keep her widow's silence. But she was sure that soon the questions and stories would filter back to her. Then she'd have to supply an answer so ordinary that his death would become as commonplace as a traffic accident. She made up her mind to petition the medical examiner again, and was annoyed with herself for not having thought of it right away.

And barely half an hour later—in which time she'd transformed herself into a helpless young widow—the medical examiner was no longer reluctant. He was making an effort to help her achieve certainty. Vagueness was tormenting, she said. No need to tell *him* that, he said. He could develop insomnia over a case that hadn't been cleared up to the last detail.

Suddenly the wife had a vision of a cut-open body, its inner recesses lit up with little lamps dangling from cords like a string of Christmas tree lights. She made an effort to listen to the helpful butcher. But by now she was feeling queasy, and wishing that she hadn't called him back, because she wasn't asking him the questions that really bothered her.

"There was a cardiac insufficiency, to start with," he said. "No doubt caused in part by a certain degree of drug abuse. Well. Asthmatics are victims of their own fear of the attack. Death during an attack is extremely rare. . . ."

"So I could tell his parents that he died of a heart attack?" she asked, longing for an end to the conversation.

"Well," said the medical examiner. "That probably is the best thing for you to say. The layman isn't comprehensively informed about death anyhow."

She almost had a laughing fit; she'd never met anyone who seemed to know less about death than this medical examiner. But maybe she was wrong. Seen face to face, he might turn out to be a demon who knew it all: knew, for example, that nothing exists but the body. And she was terrified to find that out.

She didn't phone her parents-in-law after her second conversation with the medical examiner either. She would have felt she was lying. She had a desire to go shopping. Or to the hairdresser. In the mirror, her part showed a whitish border. She'd have liked it if grief had turned her hair gray; but in fact she'd started to go gray when she was only twenty, and she'd been dyeing her hair red ever since.

"I'm not going to the funeral with a gray hairline," she said to herself, or to him. "Nobody can ask that of me." She was looking forward to delivering her head into someone else's hands for a couple of hours, and to the scent of the dye and the warm breeze from the hair dryer. You don't have to think about anything, and you spend your time looking at pictures of kings and movie stars. She also relished the prospect of the sympathetic questions the hairdresser would ask her.

In the last few days she'd felt so much her husband's wife that their three years of separation were dwindling away to nothing. Even the big dramas, like the business with Tony, seemed less important, as if other people's lives had never been anything but an adjunct to the tragedy of which the two of them were the protagonists: supporting roles in a play with a cast of thousands.

Despite her eagerness to leave the apartment, do something for herself, show her face to the world, she hesitated to go out. Since Gloucester's death, her tie to the Group had been broken. That didn't make her happy, it didn't bring her a sense of relief. They had written her off—the new boss, and the woman who had called herself Gladys, and the disguised boy whose name she had forgotten. She was no longer valuable to them.

Maybe they'd even left, maybe they'd gone to another country, to their wild Arab cohorts. She never could imagine how anyone managed to get on with *them.*

"This training camp the Group's into, with the Arabs," her husband had said once, contemptuously. "What is it they think they're training them to do? You can learn to shoot just as well hunting up in the mountains, or in the armed forces. And they can't possibly be learning to think, what with all that heat and shouting."

She realized that today was Monday and the hairdresser's would be closed. She almost cried—with disappointment this time—because there was so little she could do to brighten up the days. She thought of the bag, gone now, and felt almost sorry that her only token of resistance no longer existed.

"Did *you* know what was in it?" He would never answer her.

So, no hairdresser. Instead, thoughts of what her life was going to be like without him, completely without him. But go he must. A dead husband plants too many lies in the world. The lies come creeping out of his corpse.

The telephone stayed mute. She left her apartment almost reluctantly, because for the first time she didn't know what she intended to do in town.

She could go to the radio station and ask for a new assignment. They wouldn't say no. Or she could ask the publisher to grant her an extension on her translation. They wouldn't say no either. But she'd lost all her independence in the days since her husband's death. Paradoxical as it seemed, she no longer needed work, success, approval.

"Widowhood fills up your life," she whispered. The black clothes, the watering can for the cemetery: she had many comforting lies. The alternative to widowhood? To spend the next thirty years doing an endless series of little reports on theater productions and art exhibits, living in a self-important world that was so innocuous that no one took it seriously. Maybe revolution is better after all, she thought.

She walked through the streets that noon, indifferent to her route but keeping to the smaller, poorer districts bordering the inner city, away from the noise. Here and there in the narrow front gardens sat old dogs that had managed to get through one more winter and were turning their whitish eyes toward the sun. The houses got smaller and the gardens bigger, the farther she walked.

It was a day of inaction. No one needed her, no tasks awaited her. There was time for everything. Outside the city, broad, tidy gardens stretched along the bank of a small river. She walked beside the fences, watching the garden owners begin their new year. Cries whirred like birds or insects between the gardens. There was a smell of peat and aged chrysanthemum leaves. The young woman in black pulled along a wake of glances and silence. Her husband would have hated all this. "Going for walks—my God, that's feebleminded!" But she felt he was keeping her company anyhow.

At the end of the gardens, a large white mobile food stand was parked in an open square along with some other vehicles. She had smelled it before it came into view. A brand-new van, it had a striped awning above the service counter. The blue lettering said MISTER'S.

She had visions of grilled hot dogs, paper plates piled with greasy potato salad, frosted cans of cola. She hadn't felt as hungry as this for ages, hungry for greasy, ordinary food, and lots of it. When she approached the van, the man who was putting a row of pale hot dogs on the grill in the semidarkness of the interior suddenly addressed her.

"You, Mrs. Lawyer? How'd you get here? I'm real sorry about your old man, but life is dangerous, huh?"

"Martina," the wife said after a moment. "Martina! What are you doing here?"

"Didn'tcha hear this is where I am?" the man asked suspiciously, and drew the apron strings tighter over his belly. "Did you really come here by accident? And she's wearing black too. Are you mourning so hard you want everybody to see it?"

"That's not fair," said the wife. "I doubt you have any idea what mourning is like. And it's none of your business what I'm wearing. Besides, you have every reason to mourn too. Nobody else will ever get you out of jail as fast as he did, you know that. Where'd you get hold of this outfit? Did you beg, borrow, or steal it?"

"You found out a long time ago that I'm not scared of the jug," the man said, while the hot dogs began slowly to sizzle and she struggled to contain her hunger. "Women's jail? For me that's paradise, honey!"

"Oh, come on, don't brag," the wife said sternly. Once again she was the lawyer's widow through and through. "The last time, you moaned and groaned until you were out again. You wore out social workers by the score."

"In more ways than one," said the man behind the counter of the food van, and laughed boisterously. "So you want to know about my Rolls-Royce, my snack Bugatti? You're not the only one who's had a bereavement. But unlike you, I got something out of the deal. Or did your old man put something away for a rainy day? Mr. Counsel for the Defense, the avenger of the disinherited! My old man kicked the bucket—my father, I mean. I inherited this outfit from him. Now I have a livelihood. Business is good here, and when it isn't, I move somewhere else. People always gotta eat. And I have a steady woman now. And the money for my operation."

"Are you really sure about it?" the wife asked shyly. "Once you've done it, it's for keeps. Just think of the old days."

"It's *because* I'm thinking of the old days," Martina said angrily. "That'll never happen to me again."

Years ago, the husband and wife would continually meet Martina in town: this woman you'd never dream of calling a woman. She'd been among the lawyer's steady clients. Assault, burglary—she proved to the whole world, furiously, methodically, repeatedly, that she wasn't a woman. She was the bridge between the sexes; the lawyer had said she was the wall between them. She was something else, a third gender. But it seemed that was hard for everyone to take. She treated women and girls more aggressively than any man did. The progressive types had put up with her loud attentions, half flattered, half embarrassed.

"You mustn't be afraid of your urges," people kept reassuring her. "It's absolutely normal; some people are like that."

"You and me," Martina had said to the lawyer once, in a drunken melancholy. "Yeah, you and me."

"You're out of your head," he'd replied. "What do you and I have in common? That's something altogether different, my dear."

Then the big woman went into a rage, a dangerous rage, in her leather suit bristling with knives and bicycle chains. "You better be careful," she'd said. "It don't pay to get me mad. I'll get even later."

But her husband had laughed. "I'm not scared of women," he'd said. And when she started to go for him, wheezing like an engine, he'd given her a brief and affectionate hug.

Then she'd disappeared for months. It was as if she'd never existed. Gaps in the fringe used to close fast and tight. A person was simply gone, and nobody asked a lot of questions. If somebody came back, no one showed a sign of pleasure, assuming they felt it. People said she'd gone to join the foreign legion, and everybody laughed. "That'll suit her to a T." Then followed months of silence.

One day she turned up in the city again, fatter and brawnier than before, wearing uniform-style clothes, and with a stab wound on her cheek. She looked like hell and was proud of it. She worked in the kitchen of a night café, lugging around wine crates and pig carcasses, half a carcass at a time, and got fatter and fatter.

One day, so the female comrades said later, Martina checked into the hospital, showed the astonished nurses her ID to prove she was a woman—but only this once, only this one last time, damn it!—and said that if she wasn't mistaken, she was about to give birth to a child within the next few minutes. They didn't believe her and thought she was drunk, which in fact she was. Groaning and swearing, she bore her child without further delay in the hospital corridor. She had to be put in a private room, because the sight of her would have shocked the young mothers out of their wits. Her child, a baby girl, was healthy.

Martina disappeared from the hospital two days later, only negligibly thinner than when she came in. She refused to release her daughter for adoption. The baby was sent to an orphanage and people set about trying to persuade the young mother to give up her child. "You're perfectly normal and everything's okay with your urges and all that," they told her. "But probably the child would be better off if she were cared for somewhere else. Why didn't you tell us about it a long time ago? Then something could have been done about it." Martina told them darkly to keep their mouths shut; this was her business.

A couple of months later, the lawyer had driven his client and his wife to the orphanage to see the child. Once again, the wife came face to face with the real world, at the run-down residence outside town. Attending all those discussion groups and conferences, she had formed a firm opinion about children raised in public institutions, and about the social decline, hopeless prospects, and early criminal tendencies that went along with them. She knew all there was to know on the subject. But she'd never actually laid eyes on a child, or an infant, in an institution, or had the chance to observe these early criminal tendencies from their inception. The child's mother, who bore not the slightest resemblance to a mother nor even tried to, had spent the past few months racking her brains about the right thing to do.

As the wife stood by the food van, sometimes ignoring and sometimes giving haughty replies to Martina's brutal questions about her husband's death, she was thinking that the child, Lucie, must be over three years old now.

"Don't say anything if they think she's yours," Martina had begged the wife that day the three of them had gone to the orphanage together. "It's always such a drag trying to get it through their heads that I'm the mother, not the father!"

Consequently, the chilly glances of the infant-care nurses were directed at the wife, who, apparently, had arrived with two fathers to inspect her abandoned child.

Forty or fifty narrow white cribs filled the ward. The blinds blocked out all but a trace of the sun that shone outside. A thin whining sound, an infinitely dismal sustained wail, seemed to emerge from every crib. Martina walked straight over to one of the cribs, seeming to know exactly which was the right one.

"That's her," she said with satisfaction.

"The mother's name?" the nurse had asked in a hostile tone.

"Abramiecz," snarled the mother. "Martina Abramiecz." She actually gave her own name.

"That's correct," the nurse answered in amazement. "This is baby Lucie Abramiecz."

In the bed lay a red-haired baby, laughing out loud, making happy, gurgling notes.

"She's such a cheerful baby." The nurse appeared embarrassed. "She doesn't cry at all. It's enough to make you think she enjoys life."

"It's enough to make you think she's cracked!" the baby's mother said tenderly.

The husband had been fascinated. "You can't leave her here, it's all regimented. And you can't take her with you," he added. The nurse was at a loss, even though she was used to complicated situations. "We have to find a solution," he concluded.

"A solution!" Martina had snarled as they turned to leave. "All you do is issue a formal memo, and you think everything's taken care of. But I have to think about it, Mr. Lawyer. I have to *do* something about it, and with me, that doesn't happen so fast."

"Why don't you put the children out in the sun?" the wife had asked. "The weather is so beautiful, it would do them good."

"Easy for you to talk," the nurse had answered with irritation. "Do you have any idea how much work that would be? We're understaffed; we already have enough to do to feed them and keep them all clean. We can't go shifting them back and forth on top of that."

"I knew it," the husband had murmured softly. "An authoritarian system of child rearing, concentrated on cleanliness—the worst thing you can do to a child."

"Shall I give her a whack?" asked the child's mother.

Then they vamoosed before they incited a greater scandal. The wife had gone on thinking about the laughing baby with the red curls for a long time.

"You don't know who the father was?" the wife had asked on their way home. "He must have been nice-looking."

"What's that supposed to mean? She doesn't take after me, huh? I haven't a clue. It was a rock group and I was soused. Otherwise I'd have killed them all. But she looks strong, doesn't she?"

"She won't stay that way," the husband had said very sternly, "if you don't make up your mind to be sensible."

"She's mine," Martina had answered. "Mine. For the first time in my life I have something that belongs to me. I'll be careful. You two don't have to worry."

They didn't see Martina again, and the husband and wife ceased to be weighed down by thoughts of little Lucie's inevitable criminal career. Other problems had grabbed their attention, and people kept discussing them until they knew exactly what was what. But the problems weren't solved, any more than the case of the red-haired baby.

"You're gobbling that food like a six-headed silkworm," Martina said to the wife, who felt nowhere near full yet. "You been off your feed for the last few days? You look better. Don't gobble it all back on. Have you had the funeral already?"

"Day after tomorrow," the wife mumbled, her mouth full. "It's taken this long because of the autopsy and the holidays."

She could let herself go around Martina. She could smear her face with potato salad and eat three hot dogs in a row. She felt completely free to do as she liked, even when gardeners wearing earth-stained trousers kept coming over for a bite.

She was glad to have met fat Martina again. She could have cried her eyes out in Martina's presence, or badmouthed her husband to her heart's content. Martina had seen the world and had no illusions about it. Her thoughts ground slowly but thoroughly, and once you had gained her affection, you'd never lose it. The way the left-wing set dispensed their interest to the chosen few and then dumped them again at the drop of a hat was completely foreign to her. She hadn't understood how people could compete for her weird, boisterous company for a couple of weeks, and then pretend not to be at home when she phoned, or move on to a different place when they saw her ungainly figure standing at the bar. Martina was very loyal. If other people weren't loyal too, she'd start to hate them. Her weapons were knives and bicycle chains. She put little trust in words.

"How come they're taking so long to bury him?" she asked the wife. "That's a dirty trick. He's already starting to stink."

"No," the wife whispered. "No."

"Things are as they are," Martina said, embarrassed. "You can't help thinking about it."

"It's not proper," the wife said. "Besides, I get the impression that nobody is thinking about it." She must try to distract the fat woman. That, of all things, was something she couldn't talk about, not with anyone, not even Martina. "I have the police on my neck because of the Red Army Faction stuff."

"Your old man, huh?" You could see her brain working, slowly but steadfastly. "There were dynamite women in the Group, but what have you got to do with them?"

"Nothing," said the wife. "It's because he's dead. They're turning to me now," she said proudly. "I know a thing or two, but I'm not saying anything."

"What could *you* possibly know?" asked the fat woman. "They're bound to have told you only the uninteresting stuff. You're much too middle-class. I don't mean that as a criticism," she added hastily. "That was always the good thing about you two. You anchored your old man, like holding down a balloon. When you two split up, he took off into the air. What are you doing now?"

She would have helped me with the bag and that whole shitty business, the wife thought. But she's too conspicuous. Then the wife looked at the man behind the counter and realized that she was mistaken. If you didn't know he was a woman, there was nothing that attracted your attention. Just a bear of a guy, like millions of others on the docks of Hamburg or Liverpool, in the market halls of Lyons or Frankfurt. There were men like that all over, with big bellies and thinning hair, with big red hands and fast-moving fists. It's only that they weren't women.

The wife stared into the sunny gardens and thought again of the World Plan. "We'd have had to have her in it too," she whispered. "Him and Tony, and Eli and Martina."

"What did you say?" asked Martina.

"Nothing," answered the wife. "I've just gotten into the habit of talking to myself."

"But there's nothing to say," the fat woman retorted suspiciously.

The wife pulled herself together. "What happened to your little girl?" she asked.

"What do you mean? We have her with us, my girlfriend and me. She's a good mother. And after my operation, everything'll be just like it is for everybody else. Your grub is on the house. Just come and see me again sometime."

And the wife walked back alongside the gardens, where the work was gaining momentum as the afternoon began.

Hardenberg was always at home when you needed him. You could count on that.

"He's not a junior lawyer," her husband had said once. "He's a welfare clinic. Strange that he's such a hard-line leftist. He's a lot more like a Salvation Army worker than a revolutionary."

"They're sticking to me like glue," the wife said to Hardenberg, while the raven Isolde once again rested its evil eye on her.

"I thought they would," Hardenberg said calmly. "Although I didn't dream it would happen so fast. On the one hand, they're bourgeois, and it wouldn't go down well in the press for them to plague a widow during her time of grief. But on the other hand, the Group and their entourage don't give anybody time off out of sympathy. On the contrary. Their German hearts only melt at news photos of bewildered parents standing by the corpses of their terrorist children."

"I'm not looking for a sympathy bonus," she said. "It's just that I was never involved in that whole business. And I don't want to start now, after it's all over. But you know how it is; once they've got their claws in you they never let you go. Whenever anything happens, the first thing they think of is whether maybe you're a suitable candidate to take the flak. You," she said to Hardenberg. "You didn't get into it either. You must have had your reasons too. Or is that my legacy now? Debts and a political hero. And I don't even know what heroic deeds he did!"

"That's very unjust of you," Hardenberg said to his mentor's widow. "You know perfectly well what deeds he performed. He was more intelligent than the others. He placed his work at their disposal, but he didn't sacrifice his mind to them—or his political views either. Picture it like this: There's a very long riverbank where we're stumbling around, searching for a shallow place to cross. Since '68 we've been like lemmings, pushing our way time and again to the same spot. This place is called Political Savvy, or Critical Consciousness—call it what you will. Everybody is swarming around there. 'There's the spot,' we think, 'from which we can reach that other country across the river, the new society.' Your husband was pretty much alone, at a different place along the bank. Can you really imagine how alone he was? He couldn't see much sense in the Armed Struggle in the big cities. But the state authorities kept supplying him with reasons why he had to help the Group. Each time they almost petered out in their invisible fortresses, the other side would do something that made you feel close to them again. Take this Gloucester business right now, for instance."

"Did you know him?" she asked eagerly.

"Barely," said Hardenberg. "I read the papers. But they executed him. That's an example of what I mean. Execute isn't too strong a word. He was a gentle person," said Hardenberg. "Completely unassuming. One of those early Christian types, who never laughed. You'd be surprised," he said, "how fast that attitude is going to become outdated. In ten years his type of chaste rebel will seem almost comic. The system will kill a lot more of them before it's through."

"Ugh!" said the wife.

"You don't like that remark?" asked Hardenberg.

"I don't know," said the wife. "The system: What is that, in down-to-earth terms? In Gloucester's case, the system was probably named Willi Meier and he'd had almost nothing to eat for breakfast."

"No," said Hardenberg. "You're just parroting your husband. That's not how he saw individualism. What I meant was that a lot of the Group are going to die. Above all, they'll die from not being understood. The robber captains and Robin Hoods at least managed to drum a little historical sensitivity into people, something that would live on in their memories: you know, good revolutionaries versus bad revolutionaries, and so on. But the Group will become dated faster than all the rest, because their goals run through your fingers like water. They haven't saved anybody, they haven't lit anybody's fire."

"That's not true," she said, annoyed. "They've lit your fire, and mine too."

"We'd already gotten a bit cool," Hardenberg said peaceably.

"But believe me, your husband will never be as dead as they will, very soon now."

"Are you sorry about that?" she asked awkwardly.

"Yes," said Hardenberg. "Later on, we won't even be able to plead that we went a bit wrong. On the contrary, we'll have to admit that they were right, and the rest of us, those of us who were close to them, weren't strict enough, weren't consistent. We'll just go on paddling our canoes, when all of today's hot news items are cold as ashes. But don't you get any crazy notions," Hardenberg said sternly. "Now that you're involved with them, you can't get out again, unless you denounce them. And even that wouldn't help you. Just think about all the pathetic canaries who sang to the cops, and now have to run away from both sides."

"How come you're saying that?" the wife asked angrily. "What gives you the right to warn me about singing? You're a fool if you think there's any possibility I'd sing. It means you don't know either him or me!"

"But I *don't* think it," Hardenberg replied amicably. "I just wanted to test you. And the way you reacted was very good. Take exactly that same tone with the cops: all dignity, and you don't know a thing, not a thing. Maybe they'll believe you. That's your only chance. Otherwise you've got a lifetime subscription to their worthy company.

"Look here," he continued kindly. "Try silence. Your husband had a terrific knack for that. He didn't feel he had to prove himself by chattering away like mad, like the others, who go around talking in clandestine tones until everybody ends up getting suspicious of them. Be like him. After all, you're free to do whatever you want. And if someone calls you a coward or says you're bourgeois, if they tell you you have a legacy to carry on, or that you have to submit to group discipline—that just doesn't concern you. You must do what you want to do. And make sure that no more than one person at most knows about anything you decide to do. Otherwise, just radiate dignity: the widow of the lawyer who died so young. You should be glad about that. It's a good role."

"It's not a role, you cynic," she said. But she knew that wasn't so.

"You know what I think about death," said Hardenberg. "It's something I don't forgive, in anyone."

Early in the evening of this the tenth day, many of the shopwindows were already lit. The wife felt sad that she had no reason to go to her husband's apartment. She knew it was her duty to clear out his apartment, and his office too. But that obligation seemed very distant. Besides, she sometimes mused that one day she would open the door of the apartment in the Elbestrasse and find herself standing in front of a big empty space. Someone could very well have removed everything without a trace since her last visit. She wouldn't even feel angry at the unknown thief.

Or all his things might simply die. One day the electric typewriter could refuse to work, the computer turn silent, the steel cabinets stop locking in their contents and stand in their corners with gaping mouths. Maybe it was happening now, very fast. The stacks of paper were crumbling, the stuffing was hanging out of the visitors' armchairs, and the colors were fading out of the pictures. That, too, would be a solution.

The two of them had seen such a thing happen, when they were still sharing their small apartment and used to walk into town together every day to save the bus fare, so that at night they would have enough money for wine and taxis. The occupant of a small house in their neighborhood had died. They both felt that this little house was something they'd been waiting for for years, quite independently of each other: a dream place where they could be kind to each other from then on. Her husband tried hard to contact the new owners. This proved difficult even for someone with his perseverance. The house was small and sleek, with light-gray exterior walls and a crazy arrangement of windows. The front garden was piled high with neglected roses that went on blooming until late into the fall. The heirs wanted money as fast as possible. The lot that the little house stood on was worth its weight in gold.

"Nothing can be done," her husband had said. "They'll let the house fall apart until they can get a building permit to erect something big and expensive in its place. Besides, it's too small to stage a sit-in there. It would be something just for the two of us."

Both had an unspoken feeling that if they could only move into the little house, everything would take a turn for the better. No more boys for him, maybe. Enough money. And the rosy glow of revolution on the far horizon, without blood and gloom, behind the wildly blooming hedge.

Not that they'd ever talked about it. It was just that each day they passed by, they paused longer in front of the desolate little house, attentively noting the marks of its death agony. First the windowpanes broke, quite obviously of their own accord, without any hostile party laying a hand on them. Then suddenly long strands of moss were running down the light-gray walls from the leaky rain gutter, even though there hadn't been rain. One day the fence keeled over. And early one morning, workmen arrived and chopped down the rosebushes. The husband and wife felt as if all this were happening to them personally. But they never talked about it. A house that was too small for a sit-in was unworthy of a second thought. On the morning when the hedge came down the wife had seen her husband crying and hadn't dared to comfort him.

That had been in the long summer before their separation. She never went past the little house again.

She made up her mind not to enter her husband's apartment before the funeral. She could phone Mrs. Sattler and ask her to let Koblenz into the cellar. The apartment had to be given the opportunity to destroy itself.

She didn't feel like going home to her place either. "The cats are hungry," she said. "But they're fat enough, they can wait. I have a perfect right to a day without goals."

The city never got dark; it was simply that its brightness changed. Tired neighborhoods and wide-awake neighborhoods took turns spelling each other. The places that her husband used to visit often at night all lay in the tired neighborhoods. Tiny doors, 25-watt light bulbs, and windows boarded up with plywood. "We don't want anyone here!" the entrances said. But they were bound to open for the widow of one of their own. She knew only a few of these bars, only the nice, fairly temperate ones, with jukeboxes that played Marlene Dietrich, and friendly bartenders.

But the wife knew that there were places besides these nice bars, where he didn't take her along. Nor had she ever asked him to.

"You have no idea," her husband had said.

In an alley near the courthouse—all the worlds he loved are close together, she thought again, and they all have something in common—there were three or four of these barricaded holes-in-the-wall. At the first two, a genderless eye appeared at a peephole and refused to answer her questions, much less let her come in. For all she knew, it could have been exactly the same eye that stared at her from both doors, gave her a look of disapproval, and closed the peephole without a word of comment. There was no eye at the third bar. Someone let her in, and at first she could make out nothing in the reddish darkness.

"I know who you are," said a voice. "Do you think this is a good place for you to come?"

"But I don't know who *you* are," she answered aggressively. "And I'm not here to find out if it's a good place for me to come. I want to know if it was good for *him.*"

"It's not good for any of us," the invisible voice said cheerfully. "But I'll let you in anyway."

Metal nails glittered in the darkness. Heavy figures leaned motionless along the bar. The wife still couldn't distinguish any faces, only sections of skin, flat breasts above laced corsets, bare arms. A film was running in the background darkness. At first she couldn't make out much of what was in it.

It was very quiet in this joint, except for someone asking for a beer now and then. They all stood there like monuments, and the wife was glad that she was wearing black and so maybe didn't stand out too much.

"What do you want to drink, poor little mouse?" The voice came from an aging, exhausted-looking man in a blue evening gown that was too tight across his old man's paunch. Dead hair fell down to his shoulders.

"Whiskey," she said.

"Your old man didn't drink much. By the way, my name is Erika. He smoked a lot, but then that's not what killed him, is it?"

"I don't think so," she said. Slowly the heads of the leather statues were turning toward her.

"That's the Contessa's widow," Erika said.

The wife thought of Martina, and wished she were with her.

"You could've knocked me over with a feather," one guy said, and made a soft creaking sound as he moved. "I read it in the papers. The thing was, with him you knew the name. Usually it's best if nobody here knows your name; if something happens to you, nobody even knows it's you. But with him it was different. Besides, he didn't really belong here."

The speaker was no longer very young, maybe in his early thirties. Light-blond shoulder-length hair hung down over near-sighted eyes. A dragon sprawled across his left arm.

Everyone here was very friendly to her, and the wife wondered why.

Now she saw more clearly what the black-and-white bodies on the film screen were doing together. No one but her seemed to be paying any attention to the soundless blows, the dislocated limbs, and the horribly close-up body openings.

"What's a person supposed to make of you guys?" she said to the blond with the tattoo.

"Maybe that's not what we're here for," he said. "You didn't try to figure out how come your husband was queer, did you?"

"What gives you the right to ask me that? Why do you even want to know?"

The blond didn't apologize. He gazed over the wife's head toward the entrance, where three or four very young men were pushing their way in. The little rats, thought the widow. So there they are. Her neighbor was silent and had forgotten what she had asked him.

"Don't notice them," said the bartender, the one in the evening gown. "When the grand entrance is over, they'll all calm down again. I wish I knew what you're looking for here."

She didn't feel like replying. In the past ten days she had looked everywhere for her husband: in the courtrooms and in the political arena, in the underground and at the medical examiner's office. She had searched for him among all species and genders, and hadn't found him.

"So far, I haven't looked for him on my own ground," she finally said to the barman.

He placed his bare lower arms on the counter, and as he spoke, he too looked toward the door.

"I always had the feeling with him that he didn't know whether he really wanted to be here or not. But he did so love to dress up!" He spoke as tenderly as a grandmother talking about her grandson's Halloween costume. "Sometimes he was the lawyer and sometimes he was the tough guy and sometimes the prude. He was everything at once, you know, and that's not the usual thing with us. He didn't take anything seriously."

"He took the boy seriously . . . and me," said the wife.

"The boy? Sometimes he used to mention you, but not that he had anything solid going. . . . He never brought the boy along."

"And me? And me?" she asked, with a child's anger. "He never brought me along either. And I *was* something solid."

"Funny," Erika said, looking at her. "He always described you as incredibly grown up. I never believed him."

Now the headless bodies on the screen were bending down and thrusting at each other with vicious-looking phalluses.

"I was pretty much in the dark about all this," the wife said.

"The worst thing is that one never has time," the tattooed blond said, laughing. "There you are in the bar, waiting for *him*

—but you haven't got any patience. He could be in the sauna, or in the next toilet. And just when you think, 'Yes, he's the one,' then right away you start doubting, and wondering if someone else isn't better. Do you understand? Every night. I'm a chauffeur," the blond said. "I haven't slept longer than three hours for years. You can't keep that up without getting high on coke. But I'm not sorry I don't sleep. You're out of the running soon enough anyway, without sleeping your time away. Just get a look at her"—and he pointed his chin at the barkeeper. "Have you any idea how fast it all goes? Your old man was lucky, in a way. Not many guys manage to go at just the right time."

The others were talking inaudibly without altering their poses at the bar, while their glances were drawn again and again to the front door, as if they were being pulled along on cords. But the door opened only rarely; and it seemed to the wife that the ones who came in were never the ones who were being waited for, but only more waiters.

"You don't understand anything about this, little mouse," said the bartender. "Why are you here, really? It must be awful for you."

She said nothing, but felt ridiculous, and kept glancing back again and again to the ghastly film, in which they had now begun tying each other down.

Slowly the bar emptied. She noticed more and more figures gliding out of the darkness, paying their bills, and turning to go without looking at her.

It wasn't all that late yet. She remembered—her husband had told her—about a relentless circular motion, a nonstop rotation from bar to bar, that went on in the city at night. Like moths following a particular fragrance, they flew through the darkness, lighted for a time at certain spots, flew on, and then returned.

"Are they going on somewhere else now?" the wife asked Erika the bartender.

"No," he said. "It's not time for that yet. They've left because you're here."

"Are they that afraid of women?" she asked.

"It's not because you're a woman," Erika said, his eyes full of warmth and kindness beneath his damp wig. "Give me your hand. No, it's because they're superstitious. They believe you're bringing death with you. They don't want anything to do with death. Even without you here, they feel too close to him for comfort."

"But this isn't what killed him," the wife said helplessly, and cast a fleeting glance at the film screen.

"I don't know what he died of," Erika answered. "But it has something to do with this. We cross our fingers when we ride past a cemetery. It'd be hard to find people more superstitious than we are, and when somebody like you just walks in," he said in an almost laughing voice, "it'll take us a month to get over it."

Suddenly the wife saw her husband very clearly, standing in a rigid pose at the bar. His profile was half hidden, and nothing was visible but his sharp nose and the shadows of his lashes on the curves of his cheeks. He was standing there as if he didn't see her, and observing the door with short, rapid movements of his eagle's head. She could see his white hands distinctly, lying side by side on the bar. There wasn't any glass in front of him.

"But he wasn't there before," she whispered.

"Who?" the bartender asked, and smoothed his blue gown over his chest. "I don't know who you mean."

The wife couldn't hold her head still. On the screen, the headless bodies were vibrating in a white rain of sperm.

Day Eleven

The relatives should have arrived the day before the funeral. But no one came.

In the morning, when she phoned to find out what she needed to do for them, she learned that most of them were setting out on their journey to Frankfurt very early the next morning, from their homes in Bavaria and Franconia, the Rhineland and Westphalia. They would get to the cemetery on time, they assured her. No one planned to stay over. It would be better like that, they said. Hotels in the city were very expensive and noisy, they knew. They all intended to come. None of them intended to stay.

The wife knew none of his relatives. Only a few names had flitted past her from time to time—mostly first names. You know, Clara's daughter—yes, that one—no, not her; the one who's married to the animal doctor, the one whose son passed his exams with top grades.

She would have loved to have a horde of relatives today—familiar, mostly elderly folk to whom she could have fled for comfort.

She hadn't been able to sleep the night before, and instead of the bustle she'd feared would greet her today, nothing but stillness surrounded her. No one wanted anything of her; the flowers had been ordered, the hotel reservations canceled. Everything was silent. The cats were asleep, the boy didn't get in touch with her. The whole city, seemingly, had decided to spare her.

Very early in the morning, when it was still dark and the garden was locked in by fog, she had phoned Mr. Sable and asked if everything was all right.

"Naturally," Mr. Sable said. "You know I've been supervising everything personally. Many relatives have these fears," he said cheerfully.

"What fears?" the wife asked suspiciously. "I haven't said anything yet."

"They all think that the body in the coffin isn't their loved one, that someone else has gotten in by mistake," Mr. Sable replied. "That's an age-old concern. It's even worse with cremations. Rumors about"—he hesitated—"about irregularities are very persistent. I always favor being open with the bereaved. No, everything's just fine."

"Then let me see him," the wife said, crying. "It's been so long, and he's still around. But I don't know where, or what shape he's in. Please be brave enough . . ."

That was a slip of the tongue: She'd meant to say, Please be good enough . . .

There was a long pause from Mr. Sable, and the wife, wearing her bathrobe, warmed her hand on her teacup and looked into the spring fog that hid everything and didn't let a trace of the season show through.

"Naturally you can see your husband," Mr. Sable said in a controlled voice. "But you yourself remarked that it's been a long time. You're young. It'll stay with you a long while. Please understand what I'm saying," Sable said. "He's not disfigured. But there's no doubt that he's changed. Very changed."

"I'll come to see you this afternoon," said the wife.

"You'll have to come to the cemetery," Mr. Sable said, still controlling his voice.

"It's going to stay with me a long time no matter what, Mr. Sable," she said, "whether I see him or not. Either choice would be right, and either one would be wrong too. There isn't any right thing anymore. Please excuse my disturbing you."

"That's what I'm here for," Mr. Sable said. "Five o'clock at the main gate. I'll wait for you outside."

"It's perverse!" she said to the cats, who were yawning and staring out at the fog. "*He* spends all day getting to know dead people."

And she pictured the silky Mr. Sable wearing his dark suit. Do you suppose he ever laughs? And does he love someone? He must get the same treatment as does an executioner when people ask him what he does for a living. He scares them. Maybe he likes that. There's no such thing as a little boy who says he wants to grow up and become an undertaker. Maybe he inherited the job. I wonder if he buries his own relatives too? Or does he cremate them? "At least it's steady work," the wife said to the cats. People always have to eat, Martina had said at her food stand. "People always have to die too," the wife added.

Before they got married, during that summer when they had looked exactly like any other couple, the husband had given the wife a little tour of his childhood. The two of them had driven together to the medieval Bavarian town of Wolframs-Eschenbach, where they drank blackberry wine at a castle.

As a child, he had liked meadows and trees—the damp meadows along the banks of the Pegnitz River, and the trees in the sandy forest southeast of Nuremberg. He'd told her that there used to be mushrooms there.

In the photo album, she saw a crookedly smiling child in a knitted Tyrolean outfit. "See, you *do* like me," the little boy seemed to be saying. "How awful if you didn't like me. It's for you that I'm showing my teeth, it's for you that I'm putting my hands astride my hips just like a real little man."

"Were you a happy child?" she had asked.

"Fairly happy," her husband had replied. "Just like you, I expect."

Her mother-in-law had said that he used to play with the farm children just as if they were his equals. At that same moment, she thought, some farmer might have been telling his summertime guests in Franconian dialect that when he was young he had played with the refugee children as if they were his equals.

"I think there wasn't much to eat," her husband had said while they were drinking blackberry wine and gazing down the dark mountain from the castle top.

The wife had never tasted anything like this blackberry wine, never seen such a color. It completely filled up your mouth with sweetness, leaving behind it a feeling of faintness and the desire to go on drinking. The wine was almost violet. "We make it ourselves," the waitress had said proudly. You had to stay seated after drinking that wine.

Yes, there hadn't been much to eat. Into the late autumn the refugee women had to cook out on the open farmland, wrapped up in woolen blankets, wearing gray knitted scarves on their heads, while heat drifted outdoors like smoke from the farming kitchens. The farmers never let them in. Meanwhile the small children pushed their way through the air vents of the storage cellars to steal a couple of mealy winter apples, or two potatoes. Mothers must have found it hard to bring up their children properly in those days.

"Did you use to swipe things too?" the wife had asked.

"No, never. They all stole; a lot of them were a lot better at it than any adult. I expect children make really super criminals. But I never used to do what the others did. Too bad. I used to tell on them whenever I saw them do it. I don't know if my mother stole. But there was no other way to survive."

"You used to fink on the others?" the wife had asked incredulously.

"Always," he'd replied, laughing. "You see, it was a question of the truth. Once they didn't believe something I'd said. I don't even remember anymore what it was all about. I felt as if I were going to die of fury, simply explode. I wanted to murder somebody. I really did want to, you know. I looked around the toolshed to find things you could kill someone with. That's when it struck me that you can kill a person with almost anything."

That evening in the castle, they sat there just the way a normal couple sits, side by side, shoulder to shoulder, their heads turned toward each other, their mouths dark with blackberry wine.

He no longer remembered anything about Silesia. All he knew was the name of a country invoked time and time again, which over the years had expanded into a whole continent full of beauty and wide-ranging spaces. But lost, lost. Bytom and Katowice.

Once, after the two of them were married, the wife had gone alone to Silesia on a work assignment. In the winter, they told her, the snow was black with coal dust. Today, her husband's last day above the earth, she thought about the childhood he really ought to have spent there: a Polish childhood.

"So you're going to try and teach me about the Poles!" her mother-in-law had said. "What do *you* know? We'll never be able to forget what they did!"

"They'll never be able to forget what you Germans did, either," said the husband. It was an old quarrel that kept being resurrected —a mother-son quarrel in which no one else could ever take part. A great mystery from which wives were excluded.

"I was born in Bytom," her husband used to say.

"Bytom! He must be out of his mind! Contrariness, always contrariness! I thought *you* would get him over that habit," his mother said to her daughter-in-law.

And yet he really ought to have had a Polish childhood. Then he wouldn't have had to spend day after day in the dust of the museum when he was sixteen, tracking down Polish ancestors, the skeletons of heroes. To his misfortune, he looked like a Polish folk hero. But he had never again laid eyes on Poland, and when his wife returned from her business trip, he didn't want to hear a word about it.

His Poland hadn't been located in this world. Maybe now he was there at last. He could have grown up in the ocher-yellow cities, in the dusty streets and marketplaces that smelled of horses and vinegar. Or in one of the villages where they painted the houses sky blue. Then that childhood photo of him would never have existed.

He had never known his true country, the country of everlasting rebellion, where the Madonnas carried Molotov cocktails under their star-studded mantles.

The wife had known nothing about all this, back when she married him. She'd been embarrassed by his little altars to the Virgin. She hadn't detected the rebellion and looked away when he prayed. How alone he must have been.

In the wife's family, all religions had cohabited in a harmonious hodgepodge, and she practiced what people call tolerance, meaning that you believe nothing at all and try not to think about death any more than you absolutely have to.

"And now, and now?" the wife asked. But whom could she ask? No one had recognized his piety—the piety he later tried to conceal—for what it was: rebellion. Heaven justified revolt: The damned of the earth had to be unmasked and saved.

The wife wondered how he would have turned out if he'd lived a rebel's childhood in Poland, and then maybe met her when she went on her trip there. What futile speculation! She probably wouldn't have fallen in love with him.

She wondered where he had got his height from. Neither of her parents-in-law was tall. But ceilings had started racing to meet him almost from the start.

"The whole place is too small for me, too small!" he'd said to her, the first time she visited his home. "I keep bumping into everything. I have to duck every time I go through a doorway."

"Well, go ahead and duck," his mother had said. "And don't you intend to help your father?" The son gazed impassively at the heavy bundles that his father unloaded from the car when he came home each Friday evening.

"He has to do it alone anyhow, when I'm not here," the son had said.

At night, the oil stoves crackled in the chilly rooms.

"I'm not at home anywhere," her husband had said. "I can't remember my real home."

In Poland, the wife had seen the yellow, peeling palaces named after former owners who'd left no other memento. That's the kind of revolutionary her husband wanted to be: the kind they named a palace after. The only picture that hung in his tiny room in the student dorm was a self-portrait in green and violet, and a coat of arms he'd painted, claiming it belonged to his family.

Everything was too small for him. The attic apartment the two of them had shared had been much too small. The first and only place where he had had enough room—enough room for his day and his night sides—had been the place where he died.

"At school, I spent all my time with Joseph, no one else," he had told her once. "The others were buffoons. They didn't interest me."

Photos from that time showed a round-faced boy whose blond hair had already turned dark, with high cheekbones and tightly compressed lips. Not local stock: You could see that at a glance.

"Did the farmers use to make you feel ashamed, when you were a kid?" she had asked him. She remembered, from her own post-war childhood, the urgent entreaties of her mother, offering precious objects in exchange for food.

"I can't remember," had been her husband's reply. "I don't remember a thing about those days, except that I had trouble learning to swim."

The wife thought of the glittering Pegnitz, the unknown river.

"It should have been the Vistula; then you'd have known how to swim without being taught," she said.

She had never asked him if he was afraid of death. When the student Benno Ohnesorg was shot dead by the police in Berlin in 1967, her husband was still a member of his fraternity. He attended the demonstration against the murder—a sweet-tempered stroll with a few hundred participants—wearing a fancy cutaway coat.

"You can't belong to that fraternity and at the same time go demonstrating with the Socialist German Students Union," the wife had said. "That's crazy!"

"So what?" the husband had retorted. "So what if it is crazy? I'm against this murder. It gets to me that the same old Nazis are still running everything behind the scenes. That's no reason why I can't belong to a Catholic choir organization!"

"You're off your rocker," she'd said. "A choir organization! Nobody in the world sings as off-key as you do. You guys don't sing at all, you just booze, and one day you'll hand each other a bunch of cushy jobs!"

"You're just wall-to-wall prejudices!" her husband said. "Just like the tabloids. I've always wanted to be with a group. In the old days, it was the fraternity. I liked it, there were some bright guys in it, and I loved the house and the atmosphere."

"What do you mean, talking about the same old Nazis?" she had yelled. "*They* are the same old Nazis!"

"Fraternities were forbidden in the Third Reich," her husband answered. "And now I'm joining the Socialist German Students Union. Let's see what happens."

So he joined up, and for eight weeks he succeeded in staying a member of both organizations. Then the fraternity threw him out.

The wife hunted through the pile of condolence cards for one with an odd flourish under the signature. That would be his fraternity brothers. They had learned with sorrow of his passing, she read. I'll bet they weren't surprised though, she thought.

Outside, the fog had disappeared almost completely. I just hope it's gone for good, she thought. Otherwise we won't be able to see who's there at the funeral tomorrow. "And they won't be able to see your coffin," she said aloud. "That would be weird; it would just suit you: a funeral where no one can see the coffin. A phantom event. Everybody all by his lonesome."

She opened the garden door so that the cold would wake her up.

Her husband had kept himself hidden from her, had allowed her few glimpses of his childhood. She had been curious when his mother used to talk about him. But she didn't recognize her husband in her mother-in-law's well-behaved, sensible little boy, who was no more than a house-trained pet.

"I used to serve as an altar boy," he'd told her once.

"So you'd get to wear skirts?" she'd asked him maliciously.

"You see?" he'd replied quietly. "There's no point. You always want to hear something about trees and fishing in the river, and I suppose something about older girl cousins in white dresses. You can read Proust for that. My childhood isn't at your disposal."

The wife stood in the cold of her garden, thinking that he might still be alive if she had been able to talk with him about all the things she knew about him now.

The telephone startled her. Somebody indifferent to her need today for rest and tender loving care.

A voice that she didn't recognize at first apologized for disturbing her, but they were pressed for time; no doubt she could understand why. Did she really intend to continue following the advice of the attorney she had consulted at the time of her first police interrogation? Surely that wouldn't be smart. Of course she was only upholding her rights, but on the other hand, she must be interested in seeing their investigations move forward.

"Why should I be interested?" she asked. "What's the next thing on the agenda?"

As she stood at the telephone, she could feel the receiver getting damp in her hand. It never failed: When you've used your head to get over being afraid, your body always steps in and messes up your plans. Her knees were trembling; she could tell by the way her black skirt was moving.

"You'll be summoned to testify by the federal attorney's office," said the officer at the other end of the line.

She couldn't picture which of the officers it could be, of the ones who'd been in her apartment. Right now, her session with the police seemed very far away, like everything else, because time was no longer contracting but expanding.

"Then I'll just be summoned; there's nothing I can do about it," she said.

"We also have to inspect your husband's office," the officer said.

"Surely you've already had a good look at it," she replied.

"That wasn't us," the voice said, unperturbed. "Will you please get ready to show us around?"

The wife was silent. "Tomorrow is my husband's funeral," she said finally. "Do you really think it's necessary to pester me on a day like this?"

"That's not exactly the correct interpretation," the voice on the telephone said sternly. "We're concerned with certain plans of your"—he hesitated—"of certain people you know. It's important to prevent the execution of these plans. We have reason to believe that your husband was at least in on the secret."

"He's dead," the wife screamed. "Dead, dead! Oh, yes, he just coughed you up this time, didn't he? He really got away with something!"

She felt startled by her words. It was true, he really did use to cough, sometimes for half an hour at a time, agonizingly, his eyes wide with fear. When the two of them were still living together, she would often run out to the drugstore at night to get some Alka-Seltzer, fix it for him at home in a hurry, and give it to him with all the soothing words she could think of. She never told him that it was only a harmless patent medicine. The mere ritual of preparing the drink seemed to quiet his tormented bronchi.

"Please don't get hysterical," said the voice on the telephone. "We're only doing our duty."

"Then for heaven's sake come and get the keys," said the wife. "You can take one of my lawyers along to supervise. I'm not going to take one step out of doors today. Get a medical excuse for me if you need to. There's not a doctor in the world who'd refuse me one."

The officer turned polite, as if he'd got what he was after.

"My attorney will let you know within the next half hour," she said coldly. "Then he'll meet you at my dead husband's office."

I've learned a lot in the last few days, she thought with satisfaction, as she dialed the Kirghiz's number, and then Paul the Great's. Let *them* act as guardians. She'd done her part. But only she and the plant kidnapper knew that. She could safely abandon the evacuated fort to the enemy.

Both of her friends agreed to her request at once. Hilde the Kirghiz offered tender, maternal clucks of indignation. "The pigs!" she said. "They'll stop at nothing."

"I'm not going to his place again until it's all over," the wife said to Paul. "I'll handle everything by phone—selling the furniture, renting the apartment—no matter how much it costs me. I won't go there again, except just once, after it's all over."

"I understand perfectly," Paul said. "But that won't do you any good. You can't just make stuff vanish. They won't let you."

If you only knew, the wife thought.

"Is there anything special I should look out for?" Paul the Great asked. Hilde had asked the same question. As if the wife weren't smart enough to look out for the special things herself.

She regretted that Mr. Sable had agreed to let her see the dead man. She was scared to see him, more than she was of the police. She was beginning to shun the dead man's questions.

When he was eighteen, he'd taken a trip to Spain, equipped with a silk-bound Vatican press card. It had been hot in Barcelona, and her husband, still a boy then, had roamed the city's parks, inhaling the dense car fumes and the fragrance of unfamiliar trees. He had told his wife about it when he was drunk.

The little sins were no longer any use to him, he said; only an erotic encounter could bring him release. Someone had accosted him in the park at night. The eighteen-year-old recognized a religious habit. It was a young priest; that relieved him of the need for confession. Afterward he was very disillusioned, her husband said falteringly. But he wasn't able to leave that path. Not ever again.

"But that's a classic seduction," his wife had said. "A textbook case. You were sexually inhibited, and you were an easy mark."

"What a dope you are," her husband had replied. "You just don't *want* to understand. It was a tremendous release for me. I didn't feel guilty for a moment. The priest was more inhibited than I was. Besides, I always did want to know everything. You women, later on—that was almost too simple for me, not dramatic enough."

"Who can be dramatic all day, with bank statements and a busted washing machine?" the wife had answered awkwardly.

"But that's what I want," her husband had retorted. "I can't help it. If it isn't grand, it isn't alive. I can't change how I feel."

At around the same time that her eighteen-year-old husband was in Barcelona, an aging minister had explained to his daughter that man was full of sin and that only justice and the fight for justice could redeem him. The daughter was a thin, nervous girl. She reproached a newspaper publisher for failing to evacuate a building in time after receiving a bomb threat. The publisher was to blame for the people's getting hurt, not the bombs. At that moment, the daughter of the old minister perceived that the path of justice was littered with stones.

The wife had met the girl, Gudrun, once, when she was already on the Wanted list. They had chatted about clothes and laughed a lot in the empty room where they met. After that, the parson's daughter had looked as if she would never forgive them for that afternoon.

A childhood with lots of brothers and sisters, and always in the presence of God. Maybe, quite young, Gudrun Ensslin had had the thought that God, in his unfathomable slowness, needed a helping hand with saving the world.

Or take Hardenberg. Born 1936. After the war ended, after the currency reform, he, who had kept his mother and little sister afloat, was expected to revert to childhood. He soon saw that that wouldn't work. Leaning over his wooden train set, he dreamed of the bridges from which they used to leap down to steal from the coal trains passing underneath. His nights in the potato fields and the fruit trees, his meetings with black marketeers who bartered cigarettes in exchange for bicycle tires—things of the past.

In church, the minister said that it was wrong to steal. Little Hardenberg decided to bide his time until the day when he could investigate this stealing business more thoroughly. Fifteen years later, he read in a book: To own property is theft. It was as simple as that. And every week he visited his parents. His father still planted potatoes every spring.

One day Hardenberg told his mother that he was a Communist. "I thought so," was all she said. "Just be sure you look out for yourself." And she never mentioned it again.

Hardenberg regarded his raven and worked at the formula that would explain man's unhappiness.

"If only I knew what book he came hopping out of," her husband had often said of his intern. "The tales of Hoffmann, do you suppose, or Edgar Allan Poe?"

Occasionally the two men had gone to a café together, eaten cake, and to all appearances been friends. Hardenberg understood and forgave. It was due to him that her husband had not been isolated by his colleagues when he concocted bizarre legal statements and weird defense pleas.

"He has legal imagination," Hardenberg used to declare, and would explain her husband's motives to other lawyers behind his back.

"So there's something to it," his colleagues would say then. "It's a bit peculiar, but it has a point."

Now, as she tried to reconstruct childhoods, the wife saw how many different origins they had all set out from, on their journey to the year 1968.

Martina's childhood began in 1951 and ended in 1960. She had been her parents' first child. By the time she was born, her father had made enough money not to mind that she was a girl. She turned into a box-shaped, sturdy child.

Her father had made his money in animal waste products. He was shrouded in the scent of bones and blood. His daughter was very like him. He used to take her along to the slaughterhouse and to the dealers' offices. She inspected everything attentively, without the slightest pity or disgust. Martina occasionally got into fights with other children, but no more than any other strong little girl would have done.

In 1960 her mother gave birth to a son. From the outset he was a frail child, but tenacious. His older sister loved him dearly, and soon after he was born she took her dolls down into the cellar and left them there. She couldn't understand that the changes in her life were related to the existence of her little brother. Her father had long ago given up hope of a son and heir. Now he felt compelled to turn his daughter into a proper girl, so as to leave room for his son when the time came.

It was hard going. Martina felt bored. Her life seemed less eventful than in the past. She overheard irritated discussions between her parents over her hairdo and what clothes they were going to buy her. She didn't understand any of it. Her brother continued to be sickly and needed her protection. Dresses didn't become her, and eventually she noticed that she wasn't pretty.

At the age of ten she began to resist. At fourteen, she would start her mother trembling whenever she came into the room. She looked like her mother, with her broad pelvis, her projecting hips, and ankles almost as thick as her calves.

After her confirmation, which she attended wearing a black velvet dress that caused suppressed laughter in the church, Martina started dressing like a boy. That roused counterresistance. Her parents made no progress with their ruminations on their daughter. Martina chose friends who rode mopeds and filched the candy out of train vending machines. In 1966 it was still unusual to see a girl in a motorcycle gang. It was to her advantage that she outweighed the strongest guy in the gang by more than twenty pounds, and that by now it was hard to recognize her sex.

Martina looked after her little brother with jealous affection. Many afternoons, she would drag him along through the alleys by All Saints' Gate. She was completely unaware that these streets were dark and dismal; she felt at home there. Occasionally the prostitutes standing in the area would send her on little errands

—to fetch a Chinese meal, to get cigarettes and schnapps from the American GIs, who frequented a bar at the upper end of the street.

Martina was sixteen and was no longer satisfied just with protecting her little brother. She felt strong, and ever since the boys in the gang had given her a knife, she wanted to have it on with strong adversaries. What with all these other obligations, school came off the loser. She left it without regret and immediately got a job as a butcher's apprentice. She didn't mind the work; she just felt that it took up too much of her time.

By now she was a little short of six feet tall, had got into the habit of talking in a very loud voice, and smoked, even though she hated the taste and the smell. The time had come for her to take an interest in love. When no one hit on the idea of falling in love with her, she got restless.

Her need to protect others grew along with her physical strength. She could carry half a pig carcass with ease. She didn't have to turn over any of her earnings to her parents, so she was soon able to buy a moped. Every few months she replaced it with a heavier machine.

She still spent a lot of time at All Saints' Gate, but she had stopped running errands for people. Instead she leaned on the bar along with the men, and suppressed every sign of her loathing for alcohol. If anyone teased her, saying she was only drinking cola, she'd knock him to the ground without further ado.

By that time—just on the threshold of her eighteenth birthday—her sexual affiliation was already unclear. She was still looking for someone to fall in love with, and found a dark-haired prostitute called Pauline Borghese. Now Martina needed money, and that never changed from then on.

It was due to that need that she had met the lawyer one year later. Martina was everything that a young left-wing lawyer could wish for—badly reared, exploited, exposed to cruelty at a tender age. But his new client coolly dodged all displays of solidarity.

"It's about a break-in. I'm in jail on remand. Come get me out," she said. "My old man'll pay."

The two worlds were still far apart, but the student movement was coming, to bring them together. Pauline Borghese, who had fleeced and mocked the young girl for a year and a half and only occasionally yielded to her caresses, was found murdered one day. Martina was interrogated without result.

The husband had counseled her indignantly. "Things are going to get to the point where one day they really will pin a prostitute's murder on you."

Martina laughed. By this time she had already served a couple of short sentences for various property offenses.

Somewhere the wife had a photo of Martina, laughing, standing on a tie beam in some meadow. The beam was bending under her weight. By then she'd already adopted an unvarying uniform consisting of a T-shirt, jeans, and a stiff motorcycle jacket that was too tight for her.

The wife had set down in front of her a large, empty notebook with sturdy pages. Onto the first page she glued the still incomplete list of those who had loved and hated him. Then she drew colored lines connecting some of the names to other names. She planned to paste into the notebook all the photos that had something to do with the dead man. She was still vague about the underlying system; but the book had to start with the childhood photo of her husband in the Tyrolean outfit.

Then it occurred to her that very likely the cops were in his office right that moment, touching all his things—maybe even photos she didn't know were there. She'd taken home the notebooks with her husband's poems in them, as well as one or two files; but no photos. She grew uneasy, forgot her quest for Martina's photo, and decided to phone his office.

It's a strange experience, telephoning a dead man's apartment. She hadn't yet got over the sneaking feeling that he might still answer the phone, as if a trace of him might have been left behind in some machine. It wasn't such an off-the-wall notion. His voice was sleeping on tapes there, his movements were caught in amateur films. Anyhow, she intended to save the photos.

Paul the Great answered the phone so fast that she felt he'd been waiting for her call.

"I thought you might have forgotten something," he said. "Everything here is humming along; you know how it is. The gentlemen aren't especially amused."

That was a sort of code phrase from their days of playing cops and robbers, when the two men would bamboozle the cops tailing them by going on boring, convoluted errands, and the cop cars had to wait around on deserted corners for hours. "The gentlemen aren't especially amused."

"You still have to give the Kirghiz your power of attorney," said

Paul. "She's prowling through his rooms like an offended guard dog."

"Save the photos!" the wife said.

"Which photos?" Paul asked, surprised.

"There must be some photos!" she said, sobbing. "There must be a bunch of photos somewhere. Some from a long time ago. I don't have any—that is, only a few. None of them looks like him. Please, save the photos!"

"Take it easy," said Paul, satisfied that she was at last behaving correctly and losing control. "Take it easy. Before I can save them, I have to find them. If they're here I'll find them, you can count on it. I'll bring them to you first thing."

"Not at five o'clock," the wife said. "I have something else to do then."

She continued leafing through her photographs, and pasted a chaotic selection into the scrapbook.

She knew nothing about Gloucester's childhood. She imagined him as fatherless. He had grown up in East Germany. Maybe he didn't even know how his father had died. His mother had learned fast the value of keeping still, and brought up her son to be unobtrusive. Gloucester read the Russian educational theorists and found out that revolution was an education. Who educated him?

At the start of the sixties, Gloucester had gone to West Berlin. He had probably met her husband earlier than she was aware, in Berlin, when her husband still belonged to his fraternity and Gloucester had landed himself in a Protestant student group whose avowed objectives made less sense to him than their rigorous morality.

Back then, the two men were thinking not about revolution but about education, and they were enraged by the impudent way their nation was still held in the grip of the old Nazis. They used to attend political trials in West Germany. In their student newspapers, they wrote concerned commentaries about certain tainted government ministers, and quoted witnesses from the concentration camps.

Where might her husband and Gloucester have met? The wife hadn't known the revolutionary well enough to be able to imagine a place, a situation, where these two dead men had lived side by side.

The solitary Gloucester began to study to be a teacher. He

wanted to find out, at long last, whether revolution really was a great education, and where one could get hold of suitable educators. His friends didn't understand the trouble he had laughing. Many women from the communes fell in love with him because they wanted to get behind the secret of his stillness and they believed he was capable of great passion.

The wife didn't know if Gloucester had deliberately sought out her husband's company. Later the far left noted with surprise and disapproval the way Gloucester had secured the help of a bird of ill fame like her husband before he went underground. There were whole firms of lawyers whose philosophical views would stand up to Marxist-Leninist scrutiny better than her husband's. An anarchist was, at best, good enough only for other anarchists, for the patients' collective, the Black Panthers, and the groups of former reform school inmates who now were burning their draft notices.

The wife began a collage of the faces of people who had surfaced in the couple's lives and then disappeared. She had set down the box of photos right next to her, and was cutting heads out of gray snapshots from the sixties, to create an entourage for her husband. She was making a book—the book of childhood—and she wanted to finish it in the few hours she had left.

How many different childhoods they had come out of; all of them approaching, like orbiting stars, a single point, where they then converged. Their childhoods hadn't been dream kingdoms. They had come from fine homes or from lower-middle-class obscurity; they had had anxious or megalomaniacal mothers; rich fathers or maybe no fathers at all—railroad conductors and generals, tradesmen and poets of the Thousand-Year Reich—and yet all of them, coming from far away, had met at this same point, a place of enchantment. There had been joy in the land for that brief spell in 1967, when all over the country they listened to the radio and heard how many they were and how, at least for that moment, the streets belonged to them.

She meant for the book to show them all, as well as it could. Hurriedly now, she cut out and glued in whatever she could find. She wanted to lay the scrapbook in her husband's coffin, and she hoped that she would be left alone with him long enough to do it. But some important pictures were missing—the ones of the boys.

"If I find one I'll put it in," she said. "But I won't spend a long time looking."

In the box she found two photos she hadn't thought of for ages. Eike, the best man at their wedding, looked like a ballerina with his long neck and his tragic expression as he gazed past the camera. He hadn't approved of their marriage, and had been as emotional as a grandmother at the wedding.

He, too, had disappeared, inside a profession that kept him from thinking because it ate him up. He'd become a doctor of socialized medicine in Berlin, and they hadn't heard from him in years. But now she included him in the book of friends that she was putting together so hastily, as if by her zeal she could prove something to the dead man. Eike had lived in a summer house that he kept as neat as a sewing box. While he was studying medicine, he'd been so poor that it had been easy for him to keep in trim. But there'd always been wine, and he'd always had time for them.

The second photo was of that friend of her husband's whose carefully planned trip to Florence had ended with a self-inflicted gunshot in a hotel. That trip had preyed on the minds of the couple for a long time. She glued the two images side by side, taking the cheerful little amateur photo of the friend who'd preceded her husband into death, and setting it into the big post-card photo of the friend who had vanished.

She jumped when the doorbell rang. She'd forgotten that people weren't going to leave her in peace forever. It was Paul. He was holding a package triumphantly.

"I talked them out of keeping it," he said proudly. "Not exactly a snap!"

The wife hid the scrapbook. She felt that Paul the Great might think her planned gesture was childish, or—what would be worse and also closer to the truth—belated.

Together they looked at the photos that had been in her husband's apartment. The first one that caught her notice was a large newspaper photo showing her husband, his secretary of those days, Paul the Great, and a man friend, together outside a house where they were staging a sit-in. They were all sitting on the ground outside the front door, holding banners that explained the purpose of the demonstration. The fighters' eyes were squinting against the sun, and Paul was wearing a battered straw hat and looked like a fish vendor from the street where they used to sell sardines in olive oil. His belly was cheerfully rotund under a bright-colored summer shirt. Her husband had a straw hat too. He held it in front of his chest as if he were waving a greeting. At that time—it must have been '73—he had had long hair, thick, streaming long hair. He was smiling into the camera. He'd left the spasmodic, approval-seeking smile of his childhood photo far behind him now; he was happy in the little revolution outside the door of No. 94 Schubertstrasse. They'd won their battle this time, and the people living in the house would be allowed to stay there, for the time being at least.

The wife couldn't stop looking at the laughing, radiant face of her husband.

"It really hits you in the gut, doesn't it?" Paul the Great said. His voice caught. "It was so rare that he was able to let himself go."

"Is that something you find it easy to do?" she asked maliciously.

Paul, too, figured among the childhoods. She had pasted his massive head, cut out of a news photo, into the scrapbook along with the rest.

"What were you like as a child, Paul?" she asked their comrade.

"Alone," he said after thinking it over. "We were very well off financially. My mother is a terrific woman. I was always on very good terms with her, but I don't think she found me especially interesting. For me, the political stuff only came along on account of art," said Paul. "You can't be as crazy for art as I am and be a right-winger. To begin with, I was always concerned about that kind of freedom; the political part didn't interest me at all. Until I noticed that you can't separate the two. But don't fool yourself: Your old man wasn't primarily interested in the political angle either, or in the liberation of the Amazonian Indians. For him, it was the erotic. It's incredible how together he was in that area. He didn't enjoy forbidden fruit; it made him angry. Most people didn't see that about him. The laws relating to sexual crimes always seemed to him like punishing an amputee for using an artificial limb. And it was by that route that he got to the Amazonian Indians and the Vietnam War."

The wife didn't answer. "I have to go to the cemetery," she said then. "Can you drive me?"

"Why are you going today?" Paul asked suspiciously. "Isn't tomorrow enough?"

"I still have something to talk over, to do with the flowers," said the wife, feeling sick with fear. "Koblenz is bringing trees, and I have an appointment with the funeral guy."

Paul the Great dropped the subject.

Dusk was just falling, and the freshly painted white portal of the cemetery glowed threateningly.

"It looks positively Wagnerian," said Paul. "Think it over. Whatever you have in mind, think it over."

She hadn't quite completed the book of friends, but she'd brought it with her, in a plastic bag.

The dark figure of Mr. Sable was waiting inside the portal.

The wife didn't say goodbye to their comrade. She walked slowly and reluctantly through the gate and stared for a long time at a panel that said "Cemetery Layout." Mr. Sable came toward her.

In a long low hall, the dead were waiting for the next day.

It would have comforted the wife if Gloucester had been here too. But his remains would no doubt be shipped back to East Germany.

Her husband was alone with the other dead. He was bound to be the youngest one there.

"You're looking unwell, if you don't mind my saying so," said Sable. "Think it over once more."

"No," said the wife.

They passed through several doors before arriving at a small room. There stood the light-brown coffin, slightly elevated, with the lid standing upright beside it like a guard.

The wife saw nothing except layers of white linen. Then she saw some hands. They weren't his. They were very dark. She saw a face too, but through a thick veil of tears. The tears caused it to move. No smile was visible, only an expression as of someone being inconvenienced.

"I'm sorry," she said.

She laid the scrapbook on his hands. It looked very ugly on the snow-white shroud. Mr. Sable had stayed in the background. She sensed his disapproval.

"We can go," said the wife, and didn't look back.

Mr. Sable took her elbow with the practiced grip one used for widows.

"This stranger has got to disappear," she said.

Why did I say something like that? she thought in horror.

But Mr. Sable seemed to agree and didn't ask her what she meant.

Day Twelve

It was a frightful day and it began very early. The wife had slept, but she woke up when it was still pitch dark, and she didn't know what to do with all the time she had left. Late yesterday evening, she had washed her hair and laid everything out ready in the bathroom. This included two pairs of black nylon hose. She knew that she was bound to get a run in one when she put them on.

The flowers had been ordered. The coffin was closed. The guests were invited. It was six o'clock in the morning. The cats had gone back to sleep after giving her a couple of amazed glances, and the wife looked out the window to see if it was going to rain. But there was no sign of storm, only gloom. Appropriate, she thought.

The time of the funeral was appropriate too. Eleven A.M. Her husband had hated to get up early. She turned on the radio, even though very likely that was not appropriate. She drank her tea much too hot, but it didn't warm her up. She set down a pair of dark glasses and a small pack of tissues on the hall table.

She and her husband often used to get home around this time, back in the old days: the time of their lives. She thought about their early-morning jaunts, their long excursions past the wall of the zoo, with the sun just rising above it, greeted by strange cries from the animals. Occasionally they had caught the first streetcar and had breakfast in a taxi café as if they were living in the Paris of fifty years ago. The taxi drivers had laughed to see her husband eating cream cakes—the sagging leftovers from yesterday—at five A.M. Back then, the couple had put their guilty consciences to use as a soft pillow, and slept on into the afternoon.

"We'll never make it to the top this way," her husband had said. "But then I like going downhill better than climbing to the top."

It won't end now, the wife thought, not even today. But that doesn't matter. Since yesterday, since I saw him, it doesn't matter anymore.

She had decided not to tell her parents-in-law about the final visit to her husband. After all, they'd been satisfied with the old saw that it's better to remember people as they were. And maybe a son goes on living if you've never seen him dead.

The wife didn't want to be the one to tell them: It's really true. I've seen it with my own eyes, it's true. She wasn't going to tell anyone about it.

"A person has to keep too many things to herself," she said to the sleeping cats, while she waited for the day to grow light at last. But it didn't grow light.

"No, it's not easy to keep your mouth shut. One day," she said, "something's gotta give. And when it does, I'm afraid I won't care who I blurt everything out to."

She was glad when the Kirghiz phoned.

"I won't bother you after the service," she said. "I just want you to know that I'm thinking about you. Let's hope it's all over fast."

The wife was grateful and embarrassed. Today she would get her share of sympathy. But she couldn't stop feeling that she wasn't playing fair with her husband. He couldn't do a thing to stop her from having feelings she wasn't entitled to. "Over your dead body," she said in her gloomy kitchen, and laughed.

She put on her clothes: black, black, black. "Those cat hairs!" she said reproachfully. "I don't dare sit down." But black makes you look intriguing.

Her face in the mirror looked like someone else's. "You phony widow," she said.

Her husband gave no sign of his presence today. She fought the urge to speak to him as she'd been doing over and over during the past few days. A dead man wouldn't take much interest in his own funeral.

"In India they feed you dead people to the birds," the wife said. "That way, they don't have to put up with any relatives and priests. In India, maybe they'd burn me along with you. But that's going too far."

Unequivocal customs like that had really appealed to her husband. No matter how crazy it was, he liked it, as long as it had grandeur.

"I guess you're not worrying much about grandeur anymore," said the wife. So she was talking to empty space again, as if she couldn't accept his absence, as if he had an obligation to listen to her.

"I'm coming back soon," she murmured, saying goodbye to the cats just as on any other day. But this time she felt that she was lying.

She walked out of the house feeling as if she were leaving for weeks. The door seemed to close behind her with finality, the garden gate gave a sad creak.

In the last few days, a lot of people had offered to pick her up in their cars and accompany her to the funeral. It wasn't out of coquetry that she had rejected their help, even though her wish to be alone fitted very well the image of the phony widow, the theatrical widow. It was just that the cemetery was a half-hour walk and she wanted no company.

In the florist's shop where she used to buy herself a bunch of flowers each week, they knew what she was there for. Artificial blooms lit by blue neon filled half the shop. The Americans liked to buy them.

"It's a tough road, all right," one of the two florists said in an emotional voice. "We have everything under control. Here are the roses you ordered. And would you like a small nosegay to carry?" Suddenly the wife detested the word "nosegay."

"Lilies of the valley," she said. "Those are beautiful lilies of the valley."

"Very suitable," said the florist. "I'll just tie them together for you."

"Actually, it's April," the wife said, "and they're May flowers."

"That doesn't matter," the florist said. "It just makes for an exclusive touch. They came from Holland. A lot of orders have come in for your good husband."

Suddenly the wife loved him, with his tuft of upswept hair and his red face, because he had said "your good husband," and acted as if everything were normal.

"It must look really beautiful," she said clumsily.

She had so much time to go yet that this conversation seemed like a rescue.

"Ah yes, how fast it can all go by!" The florist looked over at his black-bearded friend, whom the wife had never heard utter a word. "We work too much too. And you can't take it with you! Your last shirt's got no pockets, eh, Karli?"

But Karli gave no indication that he'd been listening.

"Don't bother to wrap the flowers," she said. "One doesn't know what to do with the paper."

She had a sensation in her stomach as if she were being wheeled slowly into an operating room.

She held the white flowers against her black coat, and walked like that along the noisy, dead-straight road, while the breeze from passing cars pulled her hair out behind her.

"There goes the poor young widow," she said softly, "dressed in black and carrying white flowers."

The cars roared along and she got dust between her teeth. It had never struck her before that this street connected her apartment with the cemetery like a vein. She didn't have to turn corners, hunt for streets, ask people for directions. The way was there, had always been there.

There were more attractive routes than this to the cemetery: quiet detours through residential areas and gardens. But there was no route shorter than this terrible long road where you rarely saw anybody on foot.

"Here is the truth," she heard her husband say suddenly. "This is reality. Don't go on to me about how beautiful the Taunus forests are. Trees are only important to people who haven't the brains to think of something better!" He had known every inch of the road where she was walking now, and had inhaled its dense fumes ecstatically.

"But your asthma!" she used to say.

"My asthma has nothing to do with fumes! It's not the gasoline, it's not my Camels! It's something else, but I'm not sure what."

Once they'd been in Asolo, in the second year of their marriage and in the first of their cars. They had run an experiment to see how long they could vacation on five hundred marks. Not long, it turned out—only a couple of days, because they were so drawn to Italy's beautiful old hotels.

"They suit us," her husband had said. "It's just that we can't afford them yet. But that day will come."

In an attic room in the town of Asolo, they had gone to look at the clothes and shoes, the photos and the yellowed theater programs of the actress Eleonora Duse. In a little box on the wall stood a number of oddly shaped tiny glass bottles.

"Her asthma!" the woman custodian had said in an emotional voice. "They were for the Signora's asthma. *Respirare, respirare!*"

The wife had seen her husband inhale deeply in the little room, as if he were experimenting to see if he could still breathe. He was dead set on stealing one of the little bottles of smelling salts.

"I'm positive she wouldn't have minded," he had said to his wife. "She looks as if she could understand." He appeared to feel that some special power resided in the actress's little bottles.

As she walked away, the wife wondered whether she oughtn't to have encouraged him to steal one. Maybe then he'd still be here! Black magic was helpful against illnesses like his.

She walked neither hesitantly nor especially fast. She walked like a person with a definite destination that she doesn't want to reach.

And what if I simply don't turn up? she thought. I could turn off the road right up ahead there, and go down into the subway. And then I could take some train or other at the station.

It struck her that she was having exactly the same thoughts she'd had many years ago when school report cards came out and she couldn't think why she should take the road home, where there would be nothing but trouble.

"Then you think that one day you'll be free," she said. "But that's a big mistake. I'm not any freer now than I was then."

She could see from a distance the gate of the cemetery, with small black figures crowding around it. But it was still too early. She walked more slowly.

There was another, smaller group—they, too, were still only tiny figures—who seemed not to be dressed in black.

"They're our people," she said. "I might have known. But nothing can be done about it now. And you're going to have your day, just as you might have imagined it."

At first no one paid any attention to the approaching woman. That gave her time to pick out friend and foe from behind her dark glasses. She distinguished four groups, whose mourning took very different forms.

First there was a dull-black group, where she saw her parents-in-law standing at the center. Those were his relatives, stranger to her than any of the others. Her husband had never introduced his relatives to her.

"Actually, you'd have preferred to have sprung into the world full-grown," she'd said to him.

What were they thinking, in their mourning clothes? Were they hostile to her? The wife was sure that they didn't like her. She was too close to the disaster, it was too tempting to pin the blame for her husband's misguided life and early death on her. These unfamiliar men and women had all known him when he was a child. It was to say goodbye to the child that they had come here today.

No one had seen her yet, no one was running over to embrace her.

A dozen heavy motorcycles stood in a neat row at the cemetery entrance, with a figure from the old days standing beside each machine. The bikers had come to say goodbye. It was easy to recognize Blutwurst and Mike and the rest, even though they'd got very fat in the years that she hadn't seen them. Their tattoos, grotesquely distorted by the fat, glittered along their forearms. This second group was shiny black, their enamel and leather gleaming with a gloomy festiveness.

The third group was brightly colored. At its center stood the boy, the only one of them dressed in black. His male and female friends milled around him like flowers, wearing Indian-style outfits, red and blue and white. Those are mourning clothes too, she thought.

By now she was getting the feeling that she had on a magic cloak of invisibility, because she'd come very close to all the groups, holding out her flowers like a sword, yet they still hadn't seen her.

In the fourth group, her husband's friends and colleagues stood assembled around Paul. Theirs was a dark, subdued group. They had good manners but they didn't want to exaggerate. In dark-blue, brown, and gray, they were paying their final respects to one of their own.

"They're carrying four different men to the grave," she whispered to the stubborn silence that was making this day so hard for her. "Which one are you?"

Then she saw two more groups of mourners who belonged to her husband, but who were keeping their distance from the rest and from each other. Far behind the last of the relatives, half hidden by waiting taxis and stationed so that she could climb into one anytime she chose, stood an unusually tall young woman wearing a black, very elegant velvet suit and carrying a bouquet of lilies of the valley in her left hand. The wife knew why she was keeping her other hand free.

They're still here, she thought. They, too, are proclaiming their rights to you.

On the other side of the cemetery gate stood two men in raincoats, who seemed to be studying a pot of pansies. They looked at it intently whenever they weren't scrutinizing the mourners.

"Now we're all assembled. All present and accounted for," said the wife, and she decided to drop her cloak of invisibility.

She greeted her parents-in-law, who hugged and kissed her, which they had never done before. The wife offered her hand to all the suspicious elderly ladies and the men she'd never met before. No one smiled. It's hard to turn a goodbye into a hello.

Only now did she notice plump little Joseph Deutner, her husband's old friend, wearing a tight dark-blue suit. She would have liked to hug him, but she realized that something inside her was starting to slip at the sight of him. That had to be stopped.

"So good of you to come," she said.

"But of course I did," Deutner said uncomprehendingly. "Obviously I would." But he wouldn't allow himself to be hugged.

"I have to go greet the others," the wife said to her mother-in-law. "I'll be right back."

"I brought him some tulips from our garden," her mother-in-law said, as if to detain her. "He was so fond of the garden."

The tulips, looking wearied by the long journey, finally broke her down. Moisture gathered under her dark glasses. That she didn't want; she had to conserve her tears. In the distance stood the tall, admonishing figure of the woman revolutionary.

"I'll come back right away," the wife repeated.

Her father-in-law pointed with his chin. "Did *they* have to be here?"

"I can't forbid anyone to come," the wife said. "There's nothing to be ashamed of. They're his clients, his friends."

"What right have they?" The old man was bitter.

"They were important to him," she said softly. "Maybe more important than we were."

"It's all too late," the father-in-law replied. "There's no point in talking about it anymore."

He looked at the strangers who had taken over his son, who had made him even more of a stranger than he had always been.

"What could those people have given him?" he asked.

The wife went over to Paul the Great and let him hug her. Paul was crying openly.

Only now did she see the flagstaffs with their rolled-up fabric, jutting out of the group of his friends.

It's a demonstration, she thought, and she couldn't help laughing. It was better to laugh than to cry. Let the last drama play itself out; there was nothing she could do to change it.

The bikers were standing meekly next to their machines, waiting. Monkeyhead, who had tears running down his cheeks, carefully unfurled a black and red forked banner.

But those who had come here to say goodbye were far outnumbered by the absent comrades who had already said their goodbyes. In faraway prisons, in tiled vaults of profound stillness, they surely knew who was going to his grave today: one who had joined their ranks only reluctantly and never managed to become a proper hero.

"Too bad," said a friend of her husband's. "Anarchists have no flowers."

"What do you mean?" she asked, surprised.

"Oh, well," the woman said, embarrassed. "The Social Democrats have red carnations as a symbol. Anarchists ought to have a special flower too."

"And what kind of flowers did you get?" the wife asked.

"Lilacs," said the friend. "Somehow I had the feeling that anarchism is lilac-colored."

No flowers. What nonsense, the wife thought, looking around at the tulips, lilacs, lilies of the valley, narcissi, red carnations, roses, and yet more red carnations. All the flowers you could ask for.

An attendant appeared above them on the stairs of the funeral chapel and called out her husband's name. No one moved.

"You come with us," said her mother-in-law, resolutely ignoring the whole alien tribe who had convened here.

"Yes, all right," said the wife. "But let me walk alone. I don't like walking arm in arm."

The attendant called out her husband's name again.

Mr. Sable wasn't to be seen, even though he must surely have been watching his production from some concealed spot.

The wife climbed the stairs, followed by the dense group of unknown relatives, who knew that they had pride of place. Estranged or not, theirs were older rights, after all. The school friend Joseph Deutner had disappeared.

Now I have them all at my back, the wife thought, and felt an unpleasant sensation.

She passed the threshold, and saw the light in the hall. Not one ray of sunlight, none of the light of heaven, had ever penetrated these little panes of brown glass. Christoph Koblenz's big plants guided one's gaze to the coffin, which stood raised and inclined slightly forward on the catafalque. Candles were burning. A big bouquet of roses bristled on the coffin lid. Her mother-in-law could hardly bear to look at it.

I'm the only one who knows what's in it, the wife thought. But it didn't matter. Sobs were collecting behind her.

"Close relatives this way, please," said an attendant, and ushered her to a row of pews that stood parallel to the coffin, while the others were left with a frontal view of it. A lake of flowers was spreading slowly out from the foot.

One after the other, the respectable people, the black-clad, middle-class folk, filed between the pews, between Christoph's little trees, paused in the dim light before the coffin, laid flowers at the coffin's foot, folded their hands briefly. The Kirghiz bowed her head and stood that way for a long time. Paul the Great was wearing a heavy coat and looked like a Russian landowner.

The brightly colored group had sat down right in front, with the boy at their center. The wife could hear him distinctly, and made an effort not to look his way. The bikers entered the hall one by one, helpless without their machines, and stood quietly in front of the coffin. Monkeyhead and her husband's other clients, some of whom the wife didn't know, raised their fists above the pale-brown box in salute.

There were barely enough seats in the hall for everyone, because people were still piling in, to the accompaniment of a little tinkling bell. There were even some old people among them. She recognized Mrs. Sattler. The cops seemed to be having a conversation.

She could hear her parents-in-law beside her. Her mother-in-law kept her eyes stubbornly turned away from the coffin. She still couldn't face her son's death, and seemed to feel trapped in a nonsense ritual as in a net. The father-in-law stared into space. No word could reach him, no comfort.

The girls in the front row were flocking around the loudly wailing boy. They stroked the hair out of his face, hugged and kissed him, and threw angry glances at the pew where the wife had taken her seat with the parents. Whatever can have got into their heads? the wife thought, furious. As if he had belonged to *them.*

The little bell still tinkled, even though everyone was seated now. The flagstaffs stood in the corners, their banners still peaceably furled, and the smoking had largely subsided, though a few stray puffs hung on in the dim air. A mousy-looking older woman, probably one of the relatives, took out a cassette recorder and started fiddling with the buttons.

So the cops aren't the only ones taking notes, the wife thought.

She looked at the coffin from behind her dark glasses and tried to concentrate. At last the music took over from the tinkling bell. It was thoroughly nondescript music, someone or other's Largo, a sugary piece played on a mechanical organ. In the jumble of her other chores, her energy hadn't extended to the choosing of music.

She saw distinctly the indignant movements on the seats occupied by her husband's friends. They wouldn't have put up with the music even if the wife had chosen it. As the organ continued its unctuous din, she remembered the words to the Scott McKenzie song her husband had loved so much: "Who's gonna miss us/ in a year or so?/ Nobody knows us,/ all the things we've been thinking./ So what's the difference if we go?"

He would listen to that over and over, never dreaming the words might someday apply to him.

Out of the corners of her eyes, along the rims of her glasses, she saw that some of the funeral guests were consoling themselves with big joints of hash or marijuana. They were sending clouds of aroma over the coffin, without shocking the relatives because the relatives thought they were cigarettes. Cigarettes were unsuitable enough.

The boy had become invisible behind all the comforting arms and hands, behind the kissing faces and whisking handkerchiefs. But you could still hear him.

Stiffly the Catholic relatives followed the start of the ritual. The cassette recorder clicked on. One of the cops crossed himself when the priest entered.

In his surplice, the priest seemed even taller than he was. He appeared to smile toward the coffin before he scrutinized the smoking, sprawling congregation. He barely glanced at the respectable . . . relatives. It was the others he had prepared for. He wanted to move them, or at least to silence them. He was a fisher of men.

The wife scarcely listened to him. She kept looking over at the subgroups of mourners who were fighting their discomfiture and remembering the lesson they'd learned over the years: Don't let them put anything over on you, show up every ritual for what it is, a narcotic pumped out by the powers that be. Keep your head, keep your head at all times. The candles were so close to the wife that she could smell them.

"Shit God," a girl in the second row said suddenly, holding her cigarette in the air like a pointing index finger. "Don't bother us with your shit God! *He* didn't believe in all that."

Father Lächler went on speaking, imperceptibly louder. The mother-in-law asked in a whisper whether they couldn't throw people out: "I won't stand for that!" The wife shammed immobility, like a tortoise.

It's running its course now, she thought. There's nothing more I can do. "You couldn't have dreamed up a better funeral yourself," she said softly in the direction of the coffin.

The funeral hall was divided into two halves. The wife would have loved to know what the old lady next to the cassette recorder was thinking, while the machine went on capturing the unfathomable for posterity. Or maybe only for other relatives who had stayed home.

The relatives were silent. They disapproved of everything: the priest, the other mourners, the brown light of the hall, the gaudy red roses on the coffin lid. They sat there, immobile with disgust. The wife wished they would give her a comforting smile, some kind of sign. She didn't know why.

"Stop it!" the boy yelled at the priest. "For heaven's sake stop it! You don't believe all that yourself!"

"Whoever you may be," the priest said firmly, "whatever your political opinions may be, and whatever the dead man's opinions were—it's a matter of complete indifference. It means nothing in the face of what has happened."

The bright-colored crowd weren't about to put up with that. They defended themselves noisily. None of them could stand the notion that the same thing could happen to them as had happened to whatever was in the box. And not only that: At last, after days of confusion, they'd found an enemy. It was this shit God whom the priest there was talking about.

"Fascist window dressing!" they shouted. And: "We're here to protect him from that."

But they were tired too, and not as belligerent as usual. The unfamiliar air, saturated with hundreds of the dead, subdued them. The smell of candles and the silent black group on the other side, made them insecure. Paul the Great hissed a couple of words. They listened to Paul.

But the priest didn't need his help. This was just what he'd been waiting for. He gave his talk a twist that reduced them to silence. He showed his contempt for them. They weren't used to contempt. He showed that he considered them all stupid, as they sat there smoking and protecting themselves from the box. In the end, they couldn't help but feel like schoolchildren.

"Any worldview that won't look at death is folly," the priest said. He had no need to speak of God to reveal this folly for what it was. Mortality, our common ground—how could one turn away from it, as though one's thoughts were fettered? He hadn't known the man in the coffin, he said. It was his responsibility to see that this man was returned to God's hands in accordance with his religion—he assumed, in accordance with his faith.

"Oh, dear God!" the girl in the second row said obstinately. But nothing more occurred to her.

The priest went on. The dead man had surely not been as shortsighted as these friends of his, who refused even to grant him and his family quiet, and time for reflection. People could shout anything they liked, said the priest; that didn't make what they said any truer or deeper. It wasn't his intention, he said, to force God on them. He asked only for quiet.

And he got quiet, a reluctant, embarrassed quiet. The priest then asked everyone to pray.

The wife didn't pray. She heard the voice of her mother-in-law beside her, and then music again.

A door opened at the side of the hall. The attendants piled the wreaths into a cart and started the soundless motion of the coffin on its wheeled catafalque. The priest followed behind the coffin, carrying a silver crucifix.

"Go on," her mother-in-law said softly.

That's so hard to do, the wife thought. But she walked after the coffin, through the silent crowd, through the lane of friends.

Following the coffin, the priest, and the wife, all the others walked down the long road.

At the first bend, the wife turned to look behind her. It was hard to tell the procession from a demonstration: perfectly fitting! Banners, black and forked black and red, fluttered in the April air. The ranks of friends, elective kin, had formed up behind the authentic relatives. They walked in orderly rows, four abreast: the lawyers and the clients, the boys and the girls, the motorcycle gang and the policemen. The scraping of feet on the gravel behind her sounded to the wife like a rush of water. The wheels of the catafalque made no sound as the coffin swayed gently over the uneven spots in the road.

The wife marched like a soldier, looking at the box, listening to the crowd behind her. She would have liked to bring up the rear so that she could enjoy the view of her husband's triumphal last procession.

Alongside their route stood the cemetery workmen, leaning on their shovels, their caps off. Their eyes grew astonished as they saw the procession approach. A squirrel crossed the path. It waited for the coffin to pass and then darted between the priest and the wife. She looked behind her. The demonstration had halted, and all heads turned as the demonstrators looked after the vanishing squirrel.

"Come on!" her father-in-law said desperately. "We have so far to go!"

The distances in this cemetery were like those in a small city, and like a city, it had its separate neighborhoods.

Probably he won't end up in an especially good neighborhood, the wife thought. So much for the Taj Mahal. No mausoleums, just what they call a row grave.

They were still walking through patrician lanes, lined with columns and bowing angels, where no effort had been spared on marble and flowers. In the distance, a second funeral train could be seen, a very small one, with barely a dozen doleful black figures in attendance. The wife felt proud.

I mustn't turn around so often, she thought. But it's awful to have to chase along after a coffin all alone.

She remembered that like all children, she had considered suicide, just so that she could witness her own funeral. All children want to kill themselves when people hurt them, to enjoy the grief of the adults. All those feet continued to slide along behind her.

I hope he can see this, she thought. It's better than he could have dreamed. But though she tried, she couldn't feel his presence.

Meanwhile they had emerged from the shady path where the tops of the ancient mourning trees, the dark yews and the copper beeches, had long since grown together overhead, and they entered a comparatively open, bright field covered with row upon row of modest stone tablets. In some cases, resources had extended only to a wooden cross. Yellow Easter lilies shone from almost every grave.

"That's where he's going now," the wife said to her mother-in-law, who by this time was walking almost at her side, breathing heavily. The mother-in-law seemed to have decided to ignore the whole spectacle. There was only one thing she couldn't banish: her dead son.

"What does that mean: That's where he's going now?" her mother-in-law answered. "That's just it—he didn't have to go at all. None of this had to be."

"I feel sick," said the wife.

"You can stick it out a little longer," said her husband's mother. Only it was his voice, they were his words.

They came to the banks of earth next to a dug-out hole. There was a bowl of sand with a spade in it, and a bowl of flowers. The priest was blessing the coffin. The pallbearers didn't hesitate; they lowered the box rapidly into the hole, along with the roses.

There was a sound like a gust of rainy wind. It was the breath of those standing around the coffin. Others were still arriving, continually expanding the broad ring of mourners.

The priest was speaking. The wife didn't listen to him but tried to hide behind a row of people. The stems of the lilies of the valley she was holding had been crushed into a green pulp and were staining her coat.

The priest has won, she thought. The black flags have turned into banners of mourning. They looked as if they were always carried at funerals. The forked banners of the syndicalists seemed to be hiding their red halves. The flags looked as if they'd gotten together over a dead man and were no longer in enemy camps.

Her mother-in-law's moans were drowning out the quiet words of the priest. It sounded as if her heart was breaking. The boy had disappeared into his group and was no longer audible. The protagonist of the drama had dropped out of sight.

"The resurrection and the life," said the priest. The wife hadn't caught what preceded the ancient words.

Then the priest was silent and stepped back from the grave. His eyes searched her eyes before he gave her his hand. There seemed a note of interrogation in his face, as if he wanted to know whether she was satisfied. She nodded. He spent a moment longer with the parents.

The wife was just about to go over to the hole to toss the remains of her flowers into the grave and throw earth to earth with the little spade, when she saw a white-haired man already standing there and starting to speak.

She stepped back again. She might have known that his second family, too, would have arranged for an orator.

It took her a moment to recognize the old man. It was the Cologne steelworker, newspaper publisher, and anarchist August Klages, whose paper, *Liberty*, had bravely championed the liberal cause against right and left for thirty years. Klages wrote and printed his little news sheet single-handed. He had been sent to a concentration camp on account of it, and even in the camp he had continued his struggle. He was alone here too. And he was holding red carnations. When it came to fundamentals, he and the rest were fighting on the same side.

"*We* don't believe in the resurrection," he clarioned into the grave, and even in the outermost rows people grew silent. "And *here* is the life. And it's *here* that we must fight for it. You did your part," he called down into the pit, seeming to believe more than anyone else present that her husband was still there. "You fought the good fight for justice. Fare you well, my dead friend!"

He threw his Social Democratic flowers onto his dead comrade's coffin, then shook the wife's hand. He said nothing more. The wife, taken by surprise, was torn between the two camps.

"I'd like to join the others," she said.

But today she wasn't allowed to decide even that. She felt that her husband was leaving her alone, alone with the life that he had outlived. She had to stay with the people who were burying a dead little boy whom she had never met.

"Who was that person?" her father-in-law asked, his voice exhausted.

"That was a very important man," the wife said defiantly. "I'm happy he could come."

"That's funny," said her mother-in-law. "I could have sworn that you had no idea he'd be here."

Everyone waited for something to happen, for somebody to deliver another speech, or call for the overthrow of the government.

"Go on," her mother-in-law said for the second time.

But the wife remained standing by the graveside. A hole, full of flowers. She tried to say something: After all, nobody could see her. She heard bird calls distinctly.

"How long shall I stay here?" she asked her husband, and using her hand, she threw sand down to him three times.

Then she turned and looked at the forest of flags. Her parents-in-law were holding hands, standing side by side next to the pit that had swallowed their son. The tulips from their home garden fell down to join the roses, carnations, and lilies of the valley. The father held the mother in a firm embrace. That'll make it easier for him, the wife thought. He has someone to comfort.

Beside her stood Paul the Great, with a furrowed, moist face.

"You're good to hold on to," she said. "You won't fall over so easily."

"Looks are deceptive," her husband's partner said hoarsely.

Someone she had been looking for all along now appeared: the school friend Joseph Deutner. He seemed not to want to part with his bouquet of flowers. He hadn't yet gone over to his old friend's grave, where the comrades were lowering their black flags into the hole one by one. Black banners silently covered the colored flowers.

"He doesn't deserve that!" Joseph Deutner said furiously to his dead friend's wife.

"What do you mean?" she asked, startled.

Paul the Great gave the angry little man a suspicious look.

"That spectacle is unworthy of him," Deutner said. "It's an insult to a faithful Christian. How could you allow that . . . that . . ."

"Rabble?" the wife asked, furious. "Is that what you mean to say?" Deutner was silent.

"They're his friends! They were more his friends than you were, right up to the end. They're people he helped. And people who helped him. What gives you the right to be so arrogant?"

"Look at his relatives," Deutner whispered with steadily growing anger. "How are his parents supposed to get over this? Their last impression of him? And his aunts! The people who truly loved him."

"You little Pharisee," said the wife. "They never knew him! He'd made himself invisible to them. I suppose you people expect everyone to go on lying right into the grave, just for your sakes."

Out of the corner of her eye she saw Monkeyhead, carrying a syndicalist's flag, pause at the grave with his fist in the air, crying loudly, and then hurl the flag with a violent motion after his dead comrade. There was a knocking sound as the flagpole hit the coffin like a spear.

"Sure, you all like to think you've got a monopoly on the truth," said Deutner. "But you're fooling yourselves. He'd gotten onto the wrong path, in every way. You think I didn't know that?"

"I suppose you think I'm to blame?" the wife asked.

"I didn't say that," Deutner answered. "But you're part of it.

You can't put on this show now, as if he'd done some heroic deed, as if he'd died in a war. The show-offs here aren't worthy of him. You despise the philistines," said Deutner, "and us solid middle-class citizens. That's like despising the ground you walk on or the bed you sleep in. You're all nothing but a bad joke."

"Do you think this is the right place to hold political discussions?" asked Paul.

"I wasn't the one who started it," said Deutner. "But it's the only thing that matters to these people here. I admired the priest," he went on. "But even he is probably infected."

"Oh, come on," the wife said quietly. "You're just like the others. It's just disappointed love, that's all. You all talk away, in political jargon, or sociological, or Catholic, it doesn't matter which. Actually, the only thing that matters to any of you is that he ran out on you. He abandoned you. And me too. And every one of us still wanted something from him. Needed something from him."

Then the fat little school friend started to cry. He walked away without saying goodbye, still holding his bunch of flowers.

A delegation from the Union for Progressive Equality came to the grave next, young men with their arms around each other, or walking arm in arm to support each other.

Her husband had often met with them, not without amusement at how seriously they took themselves. "They do the most incredible mental gymnastics," he had said. "You should hear how they twist *Das Kapital* until they manage to unearth proof that it's revolutionary for them to go to bed together. Poor Marx gets saddled with everything. He probably didn't give a hoot who goes to bed with whom."

"But discrimination," his wife had replied. "Surely you're all fighting discrimination."

The pattern in the pit was changing once again. The Progressive Equals were tossing white lilies in on top of the black banners. Every one of them had brought lilies.

"Discrimination?" her husband had said. "Without discrimination, a lot of people wouldn't get any fun out of life anymore."

The wife envied the calm, earnest group of Progressive Equals, who so visibly belonged to each other and were bearing their loss together.

"Oh, my God," said Paul. "The aunts in mourning. I can't stand to watch. Where *did* he belong?"

"I don't know," the wife said. "I really can't tell you. Now I know less than ever."

Slowly the mourners split into two circles, a large circle and a somewhat smaller one. The relatives had formed their ring around the parents-in-law, who were standing half turned away from the grave, apparently just waiting to be left alone at last, to spend half an hour in the cemetery without banners, without young people, without slogans. But the second circle, the brightly colored one, wasn't getting any smaller.

The wife noticed that she hadn't seen the boy at his friend's grave. Again, she felt torn.

"Where do I belong?" she asked Paul. "With this group or that one?"

"With no one," he said. "You can go it alone. Letting others support you isn't your thing."

"Oh, I know that song by heart," she replied. " 'You're strong' —that's what they all say. It makes me sick. *He* didn't say that."

"Are you already starting to lie to yourself?" Paul asked. "He said it more clearly than anyone. I'm sorry, but the boy needs help. You don't."

"The boy," she said, furious. "He's tough as a weasel."

Then she saw him, standing alone and comfortless, turned away from his friends, who had scattered under the pale willows, smoking and talking.

Maybe it's true, she thought. Maybe he was somebody only when he was with him. And now he's floundering like an amputee.

The boy didn't notice her looking at him. He was standing about six yards from the hole, staring into space as if further thought were an impossibility.

"He freed you," Paul said. "You'll realize that soon. He freed you from himself. There wasn't room enough for you both, so he left you on your own. You'll understand in time."

"I already feel sorry for the kid," the wife said softly, pointing at the boy. "But I can't tell him."

"It isn't necessary," Paul said. "You don't have to play the role of a saint. You're not a posthumously appointed social service agency for your old man."

The wife felt better as the big, loosely knit group of funeral guests began to circulate around the cemetery as if they were at a party. It comforted her that they had started talking to each other. But when she looked back at the grave, she was startled by what she saw. In a flicker she realized that only she could see how strange it was.

The two cops had approached the grave with a deferential air, probably trying to get a better view of the mourners, now minus their flags. But at that same moment, the tall woman walked quietly between them up to the graveside. She peered in, dropped her lilies of the valley onto the jumble of flowers and banners. The cops looked respectfully at the young woman in her elegant mourning outfit. One of them said something to her; she bent her head gracefully in response and walked slowly over the white gravel walks, to disappear in the distance.

The wife thought of the Wanted posters downtown. A few seconds more, a flash of recognition, and another of the photos might have been crossed out. She saw Hardenberg beside her. He had followed her gaze and was laughing.

"Have they got their wires crossed!" he said. "They'll have their work cut out for them, trying to explain a bungle like that. But he's left them on their own; he won't bail them out."

"He wasn't all that fond of clearing up mysteries. Anyway, he's completely gone now," the wife replied.

"Gone where?" Hardenberg retorted. "Don't fool yourself. No one can disappear under flags and wreaths."

"But he's gone!" the wife said desperately. "You know that!"

It was the first time that she'd ever addressed the intern with the intimate *du.* Hardenberg gave no sign of recognizing any change in their relationship.

"We'll see," he said, and for the rest of their conversation managed to avoid using the word "you" altogether. "We'll see if he's gone or not. I don't believe it. You can tell just by watching this weird show that there's still something going on here."

Then Koblenz came over. The wife was now surrounded by three male friends and felt for the first time that she was being well looked after and shown enough respect.

"Your cellar was good for the trees," Koblenz said. "They looked nice here. I'll take them away again afterward. Will you keep one as a memory?"

She was a bit confused.

"It wasn't my cellar," she said. "It was *his* cellar. No, I don't want any of the trees. Don't be angry. I can't explain why. It's just that I can't let myself start treating this place as important."

"You can't help that," said Koblenz. "Here, in the cemetery, is where the plants take their revenge. Here they triumph over us! Here they eat us up once and for all. That's why people don't like cemeteries. They see that plants grow especially beautiful here. They know they're going to be eaten by the plants. Cremation doesn't help; the plants eat the ashes."

"Can't you leave her in peace?" said Paul. "You make a person feel really queasy."

She saw her mother-in-law approaching hesitantly. Who were these men with her daughter-in-law? They didn't look like the hippies over there, but they didn't look the way people normally look at a funeral, either. "Have you invited the priest for dinner?" her mother-in-law asked.

"Is that customary?" the wife asked, a bit confused. "He's gone."

He had disappeared like a ghost in his white surplice.

"We can make up for that later, dear lady," said Paul the Great.

"Oh, you!" said the mother-in-law. "Always in such a hurry to smooth things over! But here in the city, people probably do things differently anyhow." Her face had red blotches on it, from fatigue and tears.

"We're going to a restaurant with the rest of the family," she said. "I'll come back later, when there's no one else here. I can't stand to watch when they fill in the grave."

The wife saw the cemetery workmen with shovels and a grader, noiseless and half hidden behind the trees.

"I'll join you," she said. "I'll join you in half an hour."

"You want to be alone here too," said the mother-in-law. "But you won't get your way. They're around him like flies now, visible and invisible. In six months he'll be all alone, believe me."

And she left without saying goodbye, without glancing at the grave, which the workmen were approaching stealthily, as if they were still undecided which had priority, speedy labor or respect for the dead.

The party was over and the guests were leaving in large, loosely strung-out groups.

"Maybe I should load up the trees right now," said Koblenz. "What I said is true. There's no place where people swipe more stuff than a cemetery."

"I ought to drop by his office," said Paul. "I'll look things over, so that you can clue in the guy who's winding up his cases. Actually, Hardenberg ought to come along too."

"Not a bad idea," said Hardenberg. "Or are we still needed here?"

"No," said the wife. "Who could possibly need you?"

She saw the boy standing some distance away. Like her, he had been abandoned by everyone.

"Go on, all of you," she said, and walked over to the boy, who was now watching the workmen begin to close the grave. The clods of earth fell heavy and moist onto the soft flowers.

"It's over now," said the wife.

The boy didn't reply.

"I still don't get it," he said softly. "Just now, just when a couple of things were getting clearer—*now* he takes off."

"Maybe they're only getting clearer *because* he took off," the wife said, feeling foolish and obsequious for borrowing his jive.

"No," said the boy. "Not clearer to *us*—to himself. He'd figured out a lot of things just recently. He'd learned to fight."

"What do you mean?" the wife asked, and sat down on a bench without taking her eyes off the shoveling workmen. "He was always a fighter."

"That's not true," said the boy. "He'd only just figured out that he didn't need to fight to be liked. It used to be that he'd do anything to get people interested in him. He wanted everybody to love him, no matter how stupid they were. But he didn't need that anymore. He didn't care if everybody understood him or not. He understood himself."

"You're pretty arrogant," the wife said softly.

"Maybe," the boy said, unperturbed. "But he was always so anxious to please. That makes you miserable, and . . . it gets in the way of fighting for the revolution."

"You guys and your revolution," the wife said tiredly. "What good does it do you when you're lying in a box? That struggle wasn't really his thing. He wasn't obsessed enough."

"Oh, God," said the boy. "You all think effort is the same as obsession, and a cool head means you've got no feelings. Meanings wobble so when you get hold of them. But he'd gotten over that. He could think so clearly, just recently."

"Due to your intellectual influence, no doubt," the wife said furiously.

"No," said the boy. "It was all his own doing. It's just that he couldn't fool himself about the world anymore. About the contradictions. He really saw them."

"And now?" she asked.

"That's just it," the boy said desolately. "What was it all for?

I can't figure it out. Gloucester's dead, and the rest of the Group are in quarantine. I can't figure it. I guess only pigs are cheerful and happy in this world."

"Pleading the cause of the next world?" said the wife.

"I'm going now," said the boy. "We probably won't see much of each other after this."

"Can I do anything to help you?" the wife asked, hating him.

"You could pay the vet's bills for Icru. That would take a load off me."

He said goodbye softly, and the wife felt guilt for having squandered her inheritance, the legacy of love that her husband had offered and she had knocked out of his hand.

The workmen were through. A couple of curious types were creeping around between the flat rows of graves as if they were expecting one last belated scandal.

Now the wreaths were blooming, piled up on the knoll of earth, and a wooden cross, bearing his name and the date of his death, rose at the head.

"Such an awful weight to have on top of you," said the wife. "Six feet of earth. Oh, don't go," she said to the mound. "Don't go."

Then she left, walking the long road back, along the dark avenues, past the sorrowing angels. It had begun to rain a little. A small group was waiting for her at the cemetery entrance.

"We just can't leave you alone," said the Kirghiz.

And another, fainter voice said, behind her as if the words weren't meant for her: "Is she ever going to be surprised! The fun is only just beginning."

Translator's Note

It may be helpful to English-speaking readers to glance at these notes on the Baader-Meinhof group, a leftist terrorist organization that grew up in West Germany in the late 1960s and by the mid-'70s had affiliations with international terror, including Palestinian and Arab groups. Officially called the RAF (Red Army Faction), it was popularly named after two of its early leaders, Andreas Baader and Ulrike Meinhof, both of whom figure as characters in *Dead Alive.* The RAF survived the imprisonment and death of Baader, Meinhof, and other core members and is still operating today—dead yet alive, like the issues that gave rise to it.

Main Historical Events of *Dead Alive*

The mid-1960s: The student protest movements in West Germany show increasing disaffection with the German and international political scene (anti-Vietnam War demonstrations, etc.). The novel's characters are caught up in the unrest, especially at its center, Berlin.

1967: Benno Ohnesorg, a peaceful student demonstrator, is shot to death by police in Berlin, causing some young Germans on the left to begin organizing armed resistance. They include Gudrun Ensslin, the "parson's daughter," who politicizes her lover, Andreas Baader.

1969: Baader and Ensslin go to Frankfurt, center of the Frankfurt School of radical social thought (Marcuse, Adorno), where student activists have encouraged the young inmates of Frankfurt boys' homes to agitate for reform of their institutions.

1972: The RAF leaders—Baader, Ensslin, and Meinhof—are all captured and imprisoned, charged with the bombing-killings of U.S. servicemen, other murders and attempted murders, multiple robbery, and criminal association. They are not brought to trial for three years because security requirements demand that a special courthouse be built for them next to a prison in the Stammheim district of Stuttgart. Meanwhile they are guarded in separate prisons, sometimes in solitary confinement. Rumors of ill-treatment arouse widespread sympathy in liberal and radical circles, triggering protest demonstrations. The unimprisoned gang members flee abroad, some to join Arab terrorist groups.

Readers looking for a concise history written in English might consult Jillian Becker's *Hitler's Children: The Story of the Baader-Meinhof Gang* (New York: Macmillan, 1977), on which these notes are largely based.

About the Author

Eva Demski was born in Regensburg, Germany, and now lives in Frankfurt. She is a well-known journalist, both in print and on the air.

Dead Alive is her third novel.